Joseph Hocki

The Passion for Life

Joseph Hocking

The Passion for Life

1st Edition | ISBN: 978-3-75233-262-9

Place of Publication: Frankfurt am Main, Germany

Year of Publication: 2020

Outlook Verlag GmbH, Germany.

Reproduction of the original.

The Passion for Life

By JOSEPH HOCKING

I

THE DOCTOR'S SENTENCE

I am in a restless mood to-night. There seems nothing to explain this, except that perhaps I am growing tired of the life I am leading, or it may be that there are influences at work of which I have no cognizance, but which affect my nerves. As I look out of my window I can see storm-clouds driven across the wild sky, while distant lights on the heaving sea are suggestive of mystery. The wind howls around my little wooden tenement, while above the roaring of the waves I can hear the dismal screech of the sea-birds, which, for some reason or other, have left their rocky resting-places. I do not know why it is, but the cry of the sea-birds is always suggestive of the wail of lost souls as they fly through the infinite spaces.

I did not mean to begin this way at all, for I want, as far as I can, to put all sad thoughts behind me.

Let me begin again then, and, if possible, strike a more cheerful note. I want something to interest me, and it has struck me that if during these long, dark evenings when I have to be alone I can place on record some of the events which have taken place since I have drifted to this part of the country, I shall be able not only to forget the shadow which hangs over my life, but to see streaks of blue sky amidst the storm-clouds, and to catch the bright rays of the sun which are constantly shining, even although the world says that we are living in a dark time.

But I am writing this also because, as it seems to me, the happenings of the last few months are of sufficient importance to record. Even although I were sure no one would read what I am going to write, I should still go on writing. Some one has said, I do not know who, that the life of a village is the life of a nation in miniature; and even although that may contain only a suggestion of the truth, certain am I that if I can faithfully record the events which have taken place in the little village of St. Issey, I shall have written something of the history of the great world outside.

Now that I have started writing, however, I immediately realize that, if I am to make my narrative comprehensible, I shall have to give some kind of personal explanation. Who am I, where am I, and why am I here? I promised just now that I would, as far as possible, avoid the sad things of life and dwell on the sunshine rather than on the shadow. But why should I? Life is made up of sunshine and shadow, and no one can give a faithful account of life without dwelling on both. Besides, what are the things we call sorrow and joy but contrasts? And life without contrasts would be unbearable. I will tell my story just as it is, then: its light and its shade; its hope and its despair.

"Simpson," I said to my one servant and factotum, who has been with me for several years, and whom I regard more in the light of a friend and counsellor than as a paid hireling, "the doctor tells me that I have at most a year to live."

I was sitting in my chambers in London as I mentioned this interesting piece of information. Simpson had just placed my coffee and bacon before me. He stopped suddenly as I spoke, as though the news had startled him. Then he went on with his work.

"I beg your pardon, sir."

I repeated the information.

"The doctor tells me I have at most a year to live. I may not last so long. Possibly a month will see the end of me."

I thought Simpson's hand trembled, but he repeated the formula which had almost become second nature to him:

"Yes, sir; thank you, sir," he said.

"I have been thinking, Simpson," I went on, "that as I have but such a short time before me in this world I may as well spend it comfortably and in a congenial place; indeed, the doctor insists that I should."

"Yes, sir; thank you, sir. Is there anything more you want, sir?"

"Simpson," I said, "you don't appear to believe I am serious. I am simply telling you what Dr. Rhomboid told me last night. By the way, how did he ever get the name of Rhomboid? A rhomboid has something to do with mathematics, hasn't it?"

To this Simpson made no reply.

"How long did you say, sir, that the doctor gave you?" he asked presently.

He seemed by this time to have quite recovered himself.

"He is of opinion that a year at the outside will see the end of me," was my reply, "but it may be that I shall only last a month or two. There is something wrong with my inside. He gave it some sort of a name, but I won't try to repeat it. I might pronounce it wrongly. But why do you ask?"

3

"Well, sir, you have got an important case on, and I heard that it would last a long time. It would be a pity if you didn't live to see the end of it."

"I shall have to drop the case, Simpson," I said.

"What, Mr. Francis, drop the case? That would be a terrible pity, and you having had to wait so long for cases, too."

"You seem more interested in the case than in the tenure of my existence, Simpson," was my response.

"Yes, sir; thank you, sir," replied Simpson, after hesitating some seconds.

"How long have you been with me, Simpson?" I asked.

"Ever since you went to Oxford, sir—eleven years ago last October."

"That is a long time, Simpson."

"Yes, Mr. Francis. Your father—that is, Mr. Erskine—made me promise that I would stick to you. That was before he died, sir."

I may here remark that my father, John Erskine, died just as I left Winchester. He did not make any fuss about dying. He simply called me to his side and said, "Frank, I have sent you to a good school, and you have done very well. I have left you enough money to go to Oxford, where I want you to take a good law degree. After that, I want you to read for the Bar, and, if possible, rise to be Lord Chancellor. There will not be very much money left when you finish at Oxford—something over a thousand pounds, I believe; but that should last you until your briefs begin to come in. Simpson, our old servant, will go with you. I think that is all, my boy."

The next day my father died, and I, as arranged, took Simpson to Oxford with me. Simpson is not very handsome, but he is a very valuable friend, and in his way has glimmerings of sense.

I toyed with my breakfast, for although I spoke calmly enough about it, I was not altogether pleased at the idea of dying so soon. After all, I was only just thirty, and, as Simpson had said, the briefs had only just begun to come in.

"I beg your pardon, Mr. Francis, but will you be leaving London soon?"

"I have decided to leave at once," I replied, "but the question with me is, Where shall I go? I have been thinking a good deal about it during the night, and I cannot decide. Where would you suggest?"

"Well, Mr. Francis," replied Simpson, "if you will forgive me for making a suggestion, sir, I should say that, as yours is a Cornish family, Cornwall would be a suitable place to——"

Here he stopped, and seemed in a difficulty as to how he should conclude the sentence.

"That is, sir," he went on, "would it not be appropriate?"

"Exactly," was my answer. "Cornwall it shall be, then; but I don't know Cornwall, although, as you say, I am of Cornish stock. You are also Cornish, Simpson?"

"Yes, sir; thank you, sir."

"I have been looking through my accounts," I went on, "and I find that by economy I can manage to pay my way for about a year. That fits in exactly, as you see; but I am afraid it won't include you, Simpson. You have rather a good appetite."

"My appetite can depend very much on the state of your funds, Mr. Francis," he replied.

"That means you are inclined to go with me?"

"Certainly, sir; I could not think of leaving you alone."

I confess that I was somewhat relieved at this, because, although I determined to put a brave face upon everything, the thought of spending my last days alone was not pleasant.

"That is awfully good of you, Simpson," I remarked, "but if you come with me, although, as you say, your appetite can be regulated, we shall have to be careful. I like your idea of going to Cornwall, but I don't know what part of the Delectable Duchy to go to. The doctor suggests that, in order to extend my existence as long as possible, I ought to go to some spot where the air is warm, yet bracing; that I must have no excitement, but at the same time must have interesting and pleasant companionship; that, while I ought to be out of the world, I must at the same time be in it. This fellow with a mathematical name seems to be intensely unreasonable."

"Excuse me, sir, but could you give me a short holiday?" asked Simpson.

"For how long?"

"Say four days, sir. I will arrange for you to be well cared for while I am gone, sir."

I didn't ask Simpson why he wished to go away, or where he was going. I am afraid at that moment I hadn't sufficient interest to inquire. Of course, I gave my consent, and that same day Simpson packed up his bag and left me. Here was I, then, Francis Erskine, aged thirty, barrister-at-law, member of the Inner Temple, who, a week before, had good prospects, alone, with my death-warrant signed. I hadn't felt very well for some time, but had paid no heed to my ailments. For the past twelve months I had been, for a young barrister, very busy. It so happened that I had been engaged upon a case which appeared hopeless. All my brothers at the Bar declared that my client had not the ghost of a chance, and then, by what people called a stroke of genius on my part, but which was really a pure fluke, I carried off the thing triumphantly. From that time briefs came in fairly rapidly, and I was more than once referred to as a rising young man of brilliant parts. Then came the doctor's verdict, and there was an end to everything.

What I did during Simpson's absence I cannot remember. I tried to take a philosophical view of the situation, and although the disease from which I suffered was, the doctor declared, past all cure, and had made great ravages upon my constitution, I went about as usual. After all, what was the use of bothering about death?

At the end of four days Simpson came back. I thought he appeared somewhat excited, but his manner was quiet and respectful as usual.

"Enjoyed your holiday, Simpson?" I asked.

"Yes, sir; thank you, sir. When will you be ready to start, sir?"

"My tenancy of these chambers expires in three days, Simpson."

"I hope Mrs. Blandy looked after you all right while I was away, sir?"

"I really don't remember," was my reply. "I dare say."

"Could you start to-morrow morning, sir? I can get everything ready by that time."

"Where are we going, Simpson?" I asked.

He looked at me as if in surprise.

"To Cornwall, sir."

"You have made arrangements for me, then?"

"Yes, sir; thank you, sir."

I did not ask him any further questions. I did not think it worth while. After all, when one came to reflect, nothing was worth while. If Simpson had suggested the Highlands of Scotland or the Flats of Essex, I should have made no demur. On the whole, however, I was pleased that we were going to Cornwall. Both my father and mother were Cornish people, and although I had never visited the country, it seemed less disagreeable to me to go there and spend my few remaining days than to any other place. I knew that Cornwall was a narrow strip of land at the extreme west of the country, and I had heard vague reports about the fine coast-line and beautiful air, but, beyond that, very little.

"Perhaps, sir," said Simpson, "we had better put off our journey until the day after to-morrow."

"Why?" I asked.

"You will want to say good-bye to your friends, won't you, sir?"

"I think I have a remembrance of doing that, Simpson," I replied.

"You have a lot of friends here, haven't you? Excuse me for asking, sir."

"I have a lot of acquaintances, Simpson," I replied, "but only two friends—Bill Tremain and Tom Esmond. The rest don't count. I should not be surprised if they came to see me when I am in Cornwall—that is, if their wives will allow them. Have you ever reflected, Simpson, that marriage is a tremendous hindrance to friendship? Wives always make it difficult."

"Excuse me, sir, but what a pity it is you have not got a wife."

"I have never regarded the matter in that light, Simpson. Why do you say so?"

"Women always save a man from brooding. They never give him a chance of being quiet, sir," and Simpson shook his head impressively.

"You speak as one having authority. Have you ever been married?"

"Yes, sir," replied Simpson.

"I didn't know that. Why have you never told me? How long were you married?"

"Two years, sir. I never talk about those two years, but I shall never forget them."

I asked Simpson several questions, but his replies did not contain much information.

"You don't seem to be very communicative with regard to your married life."

"There's nothing to say, sir, besides what I told you. Women save a man from brooding. You see, sir, they don't give him time to brood. I have never noticed that you have paid much attention to young ladies."

"Not very much," I replied. "I don't seem to have had time. I have always been too busy with my work."

"If you had married, sir—at least, if you had married the woman I did—you would never have had any time for your work."

Next morning I found that all my bags were packed, while a taxi stood at the door. I made no inquiries as to Simpson's intentions or plans. When he went to the booking-office at Paddington I did not even ask him the name of the station for which he was booking. I remember entering a first-class carriage, where Simpson made me as comfortable as possible, after which I saw him talking to the guard, and heard him tell that worthy official that I must not be disturbed if it could possibly be helped.

Of my journey to Cornwall I remember practically nothing. I think I slept a great part of the distance. Towards evening we stopped at a little wayside station, where Simpson appeared and told me I was to alight.

"Have we come to our journey's end?" I asked.

"To the end of the railway journey," was his reply.

"I seem to smell the sea, Simpson," I said.

"Yes, sir, we are close to the sea."

He led the way to the station-yard, where a carriage stood, evidently waiting for me. This I entered, while Simpson, after attending to the luggage, and expressing the hope that he was not inconveniencing me, took his seat by my side. Once in the carriage I began to take more interest in my surroundings. I saw that we were in a beautifully wooded country, while away in the distance rose giant hills and rocky tors. I heard the roll of the waves, too, while the air was like some life-giving elixir. Presently we entered a village, which nestled among the trees.

"Simpson," I asked, "what is the name of this village?"

"This is St. Issey, sir."

"It is a very pretty place."

"Yes, sir; thank you, sir."

I saw a number of cottages, built in higgledy-piggledy fashion, each surrounded by its own garden. I saw the villagers standing gossiping with each other, heard the laughter of little children as they played in the lane, smelt the sweetness and purity of the air. After all, it was good to live.

"Is there no hotel here?" I asked.

"No, sir; no hotel, sir."

I did not ask him where we were going, or how I was to be accommodated. After all, it was not worth while. One place was as good as another. We passed some lodge gates, which evidently appertained to a big house, and I noted the great granite pillars and the heavy palisading.

"The Squire of the parish lives there, I suppose?"

"Yes, sir, Squire Treherne. That, sir," pointing to a comfortable-looking house which stood back from the road, "is the Vicarage. Mr. Trelaske lives there. And that, sir, is the Wesleyan Chapel. I am of the Wesleyan persuasion myself —at least, I was when I was a boy."

"That is a long time ago, Simpson."

"I am fifty-five, sir, but it doesn't seem long since I was a boy—that is, except for those two years when I was married; those seem very long."

Simpson's face looked so comical that I could not help laughing. It was the first time I had laughed since my interview with the doctor.

We passed by a great square tower and a low, many-gabled church, with the churchyard around it. I turned my eyes away. The place was not pleasant to me. Presently we began to descend a steep hill, and the sound of the waves rolling upon a hard and sandy beach became more and more clear. The carriage entered a narrow lane, which ended in a kind of copse close to a rugged cliff. A little later I saw, built within a few feet from the edge of the cliff, a wooden house. At the back of it a steep and almost precipitous piece of country, covered with brushwood, rose skyward. In front was the Atlantic. The house was in a bay looking towards the sea. The cliffs on the right side were not very high, but on the left they rose up almost perpendicular, rugged and imposing. I noticed that the rocks of which the cliffs were composed were in one place discolored, and I pointed it out.

"Yes, sir," replied Simpson. "When I was a boy there was a copper-mine here. There's a level under the hill now—at least, I believe so, sir. This is the house I have settled on, sir."

I alighted from the carriage and looked more closely at what was to be my future dwelling. As I have said, it was a wooden erection, and was evidently built with some care. All along the front was a veranda, the floor of which was roughly paved with granite slabs. The few yards of land between the veranda and the edge of the cliff had been cultivated, and flowers grew in wild profusion. At the back of the house many kinds of wild flowers bloomed. In the near distance, on the top of the cliffs, the land was covered with furze bushes and heather. I stood and took a deep breath and listened while the waves rolled on the golden sand hundreds of feet down.

"Won't you come into the house, sir?" asked Simpson. "I have paid the driver, and there is a man coming along with the luggage in a cart."

"Not yet," I replied. "I want to take my fill of this. This is wonderful—simply wonderful. I want to live."

Simpson stood watching me. I thought I saw his lips tremble.

II

MY NEW HOME

I liked the house the moment I entered it. It was snug, cozy, and warm. It had the feeling of home, too, and felt so quiet and restful that I threw myself into an armchair with a sigh of relief.

"You spent your holiday in getting this, I suppose, Simpson?"

"Yes, sir; thank you, sir. I hope you like it, sir. It is not altogether what I would like, sir, but directly I saw it I thought it would suit you."

"To whom does it belong, Simpson?"

"Well, sir, I would rather not tell you, if you don't mind. You may rest assured that I got it on favorable terms, and everything is in order."

"But I do mind," I said, for by this time I had quite an interest in my surroundings. For days nothing had seemed to matter, but now I was quite eager to know how Simpson had happened upon this quaint yet comfortable place.

"You are sure you wish me to tell you, sir?" and Simpson looked at me almost beseechingly.

"I insist on it," I replied.

"Well, sir, I am afraid it was built by a kind of madman who came down to St. Issey about six years ago. Who he was I don't know. No one seems to know. But he took a lease of this piece of ground from the Squire and built the house with his own hands."

"He must have been a carpenter," I suggested. "It seems very well built. But what has become of him?"

"He is dead, sir."

"Was he old or young?"

"Quite an old man, I think, sir. Anyhow, he built it himself and would have no one near him. After it was built he lived here alone for several years, speaking to no one but the village idiot, who went by the name of Fever Lurgy, who bought all his food and did all his errands. No woman was allowed near the place, sir."

"Then he cooked his own food and did his own house-work?" I asked.

"It would appear so, sir. He seems to have made himself very comfortable, too. As you see, the furniture is not at all bad, and nearly everything is just as he left it."

I must confess to being interested. The thought of a man coming to this place and building a house for himself and living there without companionship of any sort appealed to me. I wondered how he spent his days and nights.

"Let me have a look around the place," I said, rising from the chair. "I want to see what rooms it contains."

"Yes, sir; thank you, sir," was Simpson's reply.

The room in which I had been sitting was about fifteen feet square—it might be a little more—and looked out upon the veranda, beyond which stretched the great Atlantic. It was comfortably furnished, and possessed an old-fashioned fireplace, evidently intended for logs of wood, and revealed the fact that the builder was not only ingenious in the matter of house-building, but that he possessed a good deal of taste. The whole apartment was carefully match-boarded, and was, as I said, snug and comfortable.

"This, sir, is the bedroom," said Simpson, opening the door at the end of the living apartment.

It was much smaller than the other, but quite big enough for a single bed, together with the simple necessities of a man living alone.

"And did he die here?" I asked.

"Yes, sir; no, sir—that is—I don't know, sir."

"What do you mean, Simpson?"

"Well, sir, that is why I didn't want to tell you about him; but there are all sorts of stories afloat. You don't mind, do you, sir?"

"Not a bit," I replied. "Whatever my ailments are, nerves don't trouble me."

"Well, sir," went on Simpson, "the fact that he lived here all alone caused people to talk about him—especially the women. You know what women are, sir, and people used to come and look from the hill above and see what he was doing. One day two women were bold enough to come close to the place, and they knocked at the door. There was no answer, sir. They knocked again and again and made a great noise. Still there was no answer. Then they rushed away to St. Issey and gave it as their opinion that something had happened to him. They hadn't been back in the village more than half an hour when Fever Lurgy came, pale as a ghost, and trembling like a leaf. He had gone to inquire whether he was needed for errands, and, on being unable to make any one hear, had burst open the door. In this bedroom he found evidences of a great struggle. He found blood, too, but the man was nowhere to be seen."

"That's interesting," I said. "What was the name by which this old fellow was known?"

"Fever Lurgy called him Father Abraham," was Simpson's reply.

"Well, go on," I urged.

"There's nothing more to tell you, sir. From that day he has never been seen. People believe, however, he was murdered here; that some tramps came and found him alone, stole his money, killed him, and threw his body over the cliff."

"And how long was this ago?"

"About four months, sir."

"And since that time no one has lived here?"

"No, sir, no one. Most people have been afraid to come near the place. That is why none of the things have been touched; besides, the Squire, as soon as he discovered what had taken place, told his men to keep an eye on it."

"And so you thought, Simpson," I said, "that this was the sort of place I would like to come to and end my days?"

"Well, Mr. Francis," was Simpson's response, "for one thing you told me you wanted a place that was cheap, that you wanted a place that was out of the world and yet in the world, and I immediately thought of St. Issey. When I came down here, however, I found that any lodgings you might like would be rather dear, and then, hearing of this place, I determined to come and see it."

Here Simpson stopped.

"That's not quite answering my question, Simpson," I remarked.

"Well, sir, I have not lived with you going on for twelve years without knowing something of the kind of gentleman you are. I have never known you trouble once, sir, about ghosts or anything of that sort, while your nerves have always been as steady as old time. Besides, I was able to get it dirt cheap, sir—in fact, the Squire's steward was glad to have it tenanted at any price. The place is very pretty, too, sir. There is not a finer view along the coast of Cornwall, and that is saying a great deal. It is out of the world, and it is only half a mile from the village. Still, sir, if you don't like it, we can easily leave. Over at St. Eia there's a nice cheap hotel where——"

"Hang the hotel," I interposed. "I am going to stay here."

"I think I ought to tell you, sir," went on Simpson imperturbably, "that people say they have heard curious noises around here of a night, and it is believed by many that the ghost of Father Abraham haunts the place."

Simpson looked so solemn as he said this that I laughed again. I don't know why it was, but, in spite of his dreary story, my spirits rose unaccountably.

"The ghost of Father Abraham doesn't trouble me a bit, Simpson," I said. "This place suits me down to the ground. But this is not all? Surely there must be a kitchen somewhere."

"Oh yes, sir. This way, sir," and Simpson spoke quite eagerly. Evidently my approval of his choice removed a load from his mind.

Father Abraham had evidently determined to make himself comfortable, for the kitchen, though small, seemed to have every requisite. As I entered it, an old woman rose from her chair and curtsied in the old time-honored way.

"This," said Simpson, "is Mrs. Martha Bray. I asked her to come in and make everything spotlessly clean for you by the time you came."

"And Mrs. Martha Bray has obeyed orders," I remarked. "Everything is as perfect as a new pin. But, Simpson," I continued, "where will you sleep?"

"There's a little place here behind, sir, where I have made up a bed for myself," replied Simpson. "It will be nice and handy for my work."

"Yes, sur, and plase, sur, I can come in an' help 'ee any time," remarked Martha Bray. "I do'ant live fur away, an' I can come 'cross the fields in a few minutes."

"Excuse me, Martha," was Simpson's rejoinder, "but we shall need no one. I can do all that is necessary for Mr. Francis."

"Oh, plase yerself," replied the old woman, "but it'll be ter'ble wisht for 'ee doin' everything yerself without a woman to help 'ee. I do always say that a man wethout a woman to do his chores for en es like one side to a pair of scissors. I have got some tay ready, sur, and I have toasted a piece of ham rasher. It's raal ham, too, not like the stuff you buy in the shops. I do'ant hold with these new-fashioned notions about feedin' pigs, and do always feed mine meself like my mother and grandmother used to do before me. And you'll find, sur, that tes deffrent from the ham you do buy in the shops. My b'lief, sur, es that ef old Father Abram had had a woman to look after en, he wouldn't be dead now."

Having delivered herself of this long speech, the old woman curtsied once more, and prepared to take my meal into the little living-room.

"Excuse me, Martha, I will do that," said Simpson, "and there's no reason why we should detain you any longer. Here are your wages, and thank you for what you have done."

"All right," said Martha. "Ef you can do without me, I can do without you. The tay is in the caddy up there. There's some bread in the cupboard there, and the other things be in this drawer. Good-night, sur. I will look over again to see whether there is anything I can do for 'ee.'"

I returned to the sitting-room, and sat while Simpson prepared my evening meal.

"I want to wash, Simpson," I said, when he had nearly completed his work. "Besides, it has struck me that there is no such thing as a bathroom in the house. What are we going to do?"

"This way, sir," said Simpson, and I followed him out of the house towards what I call the cliff end of the building. Here I found, gurgling out of the hillside, a stream of the purest water I had ever seen, which flowed into a pond.

The idea of outdoor ablutions appealed to me, and I almost forgot my ailments as I bathed my hands and face in the pure spring water. A few minutes later, I was eating the sweetest ham I had ever tasted.

"If this is the result of the old-fashioned way of feeding pigs," I remarked to Simpson, "I shall make a closer acquaintance with Mrs. Martha Bray, and shall buy all the hams she can dispose of."

The time was spring. To be exact, it was the 14th of May, and although the evening air was somewhat chilly, the days had become long, and I remembered standing a long time at the front of my little wooden hut, looking at the giant cliffs at whose feet the waves of the broad Atlantic rolled. When I had returned to the house, Simpson had lit a lamp, while in the grate a wood fire burnt cheerfully.

"Do you think it will do, sir?" asked Simpson.

"Do!" I replied; "it's just perfect."

"Then, sir, if you don't mind, I will go to bed. I am a little tired, sir. There's nothing more I can do for you, is there?"

"Nothing, thank you, Simpson. Good-night."

A few minutes later I judged, from the silence which prevailed in the kitchen, that Simpson had retired, and that I was practically alone in the little wooden hut.

I was still in utter ignorance of my whereabouts, beyond the fact that I was somewhere in Cornwall on the edge of a cliff, and close to a little village called St. Issey. Where St. Issey was situated I did not know. Cornwall, I reflected, was a county nearly a hundred miles long, with the main portion of it surrounded by the sea. I knew that I must be somewhere in the vicinity of the main line of the Great Western Railway, as I did not remember changing anywhere, but beyond that I had little or no knowledge. Still, this did not trouble me. I reflected upon what Simpson had told me concerning the cheapness of my place of residence, and I had absolute trust in him concerning all arrangements for the future.

The night was very quiet, I remember. Scarcely a breath of wind stirred, although the air which came into my open window was pure and exhilarating. The splash of the waves was still heard on the sandy beach, although I judged the tide had receded somewhat. Now and then the cry of a disturbed sea-bird reached me, but beyond that, nothing. Somehow I could not make up my mind to turn in for the night. I had too many things to think about, while my new surroundings drove away all desire for sleep. I took one of the books I had brought with me from London, and tried to read, but that was impossible. I could not scan a dozen lines without my mind wandering from the printed pages. After all, when one comes to think about it, my position was somewhat strange. It is easy to talk about coming to a place to die; but when one has actually heard the death sentence pronounced, and is told that, at the most, he cannot live more than a year, it is not a pleasant experience, and, in spite of all my endeavors, my thoughts were constantly reverting to Dr. Rhomboid's verdict.

Presently I could bear my thoughts no longer, and, quietly opening the door, I went out into the night. How still, how solemn it was! On my left hand the great beetling, rugged cliffs rose, imposing and awe-inspiring. Behind me, the hillside rose steep and high. In front was the wide Atlantic. I could see the waves breaking into foam some little distance from the shore. I could, in the pale light of the moon, see the discolorment in one place in the rocks, which reminded me of the mine which Simpson had told me was working there when he was a boy.

How long I stood there I do not know, but presently, in the silence of the night, I heard a cry. It might be that of a sea-bird, although it made me think of other things. A little later I heard what might be described as a moan, although that does not truly convey the impression it made upon me. In spite of myself, my mind reverted to the story which Simpson had told me about the man who had built the house, and of his supposed tragic end. Could it be, I wondered, that this man's spirit visited the scene of his death, drawn there by some laws yet undiscovered by the student of psychic phenomena?

I had no superstitious fears; indeed, I had no belief in a life beyond this present existence. If ever I had believed in this, the belief had died years before. In a vague kind of way I imagined that death was the end of everything. Perhaps that was why the doctor's verdict was so grim and forbidding.

I heard another cry, not loud, but quite distinct; and then I thought I saw forms moving along at the base of the cliff some little distance away, but the moon, which was on the wane, gave me insufficient light to be certain. A cloud passed over the sky, and then I could see nothing.

"Surely I could not be mistaken," I said to myself, "yet who could be crawling along at the base of the cliffs? No. It was all pure fancy."

As if in contradiction of my thoughts, however, I heard noises which seemed to be directly under my feet. These noises seemed to continue for three or four minutes, and then all was silence.

"Events have been too much for me," I reflected, "and in spite of all my boasting about my nerves, they are playing me tricks."

I turned and looked at the little house, and I doubted whether, in spite of all my brave words, I should be able to continue living there. To be alone day after day and night after night, with no one to speak to me and no one to care for me, save this unimaginative man, was, to say the least of it, anything but exhilarating. Then I felt the gnawing, deadly pain which had led me to visit Dr. Rhomboid.

"I must not be a fool," I reflected. "What has to be has to be, and I must go through with it. Besides, one place is as good as another. I will go to bed."

All the same, I made up my mind that I would not live like a hermit, and that I would become acquainted with the life of this little village into which I had been cast.

III

THE CHURCHES' ANSWER

I suppose my long journey must have tired me, for I slept soundly, and on the following morning when I awoke the sun was shining through the windows, while the splash of the waves sounded pleasantly to my ears. A few minutes later I was up and dressed. Walking to the edge of the cliff, I looked towards the spot where, the previous night, I fancied I had seen dim forms moving; but in the light of the sun nothing was visible. The shadows, too, of a few hours before had entirely passed away. The fresh, pure spring air exhilarated me in spite of myself. I almost forgot Dr. Rhomboid's verdict. Indeed, so far did I ignore his instructions that I found my way to the highest point of the cliff and looked seaward. Never in my whole life had I been so entranced as on that morning. The blue sky was reflected in the water in such a way that I felt I had never really seen the sea until then. To the right and to the left of me stretched the giant cliffs until they were lost in the horizon. At their feet rolled great waves. Landward, hill rose upon hill, and the whole countryside was fast assuming its garments of summer glory.

In a sense, Cornwall did not seem a beautiful county to me at all. At least, it did not possess the beauty I had expected. Compared with Surrey, it looked bare, and in some senses almost drear, and yet it possessed a charm which I could associate with no other place. There was something in the air one breathed, some strange charm, something in the very essence of the county which differentiated it from the rest of the world. Cornwall is as different from other counties as England is different from Spain. I felt my blood tingle as I looked, and realized that a mysterious hand had been laid upon me. Perhaps it was because there was Cornish blood in my veins, and that for many generations my ancestors had lived amidst associations similar to these. In any case, my heart thrilled its recognition, and I knew that I was a part of what I saw, that the spirit of my county was speaking to me, and that the innermost depths of my being realized my homeland.

Years seemed to slip from me, and with a recrudescence of youth came a passionate desire for life—more life. While I had been in London I seemed to be largely indifferent to the doctor's pronouncement, even although I was beginning to sip from the goblet of the world's success. But a numbness had possessed my being, and I had been able to speculate grimly upon my approaching demise. Now, however, it was different. The world seemed wider, the sky higher, and life promised infinite things. I could not formulate them into words; nevertheless, they surged up in my being like a mighty torrent, and I longed to live. My whole soul revolted against cessation of life, and all the time I knew that a dread disease was slowly working within me.

But I would not think of it. By an effort I threw my forebodings from me, and, seeing a precipitous pathway down to the beach, made my way thitherward. I wanted to interest myself in the happenings of the world.

A little later I found my way to the base of the cliffs where, on the previous night, I thought I had seen living beings. No marks of them were evident. The hard, yellow sand was smooth and trackless. There was a stretch of a hundred yards between the foot of the cliffs and the foam-crested waves, and, calling to my mind my impressions of the previous night, I determined to put them to test. Without avail, however.

The great heap of débris caused by the working of the mine which Simpson had mentioned had now become covered with verdure. I saw the green stains on the cliff which Simpson had said betokened copper, but nowhere could I see the level which he had mentioned. I peered curiously around, but in vain.

Presently I saw a fissure in the rocks which ended in a cave. This I entered and made my way for a few yards, peering curiously around me. Nothing of importance struck my eye. I reflected that this might be almost immediately under my house, and it was here, according to my fancies, I had heard voices on the previous night. I fancied, too, that, except in the case of very high tides, this cave would always be dry. I lit a match, and, looking at the sand at my feet, discerned footmarks. This struck me as somewhat curious, especially as these footprints were apparently fresh, and some of them gave evidence that they had been made by a woman. Still, there was nothing to wonder about. I had frequently heard that the Cornish cliffs were honey-combed by caves, and that pleasure-parties visited them out of pure curiosity.

Then something bright caught my eye, and, stooping down, I picked up a woman's brooch. I went outside and examined it, and saw immediately that it was apparently of value. It was quaintly formed, and suggested great age. I concluded that it was composed of dull gold fashioned centuries ago, while two stones of considerable value had been set in it. I speculated a little to whom it might belong, and, thinking that I might hear of some one who had lost such a valuable trinket, I placed it carefully in my pocket so that I might be able to return it to its owner.

The sun by this time had increased in power, and, as the place was warm and sheltered, I sat on a great rock near, and gave myself up to fancy. How long I sat there I have no conception, but presently I was awakened to the fact that Simpson had become anxious about me.

"It's all right, Simpson," I shouted in reply to his call. "I will come immediately."

"Breakfast is quite ready, sir," I heard him say, "and I have been wondering where you had gone."

As I made my way towards the lower part of the cliffs, where I thought I saw an easier way to my house than that by which I had descended, I happened to look back, and there, seated in a crevice at nearly the highest point of the cliff, I saw what seemed the form of a woman, and that she appeared to be watching me. A few seconds later I was hidden from her view by the copse into which I had entered. When I had descended half-way towards my house I was able to catch another glimpse of the place where she had been sitting, but she was no longer there.

"I hope you haven't been anxious about me, Simpson?" I said, when I returned to the house.

"Well, sir, I was a bit worried. You see, the cliffs are dangerous, and you didn't tell me you were going out. I am glad you are all right, sir. Breakfast is quite ready, sir. I cooked some more of that ham, as you seemed to like it so much last night, sir."

"That's all right, Simpson; but before I have breakfast I must have another wash at the fountain." When I had taken off my coat I looked at my arms, and was shocked at their thinness. I looked into the little pond and saw the reflection of a tall, thin, attenuated man. I was positively ghastly. When I had finished my toilet I again glanced in the direction where I had seen the woman's form, but the place was hidden from my view. Nearer to me, however, and swayed by the breeze, I saw what I thought was like a woman's dress fluttering. It might be that she was interested in my movements. "I expect the people of the village have fears about me, as they had about Father Abraham," was my thought as I entered the house.

No visitors called to see me, and I spent several days in absolute quietness. Although I had at first made up my mind to do so, I paid no visits to the village, and beyond the furtive watcher I have mentioned, I saw no one but Simpson.

My first feelings of exhilaration had passed away, and I settled down, in spite of my resolve, to a kind of hermit's life. I still rejoiced in the beauty of the scene and took short walks in the neighborhood of my little dwelling-place, but saw no one.

When I had been there a week a bad attack of my malady sent me to bed for three days. Simpson urged me to send for the doctor, but this I would not do.

Rhomboid, who was at the head of his profession, had warned me that I should be subject to these attacks, and that they would come to me with increasing frequency until the end. He had also given me general instructions as to what I must do. What was the use, then, of calling in a local practitioner who would be utterly ignorant as to what to do in such a case as mine?

At the end of three days I was better, and informed Simpson that I intended getting up.

"Simpson," I said, as I sat in the comfortable chair which he had prepared for me, "you told me on the night we came here that you had been brought up a Wesleyan Methodist."

"Yes, sir," was Simpson's reply.

"Are you of that persuasion still?"

"Well, yes, sir; I suppose so, sir."

"Have you been to any of their chapels lately?"

"Not very often, sir."

"Is there a Wesleyan minister who lives at St. Issey?"

"No, sir. You see, St. Issey Chapel is only one of the little places in the circuit. A minister, sir, lives five miles from here, and only comes about twice a quarter. I have the circuit plan here, sir. Would you like to see it?"

"It would be a curiosity, anyhow," I replied, and a little later Simpson put a sheet of printed paper in my hand. This sheet informed me that St. Issey was in the Lanhydrock Circuit, and, with twelve other chapels, was supplied by two ministers and a number of other men called local preachers.

"I see that the superintendent minister is called Mr. Bendle. Have you ever met him?" I asked.

"No, sir; but I have heard that he is a very good man. When I was a boy, sir, St. Issey Chapel was crowded; but people don't go to Chapel as they used to."

"No? How is that?" I asked.

"Well, sir, it seems as though people have become very worldly, and many have given up Chapel-going altogether."

"And the Parish Church—do many people go there?"

"Just a few, sir; but not many, I am afraid."

"I should like to know," I said.

"Indeed, sir?"

"Yes. The truth is, Simpson, seeing that the doctor tells me I have to die very soon, I should like to know whether any one could tell me about what happens after death."

"I have a Bible here, sir," said Simpson. "It tells you all about it there."

"Indeed," I said, "I have not read the Bible for years. I don't think I have looked inside one since I left Oxford. Do you read it, Simpson?"

"Yes, sir. I read a chapter every night before going to bed."

"Are you a Christian, Simpson?"

"I hope so, sir," and he looked at me curiously.

"Excuse me for asking," I said, "but as you are a Christian you will have ideas about these things."

Simpson hesitated a few seconds, and then called to his aid his old formula, "Yes, sir; thank you, sir."

"That being so, Simpson," I continued, "I want your opinion. Supposing I were to die to-night, what would become of me?"

Simpson gave no answer. I think he wanted to be polite, but could not be truthful at the same time.

"You see, Simpson," I interposed, "I have just had a severe shaking up, and, as Rhomboid told me that these attacks would come with increasing frequency and hasten the end, I have a natural curiosity as to what will happen when the end comes. It is not pleasant to think of becoming nothing, and as a belief in a future life is one of the tenets of the Christian faith, and as you tell me you are a Christian, I want to know, from your standpoint, what you think my destiny will be."

"Excuse me, sir," said Simpson, "but you will not be offended if I ask something?"

"Oh, no," I said, "go on."

"Well, then, sir, have you ever been converted? Forgive me for asking, sir; I know you have always been a well-conducted young gentleman, and you have never gone wild like lots I know of, but all the same, sir, I have been taught that there are two places to which people go when they die—heaven and hell. The sheep which are on the right hand go straight to Abraham's bosom, and the goats which are on the left go into outer darkness, where there is weeping and gnashing of teeth. The question is, sir, whether you belong to the sheep or the goats."

"Exactly," I said; "but what constitutes the sheep and what constitutes the goats?"

"That is where the question of conversion comes in," replied Simpson. "Except we become converted we cannot go to heaven."

"Then your opinion is, Simpson, that as I have not been converted I must go to hell?"

"Yes, sir; thank you, sir. I don't mean to offend, sir."

"No, I am sure you don't, Simpson. Besides, I wanted a straight answer. Just now, however, the question of heaven and hell does not trouble me at all. It is rather a question as to whether there is anything at all after the grave."

"Do you doubt it, sir?"

"I am afraid I have had no opinions about it in the past, Simpson. You see, I have been so busy with my work that I have had no time to think about it. Now, however, when death stares me in the face, I am—well, a little bit curious. How do I know, and how do you know, that the millions of people who are dying every week in this world do not die just like flies? How can we prove that we are any better than they? Do we not sport in the sunshine during a brief space and then cease to be?"

"Life would be a miserable one-sided business if it were so, sir. Wouldn't it?"

"That is the question, Simpson. Did you ever read Omar Khayyam?"

"What is it, sir?"

"Ah, I see you have not read him. Omar Khayyam was an old Eastern poet who, in his philosophy and poetry, taught that we are just a part of an eternal round of things. We are born, we live, we propagate our species, we die, and so the thing goes on. But it is not a very cheerful doctrine, Simpson, and that was why I wondered if you, who profess to be a Christian, could give me some information."

Simpson was silent.

"Ah! I see," I said with a sigh. "You have a sort of traditional hope that there may be a sort of future life, and that you may get to what is called heaven, but you are not sure about it."

"Well, sir, I am a very ignorant man on such matters," replied Simpson, "and, to tell you the truth, religion doesn't seem to be the fashion nowadays. All the same, it would be a grand thing if it were true."

"Just so," I said, and for the first time I realized the necessity for some sort of faith which should be an anchor amid the storms of life.

"Are you better now, sir?" asked Simpson.

"Oh yes, considerably better," I replied. "I shall be able to walk about for the next few weeks, I hope."

"Then, sir, may I advise you to go to Church or Chapel? The preachers there might be able to tell you."

"A good idea," I cried. "I have not been to Church or Chapel since I left Oxford, and while there I only went because I was obliged to. I did enjoy the singing, though. Yes, Simpson, I will take your hint. I will go to Church on Sunday."

"It's Sunday to-morrow, sir," was Simpson's reply.

"Is it? I had forgotten. Then I will go to-morrow."

"Where will you go, sir, to the Established Church or the Wesleyan Chapel?"

"I will go to both, and hear what they have to say at both places."

The next day was gloriously fine. A cool breeze blew, and out at sea "white horses" rode on the crests of the waves. Near the coast-line, too, was a long streak of foam. The air was pure and invigorating. In sheltered places it was warm and gracious.

I allowed myself plenty of time to reach St. Issey by eleven o'clock, and, if the truth must be told, I was a little excited. I felt as though I was going on a tour of exploration.

I had never been what is called a religious boy, and though I inherited from my father a high code of honor, religion made no appeal to me. I suppose that at the back of my mind I had an impression that there might be a life other than this, and that some great Eternal Force, which might or might not be personal, had created this and all other worlds. As to whether this Eternal Force had any interest in created life I did not trouble. The question was too remote, and, as far as I could see, admitted of only a conjectural answer. After leaving Oxford, I was too absorbed in my plans and ambitions to trouble about what seemed to me to be something really apart from life.

I had never been a bad fellow. I had, as my acquaintances said of me, gone straight. Not that I had been a recluse in any way. For two or three years I went a good deal into society. I never had any serious love affairs, although I am afraid I indulged in some mild flirtations. I had a fair knowledge of current literature, and, although far from being a scholar, I had at the same time scholarly instincts. I had travelled on the Continent of Europe, had a fair knowledge of German and French, and during a long visit to Italy had managed to pick up the language of the people.

I had also visited the old churches on the Continent, but had never troubled about what these churches stood for. As far as I could see, the old, stately cathedrals represented something that might have been a power at one time, but which had now passed away. They were interesting from an architectural and from an historical point of view; but as for anything deeper, it never came within the horizon of my vision. I was young, and, as I thought, healthy, and death seemed a long way off. Therefore, why should I trouble?

But now death had come near. I do not know that I was frightened, and I was able calmly to face the prospect of annihilation. Nevertheless, that prospect was grim. I longed for life, more life, the completion of life. The life I had lived was, it seemed to me, fragmentary, incomplete, and, to a certain extent, chaotic.

I do not know that I attached very much importance to my visit to the little Wesleyan Chapel. All the same, I was curious. If there should be anything beyond, if the man who got up to preach could tell me something which had been hidden from me, I would like to hear what he had to say.

I walked very slowly and rejoiced in the glorious morning. As I drew near the village I noted the quiet restfulness of everything. The Church bells were ringing, and a few people were wending their way towards the old time-honored building. Very few people seemed to be making for the Wesleyan Chapel. Groups of youths were lounging around the lanes, smoking cigarettes and passing rustic jokes. Women were gossiping with each other from their cottage doors. There was no squalor anywhere, no poverty visible. Every one seemed to have enough to eat and drink. Every one seemed to be comfortably housed.

I entered the little Chapel—a square, plain building, capable of seating perhaps three or four hundred people. It was five minutes to eleven when I entered, and not a soul was there, except a man whom I took to be the Chapel-keeper. He looked at me curiously. By eleven o'clock there might be, all told, thirty people there, mostly elderly men and women. Some young girls were there, and a few children; young men were conspicuous by their absence. When eleven o'clock came perhaps a dozen more came from some vestry, and entered what I took to be the choir-seats. They were nearly all young women. Perhaps during the first ten minutes of the service half a score more came into the Chapel. I am giving these details because I want to tell exactly what I saw, especially as I have discovered that from a religious standpoint St. Issey village is typical of hundreds more all over the county. At about three minutes after eleven a man entered the pulpit. As far as I could judge he was a working man, or he might be a farmer, a carpenter, or a tradesman of some sort.

Let it be understood that I came to this place of worship hungering to know something of the deeper things of life. I wanted to be assured that there was another life greater than this, a life which should be the consummation and explanation of this.

The preacher commenced by announcing a hymn; a lad at the harmonium played over the tune, and the people sang. Let me confess here that the singing moved me. The Cornish people, whatever their defects or virtues, possess the gift of song. They had sweet, musical voices, and they sang heartily. The words, as I remember them, were of an emotional nature, and were evidently written by some one who deeply believed in what he wrote; but it was evident that very few of the congregation realized the meaning of the words they were singing. There was no sense of reality, no great assurance, no vision. It seemed to be a repetition of something which had been, rather than the expression of something that was vital to them then.

Still, I was interested. The hymn made me think of far-away things. At any rate, while no mighty conviction possessed the singers, they accepted the words as containing a kind of traditional truth. I reflected that the hymn *had* meant something, whatever it might mean now.

While the last verse was being sung, I noticed that the congregation turned round, as if some one of importance had entered. I also turned, and saw a man and woman just making their way into a back pew. The man was about fifty years of age, and was evidently a personality. At first I did not know how to classify him. He might be the Squire of the parish, but I was sure he was not. There was something lacking in him; something positive, too, which did not suggest an old landed proprietor. That he was prosperous and important there could be no doubt. He looked like one accustomed to command, and suggested a big banking account.

His companion was, as I imagined, his daughter, a young woman of, say, twenty-three or twenty-four years of age. I saw by her dress that she did not belong to the class of which the rest of the congregation was composed. Although by no means a connoisseur of such things, I knew enough of woman's attire to be sure that her clothes had been made by an artist, and probably came either from London or Paris. During the next few minutes I gave furtive glances towards her, and was not impressed favorably. She was good-looking, almost strikingly so; but she seemed to me to have no soul. She looked around the building as though she had come there under protest. She gave not the slightest evidence that the service meant anything to her.

The man in the pulpit was, I suppose, of more intelligence than the ordinary man of his class, and having said that, I have said all. I did not want to be critical. I hungered for food, for light. I reflected that Simpson had told me that congregations had fallen off and that there seemed to be no eagerness about religion as there had been thirty years before. I did not wonder at that if this man was a fair exponent of it. By what right or by what authority he was there I do not know, and how he dared to pretend to tell people about the deep things of life I could not imagine. After he had been preaching a few minutes he appeared to get, according to the phraseology which I have since heard, "warmed to his subject." This meant that he shouted, and on two or three occasions struck the Bible; but, taken as a whole, it was the parrot-like utterance of an ignorant man. I am almost tempted to give a detailed description of his discourse, but I will not do so. I am too heart-sore at the thought of it. What help was there for me, a poor wretch with his death-warrant signed? What help was there for the people who sat stolidly in their pews? Why should the boys and girls of the villages or the toil-worn laboring men and women go there? I could see no reason.

As far as I could judge, the presence of the man and his daughter in the back pew and I myself, the stranger who had taken up his abode in a wooden hut, attended only by a man-servant, was of far more interest to the people than what the man had to say.

I left with a heavy heart. At any rate, I received no assurance of any life after death. I was no nearer conviction of anything which goes by the name of spiritual. As I made my way to the door an old man came up and spoke to me.

"Mornin', sir. Glad to see you."

"Thank you," I said.

"You bean't from these parts, be you?" he asked curiously.

"No," I replied.

"I hope you enjoyed the service," he ventured.

"I enjoyed the singing very much," was my reply.

The old man's eyes twinkled. I saw that he understood.

"You ded'n feel the presence of the Maaster, ded 'ee, then, sir?"

I was silent. He seemed to be on the point of saying something more, but he refrained. Perhaps he thought he would be taking too great a liberty. As I left the building and walked quietly away, I noticed that the man and the girl whom I took to be his daughter were watching me. They evidently wondered who I was.

I did not say anything to Simpson on my return about my experiences at the Chapel, and he asked no questions.

When evening came I made my way to the Established Church. Somehow, the memory of the old man's eyes when he spoke to me at the Chapel door remained with me. I had a feeling that he knew more than the preacher. Directly I entered the time-honored building, which had stood there since pre-Reformation days, a feeling of restfulness came into my heart. Architecture has always made a strong appeal to me, and this low-roofed, many-pillared edifice, with its worm-eaten pews, its granite flooring and its sense of age, brought a kind of balm to my troubled spirit. I noticed that time had eaten away even the old gray granite of which the pillars were composed, that the footsteps of many generations had worn the hard Cornish granite slabs which floored the aisles. The evening light was subdued as it shone through the stained-glass windows. The ivy which grew outside, and partially covered some of the leaded lights, somehow gave a feeling of restfulness to everything. I heard the birds twittering in the tree-branches in the churchyard, while the bell which called the people to Church was reminiscent of olden time. In my imagination I saw people who lived hundreds of years before, with the light of unquestioning faith in their eyes, coming to worship in the Church of their fathers.

A few people entered, and my vision vanished. This old Church represented only something that *had* been; something that had had its day, and was gone; something that was maintained because of its past, and because nothing better had appeared to take its place.

A dozen choir-boys found their way into their stalls. The clergyman assumed his appointed place. The congregation was very small. All counted, I suppose there would not be forty people present, and most of these looked to me like servant lads and girls.

I remembered the clergyman's name. Simpson had told me he was called Trelaske. A good old Cornish name, and I reflected that, anyhow, he would be a gentleman. I watched him closely, and I saw a fine, aristocratic-looking man, with a clean-cut, almost classical face. He conducted the service with dignity. He read the sentences of which the Church service is composed correctly and with intelligence. While he read in his natural voice, I was interested; when he intoned, a sense of unreality possessed me.

As we went through the service a thousand memories flooded my mind. I had heard these prayers, and read the Psalms a hundred times at Oxford and at Winchester. Memories of old days came flashing back to me, and I was a boy again in the school chapel, listening to old "Thunder and Lightning," as we used to call him, preaching to us. Presently Mr. Trelaske entered the pulpit and gave out his text: "If a man die, shall he live again?"

"Now," I thought to myself, "I am going to get something. Here is a man who is set apart to teach people the Christian faith, and he is going to deal with that phase of his faith in which I am really interested."

I think he noticed me in his congregation, for he looked curiously towards me more than once. I rather liked him, too. As I said, he was evidently a gentleman, and doubtless had been to Oxford or Cambridge. Possibly he had been at my own College.

In about ten minutes his homily was finished. When I try to remember what he said, I am reminded of a story I have since heard. A popular preacher came to Cornwall and preached to a crowded congregation. On the following day this popular preacher saw an old miner, to whom he spoke in a familiar fashion.

"Well, Tommy," he said, "what did you think about my sermon last night?"

"What ded I think about it?" repeated Tommy.

"Yes," said the popular preacher, "what did you think about it?"

"I ded'n think there was nothin' to think about," was Tommy's reply.

That was my summing-up of Mr. Trelaske's sermon. There was nothing to think about. I had come to Church curious to know—ay, and more than curious; I was longing to know if life promised anything beyond the grave, but the Church gave no answer to my question. In place of burning conviction, there were empty platitudes. In place of vision, there was only the sound of a child crying in the night.

"In God's name," I asked myself as I went back to my little habitation, "why should people go to Church or to Chapel? What is there for them but boredom?"

I did not want argument, I did not want learning; but I wanted conviction, light, vision—and there were none of these things.

When I got back to my house I found that Simpson had returned.

"Have you been to Chapel, Simpson?" I asked.

"Yes, sir; thank you, sir. People have been asking a lot of questions about you, sir."

"Oh, indeed!"

"Yes, sir. Mr. Josiah Lethbridge asked me about you, sir. He lives in that big house up by Trecarrel Lane. He is a great mine-owner and ship-owner, sir."

"Indeed," I said. "Has he any children?"

"Yes, sir. One son and one daughter. Is that all you need, sir?" And Simpson gave the finishing touches to his arrangement of my supper-table.

Before I went to bed that night I stood under the veranda of my little house and looked seaward. In the dying light of the day I could still see the giant cliffs stretching away northward. I could also see the long line of foam where the waves broke upon the shore. I heard the sea-birds crying, too. "If a man die, shall he live again?" I said, repeating the words of the text I had heard that night, but no answer came. I went to bed wondering.

IV

THREE VISITORS

On the day following nothing happened, and excepting Simpson I did not see a single person. Indeed, but for one occasion, when out of curiosity I clambered down to the beach, I did not leave the house; but on the Tuesday I had a regular influx of visitors. No less than three persons came to see me, to say nothing of Mrs. Martha Bray, who, in fulfilment of her promise to Simpson, came over to see whether her services were further needed.

My first visitor was an entire stranger. He came ostensibly to ask for a drink of milk, but really I believe out of curiosity, for when Simpson had, at my request, supplied him with the milk, he showed no desire to leave. Rather he appeared much interested in my reasons for coming to St. Issey. He was a middle-aged man, say from forty-five to fifty, and lived, he told me, at St. Eia. He proved a rather clever conversationalist, too, for in spite of myself I found myself talking to him freely. There were all sorts of rumors about Father Abraham, he told me. Some had it that he was mad; some said that he was a refugee; others, again, thought he had in the past committed some crime and was hiding from justice, while more than once it had been whispered that his end was the result of a kind of vendetta which was sworn against him because of something he did in his young manhood.

"Have you any theories yourself, sir?" he asked.

"No," I replied, "I have no theories. I must confess, however, to being a little interested. The old man evidently had a purpose in building the house, and, I think, intended it to be a permanent residence. As you see, although it is composed of wood, it is very carefully built, and was intended to last. For the life of me, however, I can hardly believe he was murdered. Of course, there was blood found upon the floor, but it is not easy to dispose of a body even so near the sea. From what I can hear no one has been washed up here, and but for the marks of struggle and the blood no one would have thought he was murdered."

"Exactly," replied my visitor. "But many things are going on of which we know nothing, and many people have purposes in life which they have no desire to make known. What is your opinion of European politics?"

"I cannot say I have any very fixed ideas," I replied.

"A section of the Press," went on my visitor, "would have us believe that we are on the verge of war, and certainly there have been indications these last few years that we are standing on the brink of a volcano. Do you believe in the stories told about Germany?"

"What stories?" I asked.

"Oh, that the Germans are preparing for war, and that they mean to go to war with England."

To this I gave no answer.

"Have you read those articles in *The Daily*——?" he asked. "I mean those articles which told us frightful stories of German preparations for war, of their avowed determination to bring about war with England, and of the toast which the military and naval people in Germany drink on every great occasion."

"You mean the toast to 'Der Tag'? Of course, one has heard such stories, but what do they amount to, after all?"

"That is my own attitude," was his answer, "and as far as stories about German spies are concerned, I think they are worked up by the Press in order to increase the circulation of the papers. By the way, have you ever seen anything suspicious in this neighborhood? This," and he looked towards the bay, "would be a splendid spot for German boats to land if they wanted to do so."

"Why should they want to land in a remote corner of the world like this?" I asked.

"Exactly," he replied, "only I was wondering whether you, who live here alone, had ever seen or heard anything which aroused your suspicions?"

"No," I replied, not thinking it worth while to tell him anything about the brooch I had found.

"You have seen nothing and heard nothing, then?" he persisted.

"I have only been here a short time," I replied. "Why do you ask?"

"I only wondered, that is all. The people over at St. Eia say that foreigners have been sneaking around trying to pick up information, and I wondered whether you had heard anything."

"No," I replied, "nothing at all."

"I suppose," he said, "that these cliffs here are honey-combed with caves? Have you seen any of them?"

"Yes," I replied. "I saw one the day after I came here. I came upon it suddenly, for the entrance to it is only a fissure in the rocks."

"Ah!" he cried. "Did you enter?"

"Yes," was my reply, "but it was not at all mysterious. I could see all round it by the aid of a match, and it contained nothing. Of course, it was very curious and very interesting."

"But you saw nothing suspicious?" he asked.

I shook my head.

My visitor did not remain long after this, and although for a time I wondered why he should be so interested, I soon ceased to pay attention to his questions.

Perhaps I should have thought more about him, but just before noon I had another visitor. This was a young fellow about twenty-two years of age, whom I knew to be an Oxford man before he had spoken a dozen words.

"My name is Lethbridge," he said. "My people live up at Trecarrel yonder, and I came—well, I came really at my pater's request."

"Indeed," I said, looking at him curiously.

"Yes; you were at Chapel on Sunday morning, weren't you?"

"I was," I replied.

"Well, my pater and sister were there, and the pater wondered very much who you were. In the evening, contrary to his usual custom, he went a second time, and saw your servant, who told him who you were. Directly the pater mentioned your name, I remembered hearing it in Oxford. You are an Oxford man, aren't you?"

"Yes. I was at Balliol."

"So was I. I left last June. You are often spoken of by the men. Indeed, I had your old rooms. You will excuse the liberty we took in talking about you, won't you? but really we have very little to interest us in this corner of the world."

"You are very kind to come," I replied.

"When I told my father who you were, he suggested that I should come down and ask you to come up to dinner. You see, we had heard of some one coming to live in old Father Abraham's hut, and when it turned out to be you, we got interested. You will forgive this informal method of procedure, won't you? But if you will come up and spend an evening with us soon, we shall all be jolly glad."

"I am afraid I am too ill to come," I replied.

"You do look a bit seedy," was his response, "but the air down here is ripping. It will soon set you up again."

"I am afraid I am too far gone for that," was my reply, "but if I am well enough, I shall be only too glad to come."

"Say to-morrow night," he said.

"If you will leave it an open question," was my reply, "I will say yes, but if I am too ill, you will understand the reason for my absence."

He looked at me closely.

"Is it as bad as that?"

"I am afraid it is," and I sighed when I spoke, for at that moment a wave of desire for life rolled over me.

"May I smoke?" he asked, pulling out his pipe.

"Please forgive me," I said. "I will tell Simpson to bring some cigars."

"Oh no, thank you. A pipe for me, please. By the way, I did not know you were of the Chapel-going order. The one reason I doubted it was you was because my father said you were at the little Wesleyan Chapel."

"I went there out of curiosity, I am afraid. I was wondering whether these people had anything to say to a man whose days were numbered."

"I go there twice a year," was his reply. "I used to go regularly when a boy. Do you intend to stay long down here, by the way?"

"To the end, I expect," I said, shrugging my shoulders.

"Come, now, we will not talk like that. I am sorry to see you looking so seedy. You were always spoken of in Oxford as an athlete. You got your Blue, didn't you?"

"Yes," I replied; "but one never knows what germs of disease one has in one's system. However, we will not talk about that. It is awfully good of you to ask me to come up to your house."

"Rather it will be awfully good of you if you come," he replied. "What a jolly fine view you have here. The old man who built this hut chose one of the most beautiful positions on the whole coast. How did you find it out?"

"Simpson, my man, did that for me," was my reply. "He was a boy down here, he says, and when I told him I had to get away from London, he came down here on spec. I consider myself very lucky."

"I am afraid you will find it a bit lonely in the winter, won't you? The sea is all right when the sun is shining on it, but in winter, when the clouds are black, I know of nothing more dismal. Besides, those black, beetling cliffs are enough to strike terror into one's soul."

I must confess to liking young Lethbridge. He was an athletic, healthy-looking young fellow, tanned by much exposure to the sun, and his every look and movement suggested frankness and honesty. I did not judge him to be very clever, but he was certainly likeable.

"You were doing very well at the Bar, weren't you?" he went on. "Our chaps at Balliol spoke of you as one who would bring added lustre to the old College."

"I was only just beginning to see light," was the reply. "I was lucky in one of the cases I had, and won it by a fluke. That was why briefs were beginning to come in. But I have got to the end of them now. What do you do with yourself?"

"That is the hang of it," he replied. "I am doing nothing. The pater wanted me to go in for the Law, and then try for Parliament. He has an idea that I ought to represent one of the Cornish constituencies, but I am not cut out for that sort of thing."

"What would you like to be?" I asked.

"Oh, a farmer," he replied. "If, instead of spending all the money he has spent in sending me to Oxford, the pater had bought a thousand acres of land and set me up farming, I should be as happy as a king, but law books are just Sanskrit to me. I love an open-air life, and I love horses and animals generally. The pater won't see things in my light, however; that is why I am doing nothing. I wish you would tell him when you come up that none but brainy men can do anything at the Bar. Well, it is close upon lunch-time, and I must go. But you will be sure to come, won't you? Look here, let's have an understanding. I will send the motor down to the end of the lane to-morrow evening at seven o'clock, and then, if you cannot come, you can send your man out to tell the chauffeur. But be sure to come, if you can."

When he had gone I somehow felt better. His very presence was healthful, and I looked forward with pleasure to meeting him again.

"You have been quite busy this morning, sir," said Simpson when he came in to lay the table for my lunch. "Two visitors in one day in a neighborhood like this is something wonderful."

"Yes," I replied, "and I like young Lethbridge."

"I hear he is a great trouble to his father, sir."

I did not reply to this.

"You see, sir, old Mr. Lethbridge wants him to marry into a county family. The truth is, when I was a boy down here he was only a poor lad. How he has got on in the way he has is a mystery to every one. Somehow or other everything he touched turned to money, and now he is richer than Mr. Treherne, the Squire. He is very ambitious, too, and wants to get in with the county people. That is why people wonder at his sticking to the Wesleyan Chapel."

"But how has young Lethbridge caused him trouble?" I asked.

"Well, sir, it is said that he's in love with a farmer's daughter, and that the old gentleman says he will cut him off with a shilling if he doesn't make up to Miss Treherne. Of course, people will talk, and maybe it is only gossip."

I felt more interested than ever in young Lethbridge after this, although I was rather annoyed with myself that I had listened to servants' gossip. All the same, I believed there might be some truth in what I had heard. There was a look in the young fellow's eyes which suggested that the deepest longings in his heart were unsatisfied.

Before the day was over, the old adage which says that it never rains but it pours was fulfilled in my case. Simpson had only just brought my tea when he came to me with an important look on his face.

"Mr. Trelaske, the Vicar, has called to see you, sir."

"Good!" I replied. "Show him in."

"I hope you will forgive the liberty I am taking," said the Vicar on entering, "but, as you are one of my parishioners, and I was told you were at Church on Sunday evening, I thought I might call."

"It is very kind of you," I said. "You have just come in time for tea, too. Won't you sit down?"

Mr. Trelaske did not look so imposing, as he sat in my little room, as when wearing his clerical robes in Church. He seemed a smaller man, not simply physically—his personality seemed less as he drew a chair up to the table and took a cup of tea from Simpson.

"I suppose you know that you are the subject of a great deal of discussion in St. Issey?" he said presently.

"I'm very flattered," was my reply.

"Well, for a man to come to St. Issey with a man-servant, and take up his abode in old Father Abraham's cottage, has set all the gossips in the village working overtime."

"Mrs. Grundy lives here, then?"

"Well, you know what we country people are. St. Issey is out of the beaten track of tourists, although there isn't a prettier spot in England, and no healthier for that matter. As for the coast scenery round here, it is, in my opinion, the most beautiful in the whole country. Anyhow, a stranger attracts a great deal of notice. Then, you see, this hut is a mystery."

"Yes, I have heard all about that," I replied, "but I dare say a great deal of the mystery has been magnified. Anyhow, it suits me entirely; it is situated in one of the most lovely spots in the vicinity. It is utterly quiet, and yet it is not altogether out of the world."

"Might one ask, Mr. Erskine," he said, turning to me suddenly, "why you came to this part of the world?"

"I came here to die," I replied.

He stared at me curiously.

"To die, Mr. Erskine?" he said.

"Yes," I replied. "I have been given a year to live—at the outside. It may be that I shall only last a month or two. When I told my man Simpson about it, and said I wanted to die in the most pleasant place possible, and to do it rather cheaply, he came down here and took this house."

"Y-you do look rather seedy," he stammered. "But surely it is not so bad as that?"

"Dr. Rhomboid, who is at the head of his profession, examined me very carefully, and that was the verdict he passed. That was why I went to Church last Sunday night."

"I don't think I quite understand you," and the Vicar looked at me as though he doubted my sanity.

"You are an Oxford man, aren't you?" he went on. "At least, that is what I have heard; and you were a barrister, and have won some repute in that direction?"

"With the exception of your last sentence, you have been correctly informed," was my reply. "What I have told you is quite true, nevertheless. It is also true that I went to Church last Sunday night because of what Dr. Rhomboid told me," and I looked at his face curiously, because I wanted to see how he would take it.

37

"No," I continued, "I am not an illustration of the old rhyme:

> "The devil was sick, the devil a monk would be,
> The devil was well, and the devil a monk was he!

It is not that at all; but do you know, Mr. Trelaske, when a man is suddenly told that he has only a year to live, and may possibly die in a few weeks, he is, to say the least of it, somewhat curious to know what will happen after he is dead. I repeat, that is why I went to Church last Sunday night."

"Yes, yes, certainly," and I thought he seemed a little bit uneasy.

"Mr. Trelaske," I said, "what happens to a man after he is dead?"

He was silent for a few seconds, and again he looked at me as if he doubted my sanity.

"I am not joking," I persisted. "After all, it is a matter of some interest to me, and as you are a clergyman, and as a belief in a future life is one of the articles of the faith you preach, I thought I would ask your opinion about it."

"But surely, Mr. Erskine," he said, "you are not a heathen. You are an old 'Varsity man. You took an arts degree, and would, to say the least of it, have had to study the Greek Testament. You know what is taught there."

"Excuse me," was my reply, "but that doesn't quite meet the situation. It is quite true, as you say, that I had to study the New Testament at Oxford, and also while at school at Winchester I was in a Confirmation Class; but all that kind of thing is a long way off. It is simply traditional, and when a man comes down to the depths of life traditions don't count. It is true that I have not read the New Testament lately, not, indeed, since I left Oxford. I am like thousands of other fellows, who, on going out into the world, give these things the go-by. Years ago I suppose I held to the traditional faith, although I have troubled very little about it; but now, as things are, I am interested—I am more than interested. What will happen to me a few months hence, when I am dead? Anything?"

I could quite see that he was surprised at the course the conversation was taking, and that he had no expectation of being asked such questions; but now that I had spoken, I meant to know all that he could tell me.

"Our state in the future," was his reply, "depends on the life we have lived here."

"Isn't that rather begging the question?" I asked. "You are assuming something which, as it seems to me, is a matter of doubt. No, do not mistake me, I haven't lived a bad life. I have not descended to the vulgar vices which are supposed to be so common to men in these days. I have, as my acquaintances say of me, 'gone straight.' I listened very attentively to your sermon on Sunday night. You see, I was more than ordinarily interested. Your text was, 'If a man die, shall he live again?' Will he, Mr. Trelaske?"

"Of course," was his reply.

"Are you *sure*?" I asked, emphasizing the word.

"Hasn't it been the teaching of the Church from its earliest history?" and he looked a little indignant.

"Excuse me, but if you will forgive me for saying so, the teaching of the Church is the very thing in question. As you may imagine, I do not ask the question out of idle curiosity; I am deeply interested, vitally interested. Mr. Trelaske, are you sure, if I were to die to-night, that there would be anything after? Mind you, I do not ask for a mere opinion; we all have those, but is it a matter of certainty with you?"

"As I said on Sunday night," he replied, after some silence, "spiritual things are spiritually discerned; and immortality is a matter of the spirit, isn't it?"

"I am afraid I don't follow you," I replied. "As you said just now, I am a lawyer, and my business for several years has been to test evidence. After I have tested the evidence that has been brought in support of any particular case, it has been my business to convince the jury that the evidence is conclusive. If I don't convince the jury, of course I fail to win my case. Your answer suggests that I lack the qualities to understand the proofs in support of the doctrine you taught on Sunday night. Perhaps you are right; probably I have so neglected what you call the spiritual part of me that it has become atrophied. I will put it in another way, then, and, believe me, it is furthest from my desire to be impertinent. Supposing you were to die to-night—you, an ordained clergyman—are you *sure* there is a life beyond?"

Mr. Trelaske was silent.

"Forgive my asking you," I said. "I am afraid I have been frightfully rude; but you see, living here alone, with the doctor's verdict constantly before me, I am curious to know."

"Not at all, not at all," he said hastily, "I am very glad you asked me; but the question is so sudden. I do not think that during the whole time I have lived in St. Issey any one has asked me such a thing before, at least not in the same way."

"I was wrong," I said; "please forgive me."

I could see that I had made him miserable. The look in his eyes told me that. As I said before, Mr. Trelaske was evidently a gentleman, and he wanted to be absolutely honest with me. All the same, his silence made my heart heavy.

Although I had, in a way, made up my mind that there was nothing after death, the thought of becoming nothing was grim and repellent.

"Look here, Mr. Erskine," he said, after a somewhat painful silence, "you must come to the Vicarage and see me. I will think over what you have said, and then perhaps I shall be better prepared to meet the situation."

From that time the conversation drifted to general matters, and when the Vicar left me, it was on the understanding that I should, at an early date, spend an evening with him.

V

AN EMERGING MYSTERY

After the Vicar had gone I suffered a slight reaction. My mind was almost abnormally active, but physically I felt utterly languid and depressed. I could see that Simpson was watching me closely, and when I did not do justice to the dinner he had provided he was almost as depressed as I.

"I could not help hearing what you and the Vicar were talking about, sir," he said presently. "I tried not to listen, but some things came to me in spite of myself."

"You heard nothing very edifying, Simpson."

"No, sir; all the same, I was sorry for you."

"Sorry for me! Why?"

"Well, sir, I think I understand how you feel. I am only a poor, ignorant man, sir, but I think I should feel something the same myself. Mr. Trelaske did not help you much, did he?"

"Well, he did not seem any more sure than you did, Simpson."

"Yes, sir; I cannot understand it. I was at the death-bed of my father, sir; he was what you would call an old-fashioned Methodist. He was not clever or learned, or anything of that sort; but he was very sure, sir."

"Sure of what, Simpson?"

"Sure that he was going to heaven; sure that this life was only a school for a greater life, sir. I am afraid I have not put it very well, but he was what the Vicar says he isn't—sure. What I can't understand, sir, is that religion seems to have no meaning nowadays. I was hoping that when I got down here I should find things the same as they were when I left home forty years ago. Then, sir, religion meant something; it doesn't now. They say the same words at Chapel as they used to say, but they do not mean the same things."

"You mean that religion is dead altogether, then, Simpson?"

"I don't mean that, sir. I only mean that people seem to have lost it. It seems a terrible thing, doesn't it, sir, that when a young gentleman like you wants to know something, and you go to Chapel, and to Church, to learn the thing they ought to be able to tell you, you find out that they know no more than you do? However, sir, it isn't for me to criticize. Is there anything more I can do for you, sir?"

"No, nothing at present, Simpson;" and I turned to the book-shelves that he had fitted up, hoping to find a book that would interest me. In this, however, I utterly failed. I turned from volume to volume, but could fasten my mind on nothing. Books which a few months ago would have enabled me to pass a pleasant evening seemed meaningless and absurd. I turned from one writer to another, but always with the same result. What they had to say meant nothing. Of course, my mind was in an abnormal condition, but that was not my fault. Here was I, face to face with death, hungering for reality, hungering for truths that were vital. My law books repelled me. What did I care about old Acts of Parliament, passed hundreds of years before? Of what interest to me were the decisions of old judges, long since dead? They affected only some nice points of law, which, as far as I could see, mattered nothing. They never touched the depths of life at all. Then there were novels, many of them written by men and women I knew personally. But they had nothing to say to me. I did not care a fig about paltry intrigues, neither was I in the slightest degree interested in *risqué* situations.

I went to the door, and looked out into the silent night. Daylight had just gone, and that kind of atmosphere which can only be felt just after sunset and just before sunrise, pervaded everything. The air was full of mystery. The wondrous depths of the sky, the wide sweep of the Atlantic, the cry of the sea-birds, and that deep hush which accompanies the dying day, aroused infinite longings. What was life, its meaning, its mystery, its destiny?

Simpson came to my side.

"I beg your pardon, sir, but you are not going out, are you?"

I had not thought of it, but his words caused me to determine to go for a walk.

"Yes, Simpson, I am," I replied.

"Shall I go with you, sir?"

"No, thank you, Simpson, I will go alone."

"Excuse me, sir, but are you not foolish? Walking in the night might do you harm, sir; it might shorten your days."

"What does that matter?" I asked. "As the end is so near, of what consequence are a few days, or, for that matter, weeks? The sooner I die, the sooner I shall solve the great mystery of the Beyond, if there is a Beyond; if there isn't, what have I to live for here?"

"I beg your pardon, sir, I am very sorry." And Simpson sighed.

I put on a light overcoat, and made my way to the highest point of the cliffs.

Beneath me, far down, perhaps three or four hundred feet, the waves rolled on the black, rugged rocks. As I looked seaward, the water, as it seemed to me, became darker and darker. The lines of foam, which stretched along by the coast, became more and more distinct. Night had now fallen. The sky was star-spangled. I had never seen such a sky in England before. Once or twice down by the Mediterranean I had seen something similar, but never in my own country. I felt as though invisible presences were near me, as though they were trying to speak to me; but I could not understand the language.

Unmindful of consequences, I sat down on the heather, and gave myself up to fancy. I tried to pierce the veil which hung between me and the Beyond. I tried to understand the meaning of the far-off voices which were wafted to me by the night breezes. I wanted to read the riddle of Life and Death.

Then, suddenly, I heard voices, and I was brought back from things intangible and mysterious to things mundane.

"You are sure he knows nothing?" It was a woman's voice I heard.

"Perfectly sure. I questioned him closely this morning. I so framed my questions that he could have no suspicion—but always with the same result."

"But why should he choose a place like this? Surely, if he is ill, dying, he would never come to a madman's hut, in a place where murder was supposed to be committed."

"I tell you that there is no need for fear; he suspects nothing—he is just what he seems to be."

The voices died away. The man and woman whom I had heard talking, and whom I had dimly seen, descended the hill, and were lost in the darkness. Then it was that, in spite of myself, I became interested in things mundane. Why they should do so I could not imagine, but I felt that they had been talking about me. But why should they? What was the purport of their conversation? How had I become mixed up in the plans of people of whom I knew nothing? I felt myself at the centre of a mystery, and my interest in that mystery caused the greater mystery of Life and Death to lose its hold on me.

I recognized the voice of the man. He had been to see me soon after my arrival; but who was the woman? What interest could my movements have to her? She spoke like one having authority, and it was evident that she feared I should discover something.

I forgot my ailments, forgot the tragedy of my life, in trying to solve this new riddle. I could not help connecting it with the old-fashioned brooch I had picked up in the cave accidentally the day I had come to Cornwall. The activities and interests in this life again became paramount.

"I will get to the bottom of this, anyway," I said to myself as I made my way back to my hut. "It will be better for me, too, than to be forever brooding about myself. And, after all, while I am alive I will live, and I will keep my eyes and ears open until I have discovered what this means."

When I reached my little room again, Simpson awaited me eagerly.

"Please, sir," he said, "I have had visitors."

"More visitors, Simpson?"

"Yes, sir, a gentleman and a lady."

"Do you know who they are?"

"No, sir; they are both complete strangers. They came and asked to see you, and I told them you were not to be seen, sir. They asked a good many questions about you, but I told them nothing."

"And then, Simpson?"

"The gentleman gave me his card, with his compliments, sir."

I took the card and read the address:

> MR. JOHN LIDDICOAT,
>   THE HILL TOP,
>   ST. EIA.

"All right, Simpson," I said. "I shan't want you any more to-night."

"Please, sir," said Simpson, "I have some books here which I think might interest you."

"Hang books!" I replied. "I don't feel like reading." Then, feeling ashamed of myself for not appreciating Simpson's kindness, I added, "It's awfully good of you, Simpson, and I might like them after all. What is it you have got?"

"John Wesley's *Journal*, sir. He came to this part of Cornwall, and I thought you might like to read about it. Not that I should advise you to read to-night, sir, if I might take such a liberty, but perhaps to-morrow. Good-night, sir." And he left me.

I was just on the point of going to bed, when, on opening one of the volumes he had placed on the table, I came upon a passage which interested me. I saw that the name of St. Issey was mentioned, and a description given of this very neighborhood. In a few minutes I had become utterly absorbed. Hitherto John Wesley had only been a name to me. I had had no interest either in his life or work. I had looked upon him as somewhat of a fanatic, who had appealed to the fears of a superstitious people, and had founded a sect. Now, however, he revealed himself to me in a new light. This diary was the work of a thoughtful man, and a cultured man, too, who had lived his life to the full, and who faced its issues squarely.

My word, religion had meant something to him! It was not a mere name, a tradition, a set of dogmas, a respectable institution. It was something real, vital, pulsating with life. To him the Founder of Christianity was not a mere mystic and social reformer, who lived nineteen hundred years ago on a little strip of land on the Eastern Coast of the Mediterranean, but a Divine Person, Who lived now. This John Wesley, who was an educated man and a thoughtful man, spoke like one who knew, and because of it he had authority and power.

I went on reading page after page, until, looking at my watch, I found it was past midnight.

VI

THE LETHBRIDGE FAMILY

We had adjourned to the smoke-room, and for my own part, I was feeling better than I had felt for some time. Opposite me sat Mr. Lethbridge, while by my side sat young Hugh Lethbridge, who had been to see me the day before. I had eaten a good dinner, and felt inclined to take a bright view of everything. Mr. Lethbridge had played the part of host perfectly, and had done his best to make me feel welcome, not only as a visitor in the neighborhood, but in his house. I had the opportunity, moreover, of making the acquaintance of his wife and daughter.

The former was a well-meaning lady, whose *métier* was to manage other people's affairs. While we were at dinner she gave her husband a great deal of information as to how he should manage his men, how he should work the mines he owned, and how the vessels he controlled should be utilized. She also informed her son how he should spend his time, what his amusements and avocations should be. She greatly amused us all by describing what she would do if she were a girl again. She had opinions about everything in heaven above and on earth beneath. I found that she knew intimately the history of every family in the neighborhood, and she took it upon herself to manage the affairs of those families. She might be rather a tiresome person to live with, but for my own part I found her vastly entertaining.

Young Hugh Lethbridge told her that he intended writing to the Prime Minister, offering her services as general adviser to the Government, while her daughter laughingly remarked that she would wear herself out in attending to the affairs of people who had a distinct preference for attending to their own business. Mrs. Lethbridge took it all in a good humor, however, and seemed to regard it as her chief business to be a universal helper. She even went so far as to instruct me how I might deal with Simpson, and gave me a great deal of valuable advice on housekeeping.

I found that Isabella Lethbridge was entirely different from her mother. On the whole she puzzled me. That she was intelligent there could be no doubt whatever. In many ways she was attractive, but on the whole I did not like her. For one thing, I thought she showed bad taste in holding up her mother to ridicule, while more than once I thought she revealed an almost sullen disposition. Still, she was interesting. She was more than ordinarily good-looking, and at times became quite animated.

The family, as a whole, did not strike me as ideal. They seemed to be at cross-purposes with each other. I could see that Mr. Lethbridge did not at all understand his son, and resented any difference of opinion which might exist between them. He apparently regarded Hugh as a boy who should unquestioningly obey his father's behests without regard to his own feelings and opinions; and yet he seemed to be angry with him for not being something in the world which would give him a position among his fellow-men.

And yet I am sure Mr. Lethbridge meant well. He was, as I have before suggested, a strong, capable man, and fully bore out what I had heard concerning him. He could never have been a nonentity, wherever he was placed, and whatever he took in hand he would do with such conscientiousness and thoroughness as to make it succeed. Consequently, it was no wonder that he had risen from a poor lad to be a man of wealth and of eminence in the county. That he was exceedingly ambitious there could be no doubt, and I judged that he was a little bit sore that all his ambitions had not been realized. He seemed composed of contradictory elements. On one hand, he seemed a man of the Napoleonic order, who would make everything and every person yield to his desires. On the other, I judged him to be a man who wanted to be strictly honest and conscientious, a man who would not give up one iota of his convictions, even if by so doing he could gain the things he desired.

Although no plain statement was made at the dinner-table to that effect, I gathered that he had suffered socially because of his adherence to what he termed his Nonconformist principles, and that he would have taken his position among the county families had he not remained true to the Chapel he had attended as a boy. On the other hand, however, that same Chapel, as it seemed to me, was a fetish rather than something which vitally affected his life.

I am spending some time in recording my impressions about this family, because I was brought into close contact with it in later days, and also because the various members of it affected me considerably.

"Yes," said Mr. Lethbridge, as we sat in the smoke-room, "I am an old-fashioned man, Mr. Erskine. I do not believe in giving up my early convictions simply because they are not popular."

"What are your early convictions?" asked Hugh.

"I mean my Nonconformist principles. See what Methodism has done for Cornwall, see what it has done for the whole country for that matter."

"Yes, what has it done?" asked Hugh.

"It has changed Cornwall from being drunken and godless into the most sober and God-fearing part of the country."

"Admitted," replied the son. "But who cares anything about Methodism now?"

"I am surprised and ashamed of you, Hugh, talking like that," said the father. "What is your opinion about it, Mr. Erskine?"

"My opinion about what?" I asked.

"Don't you think a man should stand by his principles?"

"His principles, certainly," was my reply, "especially if, after having tested them, they proved to be vital; but I am rather interested in what your son says. I have been reading John Wesley's *Journal*, and I cannot help realizing the tremendous influence he wielded over a hundred years ago in this very county; but what troubles me is that it seems to mean comparatively little now."

"I don't understand you," he said, rather brusquely.

"What I want to know," I said, "is this. Does Methodism, or for that matter, does religion of any sort, vitally affect the lives and outlook of people now? If it does, why is it that its hold seems to be weakening day by day? I am told that your Chapel used to be crowded, and that while the people were ignorant, Methodism vitally influenced their lives; but now it seems a kind of corpse. It has a name to live, but is dead. This afternoon, Simpson, my man, brought me a book which belonged to his father. That book describes what the people used to do for their faith. Even the women worked to bring stones to build the chapels, while the men toiled hours after their ordinary work was over, as a labor of love, in order to erect the buildings which their children and their children's children neglect and often despise. Everything seems stereotyped. Most of the people seem to care little or nothing about what their forbears would die for, and those that do care seem to regard it in a half-hearted way, and talk about it as something that has been rather than something that is."

"Yes," said Mr. Lethbridge, with a sigh, "I am afraid you are right. The old fire has gone, faith has largely died out, real earnestness seems a thing of the past; and yet what can one do?"

"I am afraid I am not the one to ask," I replied. "You see, I am a rank outsider so far as that kind of thing is concerned."

"For that matter the Church of England is no better," said Mr. Lethbridge.

"Should that console one?" I asked. "Cornwall, as I understand, used to be the home of religious activity, of unquestioning faith, of devoted fervor; but to-day people are careless, materialistic. Faiths which at one time were held tenaciously, doctrines which were believed in unquestioningly, are now apparently a dead letter."

"I suppose you are a Churchman, Mr. Erskine," said Mr. Lethbridge.

"I am afraid I am nothing," I replied. "For several years I did not put my foot inside a Church of any sort."

"Indeed, how is that?"

"I suppose I had no interest," I said. "That was why going to Church on Sunday was something new to me. I felt like a man witnessing a strange thing, and trying to understand something which was unfamiliar."

"Yes, and how did it impress you?"

"Everything was so unconvincing," I replied. "The note of reality was never struck at all."

"But surely," said Mr. Lethbridge, "you are not an atheist?"

"I am nothing," was my answer. "I wish I were. I suppose you know why I came here?"

"Yes, I have heard," he replied, "and I am very, very sorry for you, and you such a young man too, and life opening up all sorts of possibilities. Perhaps, however, it is not as bad as you think; the doctor may have made a mistake."

"I am afraid there is no hope of that," was my reply. "The man who examined me has the reputation of being the most eminent diagnostician in his profession; but if you religious people are right, it does not matter. If John Wesley, whose diary I have been reading, is right, what we call life, that is, life here, is a very small matter; it is only a fragment of life. Death, according to him, is only an episode; but the worst of it is that here, in a county where he is so largely represented, and in a village where he has visited, his power is gone. The old words are used, but the old convictions are gone—that is why such a man as I am left stranded. But really, I am ashamed of myself, talking like this. Believe me, I am not in the habit of boring people with my ailments and foolish speculations."

We joined the ladies shortly after, and our conversation, I am afraid, was of a very uninteresting nature. I noticed all the time we were talking, too, that Mr. Lethbridge was paying no attention whatever. He seemed to be thinking deeply about something else. Presently, while his wife was engaged in a long harangue about the inferiority of girls, comparing them with what she used to be when she was a girl, Mr. Lethbridge broke in suddenly.

"Yes, Mr. Erskine," he said, "you may be right in what you were saying—that is, up to a point—but you don't go deep enough."

"I am afraid I never do go very deep," was my reply. "The deeper one goes, as a rule, the greater the muddle."

"Not in this case," and he spoke quite eagerly. "Why, the whole life of the county is what John Wesley and Methodism have made it. People, as a whole, may seem to have discarded his teachings, but they are in the very air we breathe; the people's thoughts, the people's lives, are what they are to-day because of the work he did."

"I dare say," I replied, for, to tell the truth, I was anxious to avoid anything like a theological discussion.

"Yes, don't you see? In the background of people's minds there is the impress of his work; his influence is felt everywhere. Even the people who never enter a place of worship have been shaped and moulded by Methodism."

"In what way?" asked Hugh.

"Well, take such a question as war," replied Mr. Lethbridge. "John Wesley killed the very possibility of war."

"I wish I could see it," I could not help exclaiming.

"It is plain enough," he replied. "Methodism and war cannot go together. The love of peace has entered into the very essence of people's lives. Is not that something to be thankful for?"

"I am not so sure," replied Isabella Lethbridge. "May not war be a very good thing?"

"A good thing!" cried her father—"a good thing! Why, it's hellish! I would rather see a son of mine dead than a soldier! And that is the feeling Methodism has created throughout the county. You scarcely ever find a conscientious Methodist becoming a soldier. A soldier in this county is looked upon as a kind of legalized murderer."

"Surely," I said, "it is not so bad as that?"

"It amounts to that," was his reply. "For my own part, I have an utter abhorrence of anything which savors of militarism, and I know it is because of the impressions I received as a boy."

"But supposing war were to break out?" I said.

"War break out!" he interrupted. "How can it break out, unless some of our so-called statesmen make asses of themselves? No one wants war."

"No," I said—"that is, as far as the general feeling in the country is concerned; but supposing war were thrust upon us?"

"Who would thrust it upon us?" he asked, almost angrily.

"Germany, for example," was my reply.

"Impossible!"

"Not so impossible, I am afraid," I could not help replying. "Why, during the last few years we have twice been on the brink of war with Germany, and, unless I am mistaken, a war with that country is bound to come, sooner or later." This, I am afraid, I said rather for the sake of argument than because I really believed it. "Take that Agadir incident. We were within an ace of war then. Indeed, had Germany been as ready as she is now it would doubtless have come off."

"I do not believe it," was his reply. "The people of England would have refused; the whole nation would have risen up in protest against it, and not even the Government could have forced the country into a war which it detested."

"Not if we were attacked?" was my answer.

"I do not believe in the possibility of it at all," he replied. "We are essentially a peace-loving people."

"That may be, but even a peace-loving people may be obliged to defend itself."

"But we shall never be called upon to defend ourselves."

"I am not at all sure," was my answer. "Germany is just spoiling for war. Ever since she beat France she has been longing for expansion, and the military party in Germany maintain that the English people keep them from occupying their rightful place in the world."

"Yes, the military party," he said; "a negligible section of the country."

"Excuse me," was my answer, "but the military party in Germany is practically the nation. It is true there are a few Socialists who disclaim war, and profess to be at enmity with the military party; nevertheless, that party rules the nation, and if war should break out every Socialist would be obliged to fight for his country—and Germany means that it shall break out."

"And what then?" he asked.

"Then," I replied, "the power and solidarity of the British Empire will be tested as it has never been tested before. There will be such a struggle as has never been known in the history of the world. Every ounce of power that we have will be requisitioned; every able-bodied man in the country will be called to arms."

"But the country will refuse to respond," was his reply.

"If you are right, and the men of England refuse to respond, England will cease to be. There will be no England, and Germany will rule the destinies of the world."

"You seem to be very sure of what Germany will do," he said, rather impatiently.

"No one can travel in Germany, or read German literature, without knowing it. It is a nation under arms. The love of war is bred in the people. Militarism is glorified. They have such an army as was never known before, and they have utilized all their discoveries in science to make their army a perfect fighting machine. They have huge factories devoted to the making of air-ships and guns, and all that appertains to guns, and I tell you that if war breaks out between Germany and England, our country will be tried as it was never tried before. Do you mean to say that England would stand still while Germany sought to destroy us?"

"I mean that we are not a military people, and never will be." It was at this point that young Lethbridge sprang to his feet, like a man angry.

"I do not believe that you are right, pater," he said. "If England were in danger the young men of England would fight to the last man."

"No, they would not," replied the father, "because war is a devilish thing. It is opposed to the teaching of Christianity."

"But where would our Christianity be, where would everything we hold dear be, if Germany dominated the world?" protested Hugh. "Why, if I had a hundred lives I would give them for the defense of my country."

"Then patriotism would be more than your religion?"

"I cannot argue the matter from that standpoint," replied young Lethbridge. "I only know that I am an Englishman—every drop of my blood is English. God made me English, and if I have a love for my country, God gave me that love, and if there were a call for men I would respond."

"You would be no son of mine if you did," replied the father.

"But he would," cried Isabella Lethbridge. "Why, father, you are a fighter; you know you are, and I should be ashamed of Hugh if his country called him and he held back. There doesn't seem to be much in life worth being interested in, but if anything would arouse me, it would be the thought of England in danger."

"And would you believe in war, even if we were in the wrong?" asked her father.

"I cannot conceive of our being in the wrong," was her reply. "Besides, it can never be wrong to defend one's native land." The girl's eyes flashed as she made this reply, and I saw possibilities in her nature which I had not recognized before. Her lips quivered, and her features became animated with a kind of new life.

"But do you really believe, Mr. Erskine, that Germany means to force war on England?" she went on.

"No one who has been to Germany, and has studied the life there, can help knowing that they have been preparing for war for forty years, and no one can help realizing that the Germans hate the English with a deadly hatred. It may be only because of their jealousy, or it may be, as they say, that our Navy keeps them from realizing their rightful position. Anyhow, the fact remains. Our statesmen are doing their best to put off the evil day, but it is a recognized fact among those in high places that Europe at this moment is sitting on a powder magazine; and, mark you, if war does come it will not be a picnic."

"I tell you the people of England will never allow such a thing," urged Mr. Lethbridge doggedly; "we are a peace-loving people. Besides, we cannot go to war; we have no army worth calling an army, and I, for one, thank God for it."

"Of course there will be no war," said Mrs. Lethbridge confidently; "the Powers would not allow it, my dears."

"Are we sure that we have yet realized what Germany is, or what her people mean to do?" I asked. "During the last thirty years she has simply forced herself upon the life of the world; her commerce has progressed by leaps and bounds; she has placed her foot everywhere. Before Bismarck's days she had practically no voice in the counsels of the nations. To-day her voice is a dominant one, her commerce is still increasing; she has succeeded, in spite of our protests, in building a navy second to none but our own. Why did she build that navy? She can command an army of, perhaps, eight or ten million men, more perfectly equipped than any other army known in history. She has munitions, implements of war, which can practically laugh at those of any other nation."

"That shows her foolishness," said Mr. Lethbridge.

"How?"

"Because she does not know what other countries possess."

"Is not that where you make a mistake? Germany has a Secret Intelligence Service, which enables her to know the strength of every army and navy in the world. England at this time, for example, is simply riddled with spies. Germany knows the strength of our Navy to a nicety. She knows our every port, every harbor, every fortress; she has made it her business to do so, and Germany means war. Do you think that when the time comes England will sit idly by?"

"No! by heavens, no!" cried Hugh Lethbridge. "I doubt whether what you say is true, Erskine, but if England is ever in danger, Englishmen will be true to their name and their country."

"Yes, and Englishwomen too," cried Isabella Lethbridge. "I tell you nothing can destroy the old fighting instinct, which will protect home and Motherland. Dad," and she turned to her father almost fiercely, "do you mean to say that if we were in danger you would advise us to do nothing?"

Mr. Lethbridge laughed scornfully. "How can there be any danger?" he asked. "War cannot come about in these days, as it did in the old times. War depends now on the whole of the people; the democracy rules—not a few men in high places."

"Democracy does not rule," cried the girl, "and never will. Democracy is a mob which is forever calling out for leaders. No Government is democratic, it is always autocratic."

"You are talking nonsense, child," said her father. "You can do nothing to-day against the voice of the people, and the voice of the people is against anything like war. I repeat what I said just now—I would rather see a son of mine dead than that he should be a soldier! But there, there! There is no chance of it. Whatever England has been, she is to-day at peace, and as far as Cornwall is concerned, as I said just now, John Wesley has killed militarism."

He left the room as he spoke, while Hugh Lethbridge looked meaningly towards his sister.

"I am afraid I shall have to be going," I said, looking at my watch. "I have stayed too long already."

"No, no!" protested Hugh. "Stay a little longer. Do you know, Erskine, it is like a fresh breeze from the mountains to hear what you have been saying to-night. We live a starved, narrow life down here, and—and I'm sick of it. I almost wish war would break out."

"For shame, Hugh!" said his mother. "What good would you be as a soldier? No one can be an officer in an army unless he is trained; and as for your becoming a private, why, think how ridiculous you would look in a private's uniform."

"I am afraid I must be going," I persisted, moving towards the door.

"I will have the car out and drive you home," said Hugh Lethbridge.

"No," I said, "it is a beautiful night, and I think I would rather walk."

"But in your state of health, Mr. Erskine, it would be very foolish," said Mrs. Lethbridge. "Really, we cannot allow you."

"I would rather walk," I persisted. Whereupon Hugh announced his intention of accompanying me.

When Mr. Lethbridge bade me good-night he had quite recovered his equanimity, and expressed the hope that I would soon come to see them again.

"I feel like a toad in a hole," said Hugh, after we had walked some minutes in silence together.

"How is that?" I asked.

"What has life to offer a fellow? The pater insisted upon my going to the University and reading for the Bar. I am not fit for it—I know I am not fit. Then, although he pretends to be a man of the people, he is also socially ambitious. You would not believe it, would you? I know it is wrong for me to talk in this way, but somehow I cannot help it. You know, Erskine, as my father said just now, he was a poor man, and made money rapidly, and he is disappointed that the doors of the county people are not open to us. I do not care a fig about the county people myself; do you?"

"Some of them are very nice," I replied.

"You will not take it amiss of me if I tell you something, will you? And, of course, you will regard it as a confidence? It is something which means a lot to me."

"Do you think you know me well enough to tell me?" I replied. "After all, we have only met twice."

"I must tell you," he persisted. "As you say, I have only met you twice, but I seem to have known you all my life. Besides, a fellow must tell his thoughts to some one. I am in love, Erskine."

"That is interesting."

"Yes, but don't you see, everything is at cross-purposes. Old Treherne, down here, has a daughter several years older than I am. You have heard of Treherne, haven't you? He is the Squire."

"Yes, I have heard of Mr. Treherne."

"His daughter is on the shelf—has been for several years. He is as poor as a church mouse, is the Squire; but then, he is one of the big people in the county, and the pater has an idea that if I were to marry her … well, you can see, can't you?"

"The lady might not be willing," I suggested.

"Quite possible, of course; but the pater seems sure she would be. You see, she's thirty, if she's a day, and as ugly as they make 'em, and the pater wants me to sell my soul and marry her. By so doing, old Treherne would be able to pay off the mortgages on the estate, and I, in time, would become the Squire. Just think of it!"

"I thought he wanted you to read for the Bar?" I interposed.

"Yes, he does, but that is only one of his many schemes. He wants me to marry Treherne's daughter. Celia, they call her—Celia Treherne. Good, isn't it?"

"Why, isn't she an estimable lady?"

"Estimable! Estimable enough. But, as I told you just now, I am in love with a farmer's daughter, one of the class my family really belongs to, and the pater —well, I need scarcely tell you what he says."

"And this farmer's daughter's name?" I queried.

"I wish you would let me introduce you to her," he cried eagerly. "A sweeter girl never lived. I used to think of her as a sweetheart ten years ago, when the pater was poorer than he is now. I fought several boys about her. Mary Treleaven is her name. Do you think that you could persuade the governor? You see, he refuses to countenance it, and, without him, I haven't a penny with which to bless myself."

"My dear fellow," I said, "if you care anything about the girl you will make yourself independent of your father."

"Yes, but what am I fit for—what can I do? He professes to have democratic notions, and yet he has given me the education of a gentleman; sent me to a public school, where no one learns anything of any use, and then to Oxford, where I just scraped through, and got a pass degree. What is the good of all that to me? There is not a single thing I care anything about, except farming, and that needs capital. What would you advise me to do?"

"I am afraid I can't advise anything just now. You see, I know so little about either of you. Perhaps when I have been here a little longer I may be able to help." By this time we had reached the little wooded lane which led to my hut.

"You will come and see us again soon?" he pleaded.

"You are very kind," I replied. "If I am well enough, I will."

"I cannot believe you are so ill as you think," he said eagerly.

I did not answer him. Of what use was it for me to tell him of the gnawing pain which I could feel just then—pain which told me that my very life was being eaten away?

"Won't you come in?" I asked.

"No, I mustn't. Besides, you will be tired. I say! what is that?" and he pointed towards the highest part of the cliff, the base of which pushed itself out into the sea. I looked, and in the dim light saw what I felt sure to be a boat approaching the shore.

"Some fishermen, I expect," I replied.

"No, fishermen do not hang so close to the rocks as that," was his answer. "Besides, the boat is making directly for us. No one was ever known to land a fishing-boat on this beach. Fishing-boats go direct to the harbor at St. Eia."

We listened intently, and heard the steady splash of the oars, and presently I thought I heard low, murmuring voices, but I was not sure.

VII

ISABELLA LETHBRIDGE

During the next few days nothing happened, and, if the truth must be told, I am afraid I got very lonely and depressed. Simpson did his best to interest me, but failed. My books, too, seemed dull and colorless. I suppose it was natural. I was passing through a phase in my life which was the inevitable consequence of what had hitherto taken place. The malady from which I was suffering was taking rather an acute form just then, and I had neither the strength nor inclination for exercise. Thus, although the weather was glorious and the air pure and bracing, I found that sitting day after day amid the same surroundings was anything but exhilarating. Moreover, although I cannot explain it, a sense of dread possessed me. I felt sure that something was going to happen, and that I was going to be at the centre of some untoward event.

I expect I felt all the more irritable because my desire to live became stronger and stronger. It appeared to me that I had nothing to live for, and yet I hung on to life, and the hope of life, grimly.

"Simpson," I said one day, "you told me when we came here that an idiot lad, who went by the name of Fever Lurgy, waited on old Father Abraham and did his errands. What has become of him?"

"Don't know, sir."

"Does no one know?"

"Don't know at all, sir."

"It seems strange, doesn't it, that this lad, who was the first to tell of what had happened to the old man, should not have come here when he heard that the house was occupied again?"

"I did hear something of his running away, because he was afraid; but I know nothing."

"Afraid? Afraid of what?"

"You know what these idiot boys are, sir. I suppose he almost worshipped old Father Abraham, and when he knew his master was killed he feared to stay in the same neighborhood."

"Is that your conclusion too, Simpson?" I asked.

"I never thought of it before, sir."

That day I went out for a walk. Somehow the lethargy which had possessed me for a long time was gone, and my body for the time was instinct with a new life. My fancies about Fever Lurgy had laid hold of me, and I began asking myself all sorts of questions. I found my way into the village, and, seeing a group of men standing by the pump, joined them. I found them very willing to talk with me, and while at first they showed no desire to impart any information, they asked me countless questions. This, I have found since, is a characteristic of the Cornish people. They are exceedingly friendly, and are willing to show kindness to a stranger, but they will not take him into their confidence. They are curious to know everything he can tell them, but they will tell him nothing in return. While they believed I was simply a stranger from "up country," their only interest in me was to know who I was, where I came from, and all about my affairs generally. When they got to know that I was of Cornish descent, however, there was an entire change in their demeanor towards me. I was one of them.

In the course of a few minutes we got talking about Father Abraham and of his tragic end.

"It 'ave bin said, sur, that th' ould man's ghost do wander round the plaace, where you d' live, sur. Es et true?"

"I have never seen him, anyhow. Have you?"

"Well, sur, ted'n for we to say. Oal the saame, I heerd curious noises wawn night near your house."

"What kind of noises?" I asked.

"Oh, a kind of moanin' and cryin', like a gull in pain."

"Maybe it *was* a sea-gull," I suggested.

"No, sur, we d' know what gulls be like. Twad'n that. We be sure there was foul play, sur."

"What about that lad, Fever Lurgy?" I asked. "Does he live in the neighborhood now?"

"Bless you, sur, Fayver Lurgy a'n't bin seen since th' ould man was killed."

"No!" I said. "Isn't that strange?"

"Oa, he was a funny chap, was Fayver Lurgy. Do you know whay he was called Fayver Lurgy, sur?"

"Not the slightest idea," I replied.

"Well, sur, down 'long 'ere wi' we, when a great lousterin' chap wa'ant work, and do ait a lot, we d' say 'ee've got Fayver Lurgy. That es, two stomachs to ait, and noan to work. Tha's 'ow Fayver Lurgy got 'is name. He's as strong as a 'oss, but he wudd'n work. 'Ee wadd'n such a fool as 'ee made out. 'Ee allays was a button short, was Fayver Lurgy, but 'ee wadd'n no idiot, as people d' say."

"So you think he was afraid of being killed?" I suggested.

"Tha's what we d' think, sur."

"Who were his father and mother?" I asked.

"Nobody doan knaw, sur. He comed 'ere years and years ago, sur, weth an ould woman, who said she was 'is grandmother. When th' ould woman died, sur, Fayver Lurgy jist lopped round by hisself. Sometimes he ded a bit of work, and sometimes nothin'; but 'ee scraped up a living some'ow. When ould Father Abraham comed, he kipt with 'im reglar, and direkly 'ee was killed, Fayver Lurgy left the neighbrood, and nobody doan knaw where 'a es."

"Did you ever see old Father Abraham?" I asked.

"Yes, sur, I've seen 'im, but never to spaik to. Curyus ould chap he was. He 'ad long white whiskers and ter'ble bright eyes. Wan man I d' knaw spoke to 'un. Billy Barnycote 't was. Billy did say as 'ow he believed that ould Father Abraham was a furriner."

"I suppose he never went to Church or Chapel?" I asked.

"What! ould Father Abraham? Not 'ee. 'Ee ded'n go nowhere, so to spaik."

"And you," I said. "Do you ever go?"

"Sometimes, maaster, when there is a good praicher; but why shud us go when the praichers doan knaw more'n we do? I a'ain't bin since last Sunday-school anniversary. They 'ad a praicher from up to Plymouth. Clever chap 'ee was, too. Ef we cud allays git praichers like 'ee, we'd go every Sunday, but when a man like Tommy Coad d' git up and craake, we ca'ant stand it."

The day was beautifully fine, and, as I felt more than ordinarily well, I took a long route home. I had not gone far when, passing a stile, I saw Miss Lethbridge leap lightly into the road. I could not help reflecting how handsome she appeared in her light summer attire. When visiting her father's house a few days before she had struck me as being hard and repellent. Even now there was nothing winsome or girlish about her, but that she presented an attractive figure I could not deny. More than ordinarily tall, and finely formed, she carried her well-fitting clothes to perfection. Her features, too, while not exactly beautiful, were striking; and, flushed somewhat as she was by her walk through the fields, she seemed a part of that bright, early summer day.

"I hope you are better, Mr. Erskine," was her greeting.

"Yes," I replied, "I feel well enough to take a fairly long walk. I have been down into the village talking with some of the people there, and trying to discover some of the romance for which Cornwall is famous."

"And have had your labor for your pains," was her reply.

"Not entirely. I feel as though I have happened upon something which will lead to interesting developments."

"Believe me, you will not, Mr. Erskine."

"No? Why?"

"If ever there was a false tradition, it is the tradition that Cornwall is romantic. I have lived here all my life, and there is no more romance in the county than in that mine-heap," and she nodded towards a discarded mine which lay in the distance.

"The Cornish people," she went on, "have no sense of the mysterious, no sense of the romantic. If ever they had it, it has all died. I suppose that years ago, when the people were entirely ignorant, they believed in all sorts of superstitions, but now that they are better educated they have discarded everything but what they can see, and feel with their own hands. I am inclined to think they are right, too."

"I am not so sure," was my answer. And then I told her of the conversation that had taken place a few moments before.

"And do you imagine, Mr. Erskine, that any romance surrounds the old man who built the house you live in, and lived like a hermit away there by the cliff? Do you think that any romance is associated with the idiot lad who ran his errands and did his bidding?"

"Why not?"

"Because none exists."

"Pardon me if I do not agree with you. After all, there is something romantic in the thought of that old man coming there alone and building his hut in a lonely place, and spending years of his life there."

"Yes, it may seem so; but, pardon me, is there anything romantic in your coming there, Mr. Erskine?"

I shrugged my shoulders.

"I am afraid not," I replied.

"And I dare say the reason why he came there was just as unromantic. As for

Fever Lurgy, every village has its idiot who is a butt for rustic jokes."

"And what about old Father Abraham's mysterious disappearance?" I asked.

"What you call a mysterious disappearance," was her reply, "I regard as a sordid crime. I expect the old man had a little money hoarded up, some tramps heard of it, and, for the sake of that money, murdered him and threw his body over the cliff."

"At any rate," I said, "it is more pleasant to think that some mystery surrounded his life, and that he left the neighborhood from some romantic cause. Do you know, I am inclined to think that he is still alive, that he will turn up some day, and that the whole thing will be the talk of the countryside."

"And yet you are a trained lawyer, and have lived in London!" she laughed.

"Perhaps that is why. Lawyers get weary of hard thinking. Besides, when one comes to think of it, hard thinking is only responsible for a tithe of the discovery of truth. Far more of it is discovered by intuition than by logic."

"Do you know, you are very refreshing, Mr. Erskine. It is delightful to think of a man coming from hard, matter-of-fact London to Cornwall, and believing in the things that we simple rustics have discarded for a generation or more."

"Then you don't find life either romantic or mysterious?"

"I find it the most prosy, uninteresting thing imaginable. There is no mystery and no romance in the world; everything is hard, matter of fact, commonplace."

"Come, come, now, you cannot believe that," I laughed.

"One believes as one finds." And I thought her eyes became hard. "The other day I read what is called a romantic novel. It had gone through numberless editions, and was, I suppose, the rage of reading circles. It told of all sorts of mysterious happenings and romantic adventures. Then I reflected on what had actually happened to myself and to girls with whom I am acquainted. I went to school in France and Germany, as well as in England, and, do you know, I really cannot find one bit of romance that has ever happened to me or to the girls I have known. I can't remember anything mysterious."

"Isn't life one great mystery?"

"Yes, mystery if you like, but simply because of our ignorance. When the mystery is explained, the explanation is as prosy as that cottage." And she looked towards a cottage door, where a woman stood by her wash-tub. "Do you ever find life mysterious, Mr. Erskine?"

"Yes, it is mysterious from end to end. Sometimes, as I sit in my little wooden hut, facing the sea, at night-time, and hear the wind moan its way over the cliffs and across the waste of waters, when the solemn feeling of night broods over everything, I feel that life is one great mystery. What is behind it all? What is the meaning of everything? Is there a Creator? What lies beyond what we call death? Surely, that is mystery enough. You may say, if you like, that this feeling of mystery is because of our ignorance; nevertheless, it is there."

"Yes," she replied. "But the trouble is that, in so far as we have discovered mysteries, they turn out to be of the most prosy and commonplace nature. Things that were once unknown, and appealed to the world as romantic, now that they are known are just as prosy and uninteresting as the commonplace. Directly a thing is known it becomes humdrum. I went to a lecture one night given by a scientist—an astronomer, in fact. He was lecturing on the planet Mars. He said that he himself had examined the planet through a powerful telescope, and he had seen what to him were convincing proofs that there were canals cut through a piece of land which was similar in nature to the Isthmus of Panama. As a consequence the planet Mars was inhabited— inhabited by thinking, sentient beings, who lived in a world millions of miles from this world. It seemed very wonderful at that time, but, when I came to think of it, it was all very prosy. What if it were inhabited? It would simply mean that people somehow exist there, just as they exist here, and think and suffer, and struggle and die. Can anything be more prosy and unromantic than that?"

"Isn't the very mystery of death itself attractive—wonderful?" I asked.

"Do you think so?" And she looked at me curiously.

"Sometimes," I replied, "although I dread the thought of death, I have a kind of feverish curiosity about it, and I would like to die just to know."

"Yet it would be disappointing in the end. When that so-called mystery comes to be explained, there will be nothing but great, blank darkness."

"And that is your creed of life and death?"

"We can only argue from the known to the unknown," was her reply.

"And do you not long for something more?"

"Long!" And there was passion in her voice.

"Then, to you, religion, immortality, have no interest?"

"Yes, interest," was her reply, "but, like everything else, it is because of my ignorance. I know I am very ignorant, Mr. Erskine, and I dare say you will laugh at me for talking in the way I do; but, so far as I have read of the origins

63

of religions, they are simply the result of a fear of the unknown. People are afraid to die, and they have evolved a sort of hope that there is a life other than this. I know it is a cheerless creed, but don't facts bear out what I have said? In different parts of the world are different religions, and each and all of them are characteristic of the people who believe in them. Wasn't Matthew Arnold right when he said that the Greeks manufactured a god with classical features and golden hair, while the negroes created a god with black skin, thick lips, and woolly hair?"

"Do you go far enough back, even then?" I asked. "You are simply dealing with the shape of the god. What is the origin of the idea?"

"I suppose man invented it," was her reply.

"Yes, but how? After all, knowledge is built upon other knowledge. Imagination is the play of the mind around ascertained facts. 'No man hath seen God at any time.' How, then, have people come to believe in Him, except through some deeper and more wonderful faculty, which conveyed it to the mind? For the mind, after all, is only the vehicle, and not the creator, of thought."

She shrugged her shoulders.

"You get beyond me there, Mr. Erskine. When you dabble in metaphysics I am lost. Still, is it not a fact that the more intellectual the race the less religious it becomes? Take France, for example. Paris is the great clearing-house of ideas, and yet the French are an unbelieving people."

"Is that altogether true?" was my reply, for I was led to take up an attitude of the soundness of which I was far from being convinced. "Is not France literally sick and tired of the atheism which surged over the nation at the time of the Revolution? France no longer glories in hard unbelief, and, as far as I know, the French people are simply longing for faith, and, for that matter, are going back to faith. Not, perhaps, the faith which the Revolution destroyed, but to something deeper, diviner."

She seemed thoughtful, and for some time neither of us spoke. Then she burst out laughing merrily.

"Don't things seem reversed?" she said. "Here are you, a scholar of Oxford, and a clever lawyer, upholding tradition, imagination, intuition, superstition, while I, an ignorant girl, am discarding it all."

"Perhaps," I replied, "that is because life is long to you, short to me. When one comes to what seems the end of things, one looks at life differently. There," I went on, for at that moment we had passed a lad with his arm round a girl's waist, "that boy lives in heaven. He is with the girl he loves. Suppose you tried to convince that boy and girl there was no such thing as romance, would they believe you?"

"Perhaps not," she replied; "but I could take you down the village yonder, and show you men and women who, twenty years ago, were just as romantic as those two cooing doves; and to-day the men loaf round the village lanes, smoking, or, perhaps, are in the public-house drinking; while the women are slatternly, discontented, standing at the wash-tub, or scrubbing out cottages. Where now is the romance, or, for that matter, the love?"

"Then you don't believe in love either?"

She was silent, and I watched her face closely, and again I was struck by her appearance. Yes, no doubt, Isabella Lethbridge was more than ordinarily handsome. Her features, without being beautiful, were fine. The flash of her eyes betokened intelligence beyond the ordinary. At that moment, too, there was a look in them which I had not seen before—a kind of longing, a sense of unsatisfaction, something wistful.

"Love?" she repeated. "No, I don't think I believe in it."

"Surely," I said, "that is going a little bit too far."

"Yes, perhaps it is," was her answer. "There is love—the love of a mother for her child. You see it everywhere. A lion will fight for her whelps, a hen will protect her chickens. But I suppose you were meaning the love which man has for a woman, and woman for man?"

"Yes," I replied, "I was. I was thinking of that lover and his lass whom we have just passed."

"I do not know," she replied. "All I know is that I never felt it, and yet I confess to being twenty-four. It is an awful age, isn't it? Fancy a girl of twenty-four never having been in love! Yet, facts are facts. I do not deny that there is such a thing as affinity; but love, as I understand it, is, or ought to be, something spiritual, something divine, something which outlasts youth and all that youth means; something which defies the ravages of time, that laughs at impossibilities. No. I do not believe there is such a thing."

"Then what is the use of living?" I asked.

"I hardly know. We have a kind of clinging to life, at least the great majority of us have, although I suppose in the more highly cultured States suicides are becoming more common. We shudder at what we call death, and so we seek to live. If, like the old Greeks, we surrounded death with beautiful thoughts ____"

"Ah yes," I interrupted; "but then we get into the realms of religion. The

65

Greeks believed in an immortal part, and love to them was eternal."

"True," she replied. "But where is the old Greek mythology now? It has become a thing of the past. Mr. Erskine, will you forgive me for talking all this nonsense, for it is nonsense? I know I am floundering in a deep sea and saying foolish things. Besides, I must leave you. There is a house here where I must call."

She held out her hand as she spoke, and looked at me. I felt as though she were trying to fascinate me. For a second our eyes met, and I felt her hand quiver in mine. At that moment something was born in my mind and heart which I had never experienced before. I confess it here, because probably no one will read these lines but myself. I felt towards Isabella Lethbridge as I had never felt towards any woman before. Even in those days when I had flirted and danced and laughed with girls of my own age, and with whom I fancied myself in love, I had never felt towards a woman as I felt towards her.

"Good-day, Miss Lethbridge," I said, as I walked away.

"I hope you will come up to Trecarrel again soon," she said. "Please don't wait for a formal invitation; we shall always be glad to see you. At least, *I* shall," and she gave me a bewildering smile.

I walked some little distance down the road, then turned and watched her till she was out of sight. I tried to analyze the new feelings which had come into my life.

"Why am I so interested in her?" I asked. "What is this which has come to me so suddenly? Whatever it is, it is not love." And I knew I spoke the truth, even as I know it now. Yet she fascinated me. I reflected that her talk had been pedantic, the product of an ill-balanced mind, and, while she was clever, she was superficial. Yet she attracted me in a way I could not understand. She had moved me as no other woman had moved me, but I knew, as I know now, that I was not in love with her.

I walked slowly along. We had come to the end of June, and the birds were singing gaily. Away in the distance I could see the sheen of the waves in the sunlight. The great line of cliffs stood out boldly; the world was very fair. A weight seemed to have rolled from my shoulders. Oh, it was good to live— good to bask in the sunlight on that summer day! I laughed aloud. No romance! no mystery! no religion! no love! The girl had almost made me believe in what she had said, although at the back of my mind I felt it was all wrong. I looked at my watch, and knew that I must be returning, or Simpson would be anxious about me. He had become quite paternal in his care.

I descended the steep hill towards the little copse at the back of my house.

Once or twice I stopped and listened to the waves as they rolled on the hard, yellow beach, while the sea-gulls hovered over the great beetling cliffs.

"I won't die!" I cried. "I simply won't!"

And yet I knew at the time that death had taken possession of me, was even then gnawing away at the centre of my life.

I entered the little copse and drew near to the house. I had gone, perhaps, twenty yards, when I stopped. Peering at me through the leaves of the bushes, which grew thick on the side of the cliff, was a pair of gleaming eyes. They seemed to me to be the eyes of a madman, a maniac. Perhaps my imagination was excited, and my mind unbalanced, but I thought I saw revenge, hatred, murder. The eyes were large and staring. I could see no face, no form. I felt no fear, only a sense of wonder and a desire to know. I took a step in the direction of those wild, maniacal orbs, and I heard a cry—hoarse, agonized. I took another step forward and looked again, and saw nothing, neither did I hear another sound. Feverishly I made my way towards the spot, but there was nothing there. No footmarks could I discover, no signs of any one having been there. I am perfectly certain I saw what I have described, as sure as that I am sitting in my little room at this moment, but although I searched everywhere I could discover nothing.

I returned to my house and began to dress for dinner; but all the while I was haunted by those wild, staring eyes.

VIII

MYSTERY

"Simpson," I said, after dinner, "do you believe in ghosts?"

"Yes, sir, I think so, sir."

"What are your views about them?"

"Well, sir, I don't know that I could put them into words. Will you have your coffee now, sir?"

"Yes, please, Simpson; and will you pass my cigar-box?"

"Yes, sir; thank you, sir."

"You are somewhat of a philosopher, aren't you, Simpson?"

"In my own way, sir. If I hadn't been I should have been dead before now."

"Oh, indeed," I said. "How?"

"Well, sir, it was during the two years I was married. It was my philosophy that saved me."

"In what way?" I asked.

"Well, you see, sir, I hadn't been married more than a month before I discovered that my wife had a remarkable command of language. While we were courting, she pretended to be shy, and had very little to say; but when we got married she developed the power of speech awful, sir—just awful. At first I answered her back, and every time I spoke I seemed, as it were, to open up the fountains of the great deep, until I thought I was going mad. Then I got to thinking about it, sir, and after careful study of my wife's character I came to the conclusion that the only way I could meet her was by silence. I didn't smoke at that time, sir, she having said as how she hated smoking; but I bought a pipe and tobacco, and every time she started talking I just loaded up my pipe and commenced smoking. I didn't say a word, sir, but let her go on and on."

"Well," I asked, "did that cure her?"

"Not at first, sir; for a time she was worse than ever, and I thought I should have to give it up. That was where my philosophy came in, sir; I just held on. The more she talked the more I smoked, never uttering a word."

"Yes," I said, "and what then?"

"She began to cry, sir. She cried and cried until I thought she was going to cry her eyes out. I almost gave in, but being a philosopher I still kept quiet. After that, she began to threaten what she would do. She rampaged round the house like a mad woman, but I only bought a new pipe."

"And did you master her that way?"

"No, sir; I never mastered her. It is my belief that if a woman has got the gift of the gab as she had, she never can be mastered. But she left me, sir."

"I thought you told me she was dead, Simpson?"

"Oh, no, sir; I never told you that; I only told you that I had a wife for two years. Yes, sir, she kept with me for two years, trying to break me down. Then, one day, when I came into the house I found a letter from her. She said that she could not live with a brute who would not answer her back, so she went off on her own."

"And what did you do then, Simpson?"

"I went to live with your father, sir, and I have lived with the family ever since. But it was my philosophy which saved my life. If I had given in she would have killed me."

"And where is she now, Simpson?"

"I don't know, sir, and I don't want to. Yes, sir, nothing but philosophy will master a woman."

"Well, to come back to where we were, Simpson. You being a philosopher, have you any explanation to offer as to ghosts?"

"Well, sir, not ever having seen one, I don't see how I can. If I had seen one I might answer. Have you seen one, sir?"

"Yes, Simpson. This evening, just before coming in to dinner, I was coming along the footpath through the copse, when I saw a pair of bright, staring eyes, like the eyes of a madman. There was no doubt about it; I am certain I saw them. I could make out no face, but I am certain I saw the eyes. When I went to the place where I saw them I could find nothing. What is your opinion about it?"

Simpson thought a minute, then he replied solemnly:

"It was an 'allucination, sir."

"Was it that, Simpson?"

"Well, sir, if you will excuse me for asking, who had you been with before you saw the eyes? Had you spoken to any one? Had you been talking about ghosts, or that sort of thing?"

"No, Simpson; I had been talking with Miss Lethbridge, a young lady who does not believe in ghosts."

"Ah, that explains, sir."

"How, Simpson?"

"A woman always upsets the mind—always. If you had said you had seen the face without the eyes, I could perhaps have believed you; but when you say you saw eyes without a face, and then tell me you had been talking with a young lady, I know just what is the matter."

"Yes; but, Simpson, that is not all. I heard an awful moan. Rather more than a moan—it was a kind of moan and cry combined."

"And did you hear any rustling in the bushes, sir?"

"Not a sound."

"Ah, well, sir, I stand by my opinion. Anything more you want, sir?"

"Nothing more, thank you." And Simpson went away into the kitchen.

He had not been gone long, when I heard footsteps outside, and shortly after young Hugh Lethbridge appeared.

"You don't mind my calling, do you, Erskine?" he said.

"On the contrary, I am delighted," I replied. "I have just been talking with my man about something which I saw this evening, and he can offer no explanation. Perhaps you can." And I told him what I had seen.

"By Gum!" he said, "that's funny. You are sure you are not mistaken, Erskine?"

"Impossible," I replied. "I saw those eyes as plainly as I see you. It was not dark—the sun had not set, for that matter."

"And were you excited in any way?" And he looked at me steadily.

"No," I replied; "I was not excited."

"It's funny. You don't imagine, do you, that there was anything supernatural about it?"

"I wish I did, but I am sorry to say that I have no faith whatever in the supernatural."

"No," he said; "I remember what you told us up at Trecarrel. And you searched the place thoroughly?"

"Yes, thoroughly. You see, I was curious."

"And you had not been thinking about supernatural things?"

"Not in the least. For that matter, I had a few minutes before met your sister."

"Oh, yes; Bella told me she had met you, and was afraid she had shocked you."

"No, I was not shocked at all; I was very interested."

"Bella is a curious girl," said Hugh Lethbridge, after a short silence. "We have always been very good friends, but I have never understood her. Even when she was quite a girl she was different from those of her own age."

"In what way?"

"She was always so hard, so matter of fact. I have told her more than once that she has no soul." He said the words lightly, but to me they were ominous with meaning. He had put into words what I had felt.

"I suppose I ought not to say this," went on Hugh; "but I don't feel towards you as I do towards other men. I don't know why it is. No sooner did I see you than I wanted to have you as a friend; I felt I could trust you. You don't mind my saying this, do you?"

"Rather it is awfully good of you."

"I am a lonely kind of fellow," he went on, "and my home life has shut me off from the society of those I might care for. Other fellows invite their college chums to stay with them, and all that kind of thing, but the pater never allowed me to do it. Why, I don't know. I know it is wrong to discuss one's people before a stranger, but, as I said just now, I don't feel you are a stranger. What do you think of my father, Erskine?"

"I think he is a strong, capable man," I replied.

"Yes, there is no doubt about that. Why, years ago he was only a poor lad, living in a district where there seemed to be very few chances of a lad making his way, and yet you see what he has done. He was a clerk in the office of a man who had to do with shipping in Penzance. Only in a small way, you know, but he gave my father the chance to learn the business. He did learn it. What the pater doesn't know about shipping isn't worth knowing. To-day he owns scores of vessels. He got into touch with the mining world, too, and he seemed to possess a sort of genius for fastening on to mines that would pay. He has not only a controlling interest in the few prosperous Cornish mines, but he is connected with the mining world in almost every country where mines are to be found. He is as keen as a razor, is the pater, and has a way of making his will felt everywhere.

"And yet he is a most conscientious man. That is, conscientious in his own way. He used to be very religious. He used to pray at the Chapel, and all that sort of thing, but he's given it up now. But he holds to the form of religion still. As you heard him say the other night, he is a very strong believer in democracy. On the other hand, a greater autocrat never lived. In reality he believes in the feudal system, even while he professes to scorn what we call aristocracy. Yes, I see you smile. Never was a man more anxious to associate with county families than he. But he never yields an inch to them. If he had, he would have been admitted into what is called county society. Even as it is, Squire Treherne seems to be afraid of him."

"How is that?" I asked.

"Oh, he pays deference to his opinions; always supports him in public matters, and all that sort of thing. I am inclined to think that the pater has old Treherne in his power. You will not say anything about this, will you, Erskine? I do not believe my father cares a fig about me," he added.

"Nonsense!" I replied.

"I don't really. In a way he is interested in me. I suppose it is because blood is thicker than water, but do you know I can never remember the time when he kissed me, or anything of that sort. He always tried to rule me with a rod of iron."

"And has he treated your sister in the same way?" I asked.

"Yes, and no. Do you know, Erskine, my sister is a strange girl."

I was silent. I felt I had no right to ask the question which rose in my mind.

"What do you think of Bella?" he asked suddenly.

He did not seem to realize that he was overstepping the bounds of good taste in asking me, a stranger, such a question, and I realized more than ever that he was only an impulsive boy, although he had reached man's estate. Indeed, in one sense, Hugh did not know what it was to be reserved, and yet in others he was strangely reticent.

I thought he seemed to be about to take me further into his confidence at this point, but, perhaps noting the non-committal nature of my reply, he desisted.

"Of course, she's a bundle of contradictions," he said; "but she's really splendid. Why, on the day after she'd—but, there, I mustn't tell you about that. Anyhow, there was an accident at Pendeen Mine. Two men were believed to be in danger of drowning by the flooding of the old workings. The miners had made every attempt—at least, so they said—to rescue them, and to do anything more would be to throw away their own lives."

"Yes," I said. "What then?"

"Bella went to them and talked to them as they had never been talked to before. She laughed all their protests to scorn, and when they proved to her that, humanly speaking, they had done all that men could do, she insisted upon going down the mine herself. It was the maddest thing a woman could do, and God only knows how she did it; but she rescued the miners. Why, it was in all the newspapers. Yes, Bella is magnificent, but—but——"

Hugh Lethbridge was silent for some time after this, neither did I speak. I was thinking of the impression she had made on me when I first saw her.

"She was never like other girls, even when she was a child," he went on. "She did not care for games—that is, ordinary children's games—so, although she is only two years older than I, we were never what you call playfellows. She is a very brainy girl, too, and by the time she was fourteen had read all sorts of out-of-the-way books."

"I wonder she did not go to Somerville or Girton when she left school."

"That's what she wanted," replied Lethbridge, "but the pater said he did not believe in women going to a university. He has always maintained that this modern craze about advanced education for women is so much nonsense. Still, Bella is an educated girl. She speaks French and German and Italian fluently, and there is scarcely a classical writer in these languages whom she has not read first hand. Yes, Bella is a strange girl, but very hard."

Again there was a silence between us for some seconds.

"She is not at all like mother," went on Lethbridge. "I wish she were. Although, as you saw the other night, we teased mother about being general manager of the world, there is scarcely a family in the parish which mother has not helped in one way or another, and in a way she is very popular; but no one would think of going to Bella in trouble."

I must confess that I wanted to ask more questions about her, but refrained from so doing. After all, it would not have been good taste on my part.

"Well, I must be going now," said Lethbridge presently, rising from his chair. "I am glad I have seen you. Our chat, somehow, has done me good, although I have done most of the talking. I was awfully restless after dinner to-night, and the walk here, and seeing you, have made me feel better. By the way"—and I saw that this was what he had really come for—"I spoke to you about Mary Treleaven the other night."

"Yes, I remember."

"I have had a row with the pater about her to-day."

"I am sorry for that."

"It was bound to come. You see, he will not hear of my marrying her. He says it would be pure madness on my part, and if I will not fall in with his wishes he will not give me a penny. I should like to introduce you to Mary; I told you so, didn't I? Will you let me?"

"If you like, certainly," I replied; "but really, Lethbridge, I cannot help you in that matter. I would not, even if I could. It would not be right."

"If you knew her you would," he said, with boyish eagerness. "She's the finest, sweetest girl in the country, and she is the only one I could be happy with. As for the pater's ideas, I won't fall in with them—I won't." He went to the door as he spoke, and looked out over the sea.

"It's a glorious night," he said; "there is not a cloud in the sky, and the light of the moon transforms everything into a fairyland."

I went to his side as he spoke, and as I did so a kind of shiver passed through me. The night was, indeed, wonderful. The moon shone so brightly that no stars appeared, and I could see the long line of cliffs stretching northward. Scarcely a breath of wind stirred, and I could hear the waves lapping musically on the hard yellow beach beneath.

"I will walk a few steps with you, Lethbridge," I said. "I will not go far. But really this is not an evening to spend indoors. How I wish I were strong and healthy!"

Putting on a summer overcoat, I walked with him along the footpath through the copse, and when at length we reached the open country, where heather-covered moorland stretched away on either side, both of us stopped and listened.

"What a noise the silence is making!" said Lethbridge. "Did you ever hear anything like it?"

"No," I said, "the hush is simply wonderful."

Scarcely had we spoken, when rising suddenly before us was the form of a man, and again those strange eyes, which had haunted me for hours, flashed before me. The man moved so quickly that I could not discern his features. He uttered a cry as he went—a cry similar to that I heard in the copse hours before.

"Do you know who it is?" I asked.

"No," replied Lethbridge. "Strange, isn't it?"

"Anyhow, it explains what I saw this afternoon. It might seem as though some one were watching me."

"I will follow him, if you like," said Lethbridge, "and find out who it is."

"Oh, no, don't trouble; very possibly it means nothing. But I think my mind must be excited, after all. I will go back now, if you don't mind. Good-night."

And I went slowly back to my little hut, wondering what the apparition might mean.

IX

AT THE VICARAGE

On my return to my room, I naturally reflected upon what young Hugh Lethbridge had told me. It may seem strange that, on such a short acquaintance, he spoke to me so freely about his family, but what I have written down is, as far as I can remember, exactly what took place. Hugh Lethbridge was scarcely twenty-three, and, although he looked older, was little more than a lad. He was the child of his mother rather than of his father, and was lacking in anything like secretiveness, especially to any one whom he liked. For some reason or another I had seemed to captivate him, so much so that he opened his heart and gave his confidence more fully than was natural on such a short acquaintance.

In many respects young Lethbridge was sensitive and self-contained, but in other ways he was so impulsive that he overstepped the bounds of good taste. I got to know him better afterwards, and found that, although he had spoken so freely to me, he was regarded by many as reserved. Besides, he was hungering for sympathy, and because he thought I sympathized with him his confidences were so personal that I almost felt uncomfortable.

Nevertheless, I pondered a great deal over what he had told me. Evidently the household at Trecarrel was not altogether happy, and an estrangement existed between Mr. Lethbridge senior and his son. As for Isabella Lethbridge, she presented an interesting study to me. As I have said, she appealed to me as no other woman had ever appealed to me before. For the moment I had thought I was in love with her, but, on reflection, I knew I was not. I was able to study her character calmly and think of her in a kind of detached way. She formed no part in my life. She was an interesting specimen of humanity, whom I took pleasure in analyzing, but the feeling I had towards her was not love. Rather she repelled me even while she fascinated me. The thought of her never caused my heart to throb, nor made the blood course through my veins one whit the faster.

Besides, it was not for me to think about such things. I had come down to Cornwall to die. In a few months the spark of my life would go out, and I should enter the great darkness.

Days and weeks passed away, and very little of importance happened worthy of record. Often I reflected upon the uselessness of my life. Why, after all, should I live? No one but Simpson was really interested in me, and only he would grieve when I had gone; then again the old revulsion against becoming nothing surged within me. I had hopes, longings, intimations which seemed to overleap the boundaries of time and sense. If this life were all, then life was a mockery, a promise without possible fulfilment, a hope born only to be disappointed.

Sitting there alone night after night, hearing the cry of the sea-birds, listening to the wail of the wind as it swept over hill and dale, or found its way across the great waste of waters, I asked a thousand questions and pondered over the problems of life and death, without ever receiving one single ray of light. Sometimes I became so lonely that I called Simpson into my room and talked with him, but I never allowed him to know how dark were the prospects which faced me. The questions I asked him, I remember, were almost flippant in their nature. I made a joke of death, as I tried to make a joke of everything else; so much so that I fancied Simpson was convinced that I did not trouble. After all, why should I worry the poor, simple-minded fellow with questions which he could not answer or understand? The best thing to do was to bear everything with a kind of stoicism, and to make a jest of what really haunted me night and day with strange persistency. Indeed, I think I sometimes rather pained Simpson with my flippant remarks, for I found that the beliefs of his boyhood were still powerful in his life. It is difficult to eradicate the impressions of youth.

"After all, Simpson," I said one day, "sleep is a good thing providing one has no bad dreams, and if I sleep for ever I shall know nothing about it."

"But if one should dream, sir?" suggested Simpson.

"You are quoting Hamlet," I said.

"I don't know the gentleman you refer to," was Simpson's somewhat indignant reply; "indeed, I never heard of him. But don't you think, sir, that education and cleverness are very poor things?"

"Doubtless, Simpson. But why do you say so?"

"Why, sir, here are you, a gentleman who has been to college and all that. You were spoken of in the newspapers as one who would do great things some day, and yet you don't know as much as my old father did, who never had a day's schooling in his life."

"How is that, Simpson?"

"Well, sir, he *knew* there was a life after death. He saw the angels, sir."

"Did he tell you so, Simpson?"

"Yes, sir, he did. He was a very ignorant man, sir, but he knew. Besides, sir—

excuse me for saying so—but aren't your opinions very foolish, sir?"

"I dare say," I replied. "But to what particular opinions do you refer?"

"Opinions about dying, sir. If a watchmaker makes a watch, he makes it keep time, doesn't he?"

"Yes," I replied; "but if one of the wheels doesn't fit, the watch stops, and somehow my inside wheels don't fit, or rather they are made of poor material, Simpson."

"Of course, sir, it is not for me to contradict you, but I don't think you have been well educated, sir."

"My teachers are doubtless to blame, but the worst of it is your Vicar here seems to know nothing for certain, neither do your preachers at Chapel. It is all a matter of guesswork."

"Yes, sir, I know I cannot answer you properly, sir, but I do not believe Almighty God is a fool."

"What do you mean, Simpson?"

"Well, sir, I have an old watch which my grandfather used to carry, and it keeps good time still. The watch was made by a man, and it has lasted nearly a hundred years. Now, I don't believe Almighty God would take so much trouble in making us and then let us last only twenty or thirty years. Excuse me, sir."

I mentioned some time ago that Mr. Trelaske, when he had visited me, told me of his intention to invite me up to the Vicarage. He had fulfilled his promise, but I had not been well enough to take advantage of his kindness. This invitation, however, he had repeated, and one night I found my way to the Vicarage. I had hoped for a quiet chat with him, but to my surprise I found three other guests besides myself. One was Squire Treherne, another was a young fellow named Prideaux, and the other was a clergyman from a neighboring parish.

Mr. Trelaske was a widower, whose household affairs were conducted by a man and his wife by the name of Tucker. He received me most kindly, and played the part of host perfectly. It happened, too, that young Prideaux knew a man who was at Balliol with me, and this fact led to many reminiscences of college life. The fact, moreover, of my being at Winchester greatly interested Squire Treherne in me. He was an old Winchester boy, and was eager to ask questions concerning the school and to compare it with the days when he was there. In fact, before I had been in the house an hour, I found myself on a friendly footing with them all, and they spoke quite freely in my presence.

"By the way, Squire," said Prideaux presently, "I hear that Lethbridge has made another big *coup*. The way that fellow makes money is simply marvellous."

"Yes," said Squire Treherne, "and he has made it at my expense, too."

"At your expense? How is that?"

"He has found tin on my land."

"Has he? That's good. It will mean mining royalties for you."

"Not a bit of it. He persuaded me to sell the farm on which the tin was discovered two years ago. I did not want to sell it, but I wanted the money, and as the farm was, in a way, outside my ring fence, I consented. Evidently, he knew of the tin, but didn't let on. Got it for a song, too. Now he has the whole thing."

"That is bad luck," said Mr. Trelaske. "He makes money at every turn. I would not mind if one of our own set was lucky, but for that fellow—a dissenter and a Radical—to do it riles me."

"Well, he is a capable man, isn't he?" said Mr. Robartes, the other clergyman.

"Capable, if you like," replied the Vicar.

"And public-spirited too, isn't he?"

"Only in a way. The fellow isn't a sportsman, and, in the true sense of the word, isn't an Englishman. That is why I dislike him. As you know, too, he opposes the Church at every corner. I suppose it is natural in a rabid dissenter, but it is hard to bear."

"Still, he is a great employer of labor," said Prideaux. "And as for young Lethbridge, he is quite a decent fellow."

"I suppose Mr. Lethbridge still goes to the Chapel, doesn't he?" asked Mr. Robartes.

"Oh yes, I suppose so," was the Vicar's reply. "I believe, if he hadn't been a dissenter, things might have been all right."

"How? What do you mean?"

"Oh, at bottom a dissenter is never really an Englishman. Did you see that speech he made some little time ago up at Polzeath? He was crying down the Army and saying that our nation was being bled to death to keep up a useless institution. That is what I cannot stand."

They went on talking in this way for a considerable time until I began to get rather bored. It seemed to me that they discussed the Church and Dissent as two rival institutions. They regarded the Church as something which should be supported because it was a State affair. As for anything deeper, it did not appear in their conversation. Churchgoing was regarded as something that ought to be a national institution, and as such should be kept up. A few months before I dare say I might have taken an academic interest in the conversation, but as I reflected upon Dr. Rhomboid's verdict upon me it all seemed paltry and foolish. Church and Chapel, as institutions, did not matter a straw to me.

"What does Almighty God, if there is an Almighty God, Who made all the worlds, care whether a man goes to Church or to Chapel?"

I remember propounding this question quite suddenly, and it seemed to take them aback.

"You are a Churchman, aren't you?" asked Mr. Robartes eagerly.

"I suppose so, if I am anything," I laughed. "I was confirmed while I was at Winchester, but for the life of me I can't see that it matters whether a man goes to Church or to Chapel."

"But surely you have no sympathy with these dissenters?"

"I hardly know," was my reply. "I have been to the Methodist Chapel down here two or three times. I went out of curiosity. You see, my lease of life is very short, and I was wondering whether any of them could tell me what lies beyond the grave."

I saw Mr. Trelaske look on the floor as I spoke. He evidently remembered our conversation.

"It seems to me that we have to leave such things as that," said the Squire. "The Bible and the Church teach us that there is a life beyond the grave, and we had better let it stand at that. As for the Church, it makes a man a good neighbor, a good citizen, and a good Englishman. Besides, the Church doesn't cramp a man. He can be a good sportsman, enjoy a glass of wine, play a game of cards, and still be a good Churchman. That is why I am glad the Methodists are still losing ground. Of course they must."

There was nothing harsh in the way he said this. He seemed to regard dissenters as a class apart—a people with a kink in their brains, who out of pure stubbornness adopted a form of religion which somehow made them outsiders. I dare say, if I had gone deeper into the matter, I should have found something which had not appeared in their conversation, but such was the impression I received.

"By the way," said Mr. Trelaske presently, "this is bad news about Serbia, isn't it?"

"Yes, very bad," replied the Squire. "I should not be surprised if it doesn't lead to complications. These Serbs are barely civilized."

I did not understand what he meant, for I had not taken sufficient interest in what was going on to open a newspaper for several days, and I said so.

"I tell you," said Squire Treherne, "it is a serious matter. Last Sunday some Serbians murdered the Crown Prince of Austria, and I am afraid it will raise a rumpus. You see, Serbia is backed up by Russia, and if Austria threatens to take reprisals there may be a row."

I did not follow with very much interest what they were saying about the trouble in the Balkan States. What did interest me, however, was the tremendous difference between their attitude to war and that which Mr. Lethbridge took. To them the defense of their country was a sacred thing—indeed, almost a religion. I found that Mr. Trelaske had two sons, both of whom were in the Army, and that young Prideaux was a captain in the Territorials. They assumed, as a matter of course, that no man could keep out of the Army in time of national danger. It was not something to argue about; it was something settled as a fixed principle in their lives. No one seemed to believe, however, that trouble between Serbia and Austria could affect England. All of them appeared to think with Lord Salisbury, that we must retain our attitude of "Splendid Isolation," whatever might take place. Perhaps I ought to except young Prideaux, who, having no fixed beliefs, seemed to have doubts about the matter.

"I wish these blessed Radicals were not in power," he reflected, between puffs of his cigar.

"For that matter, all of us do," said Squire Treherne, in response. "But still, there it is. They have got the upper hand of us now, and it seems as if they are going to keep it."

"What I can't stand about the Radicals," said Mr. Robartes, "is that they aren't gentlemen."

"Oh, I don't know about that," said Prideaux. "There's Grey, for instance, he's a gentleman, and a sportsman too."

"Yes, but he is different from the rest. I wonder how he stays with that lot! I expect if we were dragged into this trouble the present Government would adopt a peace-at-any-price attitude. The great majority of Radicals are dissenters, and nearly all dissenters seem to be fed with anti-war ideas. You remember what took place at the time of the Boer War?"

"I am not sure they weren't right about that," remarked the Vicar; "I don't mean about the war itself, but about giving self-government to South Africa. The Boers have settled down remarkably well."

"Nonsense, Parson," said Squire Treherne. "It was pure madness. Supposing war were to break out, we should have a revolution in South Africa before we could say 'Jack Robinson.' These Boers ought to have been kept under our thumb. Do you know, I had an awful row with Lethbridge about that."

"How are the Lethbridges regarded in the neighborhood?" I asked, for I was anxious to avoid anything like a political discussion.

"Regarded in the neighborhood?" replied Squire Treherne. "Oh, we have to tolerate them, you know. Lethbridge is a man of great influence, and, of course, he's very rich. That is where he has the pull. He is the largest employer of labor in this district, and as a consequence people look up to him."

"I don't mean that so much," I said. "How is the family regarded socially?"

The Squire did not reply, but the Vicar was very pronounced.

"Oh, socially," he said, "they scarcely exist. You see, Lethbridge, in spite of his money, is a parvenu and rank outsider. It is true that his wife comes of a decent family, but a few years ago he was a poor lad in this district, and people can't forget it. Besides, the fellow is such an aggressive Radical. He is constantly treading on the corns of people who would otherwise be civil to him."

"What about his children?" I said. "I happen to have met them both, and they strike me as being well educated and presentable."

"Yes, his children are not so bad, and but for their father would doubtless be well received. At least, Hugh would. He is quite a nice boy. As for the girl, I don't know anything about her."

"The girl is handicapped by her father," said young Prideaux. "In spite of everything, she is placed in a curious position."

"How is that?"

"They occupy a kind of half-way position. On the one hand, they do not associate with the people to whom Lethbridge belonged twenty years ago, and, on the other, they are not quite our sort. Still, I believe the people would have forgiven them, in spite of the father, if the girl hadn't been such a heartless flirt."

"A flirt?" I repeated.

"Yes. She's a dashed fine-looking girl, you know. Clever, too; and when she likes can be quite fascinating; but, like the rest of her class, she can't play the game."

"No?" I said, thinking of what her brother had told me.

"No, there was young Tom Tredinnick; fine fellow Tom is, too. He fell head over heels in love with her, and every one thought they were going to make a match of it, but she treated Tom shamefully. There was Nick Blatchford, too; she treated him just as badly. She led him to the point of an avowal, and then chucked him."

"That class of people have no sense of honor," said the Vicar. "Of course, we can't get away from them down here. Methodism of one sort or another is the established religion of the county, and they are nearly all Radicals. In fact, they are anti-everything. Anti-smoking, anti-drinking, anti-sporting, anti-vaccination, and all the rest of it."

"I wonder," I said musingly.

As I went home I tried to gather up the impressions the company had made upon me, and I reflected that the atmosphere of the Vicar's house was utterly different from that of Mr. Lethbridge's. In a way, both were entirely new to me. I was a town-bred boy, and knew practically nothing of country life, and as a consequence was utterly unacquainted with the thoughts and feelings of those who lived far away from London.

I had not time, however, to follow my reflections to their natural issue, for no sooner had the carriage, which I had hired for the evening, dropped me at the footpath at the end of the little copse than my thoughts were turned into an entirely different channel. I was perhaps a hundred yards from my little dwelling-place, when suddenly some one crept out of the undergrowth and stood before me.

For the time of the year the night was dark. It was now midsummer, but a change had come over the weather, and dark clouds hung in the sky. Still, there was enough light for me to discern the figure of a man, who stood directly in my pathway.

"Be you the straanger?" he said.

"What do you mean?" I asked; "and who are you?"

"Be you the straanger wot d'live in Father Abram's 'ut?" The man's voice was thick, and his enunciation anything but clear.

"That seems remarkably like my own business," I replied.

"Be you the straanger wot d'live in Father Abram's 'ut?" He repeated the words almost feverishly, and his voice trembled.

"What if I am?" I asked.

"Then go away! Go away!"

"Why should I?"

"Ca'ant tell 'ee."

"But why should I go away? Who are you?"

"Never mind that! You go away! Go away to once!"

By this time I had become more accustomed to the darkness, and saw that the man was of huge proportions, and I judged that he had a serious purpose in speaking to me.

"I tell 'ee," he went on, "that you must go away; ef you do'ant ..." Here he stopped as though he did not know how to finish his sentence. My mind worked quickly, and I remembered my previous experiences which had taken place at this very spot. His presence explained those wild, staring eyes which I had seen in the copse, and the apparition which had puzzled me on the night I had talked with Hugh Lethbridge.

What he might mean by dogging my footsteps I could not explain, but that there was some meaning I felt quite sure.

"You have been following me for days," I said.

He grunted an assent.

"I found you watching me last Thursday week. You crept away from me when I went after you."

"I dedn't main no wrong."

"Yes, but what do you mean?"

"You must go away!—go away!" he repeated.

"Come with me to the house," I said. "I want to talk with you."

He gave a cry of abject fear.

"I mustn't! I mustn't! I be afeerd!"

"What are you afraid of?"

"I ca'ant tell 'ee! You must go away!"

"Go away where?"

"Anywhere; but you mustn't stay in thicky house! I've tould 'ee. Summin'll happen to 'ee ef you do'ant!"

"What will happen to me?"

"I ca'ant tell 'ee, but you must go away!" The man repeated the words with wearisome iteration. He seemed to be obsessed with this one thought. He spoke unintelligently. He might have been a machine repeating over and over the same words.

"You are Fever Lurgy," I said.

Again the fellow gave a cry as if of fear.

"Do'ant 'ee tell nobody," he cried. "But go away!—go away! I tell 'ee, ef you do'ant…." Again he stopped, like one who is afraid to finish his sentence.

"Some one has sent you to me," I said. "Who?"

"I mustn't tell 'ee—I mustn't tell 'ee!" he cried.

"But you must tell me. Come, you are going with me to the house, and I am going to know everything."

He started back as I spoke, and then rushed from me. I heard him among the bushes; then he spoke again.

"You must go away!—you must go away at once!"

I waited for some time but heard nothing more. Then I made my way to my little house, wondering at the meaning of what I had seen and heard.

X

WIRELESS TELEGRAPHY

I did not sleep well that night. The incident of Fever Lurgy raised many questions in my mind. I felt as though I were the centre of some mystery—a mystery of which I was ignorant. I was more convinced than I had ever been that old Father Abraham was not dead. I believed, too, that he had a motive out of the ordinary in coming to this spot and building the hut, and that the reason of his disappearance was not an ordinary crime, as was generally supposed. I pieced together all the events which had taken place since I had been in the neighborhood, and tried to see a meaning in them all, but I could not find any key that would unlock the door of the mystery. I knew nothing of Father Abraham's doings. I was simply a poor wretch who had come there to die, and yet, from the vehemence of Fever Lurgy's voice, it might seem as though there were some plot against me—as though some one wished to do me harm.

Twelve months before I should have rejoiced at what seemed like an adventure. It would have added spice to life. I should have thrown myself into the work of solving the mystery with avidity. Then I was strong and vigorous, scarcely knowing the meaning of weariness. While at school I had been a boxer, a runner, and had got my school cap for Rugger. At Oxford, too, while I had been a reading man I was looked upon as an athlete, and so could have held my own whatever took place; but now all was different. While to outward appearances I was still a strong man, I knew that my flesh was wasting away, that the disease from which I suffered was eating away the centres of my life. Still, with a kind of stubbornness which had always characterized me, I resolved I would take no notice of the warning I had received. Why should I go away? If I were in danger it was because something interesting existed at the back of my life. I did not know what it was, but I would find out. To fear, in the ordinary sense of the word, I was a stranger, and in spite of what Fever Lurgy had said, I could not see how any one could wish to harm me.

Towards morning I fell asleep, and when I awoke it was to see the sun streaming through the window of my little bedroom.

I felt very light-hearted, I remember, and in the light of that new day, instead of Fever Lurgy's warning causing me to be depressed, it gave me a new interest in life. Something was happening. A mystery surrounded me. Things were taking place in this very district which gave zest to life. I jumped out of bed, and in spite of Simpson's repeated warnings against such madness, I plunged into the little pond of pure cold water, which burst out from the hill just above my house.

I had scarcely finished breakfast when young Prideaux came into the room.

"By the way, Erskine," he said, "you mentioned last night that you were interested in wireless telegraphy. I have to go over to M—— this morning, and remembering what you said last night, I came round this way to ask you if you would go with me."

My interest in wireless telegraphy had been aroused because of the case which had won for me some notoriety. In fact, the secret of my success lay in the fact that I had swatted up the subject, and was able to put questions which would never otherwise have occurred to me. I am afraid I did not know much about the system, but, as every one knows, the success of a barrister lies largely in his power to assimilate knowledge quickly, to see the vital points of a case and to insist upon them.

It seems that Prideaux had remembered the case in which I had been interested, and in talking about it I had been led to confess that I had given some attention to wireless telegraphy. This explains why he had come to me with the suggestion I have mentioned, and why I eagerly accepted his invitation to motor to M—— with him. Like every one else, I knew that Signor Marconi had erected a station in Cornwall, and that he had thereby created a new epoch in the transmission of messages. I do not know that, under ordinary circumstances, I should have mentioned this fact, but my visit to M—— that day was vitally connected with what happened afterwards.

I am by no means a scientist, and what brains I have never ran in that direction. Still, I have a schoolboy's knowledge of scientific subjects, and this went far in helping me to understand the things I saw. Presently, too, the wonder of the thing laid hold of me. The sending out of a mysterious current across the spaces, to be received hundreds of miles away, was like some fairy dream of childhood. Prideaux had a friend at the station, who was a great enthusiast, and who explained, as far as it can be explained, the principle of the thing to us.

"Look!" he said presently, "I will show you the thing in miniature. I can easily fix up a couple of these little machines here, and then you will see how it is done."

Being an ingenious sort of fellow, he soon did as he had said, and ere long I was simply captivated. My interest in the subject, too, seemed to flatter the young fellow's pride in his work. It was not often, he affirmed, that any one came to the station who picked up the thing so easily.

After spending three hours with the young operator, we had lunch together, and being in a more communicative mood than usual, I told him why I had come to Cornwall, and why, in spite of the people's kindness at St. Issey, my evenings were long and lonely.

"Why not take this up as a hobby?" he said.

"What? Wireless telegraphy?"

"Yes. These things are easy enough to fix up. Any boy with a mechanical turn of mind can manage it. I will give you all the material necessary, and you can make a hobby of it. Of course, it will be no advantage to you, but it will help you to while away the time. When I first came here I didn't care a fig about it, but now my work is a source of ever-increasing interest to me. I am always trying new experiments. Why, you and Prideaux could have all sorts of larks."

"How is that?"

"Why, if you got one of these things at your place, and Prideaux fixed one up at his, you could be sending messages to each other, and you could bewilder people by telling them what is taking place at each other's houses. Don't you see?" And the young fellow laughed boyishly at the prospect which appeared before his mind. "Why, you can have a party at your house and tell your guests how, by your gift of second sight, you know exactly what is going on at Prideaux's house, and then Prideaux, when he comes over, could confirm all you say."

"But I should have to learn the code in order to do this?"

"Of course you would. That is easy enough. I have a book of codes. A chap with a good memory like you could learn everything in half an hour."

I could see that to him his work was at once a plaything and a wonder. He must have been over twenty, but he talked like a lad of fifteen.

"It is the most wonderful thing in the world," he went on. "See what lives have been saved by the invention. You remember the burning of the *Volturno*? A man I know was on board that ship, and he told me what he felt when it caught fire, and how, in spite of his danger, his heart thrilled with wonder when he saw the vessels which had been summoned by wireless to their aid. Every one would have died an awful death but for this discovery. Besides, supposing we went to war, can't you see the advantage of it?"

"I don't know," I said. "It seems to me that it might be a great disadvantage. Supposing, for example, we went to war with France, and we wanted to send a message to one of our ships, the French would receive the message at one of their receiving stations, and they would know all our plans."

"I've made a special study of that," he said, with a laugh. "I daren't let you know how; it would be telling; but I believe I know the secret codes of nearly all the countries. Look here, you get one of these things fixed up, and I will come over and see whether you have got it right. I can put you up to all sorts of dodges. You will never be lonely if this thing really grips you."

I must confess that I caught some of the boy's enthusiasm, and when we returned that evening I brought with me the material for fixing up a kind of amateur installation. Although not scientifically inclined, the wonder of the thing appealed to me, and I reflected that during my lonely hours I could occupy myself with this marvellous discovery. Indeed, for many days afterwards I was engaged in carrying out what the boy had instructed me to do. I found what seemed to me a convenient spot on the cliff, close to my house, yet hidden from the gaze of any passer-by, and here I almost forgot my troubles in perfecting it. More than once, too, young Martin—for that was the name of the lad—came over to see me, and told me that I was getting on famously.

"I am afraid your affair is not powerful enough," he said; "but I will try and send a message to you. It will be an awful lark, won't it?"

By the time young Martin and I had met three times we had become quite friendly, and so eager was he about the work I was doing that he gave me a little book, which he himself had compiled, containing secret codes.

"I don't know whether I ought to do this," he laughed, "but really, you know, it is so fine. It is so interesting, too, and it was by the purest chance that I picked them up."

By the end of a fortnight I boasted to myself that I knew practically all young Martin could tell me about wireless telegraphy, and that I had assimilated all his boasted knowledge about codes. Although I was not a scientist, I had a voracious memory, and was not long in storing my mind with what, a few weeks before, had but little meaning to me, but was now full of mystery and wonder.

By the end of that time one of my old attacks came on, and I was too ill to care about anything. Indeed, when Prideaux and Lethbridge called on me I was too unwell to see either of them. For that matter, I had lost interest in everything. Day followed day, and I opened neither newspaper nor book, nor did I give a thought to what had so interested me since my first visit to that monument of Marconi's genius. What was going on in the outside world I neither knew nor cared. Once or twice I thought the end had come, and that I should never leave Father Abraham's hut alive.

Presently, however, a turn came for the better, and in what seemed a remarkable way, health and strength returned to me. I knew it was only temporary, and that in a few weeks I should have another attack, possibly worse than this, but I drove the thought from my mind.

"Let me enjoy freedom from pain while I can," I said to myself. "As for morbid thoughts, I will have nothing to do with them."

That was why, when Hugh Lethbridge next came to see me and invited me over to Trecarrel, I accepted the invitation with eagerness. I wanted to live while I was able, and the thought of another conversation with Isabella Lethbridge appealed to me.

At Hugh's request, I went early. I engaged a kind of phaeton to meet me at the end of the copse and take me over. I still felt weak and languid after my lengthened attack, but was much stronger than I had hoped. The thought of strange faces, too, added a new interest to my life, and I looked forward with eagerness to a pleasant evening. As the carriage entered the lodge gates and passed under a fine avenue of trees, I could not help reflecting what a fine old place Trecarrel was. It had been built hundreds of years before by the family of Trecarrels, which, like many other old families, had become poor, and had to sell the ancestral acres. Mr. Lethbridge had the good sense to leave the house practically as he found it, and had not attempted to modernize it in any way. It is true he had, as he told me, brought the sanitary arrangements and the fireplaces up to date, but the building, as a whole, remained pretty much as it had been at the time of the Trecarrels. From the front entrance it commanded a fine view of rugged tors, beyond which shone the sea, on the one hand, and of wooded dells and rich meadows on the other. It was a place to rejoice in—a place of which the possessor could say proudly, "This is my home."

It wanted half an hour to dinner when I entered the house, but I found Isabella Lethbridge already dressed, as if awaiting me. She gave me a warm welcome, and, as I thought, seemed pleased to see me. I had not now seen her for some weeks, and I imagined that the feelings she had awakened in my heart, when we last met, were a thing of the past. Now, however, I knew it was not so. In a way I could not understand she exercised a strange influence over me. I found myself eager to talk to her, anxious to be thought well of by her. I remembered what had been said about her, and I believed it to be true; yet at this time I cared nothing about it. What, after all, did it matter?

If any one should read this, I imagine he will say that I had fallen in love with her, but such was not the case. I realized the barriers between us, that, much as I delighted in her beauty—for she was beautiful that night—that much as I rejoiced in being with her, I felt no love for her. That is, love as I understand it. I knew that she repelled me, even while she fascinated me. That she had a vigorous intelligence, I could not deny. That she possessed a strange charm was just as evident, but something kept Isabella Lethbridge from making that appeal to me which caused me to be what the world calls "in love."

Perhaps this was because I knew my days were numbered. How could a man, who a few weeks before had been given a year to live, think of marriage and giving in marriage? No, no, Isabella Lethbridge was still only a problem to me, and yet I could not understand the strange interest I had in her.

"I hear you have got to know Mr. Ned Prideaux?" she said to me, after we had been talking for a few minutes.

"Yes, I met him one night up at Mr. Trelaske's. Do you know him?"

"I have met him two or three times," was her reply. "What do you think of him?"

"He struck me as a fine specimen of a young Cornishman."

"Have you seen him since that night at the Vicarage?"

"Yes, two or three times; we have become rather friendly."

"He said all sorts of things about me, I expect?" and she looked at me questioningly.

"About you! Why should he?"

"Don't try to deceive me, Mr. Erskine. You cannot succeed in doing it, although you are a lawyer. I can see that he talked to you about me. What did he say?"

"What could he say?" I laughed, "except that you are very beautiful and very fascinating, and all that sort of thing."

I know it was very clumsy, and that had I been gifted with a ready wit I should have evaded her question with a greater appearance of ease.

"That will not do, Mr. Erskine, and it is not worthy of you. What did he tell you?" There was a look in her eyes, half of curiosity, half of anger, as she spoke. It appeared that she was interested in what Prideaux thought of her, yet angry that he should speak of her.

"What could he tell me?" I asked.

She reflected for a few seconds, then said suddenly:

"Do you believe that any one should be tied down to conventional morality, Mr. Erskine?"

"Conventional morality?" I asked. "I am not sure that I understand."

"Don't you think," she said, "that one has a right to pick the flowers that lie in one's pathway? Rather, don't you think it is one's duty to do so?"

"The question is rather too abstract for me," was my reply; "one has to get down to concrete instances."

Again she reflected for a few seconds.

"I am glad you have come up early," she said. "Glad to have this opportunity of talking with you alone. You come from a world of ideas. You have met with people who are determined to live their lives at all costs."

"I have met with people, certainly, who have claimed to do this," was my reply; "but, on the whole, the so-called unconventional people, as far as my experience goes, are the most discontented. After all, life doesn't admit of many experiments, and those who make them, as a rule, have to pay very dearly for them."

"Yes, but they have been happy while they have been making them," was her reply. "You confess to that, don't you?"

"I am not sure. For example, I know a man who was determined to do as you say. He said he would live his life untrammelled by conventional ideas, that he would experiment, that he would pick the flowers that grew at his feet, no matter to whom they belonged."

"Yes," she replied eagerly, "and what then?"

"He did what he said he would do," I said, "and the result was misery. Lives were wrecked, and he obtained no satisfaction for himself."

"But did he not confess that he had happiness while he was making the experiments?"

"Perhaps he did, until his deeds bore fruit," was my reply.

"Ah yes, that is it," and her voice was eager. "After all, what is the use of a humdrum existence? Some people," and she spoke almost bitterly, "are born handicapped. I think with you that, for most people, our present mode of life is the outcome of a long period of evolution. Customs have become laws, and these laws have hardened until, if one breaks them, he, or she, is banned— condemned. All the same, they are artificial and they should not apply to exceptional circumstances. Do you believe there is a God, Mr. Erskine?"

"There seems to be a consensus of opinion that there is," was my reply.

"If there is, do you think He intends us to be happy? Do you think He would condemn us for snatching at our only means of happiness?"

I tried to understand the drift of her mind, but could not.

"I don't know whether there is a God or not," she said. "Even all feeling of Him is kept from me. Neither do I believe there is a future life. Do you?"

I was silent, for she had touched upon a sore spot.

"We have only this little life, and that being so, ought we not to snatch, as a matter of duty, anything that will make this life happy? Let me put a common case to you. I knew a lad who was doomed to die between twenty and thirty. He was the victim of an hereditary disease. A year before he died, and knowing that he would die, he married the girl he loved. People called it a crime, but to me it was his only chance of happiness, and he seized it. Was he not right?"

"I don't know," I said.

"Some people are handicapped, Mr. Erskine. They are born into the world with limitations, kinks in their characters, and a host of wild longings—things which make life a tragedy. They cannot obtain happiness in the way ordinary people do. Why, then, is it wrong for them to try and snatch at the happiness they can get?"

"That sounds all right," I said, "only I doubt the happiness."

"Napoleon broke through conventional barriers," she urged. "He said he could not be governed by ordinary laws."

"Exactly," I replied. "But then, for one thing, Napoleon was a genius, and, for another, his great career ended in a fiasco."

"Yes; but if being a genius justifies breaking away from the established order of things, do not peculiar limitations also justify it? Do not abnormalities of any sort justify extraordinary measures? If there is a God, Mr. Erskine, we are as God made us, and surely He does not give us life to mock us?"

"The worst of it is that facts laugh at us. As far as I can discover, nearly all these experiments end in bitter failure. It is by abiding by the common laws of life that we find what measure of happiness there is."

"If I were sure there was a God and a future life I think I could agree with you," was her reply.

"And you are not?"

"How can one be?" she replied. "It all seems so unreal, so utterly unconvincing. My father sticks by his Chapel, but does he believe what he hears there? Most people accept for granted what isn't proved. They say they believe, but they have no convictions. No one is certain. Sometimes I go to hear Mr. Trelaske, and it is just the same at the Parish Church. If religion were true, it should be triumphant; but there seems nothing triumphant about it.

Everything is on the surface. Again and again I have asked so-called Christians if they believe in a future life, and when one goes to the depths of things they can only say they hope so. Were not the old Greeks right when they said, 'Let us eat, drink, and be merry, for to-morrow we die'?"

"You are in rather a curious mood for a young lady," I said, with a laugh. "Here you are, situated in this lovely home, with health and beauty and all that makes life worth living, and yet you talk like this."

"What is the good of anything, everything, if you are forever yearning for something which you never realize, when you find that at the end of every road of desire is a great blank wall: when the things you passionately long for only end in disappointment?"

"Surely that is not your condition, Miss Lethbridge?"

"I don't know," she replied, and there was a touch of impatience in her voice. "One doesn't know anything. We are all so comfortable. Every one seems to have enough to eat and to drink; we have houses to live in; we are, in our way, very prosperous, and, superficially, we are content. But life is so little, so piteously mean and little, and no one seems to know of anything to make it great. We never seem to overstep the barriers which keep us from entering a greater and brighter world. Is there a greater and better world?"

At that moment Mr. Lethbridge senior entered the room, and our conversation ended.

XI

MARY TRELEAVEN

"Seen to-day's papers, Mr. Erskine?" he said, after our first greeting.

"I am afraid I haven't."

"You do surprise me."

"I fancy I have become pretty much of a hermit, Mr. Lethbridge, and I have scarcely enough interest in what is going on to open a newspaper."

"Things are very bad," he said gloomily.

"Bad! How?"

"We are threatened to be mixed up in this Eastern trouble. The whole thing has got entangled. Some Servian assassins have murdered the Crown Prince of Austria. Austria made certain demands on Servia. Russia supports Servia, whereupon Germany steps in and threatens Russia; but the thing doesn't end there. The alliance between France and Russia drags France in, and then the *Entente Cordiale* between France and England causes us to interfere. Sir Edward Grey made a most pessimistic statement last night. It seems as though we might go to war."

"You remember what I said the last time I was here, Mr. Lethbridge?"

"Yes, I know; but it is madness, pure madness. Think what it would mean. The whole trade of the country would be crippled. For that matter the trade of the world would practically stop. We were just beginning to recover ourselves from the effect of the Boer War, and to place the finances of the country upon a solid foundation, and now——It's madness, pure madness. Just as our country seemed to be entering upon another era of prosperity. If there is a war hundreds of people will be ruined. Great firms will come tottering down like ninepins. Besides, think how we should all be taxed."

"That is the way you look at it, is it?"

"How can I help looking at it in that way?" he replied. "Why, think, I have just formed a company for working a petrol mine in Austria. Nearly a million of money has been raised, and is practically in the hands of the Austrians. We shall probably never see a penny of our money back. What right has England to go bothering with what Germany, or Russia, or Austria does? Why can't we attend to our own business?"

"I must get hold of the papers," I said. "I must try and see how we stand."

"Oh, of course, Grey makes a good case. Here is the difficulty, you see. We signed a treaty in which we are engaged to protect Belgium; Germany won't promise not to invade Belgium in order to attack France. But why should we bother about old treaties? What have we got to do with Belgium? I did think this Government had the sense to avoid war. If the Tory party had been in we might have expected it; but there it is."

"Then Sir Edward Grey really thinks there is danger of war with Germany?" I asked.

"Things look very black," was his reply.

"If such a thing comes to pass," I could not help saying, "the whole Empire will be in danger."

"What, the British Empire in danger! You don't mean that?"

"I do," I replied. "I am not sure that war is not inevitable. Germany has been hungering for war for years, and she can place at least eight million men in the field, armed as never a nation was armed before."

"Oh, I have no fear about the Empire," he said. "The British Empire is as firm as a rock, and as safe as Gibraltar."

"We shall have to utilize every pound of power we have if it remains safe."

"Nonsense! nonsense!" he replied impatiently; and I could see he regarded my opinion as of very little value.

"Where's Hugh?" he went on. "Late again, I suppose."

Hugh entered the room as he spoke, and behind him came his mother. A few minutes later we found our way into the dining-room. Hugh was full of the news which had that day been recorded in the newspapers.

"It appears that war is certain," said Hugh. "You were right, Erskine, in what you said the last time you were here. It is evident that the Germans mean war, and are forcing it. They still hope that we won't come in, in which case they think they will soon be able to settle with France on the one hand and Russia on the other."

"Of course we shan't come in," replied Mr. Lethbridge; "it would be a crime if we did. Besides, it would be bad policy. We should be missing the opportunity the war would give us. If Germany went to war with France and Russia, her trade, for the time, would be stagnated, and we should be able to get it. If we get embroiled, America will steal the trade of the world."

"I have been to Plymouth to-day," said Hugh, "and, as luck would have it, I met with a man who is in the know. He says he knows for a fact that Germany means to fight us, that if we do not come in now she will simply force a war on us in two or three years' time, and then she will smash us."

"Nonsense! nonsense!"

"He is a great believer in what Lord Roberts says," went on Hugh. "He believes that every man in the country ought to have been trained to defend the country."

"And then we should have become a military nation," was Mr. Lethbridge's reply. "No, no, that won't do, and I simply can't believe what the papers say."

"Anyhow, our fleet is mobilized," said Hugh, "and I hear that the Territorials are being called up. But that is nothing. Our Army is a mere bagatelle. It is on the board that a million men will be called for. Some say there is going to be conscription."

I will not record anything further that took place that night, for, truth to tell, I felt anything but comfortable. It was soon evident that Mr. Lethbridge and his son were entirely antagonistic, and, as a consequence, a strained feeling existed. Indeed, I was glad when the time came for me to return home, and but for the few minutes' chat I had with Isabella Lethbridge, I should have wished I had not accepted the invitation. There could be no doubt about it that Mr. Lethbridge was in a very bad temper. I imagined that he had lost a lot of money, and he saw the possibility of losing more. The fact, too, that Hugh, his only son, was not interested in his schemes, angered him.

"I say, Erskine," said Hugh, just before my leaving the house, "you have no objection to my bringing Mary Treleaven over to see you to-morrow night? I want you to know her."

"I shall be delighted," was my reply. "But do you think you are wise in opposing your father?"

"How can I help opposing him?" asked Hugh. "I am of age, and I have my own life to live. She is the only girl in the world to me, and I am not going to live in misery because of the pater's fads."

As I left I had a few seconds alone with Isabella Lethbridge.

"You have been bored to death, Mr. Erskine," she said. "No, don't try to deny it. You have played your part very well, but your boredom is written on your face. I don't wonder at it."

"Then I apologize for an unforgetable breach of good manners. But did I seem bored when I was talking to you?"

"No, you did not; but please, Mr. Erskine, don't go away with a false impression about me."

"I hope it is not false," I said, "for it is a very pleasant one."

"That is awfully poor," she replied, "and certainly it is not worthy of you." And then she flashed a look into my eyes which, I must confess, set my heart beating violently. "Perhaps the next time you come, Mr. Erskine, we may have pleasanter things to talk about."

I went home feeling that my evening had been ill-spent, and yet I was not sure. I felt somehow that forces were at work in my life which were going to make a change in me. Why, I did not know. It is said that when people are near death, the horizon of their vision becomes widened, that the barriers which have hitherto bounded their sight break down. Was that so with me? I did not know why it was, but I felt as though I were on the brink of some discovery. I had no reason for this. My thoughts were rather intuitional than logical.

When I reached my little home I reflected upon what had taken place. I tried to gather up the impressions which had been made upon me since I had been in St. Issey. I was obliged to confess, too, that Isabella Lethbridge was right in many of the things she had said. I had come to Cornwall, supposed to be a religious county, and yet, as far as I could see, the religion of both Church and Chapel was something that existed only on the surface. There was very little that went down to the depths of life. I had been to Chapel several times since the service I have described. I had also been repeatedly to the Parish Church, but I never found the thing I wanted. The note of conviction, of reality, was always wanting. The people were so awfully comfortable, so completely self-satisfied; the life of every one seemed to be laid over with a thick covering of materialism. There was no general doubt about spiritual things, but there was a lack of consciousness. Men and women appeared to be careless about what they pretended to accept. I discovered, too, that people went to Church and to Chapel rather as a matter of form and custom than because they entered into communion with the Unseen and the Eternal.

Next evening Hugh Lethbridge brought Mary Treleaven to see me, and directly we met I did not wonder at the young fellow's determination. If I have portrayed his character correctly, I have shown him to be a simple-minded, impulsive lad, who cared little for rank or riches; one who obeyed the promptings of his heart, rather than the findings of his reason. No one could associate Hugh with Mr. Worldly Wiseman, and surely Mary Treleaven was a fit mate for such a man. As far as I can judge, she was about twenty years of age, unsophisticated and true-hearted. That she almost worshipped Hugh was evident, and that she stood in awe of his father was just as apparent. I judged, too, that Hugh had been very enthusiastic in his praises about me, for she seemed to regard me, comparative stranger though I was, as a very dear friend of her lover, and when for a few minutes Hugh left us together, she opened her heart to me.

"You know, Mr. Erskine," she said simply, "I know that as far as money and position and all that sort of thing goes, I am not Hugh's equal. My father is only a tenant farmer, and I am afraid they up at Trecarrel think that I just look on him as a good catch; but really, Mr. Erskine, it is not that at all. I almost hope they won't give him any money, and I wish, oh, I wish he was only just a simple farmer like my father! I don't care a bit about the money."

"I am quite sure you don't," I said. "You care only for Hugh."

"Oh, you see that, don't you?"

"Indeed I do," I replied.

"Do you know," she went on, as artlessly as a child, "that I have prayed about it for hours. I thought it my duty to give him up; indeed, I have offered to do so more than once, but Hugh won't hear of it. But, after all, why should I, Mr. Erskine? I love him and he loves me, and I am not afraid to work for him. Why, only give me a chance, and I will work my fingers to the bone for him," and the tears started to her eyes.

I loved to hear her talk. She had that peculiar, soft intonation, common to the fairly-well-educated people in Cornwall. She spoke perfectly correctly, but the Cornish accent, which I had learnt to love—that peculiar, sing-song lilt— was manifest in every sentence she uttered.

"Do you know, Mr. Erskine," she went on, "I have been up to see Mrs. Lethbridge?"

"Oh!" I said; "and did you have a reason for doing that?"

"Yes," she said. "I thought it right just to let her know what I felt. Hugh is talking about emigrating to Canada, and I am sure that if he went he would succeed there, and I am willing to wait five, ten years; it doesn't matter how long. You see, Mr. Erskine, I never loved any one else."

"And what did Mrs. Lethbridge say to you?"

"Oh, at first she didn't seem to like me, and, as I thought, was angry; but after a bit she got quite pleasant, and Hugh says that she has some money of her own, and that she is willing to give it to him, so that he can start a small farm of his own. You think it would be right, don't you?"

"Think what would be right?" I asked.

"For him to go against his father, and take it. It isn't as though I wanted Hugh for his money, Mr. Erskine, I only want him for himself, and he wants me."

"I am sure that your motives are perfectly pure," was my reply, "but you must remember that Hugh is his father's only son, and it is a very grave thing for a boy to disobey his father's wishes."

"Yes, I know, and that is what has made me so miserable. We should have been married before now but for that. I am so glad, Mr. Erskine, that you don't think badly about me."

"Think badly about you?" I said, with a laugh. "That would be impossible. I only congratulate Hugh on his good luck, and I jolly well wish I had his chance."

"Now you are laughing at me."

"Good gracious! No, I am not laughing at you." And I suppose I sighed, for she looked at me curiously.

"Oh, forgive me, Mr. Erskine. I did not think! Hugh has told me all about you. Perhaps it isn't as bad as you believe."

"Well, it is no use worrying," I replied, "and, believe me, I am awfully glad to have met you. Ah, here is Hugh coming."

"You don't advise me to give him up, do you?"

"No, of course not!" I said; and I meant it, for this dark-haired, soft-eyed girl had made a strong appeal to me, and I had been perfectly sincere when I said that I envied Hugh Lethbridge. What, after all, were rank and position? What was anything compared with the love of a pure girl like that, and I, whose death-warrant was written, felt a great pain in my heart, as I reflected that the love of such a girl would never be known to me, that I should die in ignorance of what it could mean.

"Hugh thinks so much of you, and he is so proud that you are his friend," she went on. "He says you were awfully clever at college, and that if you live you will make a great name for yourself. He says he never felt towards any one like he feels towards you. Oh, it would be lovely if you got well, and could be our neighbor and be near us always."

I saw the tears roll down her face as she said this, and I, who have never known what it is to have a sister, felt towards her as, I think, brothers feel towards a sister whom they love.

"You don't think badly of me, do you?" she went on. And I could see a look of longing in her eyes.

"What makes you ask such a question?" I said.

"Oh, Hugh says his father has quite taken to you too, and thinks a great deal of your opinion. I wonder if—if——"

"I am afraid Hugh is mistaken," I said. "But if any word of mine can soften his heart——"

"Oh, you are good!" she interrupted impulsively, "and you don't think that Hugh would be throwing himself away on me, do you?"

"Throwing himself away?" I cried, and at that moment I thought of Miss Treherne, whom I had seen at Church on the previous Sunday morning, and mentally I compared them. The Squire's daughter was a staid-looking spinster of about thirty years of age. She had never been beautiful, and no one by the utmost stretch of imagination could call her attractive.

"If I were Hugh," I said, "I would not give you up for anything or anybody, and I should regard myself as the luckiest fellow in the world to get you."

She laughed like a child. It was easy to see that I had gladdened her heart, and when a few minutes later she walked away hanging on her lover's arm, I heaved a sigh of envy.

"They are right, both of them," I said to myself. "What is all the money in the world, and all the rank, compared to the infinite trustfulness and affection of those two?

"Surely God, if there is a God, wants them to be happy," I reflected, and I formed a sort of quixotic resolution that I would speak to Mr. Lethbridge, and try to persuade him to withdraw his opposition to his son's marriage with this pure, sweet, simple-minded country girl.

I did not carry my resolution into effect, however. The next day I suffered a kind of reaction from the little excitement caused by what had taken place, and immediately afterwards it seemed as though all my thoughts and resolutions were scattered to the wind.

"Please, sir," said Simpson, entering my room, "here's the paper, sir. I thought you might like to look at it, sir."

"Is there anything particular in it, Simpson?"

"Yes, sir; war is declared, sir."

I took the paper from his hand, feeling strangely heavy-hearted, and on opening it, saw, staring me in large letters:

"England Declares War on Germany.
Germany Determines to Violate Her Treaty.
England Decides to Risk all for Honor.

No sooner had I read this, than a strange calm came upon me, and I scanned the paper in a detached sort of way. I seemed to have nothing to do with it; I was cut off from everything. I read what had been written, rather as one who read the history of another country, than as something which vitally affected England.

In a way I had expected it. My conversation at Trecarrel had somewhat prepared me, and yet events had moved so rapidly, that declaration of war came like a shock. The whole story was set forth in the newspapers, and from the dispatches it was made plain that, while Germany had hoped that England would remain neutral, and had been willing to offer bribes for our neutrality, she had planned this war, and made arrangements for it. There was no doubt that she believed both Russia and France to be entirely unprepared, and that both she and Austria were prepared. It was plain too that unless we were willing to violate our plighted word, and to allow our honor to be dragged in the dust, we must stand by Belgium. I saw more than this. I saw that a critical moment had come in the life of our nation and Empire.

For I realized, knowing Germany as I did, that this was not a war to be "muddled through," as had been the case with other wars. I knew that England must make sacrifices, such as had hitherto been unknown to her. I knew that before German militarism could be crushed, all the vast resources of our Empire would have to be utilized, and that we must be prepared to spend our last penny, and shed the last drop of our blood.

But even then I did not realize what this war would mean to our Island home, never saw, even from afar, how it would revolutionize the thoughts and feelings of our land, never dreamed how it would affect the lives of the people in this little Cornish village.

XII

FIRST DAYS OF THE WAR

Next morning I took a walk into the village, and just as I was entering it saw a group of youths reading a placard on the wall. It was headed by the British Coat of Arms, and contained an appeal from Lord Kitchener for five hundred thousand men. The youths looked at it stolidly. They did not seem to think that it affected them. Farther on I saw a woman brushing the little pathway which led to the front door of her cottage. By this time I had become on friendly terms with many of the people in the village, who spoke of me as "the poor young man, staying up to Father Abraham's hut." They evidently knew why I had come to Cornwall, and looked on me pityingly as I passed by.

"Mornin', sur."

"Good-morning, Mrs. Crantock."

"This es ter'ble news, sur."

"Yes, very terrible."

"I d' think et es judgment from God."

"Why do you think that, Mrs. Crantock?"

"Ah, sur, w've a forgot God, sur. Things be'ant what they used to be, and God's goin' to teach us a lesson."

She was a woman perhaps sixty years of age, and had a patient, kindly face, even although it was not without signs of determination and vigor.

"What reason have you for saying that we have forgotten God?" I asked. I reflected that she was an intelligent woman, and represented the class to which she belonged.

"Ah, sur, I've lived in Cornwall all my life, and I ca'ant 'elp seein' the deffurence between things now and what they used to be."

"Oh," I said, "and how is that?"

"Ah, sur, the young people be'ant the same. Why, sur, when I was a young woman, we didn't spend all our time gaddin' about, like young people do nowadays. We wad'n all for pleasure then. Why, sur, every Sunday mornin' I used to go to seven o'clock prayer-meetin', and there would be thirty or forty of us. The people had'n forgot 'ow to pray then, sur."

"And have they now?" I asked.

"Why, sur, there ed'n no seven o'clock meetin'; we d'ardly ever 'ave prayer-meetin' like we used to. There ed'n nobody to pray, so to speak, and when they do pray, 'tis deffurent. Ah, sur, we 'ad power then. We felt the power, too. As for the Chapel, it was full nearly every Sunday, and nearly everybody went."

"And they don't go now?" I suggested.

"No, sur, they do'ant go now. That is, nothin' like they used to. Young people do'ant seem to have no relish for the House of God."

"What is the reason of it?" I asked.

"Worldliness and pleasure, sur. Everybody be a thinkin' 'ow they shall enjoy theirselves. Yes, sur, we 'ave forgotten God, and He is goin' to bring us back to our senses. Yes, war is a ter'ble thing, but ef et will do that et'll be good for us. We d'need strong physic sometimes."

I waited, for I could see that she was in a communicative mood, and was pleased with the attention I gave to her.

"Then ther's the class-meetin's," she went on; "when I was a young woman, all the professin' Christians went to class-meetin', and everybody did give their experience. It was a means of grace to go then, sur. Men and women 'ad somethin' to tell of what God had done for them, and now, it do'ant seem as ef anybody 'ad any experience to give. Why, sur, we 'ad cottage prayer-meetin's all over St. Issey, and we was 'appy. We knawed then that God loved us, but now we do'ant seem to think about God. Religion wad'n a formal thing then, sur, it was everything to us. Yet, I dunno; people seem to have more worldly goods than they 'ad then, we 'ave better wages, and more of the good things of this life, but then we knawed God; now we do'ant."

"Do you mean to say that every one has forgotten Him, Mrs. Crantock?"

"No, sur, I do'ant go so fur as that. There be a few who 'aven't removed the ould landmarks. There's Tommy Yelland, and Mary Tresidder, and a few like they, to whom the Word of God is precious, but there be'ant many. You can remember, sur, the story of Sodom and Gomorrah. The Lord destroyed those cities because there wad'n ten righteous men. I do'ant say things is so bad as that wi' we, but we have lost certainty, sur, and we 'ave lost power. Be you a professin' Christian yerself, sur?"

"I am afraid I am not, Mrs. Crantock, but I am very interested in it."

"Ah, sur, I wish you 'ad come down 'ere in the ould days, when we 'ad Revivals. I've knawed the time when every one in St. Issey who went to

Chapel was converted."

"Revivals?" I said, for I scarcely understood her.

"Yes, sur, the Spirit of the Lord used to move mightily, and after a Sunday evening service I 'ave knawed lots of people come out and be soundly converted; but that is all over now."

"Why is that?" I asked.

"Ted'n the Lord's fault, sur; His arm is not shortened, neither is His ear heavy. We have resisted His Spirit, sur, and come away from Him. We are fulfilling words of Scripture, 'Ephraim is joined to his idols; let him alone.' Why, sur, at our last special services nobody wad'n converted."

"Special services?" I queried.

"Yes, sur, we call it a 'mission' now, and we 'ad a special preacher down, but there wad'n no results."

"And are things no better at the Church?" I asked.

"Well, sur, they d'think of things deffurent up there. We do'ant look upon they as thinking about religion, like we Wesleyans do, or used to do," she added, correcting herself. "Now, sur, we be all alike. There do'ant seem any deffurence between the Church and the world. That is why God 'ave allowed this ter'ble war to come; for 'twill be ter'ble, do'ant you think so, sur?"

"Yes," I replied, "I am afraid it will."

"I d'ear they Germans be ter'ble fighters, and that every man in the country is a sojer. Es that true, sur?"

"Yes, practically true."

"Ah, 'tis a wisht thing ed'n et, then? but ef all the people would return to the Lord I shudd'n fear, but we seem to 'ave forgot the power of prayer. Be you better then, sur, makin' so bold?"

"Not much better, I am afraid," I replied.

"You do look fine an' slight, sur," she added, looking at me pityingly.

At first I scarcely understood what she meant, but I discovered that the word "slight" was commonly used among the Cornish people when they spoke of people looking ill.

"Pardon me," I said, for although the old dame was comparatively ignorant, and lived in a narrow world of her own, her conversation had greatly interested me. She had made me realize the power of Methodism in the county half a century before, and I wondered whether, in the simplicity of her mind and heart, she had got hold of a greater truth than I had realized. I remembered some words of the Founder of Christianity, "He hath hid these things from the wise and prudent, and hath revealed them unto babes." "Have you lost the knowledge of God, which you once possessed, with the rest of the people?"

"No, sur; that is," she added, correcting herself, "I do'ant think I have. Sometimes I am in danger of forgetting Him, and then He d'seem a long way off like, but I know et es my own fault, for direckly I spend a lot of time on my knees the Lord d'come real again to me. I d'remember my ould man's death-bed, too, and, sur, he was like Enoch of old, he walked with God, and when he came to die it was like heaven to hear him talk. He was triumphant, sur, triumphant."

As I left Mrs. Crantock, and made my way into the village, I could not help reflecting on what she had said. I had now been in St. Issey ten weeks, and had had time to form some impression on the life of the people. I could not help being convinced, too, that the old woman, in her simple way, had spoken the truth. As far as I could see there was no religion in Cornwall such as she had described. The people were, on the whole, well conducted, but, as I understood the word, there was no deep sense of religion at all. Both at Chapel and Church the people were listless, and, to a large extent, indifferent. The fact of God was not real. That consciousness of the presence of God, which, as far as I could judge, had been common to the people fifty years before, no longer existed.

And yet, perhaps, I am not altogether right in saying this. The ideals and the thoughts of the people were largely because of what religion had been in the olden days. Whether the distinctive doctrines of Methodism were largely superstition I am not going to argue here, but they had, in the past, permeated the county, and their effects had not altogether died out. On the other hand, however, they were no longer a present possession, neither was religion, in a large number of cases, a distinctive factor in their lives. The people were comfortable, well fed, well housed, and, generally, well conditioned, and, as a consequence, they did not feel the need of God. The fear of hell, which was prevalent in the old days, had died out, and with its death the realization for the need of religion had died out too. They were so comfortable, so self-satisfied, that everything appertaining to the spiritual world was a long, long way off. No one seemed to be stirred to the depths of life, never anywhere was there a deep calling unto the deep; and thus, while the majority of people were respectable and well behaved, they sought for satisfaction in the life around them.

As I walked through the village I came upon a number of miners lounging around, with, apparently, nothing to do. They were, they informed me, working afternoon "core" that week, and thus had their mornings at liberty. They greeted me heartily as I came up, and willingly entered into conversation with me. The subject of conversation was the war, and the two things which impressed me were, first of all, that it would soon be over, and, second, that they had nothing to do with it. In the majority of cases they did not seem to feel that Lord Kitchener's appeal was to them at all. They imagined that soldiers would be forthcoming, and that England would be able to get all the men she wanted, but the idea that they should leave their homes and go away for training did not seem to occur to them. I am speaking now of those early days of the war, before the terror of it really gripped the country.

"I d'give they Germans about six weeks," said one miner to me. "What can Germany do 'gainst Russia and France and we? I tell you what, maaster, they have bite off a bigger piece than they can chow, tha's what they've done; do'ant you think so?"

"I hope they have," I replied; "but I think you are over-confident. You see, in Germany, every man is trained to be a soldier, and thus they have an army nearly twenty times as big as we have."

"But you do'ant think they'll bait we, do 'ee, maaster?"

"I think we shall have difficult work to beat them," was my reply, "and the sooner you chaps enlist the better."

"What! we go for sojers; do'ant you believe it. I never fired a gun in my life."

"Then I think the sooner you begin to learn the better."

But I could make no impression on them. The war, to them, was a long way off, and they had only a kind of detached interest in it. They quite agreed with me that, as we were in it, we should have to see it through, only some one else must see it through, not they. The thought of their becoming soldiers seemed utterly alien to them. I discovered, too, that all of them had a kind of feeling that they would lower themselves in the social grade if they donned the King's uniform. In the past, the Army had largely been recruited from men of the extreme lower orders. Of course, I am referring now to privates. When a young fellow got into trouble, or had disgraced himself in any way, the Army was a kind of harbor of refuge. Indeed, it was quite common for magistrates to give incipient criminals the choice between joining the Army and being sent to prison. As a consequence, these Cornish miners, who in their way were exceedingly proud, thought it beneath them to don the King's uniform. Besides, as Mr. Lethbridge had said on a previous occasion, the whole spirit of the county was utterly alien to anything like militarism.

As, towards noon, I found my way back to my hut, a great feeling of bitterness came into my heart. "Wouldn't I enlist, if I were able?" I said to myself. "I would to heaven that I were strong and well, and able to do something; but I am nothing but a useless hulk. If the spirit shown by these young fellows is the spirit of the country, the Germans will smash us in a few weeks."

For I was not blind to the problem which faced us. I knew that France was not prepared in the same way that Germany was. I remembered that, forty-five years before, Von Moltke with his perfectly trained army had swept down like an avalanche, and carried away the French army as if by a flood. I knew, too, that the German forces were far stronger now than they were then, and that, with the thoroughness which characterized them, they had prepared everything to the minutest detail. I reflected that at that time the German guns were thundering at the Liège forts, and that, except some miracle happened, the German hordes would sweep towards Paris, as in the great *débâcle* of 1870. I knew we had a little army of, perhaps, 200,000 men, but what could they do against such a mighty host? I wondered, too, whether our guns were equal to those of the Germans. Altogether, I was very pessimistic.

After this, some days passed without anything happening. For some reason or other I seemed to be left severely alone. No one visited me, neither did I go out of the house. The weather was somewhat inclement, and I was too depressed to brave the angry clouds which hung in the sky. I went neither to Church nor to Chapel, but hung around my hut, sometimes listlessly walking along the cliffs, but, in the main, staying in my little room.

"I suppose, sir," said Simpson, one evening, "that there is going to be a recruiting meeting in the village schoolroom."

"How did you find that out, Simpson?" I asked.

"Saw a bill, sir. Squire Treherne is going to take the chair, and the Vicar and several others are going to speak."

"When is the meeting to be, Simpson?"

"To-morrow night, sir."

Although I felt far from well, I determined to go. I was far away from the centres of life, and felt utterly incapable of doing anything; but I wanted to feel the throb of humanity's pulses, longed to take my share in the great world struggle.

I had not time to ask any more questions, however, for at that minute Hugh Lethbridge walked into my room, and I saw by the look on his face that he was much perturbed.

I did not ask him any questions, for at that moment Simpson was busily clearing away the dinner utensils. It was evident, however, that something had excited him greatly. He could not sit still, and his hands were constantly clenching and unclenching themselves.

"Erskine," he said presently, when Simpson had left the room, "I want you to help me."

"Help you, my dear fellow, how?"

"I have been and done it," he said.

"Done what?"

"I could not help it, my dear chap. You have seen the placards all over the place. You know the call there has been for men. What could I do? Here am I, healthy and strong, and just the kind of man that is needed. How could I hang back like a coward?"

"Then you have enlisted?"

"Yes," he cried, "I have enlisted; I could not help myself."

"As a private?"

"Yes, as a private. I am not fit to be an officer."

"But didn't you belong to the Officers' Training Corps when you were at school?"

"The pater would not allow me. No, it was no use my thinking anything about it, so I went to a recruiting station and joined up. I shall have to go to the front immediately."

"How is that?" I asked. "What is the use of your going to the front without training? They won't allow you. You will be kept in England at least six months."

"No, I shan't. You see, I know the Colonel of the regiment I have joined very well, and he is off to the front immediately, and I am going too."

"But how?"

"Well, you see, for one thing, I know French and German, and for another, I am not a bad hand at mechanics. I know all about a motor-car, inside and out, and they can find work for me."

"Then you are not going as an ordinary Tommy?"

"In a way I am, and in a way I am not; but there it is. They are going to make a special case of me. I am off to-morrow to join my regiment, and from what I can hear, the regiment is off in two or three days. I don't know exactly what my duties will be; but there it is, I am off."

"What will your father say?" I asked.

"That is what I have come to see you about. I never realized until I had done it what the pater would say. You know I am fond of him, even although we have never got on well together. He has never understood me, and I am afraid I have never understood him—there is no link of sympathy between us; but then, you know, he is my pater after all. Yes, I have joined; but that is not all, Erskine."

"Not all?" I queried. "What is there besides?"

"I have been and got married," was his reply.

"Got married!"

"Yes. I expect it was a mad thing to do, but I could not help myself. You don't know what it is to be in love, Erskine, and I could not bear the idea of leaving Mary without knowing she was my wife."

"And, of course, your father knows nothing about that either?"

"No, he knows nothing. You see, I got married by special license. I was afraid to tell the pater what was in my mind,—afraid he would interfere somehow and stop me,—so I thought I would do it first and tell him afterwards."

Our conversation was not nearly so connected and straightforward as I have described it here. What he said was uttered in quick, disjointed sentences. Sometimes he would break off in the middle of what he was saying, and talk about something else. That he was greatly excited was easy to see. It was evident, too, that his duty towards his father troubled him greatly.

"I don't mind mother," he said; "she will be all right—mother understands me. Of course, Bella and I laugh at her, and all that sort of thing, because she is always making plans for us, and mapping out our day's program, and telling us what we ought to do. We call her the general manager; but she is a good sort is mother, and she understands us, too. But the pater is different. Somehow, he cannot understand us, and we cannot understand him. I suppose, in a way, he is just, and in many things he is generous to me, but in others ——Well, there it is. I wondered what I ought to do. At first I thought I would go away without telling him anything, but that would be acting like a sneak. Mind you, Erskine, I would not undo anything I have done. If ever a man had a call to serve his country, I have, and I think it is a splendid piece of luck that I can be useful at a time like this, without going through the training of an ordinary soldier. I jumped at the chance of going to the front straight away;

but then, there was Mary. How could I leave her without being sure that I had her? I was afraid the pater would take steps to hinder me from ever getting her. You have some idea what he is—and I was afraid. Besides, she was willing, and so I—I——God forgive me if I have done wrong, Erskine, but I could not help it."

"Well, what can I do to help you?" I asked.

"There it is, and that is why I have come to-night. I have always had the reputation of having a fair amount of pluck; I do not fear death a bit, and I haven't a single qualm about going to the front; but it's the pater, you see."

"What about your father?" I asked.

"I am afraid to tell him, Erskine. I simply dare not go home and tell him what I have done."

"Nonsense!" I said; "he cannot eat you; you have done nothing to be ashamed of. For that matter you have done what thousands of other fellows have done. You have joined the Army at the call of your King and Country, and it was the right thing to do. I would to God that I were able to do it too!"

"Would you, Erskine?" he cried eagerly. "You think I have done right, then?"

"I think you should have gone to your father first and asked for his consent. Then, if he would not give it, I think you, being of age, and feeling it your duty, should go in spite of him."

"But he would not have consented."

"Exactly; still, you should have asked him. As for getting married——"

"Yes, yes, what about that?" and he looked towards me feverishly.

"Well," I said, "hundreds of fellows are doing it. I have seen scores of such cases in the newspapers. Hurried marriages have been arranged by young fellows going to the front."

"Yes, but, you see, they have been different. They have been married with their father's blessing, and all that sort of thing; but I, I am afraid to go and tell him, Erskine, unless——"

"Unless what?" I asked.

"The pater thinks no end of you," he said excitedly. "He doesn't say much, but I can see it. You see, you promised to do well at the Bar, and he thinks you are clever, and all that sort of thing. Of course he hasn't said much to you, but I know it."

"Well, what if he does?" I asked.

"Look here, Erskine, that is what I came for. Will you come with me? If you are with me, I believe I can tell him. I have got the car outside, and I can run you up in five minutes."

Although I ought to have seen what was in his mind all the time, his request came almost as a shock to me. Josiah Lethbridge was almost a stranger to me. It is true I had been to his house twice, and had met him on two other occasions, but he was not a man to whom one could speak freely. At least I thought so. As I have intimated before, he was a strong, capable man, and, like many of his class, was overbearing, almost repellent. He had risen from a poor lad by his own energy and determination and ability. He had swept difficulties out of his path. He had succeeded because he had made others yield to his stronger will. All these things had left their mark upon him. He could not bear opposition, and he took it as a personal grievance when others did not fall in with his way of thinking. I knew, too, his thoughts and desires with regard to his son, knew how he hated militarism, knew how ambitious he was that Hugh, his only son, should take a high place, not only in the county but in the nation. Therefore, when he was told that Hugh had not only joined the Army as a common soldier, but had married, against his will, a small tenant farmer's daughter, his anger would know no bounds.

Besides, what had it to do with me? I had known none of them before I came to Cornwall, less than three months before. Why should I be dragged into this imbroglio? Then I looked at Hugh Lethbridge's face, saw the quiver of his lips, saw the eager look in his eye. Although I had known him only a few weeks, I had conceived a strong affection for him, and, in spite of myself, could not help sympathizing with him.

"Will you help me?" he said pleadingly.

I nodded.

"You will come with me now and see the pater?"

"If you wish it."

"Thank you, my dear chap," and his voice became husky as he spoke.

A few minutes later we stood at the door of Josiah Lethbridge's house.

XIII

FATHER AND SON

I think Isabella Lethbridge must have realized that something out of the ordinary had brought me there that night, for when she met me in the hall there was a look of inquiry on her face. Still, she greeted me kindly, almost eagerly.

"It is good of you to come up with Hugh. Father is in the library alone," she said, "and mother and I have sat for more than an hour without speaking. Come in, will you?"

"I am afraid I can't," I said. "I have come to see Mr. Lethbridge."

Again she looked at me inquiringly, and I was sure, as her glance passed from myself to Hugh, that she divined something of our purpose.

"You said the pater was in the library, Bella?" said Hugh.

"Yes," was her reply. "Some man came up to see him directly after dinner, and has only just left. I fancy he has had some unpleasantness about business."

Hugh, whose mouth had now become firm and determined, went to the library door and knocked.

"Yes, come in."

I followed Hugh Lethbridge into the room, while he carefully shut the door. The older man looked at us inquiringly.

"Won't you sit down?" he said to me, nodding towards a chair; but I could see that he hardly knew what he was saying. His eyes were riveted on Hugh's face, as if he would read his inmost soul. Even then I could not help being impressed by the young fellow's behavior, nor, for that matter, by his general appearance. For Hugh Lethbridge was one of the finest specimens of British young manhood I have ever met. Quite a boy in appearance, he was tall, well knit, and muscular. He had an open, frank countenance, sparkling blue eyes, and brown, wavy hair. He stood before his father firm and erect. His every movement belied the statement that he was afraid. There was no suggestion of fear in his presence, except for the fact that once he looked towards me, as if to be certain that I was there, near to him. Then, without preamble, and without seeking to excuse himself in any way, he burst forth with the news.

"Pater," he said, "I have joined the Army—and—and I have married Mary

113

Treleaven."

The two sentences came like two pistol-shots. He had evidently determined to waste no time or words.

His father did not speak a word for some time. At first he looked at his son, as though he did not comprehend him, and then, when the truth came to him, felt stunned. I watched his face closely, as Hugh spoke, and for a moment could not help pitying him. I realized the pride of the man, realized, too, all the plans he had made, and understood something of what he felt when he saw that the structure he had built up was levelled to the ground like a house of cards.

At first I thought he was going to lose control over himself. I saw anger flash from his eyes, saw his face harden. Perhaps, had I not been there, he would have yielded to the passion of the moment; but he was a proud man, and would not willingly place himself in a ridiculous position. It was evident, too, that two forces were fighting in his heart. One was love for his boy; for doubtless, in his way, Hugh was very dear to him. He was his only son, and, as he had hoped, heir to his possessions. On the other hand, he could not bear opposition, and would not yield an inch in the pathway which he had chosen to tread.

The silence was almost painful. After Hugh had blurted out his confession, he seemed like one incapable of speech, as his eyes were riveted on his father's face. Neither did he feel that there was anything for him to say. I had told Hugh, on my way up to the house, that he must not expect me to plead for him. It was not my business to interfere between father and son. Indeed, I felt like an intruder all through the painful interview. As for Josiah Lethbridge, he sat in the leather-covered library chair, close by his writing-desk, motionless, for what seemed an interminable time. Then, as if by force of habit, he took a pen, and began to draw grotesque figures on the blotting-pad. He was evidently thinking deeply. Outside the night was windless, and no sound reached us save that of the roll of the waves upon a distant beach.

"Dad," burst out Hugh at length, "have you nothing to say?"

The older man moved in his chair slowly, and as if with difficulty.

"What is there to say?" and his voice was hard and cold.

"Well, I thought that—that——" And then Hugh broke down.

"What is there to say?" repeated Josiah Lethbridge in the same cold, even voice. "You know what my views are, you know what my wishes are. I have told you more than once my plans about you; but it seems that you thought yourself wiser than I. Or perhaps," he added, "you do not care about my wishes. That is why you have gone and married a penniless girl who can never be anything but a drag to you—married her, too, senselessly, madly, without a shadow of reason for doing it."

I saw then that the thing which had wounded him most deeply was not the fact that his son had joined the Army, but that he had married a poor village girl—married her in spite of his wishes, in spite of his positive command.

"You have acted in a very honorable way, too, haven't you?" he sneered. "Knowing what my feelings are in the matter, you take the irrevocable step first, and then come and tell me afterwards."

"But, dad, don't you see?" and Hugh spoke excitedly. "Yes, I ought to have spoken to you first, perhaps; but then I knew you would not give your consent, and—and I could not bear to lose her. You see, I—I love her!"

"Love her!" and Josiah Lethbridge spoke contemptuously.

"Yes, love her," cried the young fellow hotly. "I have loved her for years."

"A common village girl!" burst forth the father.

"She is not common," replied the son. "A purer, better girl never breathed. No one has ever dared to raise a breath against her. She is well educated, too, and every one respects her."

It was evident the father's contempt aroused the lad's anger. He had no difficulty in speaking now. Mary Treleaven had to be defended, and he no longer stammered in his speech; words came easily.

"I say she is a pure girl and a good girl," he continued almost angrily, "and I love her."

I thought for the moment that Josiah Lethbridge would have lost self-control here, and have burst forth in a tirade of abuse; but still he kept command over himself, and, although his lips quivered, he spoke quietly.

"Pardon me if I doubt your love," he said. "May I ask what you intend doing with her? If a man loves a woman, he should at least have some prospect of keeping her decently before he marries her."

At this Hugh was silent. The father had, by his question, pierced the weak place in Hugh's armor.

"If you think," went on Josiah Lethbridge, "that I am going to do anything for her, or you, you are mistaken. You have chosen your own way; you must follow it. I had intended another future for you, but my intentions do not seem to count. I think there is nothing more to say," and he moved in his chair as though the interview were at an end. Then, as if on second thoughts, he turned to me and said quietly:

"I do not see why you should have been dragged into this, Mr. Erskine; but I suppose you had your own reason for coming."

I felt he had placed me in a wrong position, and for a moment was at a loss how to answer him. Indeed, I felt I had made a mistake in coming, and I was almost sorry I had yielded to Hugh's entreaty.

"He came," stammered Hugh, "because I—I begged him to. I was a coward, and I—I thought you would b—be more reasonable to me if he came."

"Have I ever been anything but reasonable to you, Hugh?" asked the father. "Of course, to one like yourself, who will not listen to reason, I suppose my words have seemed harsh and arbitrary. I am an older man than you, and therefore think my way is best. Besides——But we will not speak of that. Surely, however, Mr. Erskine did not come here with the intention of condoning your action."

"I am sorry if my presence here is unwelcome," I said. "All the same——"

"Excuse my interrupting," said Josiah Lethbridge. "Did you know of my son's intention? Were you aware of his mad plans?"

"No, dad," burst in Hugh; "Erskine knew nothing. He was as surprised as you when, an hour ago, I went and told him. The truth is, dad, that you and I have never got on well together. You seem to have forgotten that you were ever a young man, and had a young man's feelings and thoughts—seem to have forgotten that you were ever in love. You have always treated me, even since I have reached a man's age, as though I were never to have a will of my own, or to think of disagreeing with you. I feared you as a child, and—and up to to-night I feared you still. That was why I asked Mr. Erskine to come with me while I made my confession."

"Did you think," asked Mr. Lethbridge, "that he would influence me in any way?"

"I don't know what I thought," replied Hugh; "but Erskine told me that you ought to know—that I ought to come and tell you everything; and I have come, and I have told you."

"Very well. That is all, I suppose?" and still the older man spoke in the same calm, measured tones. "You, I imagine, think you have done a very romantic and heroic thing. On the other hand, I feel that my only son has disgraced me."

"Disgraced you?"

"Yes, disgraced me. Every one in the county who knows me will point at me as one whose son married against his father's wishes—married without a penny—married like one who is ashamed of his action. Well, I imagine I can bear it."

"Is that all you have to say, dad?"

"I cannot see what there is to say besides. You have followed your own devices, and you must take the consequences."

"I think it may be as well to remember, Mr. Lethbridge," I said, "that, whether your son has acted wisely or foolishly, he can claim the credit of being sincere and honest. There is nothing ignoble in a young fellow marrying the girl he loves. As for his joining the Army, it is what every young man ought to do at a time like this."

"Pardon me, Mr. Erskine, if I have my own opinions about my son's actions. No doubt the old-fashioned ideas which were instilled into my mind as a boy are regarded as out of date. I was taught to believe in the Commandment, 'Honor thy father and thy mother.' That Commandment, in the present generation, is discarded; but I do not think the present generation, or future generations, will be any the better because they have discarded it. As for his joining the Army, he certainly knows my views about that."

"But surely you will give him credit for being conscientious and sincere?"

Josiah Lethbridge looked down at the blotting-paper upon which he had been tracing grotesque figures without speaking. He seemed to imagine that my question did not call for a reply.

"Hugh tells me that in all probability he will have to go to the front shortly," I went on. "It may be—although I sincerely trust he will come back in safety—he will never come back again. That being so, it is natural to hope that his father will say a kind word before he goes. After all, your son is doing the noblest thing of which he is capable: he is offering his life to his country."

"Pardon me, Mr. Erskine," replied Josiah Lethbridge, "but perhaps I may be forgiven if I hold different views from your own. I am a plain man, and as a rule do not waste words. When a son of mine deliberately flouts the deepest convictions of his father's life; when he deliberately defies and does what his father has commanded him not to do; when he tramples underfoot his father's deepest convictions—then, I say, he is no longer a son of mine; henceforth he is a stranger to my house."

I was staggered at this. I had quite expected anger—denunciation, perhaps—but not this cold, cruel treatment.

"You cannot mean that, sir?" I said.

"I am not in the habit of saying what I do not mean, and I do not speak hastily. Your presence here, Mr. Erskine, may have given my brave son the courage to speak to his father, although I have my own opinion about your good taste in coming here to support him; but it doesn't alter my opinions and determinations in the slightest degree, and I presume that, since he has chosen to defy me, he has made his own plans for the future. Anyhow, I have no more to do with him."

"Dad, you don't mean that!" and Hugh's voice was hoarse and trembling.

"I do not think I need detain you any longer," and Josiah Lethbridge rose from his chair as he spoke. "I have many things to attend to."

Perhaps I was foolish, but I could not bear the idea of the young fellow being turned out of his home without making protest. I knew it was no business of mine, and that I was taking an unpardonable liberty in interfering in any way, but I could not help myself.

"Mr. Lethbridge," I said, "you will live to repent this. That your son may have been foolish in making a hurried marriage I do not deny; but that he has done wrong in joining the Army at such a time as this I *do* deny, and it seems to me that no father should treat his son as you are treating yours. He, at least, is offering his life, while you, without a thought of sacrifice and without care for your country's need, coldly turn him out of the house."

"Sacrifice!" and for the first time there was a touch of passion in his voice. "We are dragged into this ghastly war through the bungling of our statesmen; we are made the puppets and playthings of political hacks!" he cried. "The whole country is being dragged to ruin because of the mad bungling of those at the head of affairs, and then, because some of us are sane and do not wish to see the country bled to death, we are told that we are making no sacrifice. Sacrifice! I have within the last week lost a fortune through this madness. My business will be ruined; we shall be all bled white with taxation; England will never be the same again; and my own son—or he who was my son," he added in bitter parenthesis—"offers himself as a legalized murderer! And then you talk about sacrifice! But remember this," he added, looking towards Hugh, "it will be no use your coming to me in days to come, or expecting help in any way. I wash my hands of your whole future. As you have made your bed, so you must lie on it."

Hugh Lethbridge stood in the middle of the room, looking at his father in a dazed kind of way, as though he had failed to comprehend his words.

"You—you surely don't mean that, dad!"

Josiah Lethbridge stood, resting one hand on the back of his chair, his face hard and immovable, no word passing his lips.

"Good-bye, dad," and Hugh held out his hand. The father did not seem to notice it. He stood perfectly still, with the same hard look on his face. Hugh passed out of the room, leaving me alone with the angry man.

"Good-night, sir," I said. "I am sorry, and some day you will be."

He hesitated a second, as if in doubt whether to speak, then he looked at me more kindly.

"Mr. Erskine," he said, "doubtless you do not approve of my actions, but my convictions are not of yesterday."

"I hope, when you have considered, you will act differently," was my reply. "Your son may have all the foolishness of a boy, but he is a lad of whom any father ought to be proud."

Mr. Lethbridge did not speak a word for some seconds, then he said, half apologetically:

"I am afraid, Mr. Erskine, that I have been very rude to you. I remember that you are a guest in my house, and I am afraid that, in my disappointment, I have broken the laws of hospitality. I shall always be pleased to see you here, when you care to call."

"Thank you," I replied, "but I am afraid I cannot accept the hospitality which you offer. The man who closes his door to such a son as yours, and for such a reason, forfeits all right to respect. I am told you claim to be a religious man, but I will not speak of that." And I, too, passed out of the room.

I had scarcely closed the door behind me when I saw Isabella Lethbridge standing in the hall.

"Hugh has gone in to see mother," she said. "Please tell me what has happened."

"I have no right to do that, Miss Lethbridge," was my reply. "Good-night."

I went to the door and opened it, regardless of what she might think of me. It seemed to me that I could not breathe in the house; the atmosphere was stifling, and the memory of the look I had seen on Hugh's face made me so angry that I could not trust myself.

XIV

THE RECRUITING MEETING

The human mind and heart are difficult to understand, and, in spite of all men's researches in the realm of psychology, can never be explained. I had left Mr. Lethbridge's house, angry with the owner of it, almost angry with Hugh, certainly hard and bitter towards Isabella Lethbridge; and yet, no sooner had I got outside than an entire revulsion of feeling and thought came over me. My mind seemed like a cloud of dust, while confused, whirling thoughts possessed me. But nothing was real and clear, save that I had played an unworthy part. I reflected that I had not understood Hugh, neither had I understood his father, and in everything I had bungled. I had left Mr. Lethbridge when, as it now seemed to me, he was in the humor to be reasoned with. Had I, I reflected, understood anything of the human heart, I should have known that he would have felt a sense of utter desolation at Hugh's departure, and might, if I had been wise, have repented of his harsh action; but I had not been wise. In a fit of anger I had refused his hospitality, I had insulted him, and thereby had closed the door of his house against me forever.

With this thought, too, came the realization that I had been anything but courteous to Isabella Lethbridge. She, naturally, had desired to know something about the interview which had taken place, and I had rudely refused to reply to her question. I had left the house in a way that was less than civil, and had, as a consequence, stamped myself as a clown.

Strange as it may seem, I had practically forgotten all about Hugh. I had come to his father's house in order to be near him during the most critical and difficult hour of his life, and I ought to have been with him during the period of anguish which must naturally follow. Instead of which I had left him as though I did not care how he fared.

But more than all this my mind and heart were in a state of turmoil, as I considered my feelings towards Isabella Lethbridge. I had caught the flash of her eyes as she looked into mine. In my pride and vanity I could not help believing that she had an interest in me which was more than ordinary, and I knew my heart had responded to what I believed existed in hers, even although, all the time, I felt angrily towards her.

I walked towards the Lodge gates, scarcely knowing what I was doing or realizing what had happened, except in a vague, confused way. At that time I forgot my own malady, forgot that my days were numbered. It seemed to me that life stretched out before me, full of wonder, and full of promise. Presently, however, my confused feelings subsided, and I began to think more sanely and connectedly on what had taken place. I remembered that Hugh's car was outside the house, and that, in all probability, he would be coming along in a few minutes. I determined, therefore, to wait for him. So instead of passing through the Lodge gates, I turned and walked back towards the house. I had not gone more than a hundred yards when I met Isabella Lethbridge. Why she had come I had no idea, because she could not have expected to meet me. She would, naturally, think I had continued my journey home, yet she showed no surprise at meeting me.

"Mr. Erskine," she said, "what have I done that you should—should——"

I thought I caught a sob in her voice. Certainly she seemed strangely wrought upon.

I was silent, for I did not know how to answer her. Longings, hopes, fears, and desires surged through my heart in a most unaccountable way. In one sense I felt strangely happy at being there with her on that bright moonlight night; for the clouds had now rolled away, and the moon sailed serenely in the sky above. On the other hand, I knew I was much depressed. While everything was possible, nothing seemed possible. Truly, life was a maddening maze!

She turned with me, as if to return to the house, and for some time we walked side by side without speaking.

"Won't you tell me what has taken place?" she asked.

"Your brother has joined the Army," I replied. "He has got married too— married to Mary Treleaven. He asked me to come with him to the house while he told his father."

"And——?" she asked.

"Need I tell you that?" was my response.

"You mean that my father has driven him out of the house," and her voice was hard and angry.

I do not know why it was, but at that moment I felt I must champion Josiah Lethbridge's cause. The man had angered me beyond words, and yet I found myself excusing him.

"Your father has had all his convictions trampled upon, all his hopes destroyed," I replied. "The things Hugh has done came upon him suddenly, and overcome by disappointment and grief, he—he——"

"Do you excuse him, Mr. Erskine?" she interrupted.

"I have neither the right to excuse nor condemn. I was simply an onlooker, and had no right to be there at all."

She caught my arm convulsively.

"Don't say that," she said eagerly. "You—you have the right; that is, you are interested in Hugh. He is so fond of you, and he thought, of course he thought, you might influence my father. Besides——"

"Besides what?" I queried, as I saw her hesitate.

"Oh, I don't know. Everything is in a muddle; everything is so hopeless; and yet father talks about God—talks about the power of religion—talks about providence!"

I was silent at this, for her words were but an echo of my own thoughts.

"Why should not Hugh marry the girl he loves?" she went on. "He is young, and has the right to live his own life; if they love each other, what right has my father to stand in their way?"

"I thought you did not believe in love. I remember, when talking with you about it one day, you expressed the opinion that such a thing did not exist." I said this almost triumphantly, as though pleased to get the better of her in an argument.

"At any rate," she replied, "he has the madness of love. He is willing to give all, sacrifice all, risk all, for it. That is something anyhow. Mr. Erskine, will you not come back to the house again and plead with my father? He might listen to you. Do you not think you owe it to Hugh, since you came up with him?" Then her mood altered. "After all, what is the use of it? Life can never be anything but a promise of something which can never be fulfilled. But I love him for what he has done. I am prouder of my brother than ever. It is worth living to know that one whom one loves as a brother, has dared everything, and sacrificed everything, for his love."

A strange feeling possessed me; at that moment I thought I loved Isabella Lethbridge; felt that here, at least, was a woman who, in spite of her contradictions, in spite of the fact that she had repelled me, was worth the love of a lifetime. As I reflected upon it afterwards, however, I knew that I did not love her. Between my life and hers was a great impassable barrier. Besides, what right had I, a man with one foot in the grave, a man whose days were numbered, to think of such things?

Again there was a silence between us, and during that silence such a longing filled my life as I had never known before. I longed to live, to live on and on indefinitely. I hated the barriers by which I was bounded. My whole being revolted against the thought of death. At that moment, too, I felt as though there must be something for which I could find no better name than God Who was behind all things, Who made all things, Who thought all things. Why should that Infinity give me life, only to stamp it out, according to His caprice? Why should I be the subject of such a hideous mockery?

With the longing of life, too, came the longing for something even deeper. For the moment my mind was bounded by no barriers. I saw infinite possibility, possibility which transcended all thought and imagination. It seemed to me that if man were a child of God, he possessed something of God's life, lived in Him, was part of Him, that he shared in God's Infinity and Eternity.

Then I looked at the woman by my side, and as I did so she seemed to shrivel up. She was a thing of a day, of an hour. She did not seem to share in this Eternal Life of which I had been thinking. All the time she clutched my arm convulsively.

At that moment I heard footsteps on the drive, and saw Hugh Lethbridge coming towards us.

"Where are you going, Hugh?" I asked.

"Going!" he cried. "I am going to the only place a man can go at a time like this. I am going to my wife."

"Your father has said nothing more to you?"

"I have not seen him. He has not come to me, and I could not go to him; but I have seen mother. She knows, she understands."

"Are you walking back, then?"

"Walking?" Then he laughed. "Oh, I see, you are thinking about the car. It is not my car now. My father has disinherited me, disowned me; this place is no longer my home; but I would do it again, Erskine, I would do it a thousand times. Good-night, Bella, old girl. What have you and Erskine been talking about?"

"But I shall see you again, Hugh?" said Isabella Lethbridge, without seeming to notice the question.

"You will have to come early to-morrow morning, if you do," he replied, with a laugh. "I am under orders now, and must report myself to-morrow afternoon. Don't worry, old girl."

"I will make father forgive you, I'll simply make him."

Hugh laughed sceptically.

"You might as well think of moving Routor, or Brown Willie, as think of moving my father; and you know it, Bella; but mother's a trump. Do you know, mother sees more of this business than I have ever seen. I told her just now that I was going to the front almost immediately, and I don't think she ever expects to see me alive again; but she behaved like a saint in heaven. She sees into the heart of this war—sees why England must fight, why it is our duty to crush German militarism; sees why we must save Belgium. You and I have often laughed, Bella, but her mind, or rather her heart, has probed the thing to its very depths. She has made me believe more in religion during the last few minutes I have been with her than I have believed in all my life. She quoted some words from the Bible, which opened a new world for me —'Without shedding of blood, there is no remission of sins.' She spoke like one inspired. I cannot explain the meaning of it, I only know that as she repeated the passage I *felt* its meaning;—and she made me feel I was doing a great thing. I was no longer going to the war simply at the call of my country, but at the call of God. Good-night, Bella, old girl; shall I see you to-morrow?"

"Where can I see you, Hugh?"

"At my wife's home," he said proudly. "Will you dare father's anger, and come?"

Her only reply was to throw her arms round her brother's neck and kiss him, and then, without even looking at me, she rushed rapidly towards the house.

When I reached my little hut that night, I paid the penalty for the excitement through which I had passed. At one time I thought I was going to die. Pain such as I had never suffered before racked me, and I was as weak as a child. It was not until morning that the pain subsided, and I was able to sleep. I, too, had intended to go to John Treleaven's house, and give Hugh a word of cheer as he left to join his regiment; but nature was too strong for me. I did not awake till after midday, and Simpson had been too wise to interfere with nature's healing balm.

I had expected during the time I was suffering so terribly that it would be many days before I was restored to my ordinary strength, and yet, strange as it may seem, I awoke refreshed. Evidently there was enough vitality in my system to enable me to recuperate quickly.

"There is bad news, sir," said Simpson, after I had dressed.

"Bad news! How? Where?" I asked.

"The Germans are driving us back everywhere, sir, driving the French too. Do you think the Army would take me, sir, if I offered myself? I'd like to have a smack at them."

"How old are you, Simpson?"

"Fifty-five, sir."

"It may be that they will be obliged to take you before the war is over."

"I am ready now, sir, if they will have me."

During the afternoon I tried to forget the interview of the previous night in some experiments with the hobby which had occupied my mind for several weeks. I had become quite efficient in the management of my little wireless apparatus, and I was greatly interested in the little book of codes which the young fellow from M—— had given me.

When evening came I determined, in spite of what I had suffered on the previous night, to find my way to the village schoolroom. As I have said before, I wanted to feel the pulse of humanity, longed to know what was doing in the world; and living here, in this out-of-the-way corner of the world, it seemed my only chance of fulfilling my desire.

When I arrived, the little schoolroom was nearly full. There were but few young men, not more than a score in all. The rest of the audience was made up of women and older men. On the platform was the Squire, who presided over the meeting, and near him were several of the leading people of the district. Both the vicars of St. Issey and St. Eia were there, together with one or two neighboring squires. Naturally, Josiah Lethbridge was absent.

I took my seat in a corner of the room, as far out of sight as possible, and tried to understand the little audience which had gathered together. I suppose every county has its characteristics, and certainly a Cornish audience is different from any I have seen. Years ago, I had been informed, the people were exceedingly emotional, and easy to be moved. That, however, was a thing of the past. There was no suggestion of excitement or enthusiasm, and while each and all seemed to listen carefully to what was being said, it was difficult to tell what their feelings were. On the whole, I think I never saw a less responsive audience, if one might judge from outward appearances.

A lady with quite a county reputation for singing was at the meeting, and while there are few parts of the country where there is stronger love for music than in Cornwall, she seemed to make little impression on her audience. Yet perhaps I am wrong in saying this. They appreciated the sweetness of her voice and the melody of her songs, but the sentiment which those songs expressed went for nothing. I have heard audiences spoken of as stolid. The audience at St. Issey was not stolid; it was stony. The people were keenly alert, they understood all that was being said, and in a way appreciated all the speeches; but they sat coldly critical, and unmoved.

Squire Treherne made a model chairman. He came to them, he said, as a friend and neighbor. He had known most of them all their lives, and he felt it his duty to point out to them, at this time of national danger, the needs of the times and the duties of the people. He spoke of what Cornwall had done in the history of the nation; he reminded them of stirring events in the life of the county, when Cornishmen had done their part and more than their part.

Then he went on to describe the circumstances which had led to the war. He described Germany's preparations, told the story of what had taken place in the Balkan States, and related how Sir Edward Grey had done his utmost to avert the war; but the time had come when war could not be averted, and when England had to take her part in it. Her honor was at stake, her safety was in peril, all that we loved was in danger, and every man in the country was called upon to play his part. The Squire did not give a brilliant speech, but it was full of good common sense, full of patriotic fervor. The old man did not see how any Englishman could stand aloof at a time like this.

Other speakers followed, who simply repeated what the Squire had said, and presently came the appeal for young men to offer themselves to their King and Country.

No one knows how I longed to be able to respond to that appeal. It seemed to me that, commonplace as the speeches were, no man could, who bore a British name, or had British blood in his veins, keep back. But I could do nothing; I was a useless hulk doomed to die. I eagerly scanned the faces of the young men who were near me, anxious to catch some suggestion of response to the speakers' appeals, but no one seemed moved. Each listened attentively to all the arguments that were adduced, but no man made a sign. Never, as it seemed to me, had I seen a more saddening sight, and presently, when the meeting was about to close, and the audience prepared to depart, I yielded to an overwhelming impulse. I knew it was madness on my part to do so, but I could not resist it. After all, what did it matter whether I shortened my days or not? I could not fight for my country, but perhaps I could persuade others to do so.

As the chairman was on the point of asking the people to rise and sing the national anthem, I got up and asked to be allowed to say a few words. Of course, consent was immediately given, and I saw some of the people, who were on the point of leaving, resume their seats, as I made my way to the platform. Indeed, I could not help feeling that there was a wave of more than ordinary interest passing over the audience, as they saw me preparing to address them.

I had not the slightest idea of what I wished to say. Indeed, as I stood up and faced the people, my mind was a perfect blank. I had simply yielded to an overwhelming impulse, without having any definite message to deliver.

Usually making speeches had been no difficulty to me. I had not been a barrister for several years without having had some practice in the art. Nevertheless, I felt a strange nervousness as I faced these simple country-people. I had nothing to say, and there seemed no reason why I should be there. I stood for a few seconds in silence, while the people waited; then, looking in one corner of the hall, I saw Isabella Lethbridge. She was looking at me intently, her eyes were shining brightly, and her lips were parted, as if with eager anticipation.

Immediately my thoughts took shape, and words came easily. At that moment, too, a wave of passion passed over me. I remembered what Hugh Lethbridge had done; knew that even now he had left his wife, left his home, left everything at the call of his country; and as I saw a score of stalwart youths, sitting together in the back part of the room utterly unmoved by all that had passed, a feeling of hot anger filled me. I scarcely knew what I said. It did not seem to matter; but something seemed to catch fire within me, and in a few moments I realized that the audience had caught fire too. Cheer after cheer burst forth. Only one thing do I remember saying, and that I thought afterwards was in anything but good taste.

"I have come to you," I said, "as a dying man. One of the greatest physicians in London has told me that my days are numbered, that I must avoid all excitement, that I must take care that I do not over-exert myself; that if I do, my life hangs on a thread; but I feel I cannot sit still, although this meeting may kill me, while you are unresponsive."

This gave me a kind of text for the appeal I made. I knew I spoke in hot, passionate words. I forgot everything in my desire to rouse the people to a sense of duty. I saw that the faces of the people had become set and stern, I noticed that their eyes were shining with a new light, and I felt that influences were at work which had hitherto been absent. This made me forget the madness of my action, made me careless of my own life. Nothing at that moment seemed to matter but the cause for which I was pleading.

"What are you going to do?" I cried. "Will you not respond to the call of your King and of your Country? Will you not fight for liberty, truth, and honor? As for me...." Then a great darkness came over me, and I remembered no more.

When I awoke to consciousness, I was sitting in a little anteroom, at the back of the platform, where around me stood the Vicar, the Squire, and two or three others.

"Are you better?"

"I am quite all right," I replied. "What is the matter?"

"You were overcome, exhausted. I am afraid you ought not to have spoken."

"Was it in vain, then?" I asked.

"Oh, no; half a dozen young fellows came out at the close of your appeal. I do not think it was because of what you said so much, but the fact that you were ill, and risked your life in trying to arouse them, which made them feel ashamed. Are you sure you are better?"

"I am quite all right," I repeated. "I cannot understand how I came to lose consciousness."

"I am going to run you up in my carriage," said the Squire; "I cannot think of allowing you to walk."

"There is not the slightest need for that," I replied; and as if to prove my words I walked across the room.

"Still, I am going to drive you home," said the Squire. "I am afraid I ought not to have let you speak, even although you have done what we all failed to do."

As I walked into the schoolroom, a group of people waited, evidently anxious to hear about me, and an old man came up and gripped me by the hand.

"I be glad you be better, maaster," he said. "'Twas good to 'ear ee for sure; you made me think of John Guttridge, when he used to come down 'ere preachin'. Yes, maaster, you made some of them feel what cowards they was; but we Cornish be curious people. Besides, maaster, we be'ant used to this sort of thing, and spite of all you say, we ca'ant grip it like."

"How is that?" I asked.

"For forty year we've bin tould the other thing, maaster. Tha's how it is. For forty year we've bin tould that war was wrong; and now to be tould it be our duty—well, you see, we ca'ant clunk it. It do'ant seem right. It'll take a lot to git the thought fixed in our minds that the Lord would have us do this. When you can do that, maaster, there won't be no need for meetin's; the difficulty then will be to keep the boys back."

Although I did not reply, I felt that the old man had got to the heart of the thing. One could not eradicate the teachings of half a century in a day.

Immediately afterwards, the old man's words were driven from my mind; for coming towards me, with hand outstretched, was Isabella Lethbridge. I saw a look in her eyes that I had never seen before.

"Are you mad, Mr. Erskine?" she asked.

"I expect so," I replied.

"Oh, but I did envy you!" and her voice quivered. "It must be glorious to have the power to move people, even though——" Then she stopped, as if she thought it unwise to utter the thought that had come into her mind.

"Good-night;" and her voice was like a sob as she went out into the darkness.

XV

HOW THE CHANGE BEGAN

"That was Lethbridge's daughter, wasn't it?" asked the Squire, as we drove towards my little house.

"Yes," I replied.

"I am surprised that she should be there;" and I noticed that the Squire's voice seemed tense and angry.

"Surprised! Why?"

He hesitated a second, then went on.

"I had a row with the man this morning. I—I could not help it."

"A row with Mr. Lethbridge?"

"Yes, he made me mad. I tried to act as generously as I could; but there are limits."

I was silent, although, truth to tell, I wanted to know what had caused the Squire's anger.

"I went to see him this morning," he went on presently. "You see, I wanted the platform to be as representative as possible, and knowing that Lethbridge is a large employer of labor, and therefore has a great deal of influence among working men, I thought he might be of value to us. I suppose I ought to have gone to see him before; but the meeting was arranged in a hurry, and—and—anyhow, I didn't. But I went this morning, and asked him to propose the chief resolution."

"And what did he say?"

"He refused pointblank, and added an insulting remark to his refusal."

"And then what?" I asked.

"I am afraid I lost my temper. You see, I did not understand his point of view —how could I? Whatever he is, he was born in England, and I am afraid I told him some home truths. I told him he was a disgrace to his country, that he was unworthy to be called an Englishman, and that I should refuse ever to enter his house again."

"Pretty drastic," I remarked.

"Drastic!" replied the old man. "How could I help being drastic? He abused the Army, abused our statesmen, said we had been dragged into the war by a bungling diplomacy, told me we were as guilty as the Germans were, and that we had torn up more scraps of paper than the Germans had. I asked him to prove his words, I challenged him to bring forward a single instance where we had treated any country as the Germans had treated Belgium."

"And he?" I asked.

"He couldn't answer me."

"Well, what was the upshot of it?"

"After a bit I got rather ashamed of myself for having lost my temper; besides, I thought I might have misunderstood him, and I wanted his help in the fund we are raising."

"And did he help you?"

I felt the old man's body quiver as he sat by my side in the carriage.

"Not a penny, sir, not a penny. He actually had the cheek to tell me that he had lost a large sum through the war, and that he would be bled to death with taxes. God bless my soul! What have we English people to do talking about taxes at a time like this! Besides, he is a rich man. If he lost a hundred thousand pounds to-morrow, he would hardly feel it. He has been making money hand over fist for a quarter of a century, and now, when the country is in peril, he complains about taxes; squeals like a stoat caught in a gin! I have no patience!"

"And you got no further than that with him?"

"I got no further with him because I didn't stay. I have tried to be neighborly with the man, although I hate his views. But when one's country is at stake, when a man tries to hide his meanness and niggardliness by whining about taxes!—well, you see, we had nothing more to say to each other. He proved himself to be a bounder, a rank outsider. I told him so, too. I said, 'Henceforth, Mr. Lethbridge, we shall be strangers. I shall never enter your doors again, and naturally you won't want to enter mine.' Then he turned round and asked me what I had sacrificed for the country. I suppose he thought he was going to make a point against me there, but he didn't get much satisfaction out of it. I told him I had written to Headquarters and offered everything I have. If they wanted my house for a hospital, they could have it; if they wanted my land for a camping-ground, they could have it. At that he sneered, and said I was perfectly safe in making such an offer. Think of it, Erskine, think of it! What can you do with a man like that?"

131

"His only son has enlisted," I said.

"What, Hugh! You don't mean it?"

"Yes, I do. He has enlisted as a private, although I understand that owing to his knowledge of modern languages, and his skill in mechanics, besides being a very good shot, they are going to make a special case of him. All the same, he enlisted as a private."

"God bless my soul! That's good."

"I am afraid that is why Mr. Lethbridge is so angry," I went on. "You see, he is one of those men who hate war."

"Hates war! Well, what of that? We all do. We English are a peace-loving people, and we detest war, we loathe it, shudder at it. Did I not lose my only son in the Boer War? But in this case everything is at stake, our plighted word, our honor! If we slunk out of it, we should be a byword among the nations. Besides, think what these Germans mean to do. If they are not crushed we shall have no country, no home. Have you read what they are doing in Belgium? Have you read about Louvain, Malines, Aerschot? It is devilish, man, devilish. They have violated every law, human and divine. I never thought that any fiend from hell could do what they are doing. And if they can do these things in Belgium, what will they do in England, if they get here? What would become of our women and children? No, no, it is a call of God, my boy, it is a call of God. You put it straight to-night, hot and strong. I nearly lost my head when I heard you."

"Anyhow, Hugh Lethbridge has joined the Army. And what has hurt his father even more than that is that he has married that girl Mary Treleaven."

"God bless my soul! You don't mean that!" and the old man lapsed into silence. "I am glad he did it," he went on presently. "It serves his father right. And—and Hugh is a fine lad."

"He *is* a fine lad," I assented. "But you can understand how his father feels about it."

"Yes, yes," said the Squire. "All the same, I am glad I gave him a piece of my mind. I could not help it, Erskine. I am a peaceful man, and I hate losing my temper, though, God knows, I am a bit given to it. But I was surprised to see his daughter there to-night," he went on, "and she was carried away by what you said too. Well, she has good blood on her mother's side. The Vivians are good people, and the family has owned land in the county for centuries. Ah, here we are. I hope you won't suffer for what you have done to-night, my boy."

"I do not think I shall," I replied. "I dare say I was very foolish, but I could not help it."

"I am proud of you!" and the old Squire gripped my hand heartily. "You have got good English blood in you, you have got the old Cornish feeling. By the way, I hope you will come over and see me sometimes. I am a poor man, Erskine, and we shall all of us have to retrench, but you will always find a welcome at my house."

Then he left me, and I found my way through the copse to my lonely little house.

For the next few days I was almost prostrate. I was paying the penalty for my foolishness. I knew I ought not to have gone to the meeting, and yet, I was glad I had.

So ill did I become that Simpson, without obtaining my permission, sent for the local doctor to come and see me. This doctor was a tall, gaunt Scotsman, who had, as he informed me, come to Cornwall rather for the purpose of building up his own health than for building up a practice. I was vexed that Simpson had sent for him, but I could not remain angry with the poor fellow, for I was so ill that he dare not be left alone with me without having some one to advise him. Dr. Wise was one of the most talkative men I ever met in my life, and after he had asked me a few questions about my illness, he assured me that I had not long to live, and that in all probability what I had done had curtailed the few months which otherwise would have been left to me. I found out, however, that his chief interest in me was not the malady from which I was suffering, or how he might get me better, but to have me as a listener to his views.

"The country is in a bad way," he said. "We have neither arms nor munitions. Even now the Woolwich Arsenal is only working two days a week."

"How do you know?" I asked.

"Oh, I got it from a man who knows a man who lives near Woolwich," he replied. "I got a letter yesterday morning, telling me about it."

"Has your informant an entrée into Woolwich Arsenal?" I asked.

"Oh, I know it is true," he replied. "Our house-maid has a brother who works there too, and he says the same thing. Oh, the country is in a bad way."

"It must be," I replied.

"Yes, and then there is all this talk about the Russians coming over to help us; do you know there is a plot in that, a deep-laid plot?" he asked in serious tones.

"You don't mean it!" I said, for by this time the man had begun to amuse me.

"Yes, I do," he replied. "I have heard on good authority that the Russians mean to turn round on us. They are in league with the Germans, and they are sending over half a million men to attack our Army at the back. I am not at liberty to tell how I got my information, but it is true. Then there is the Army food. Do you know, it is in a terrible condition."

"How is that?"

"Our soldiers at the front haven't got enough to eat. I know it for a fact. One of the men who went out with the Expeditionary Force wrote and told me that if it were not for the food they took from the German prisoners they would be starving."

"That is terrible," I replied.

"You would not believe it, would you?" he went on, "but the whole country is governed wrongly, and they are allowing the Germans to hoodwink us at every corner."

"If that is so," was my answer, "it seems strange that the Germans should have been driven back from the Marne. How is it that when they got so near to Paris they did not take it?"

"Ah, that is because they hated the English so. They had Paris in their hands practically, and might have been there now if they had not hated the English."

"That is very interesting," I said. "How did it come about?"

"Well, you see, the German generals had made all arrangements to march into Paris, but they gave way to a fit of anger, and determined to crush the English instead. It was a false move on their part, and but for that we should have been done for."

"How lucky for us," I replied.

"Yes, but they are arranging to get to Calais by another road now. They have everything fixed up for the invasion of England."

"What, the Germans have?"

"What they are going to do is this," and he spoke very solemnly. "First of all they are going to take Calais; then they are going to bring their big guns and bombard Dover. After that, they are going to lay mines in two lines, allowing a lane for the German boats to land two hundred thousand men in Dover. They are going to be flat-bottomed boats, and I have it on good authority that the Kaiser is coming with them."

"What! that he is coming over in these flat-bottomed boats with two hundred thousand men?" I asked.

"Yes, that is it. He is going to march on London with all these men, and dictate terms of peace from there," he added.

"And can you inform me what the British Fleet is going to be doing all this time?" I asked.

"We have no coal, man," was his answer. "Besides, think of the German submarines. They will sink all our ships as fast as we can bring them up."

How long he went on in this strain I hardly know, but that he believed in all he said was evident, and that he took a delight in his mournful prognostications was just as evident.

"Simpson," I said, "Dr. Wise has done me good. I feel better than I have felt for days."

"Yes, sir; thank you, sir," said Simpson. "Has he given you any medicine, sir?"

"Oh, no," I replied. "But he has done me a world of good; only, Simpson, don't allow him to come again."

September passed slowly away, and although I gradually recovered from the effects of the excitement through which I had passed, I did not go far afield, and beyond going into the village, and roaming round the cliffs, I took little or no exercise.

I discovered, as far as the people of St. Issey were concerned, that no sooner had the first effects of the declaration of war passed away, than they settled down to the old mode of living. Indeed, the war was not real to them at all. It was something that was happening a long way off. Only a few of them read the newspapers, and in spite of the bad news which circulated, they had not the slightest doubt about the English soon bringing the Germans to their knees. They found, too, that the war did not affect them in the way they had expected. There was neither scarcity of money nor food; work went on as usual, the harvest was garnered, and there were no prospects of a famine, which they had feared, coming to pass.

Indeed, as I think of those days, and as I reflect upon my own experiences, I do not so much wonder at the general prevailing sentiment. We are far out of the world down here in Cornwall—St. Issey is some miles from a railway station—and removed as we are from the clash and clamor of the world, it is difficult for us to realize what is going on in the great centres of life. That the war existed we knew, that a great struggle was going on hundreds of miles away was common knowledge, but it did not come home to us.

The following incidents will give some idea of what I mean.

One day, while walking through the fields towards St. Issey, I passed a cottage, by the door of which a woman of about forty years of age was sitting.

"Look 'ere, maaster," she said. "I want to ax 'ee a question."

"Well," I asked. "What?"

"Well, 'tis like this," she said. "Me an' my 'usband 'ave come to words."

"I am sorry for that," I said. "But that is not so bad as coming to blows."

"Oh, we do'ant come to blows, maaster, and 'ard words break no boans; but that is ev et; we 'ave come to words about this, and we 'ave 'ad several arguments about et, and I d'old to one thing, and my 'usband to another; and I thought you bein' from London would be able to put us right."

"If I can I will, but I have my doubts."

"'Tis this," replied the woman. "'Tis about Lord Kitchener. My 'usband d'say that Lord Kitchener is for the Germans, and I d'say 'e ed'n. I d'say 'e's for the English. Now which is right, maaster?"

Later in the afternoon I met Martha Bray, who, it may be remembered, proffered her services to Simpson on the day of my arrival.

"'Ow be 'ee gettin' on then, maaster?"

"Oh, better than I deserve, Martha," I replied. "Thank you for the ham you sent over."

"Oh, tha's all right, sur. Es the war still goin' on?"

"Yes," I replied; "still going on."

"Ter'ble pity," was her answer. "It ought to be stopped."

"The question is, Martha, how can we stop it?"

"We could stop et all right," said Martha, "ef everybody made up their minds to send them no more money. They would have to stop et."

"Send who any more money?" I asked.

"Why, Lloyd George, maaster; ef everybody in the country refused to send 'un a penny, he'd 'ave to stop et, and then the war would be over."

I could not help laughing at Martha's method for ending the great struggle of the world, neither would I have mentioned it, but to give an idea of the feelings which obtained in certain sections of the country.

But although to many the great carnage of blood which was convulsing

Europe was not real, the fact of war brooded over us like a great black cloud. In a sense we did not realize it, everything was so quiet and peaceful; but in another we did. It was in the background of all our lives, it colored all our thoughts.

Although I had given up all hope of getting any answers to the questions which troubled me either at Church or Chapel, I still went almost regularly. I could not understand how, but I had a feeling that it was here I should solve the problems which faced me.

For the first two or three weeks after war was declared there was a slight improvement in the congregations, and then things seemed to settle down to their normal condition again. And yet there was a difference, a subtle, indefinable difference. In a way I could not explain, it colored, as I have already said, all our thoughts and feelings. The services both at the Church and the Chapel were conducted just as they had been, except that some new prayers had been added to the Church liturgy, while the preacher at the Chapel generally made some mention of the war in some part of the service.

It seemed to me, too, that the people were thinking more than usual. Questions were being asked, which they had never thought of asking when I first came to the village. They did not go very deep, but they were suggestive of the new forces which were being realized. The change was so slight that a casual observer might not have noticed it; but it was there. I could not help thinking of the old Biblical story I had read at school, about the cloud the prophet saw which at first was no bigger than a man's hand, but which presently overspread the whole sky.

One day, when I went into the village, a woman stopped me rather angrily.

"Look 'ere, Mr. Erskine, I 'ave got somethin' to say to 'ee."

"What is it?" I asked.

"Well, a few weeks agone my boy Jim enlisted as a sojer 'cause of what you said at the meetin'."

"Very sensible of Jim," I replied.

"I ded'n like it at the time," said the woman.

"I'm very sorry."

"Well, none of my family have ever come so low as that before, and the mornin' after he'd enlisted I told my sister Betty, who comed over to see me about it. I said to 'er, 'Jim's goin' for a sojer,' and she says to me, 'God help us, Mary!' she said, 'to think that one of our family should sink so low as that.'"

"Yes," I said. "And what then?"

"Well, sur, he went away, and a week agone he didn't get on very well with one of the officers."

"No," I said, "that is a pity. Didn't the officer behave nicely?"

"No, 'e didn', that is, what I call nicely. He spoke to my son 'bout what I call nothin' 't 'oal."

"Well, what then?"

"Well, Jim wad'n pleased, so he gived a fortnight's notice to leave."

"What! to leave the Army?" I asked.

"Yes. You see, down 'ere wi' we, when a man d'want to leave 'is job, 'ee d'give a week's notice; but Jim thought he would be generous, so 'e gived a fortnight's notice. He went to the officer, and he said, 'I d'want to give a fortnight's notice to leave.'"

"And then?" I asked.

"Well, first the officer laughed, and then 'e told Jim to go back to 'is work, and said ef 'e left the Army before the war was over, 'e would be shot. I do'ant 'old with things like that, so now Jim 'as got to stay, whether 'e d'like it or not."

"And Jim doesn't like it?"

"No, 'e ain't bin used to bein' treated like that, and it was all because of you, too. Ef et ad'n bin for the speech you made in the schoolroom, 'e would'n 'ave joined."

But although humorous incidents were often happening, the grave realities were slowly gripping our minds and hearts. Day after day, this and that lad was leaving his home to prepare for the war, while many of the Naval Reserve men were already away in the North Sea, or elsewhere, waiting to give their lives, if need be, for their country's safety. Indeed, the Navy was far more real to us than the Army. The Cornish have never been a military people, but have always been at home on the waters. Many a time, as I have watched those great steel monsters ploughing the Atlantic, I have reflected that they were manned very largely by the Cornish, and that they were the chief bulwark against enemy invasion.

"I wonder if my boy is on her?" said an old man to me, as one day I watched the smoke from a great warship in the distance. And that question was echoed by thousands of hearts all over the county.

Week after week passed away, until the days became short and the nights grew cold. Blacker and blacker grew the clouds, while the lists of casualties which daily appeared in the newspapers made us feel that it was no game we were playing, but that we were engaged in a death struggle.

I had not been to Josiah Lethbridge's house, neither had I seen anything of the family, since the night of Hugh's departure, and then—I think it was the beginning of November—I was greatly surprised to see Josiah Lethbridge come to my door.

XVI

NEWS FROM HUGH

I thought he looked ill at ease, and I noticed that he was less ruddy and more careworn than when I had first met him.

I am afraid I greeted him rather coldly, for I remembered what had taken place at our last meeting.

"I hope I do not intrude," he said.

"It is very kind of you to call," was my reply.

"Not at all, I ought to apologize for coming."

"Have you heard from Hugh?" I asked, for I was determined, as far as possible, to make him feel his duty to his son.

I saw his lips shut, and his eyes and face grow harder, as I spoke.

"I have heard nothing," he replied. "I do not expect to, neither do I wish to."

I was silent at this, for it was not for me to interfere in his relations with his son, but I could not help feeling angry. But there was pity in my heart too, for I could not help seeing that the man was suffering. Why he was suffering I could not tell, but suffering he was.

"You have not been to see us lately," he said. "I hope what you said when we last met is not final. I—I should be sorry if the neighborly relations which I had hoped were established came to an end."

"I have been nowhere," I replied. "The weather has been very wet lately, and I have scarcely ventured out of doors."

"You must be very lonely here."

"Life is not very gay," I said. "It can scarcely be."

"I suppose friends come to see you?"

"Yes, a friend came down last week and spent three days with me," I replied, wondering what was in the man's mind.

"The newspapers do not bring us very good tidings."

"No, I am afraid we shall have a great deal of bad tidings before the good comes."

After that there was an awkward silence for some time.

"I am a lonely man myself," he went on. "Of course I have my business, and my public work, but I should be very glad if you would come up to see us sometimes. If you would let me know when you would come, I'd always send a car for you."

"What is in the man's mind?" I asked myself. "Surely he did not come here simply to say this."

"Naturally I did not think my presence would be welcome after our last interview, and——"

"Nothing of the kind," he interrupted, almost eagerly. "I hope you will forgive me for coming so informally, but my wife and I were wondering whether you would come up to-night. Could you? Of course I will send a car for you."

I reflected a few seconds before replying. It is true I had told him in a fit of anger that I should refuse his hospitality in future, but I wondered whether he was not repenting of his action towards Hugh; wondered, too, whether by going I could not bring about a better relationship between them and soften his heart. After all, I owed it to Hugh. But, if the truth must be confessed, there was another reason which made me long to go. I knew it was weakness on my part, knew, too, that I was a madman to encourage such feelings. As I have repeated in this history so many times, with dreary monotony, I had received my death sentence, and as I looked at my face each morning in the glass, and saw it become thinner and thinner, I had no misapprehension about the truth of the doctor's words. Therefore it was worse than madness for me to think about Isabella Lethbridge as I did; and yet—let me repeat it again—I was not in love with her.

"I wish you would come up to-night," urged Josiah Lethbridge. "Ours is a very quiet household."

"Are you giving a dinner-party or anything of that sort?" I asked.

"Oh no, no. I believe Bella is having one or two friends; but nothing in the shape of a dinner-party. Come, will you?"

I wanted to accept his invitation more than words can say, and yet something held me back.

"Have you heard anything about your son's wife?" I asked.

Again the old hard look came into his eyes, and he seemed to be struggling with himself.

"I have no son," he replied. "I know nothing about the woman you speak of."

"Pardon me, Mr. Lethbridge," I said, "but you have. Your son may not have fallen in with your wishes, but he is your son. Nothing can undo that fact. As for his so-called disobedience, he acted according to his conscience, and ____"

Josiah Lethbridge held up his hand, as if in protest.

"We will not speak of that, if you don't mind," he said. "I do not often alter my mind when it is once made up."

Again there was a silence, and I was on the point of refusing his invitation, when he, as if anticipating me, broke out almost eagerly.

"But you must come up to-night, Mr. Erskine," he said. "My wife is so anxious that you should. She is very fond of you. I never saw her take to a stranger as she has taken to you. Naturally, too, she is very anxious."

I tried to read his heart, tried to understand something of the thoughts which were surging through his mind.

"I suppose," he went on, "that you, who know influential people in London, know nothing more of this ghastly business than we do. That is, you know nothing more than what appears in the papers."

"No," I replied; "but what has appeared in the papers has surely made us feel proud that we are Englishmen. You have seen that we have again repulsed the German attack at Ypres?"

"Wholesale murder, I call it!" and his voice became hard as he spoke. "But there, we will not talk about that any more. I shall expect you to-night, then, and will send down the car at a quarter to seven. No, no, I shall accept no refusal. That is settled. I dare not face my wife if I had to go back and say you would not come." And a wintry smile passed over his face.

"I am like a moth fluttering in a candle," I said to myself as I put on my evening clothes that night. "Why should I be going to this man's house? Why should I eat of his dinner? Why should I throw myself into the society of this girl? She is nothing to me, never can be; in a way I positively dislike her, and yet I am always thinking about her."

"I am glad you are going out to-night, sir," said Simpson, as he helped me on with my fur-lined coat. "It must be very lonely for you night after night, sir, with no one to speak to. I hope you will have a pleasant evening, sir."

"It must be a little lonely for you too, Simpson, and I am afraid I try your patience sometimes." For the man had been with me for so long, and had served in our family for so many years, that I regarded him more as a friend than as a servant.

"No, sir, it is always a pleasure to serve you, sir."

He lit the lantern and walked ahead of me, as we went along the pathway through the copse.

"Shall I wait up for you, sir?" he added, as he held open the door of the car.

"I think you may as well, Simpson," I said. "I shall not be late."

A few minutes later I had reached Josiah Lethbridge's house, and was greeted warmly by Mrs. Lethbridge. I heard the sound of merry voices in the drawing-room close by, and was made somewhat angry that Mr. Lethbridge had asked me this evening, especially as, in spite of what he had said, they were evidently giving a dinner-party that night. When I went into the drawing-room, however, I found only three people. A young man and woman, whom I took to be brother and sister, were the only guests besides myself. They were the son and daughter of the managing director of one of the Cornish banks, and had motored some twenty miles in order to be present. The man, Edward Barcroft, was a young fellow of about five-and-twenty, and I knew him to be a rich man's son. There was nothing striking about him. He was of medium height, somewhat stoutly built, and carried himself with an air of confidence. I did not like him, however. He seemed to be too sure of himself, too aggressive. Miss Barcroft was one of those placid, even-tempered girls who made me think of a German frau.

Before the evening was very far advanced, I could not help concluding that Edward Barcroft was a suitor for Isabella Lethbridge's hand, while, as it seemed to me, she was much flattered by his attentions. I do not think I had ever seen her look so handsome as she looked that night. I was never able to describe a woman's dress, but I could not help noticing that her clothes fitted her to perfection. They seemed a part of her. She was very gay, too. She laughed frequently, but her pleasantries grated upon me. Why, I could not tell. She paid me very little attention; indeed, she did not treat me as her guest at all. I had simply come there at the invitation of her father and mother, while she devoted all her attention to young Barcroft.

I have said that I had never seen Isabella Lethbridge looking so handsome as she did that night; on the other hand, she had never repelled me more, even while she fascinated me. I understood, as I had not understood before, young Prideaux's description of her. She was a flirt. I saw that young Barcroft was greatly enamored with her; noted, too, that she laughed at his feeblest jokes, and, as far as I could judge, made him believe that she was as interested in him as he was in her. Yet I could not help realizing the artificiality of her every word and action.

As for poor Hugh, he was never mentioned. He might never have existed, although I knew by the look on Mrs. Lethbridge's face that she was constantly thinking of him, constantly grieving about what had taken place.

I could not tell why it was, but in spite of the fact that every one except Isabella Lethbridge was very kind and courteous to me, I was angry, and felt a sort of contempt for the self-assertive, unpleasant young Cornishman who made himself so much at home in Josiah Lethbridge's house.

"The war will soon be over, don't you think, Mr. Erskine?" he said.

"What makes you think so?" I asked.

"Why, the Germans have been able to do nothing for months," was his reply. "Never since their first blow have they been able to hurt us. See how we have been able to hold them up at Ypres. At present we are not ready to strike our decisive blow, but when we have more guns and ammunition, we shall be able to drive them like a flock of sheep. Besides, they are financially bankrupt, you know."

"Indeed," I said.

"Yes. It is a matter of robbing Peter to pay Paul with them now. They live by taking in each other's washing; but that will soon come to an end. On the other hand, the war hasn't been such a bad thing for us."

"No," I said. "How?"

"Oh, it has been good for business. Money has been circulated as it has never been circulated before. Instead of it meaning a financial crash to us, it has meant a boom. Have you not found it so, Mr. Lethbridge?"

"Money has certainly been circulated freely," was the older man's reply, "but I do not wish to talk about it. The whole thing is a crime." And both his face and voice hardened.

At that moment a servant entered and brought Mr. Lethbridge an official-looking document, which he opened eagerly. He read it through twice, and then calmly and deliberately folded it again and placed it in the envelope.

"What is it about, Josiah?" asked Mrs. Lethbridge.

I thought he looked pleased, but I could not tell. He did not answer his wife's question.

"Is it about Hugh?" she asked.

Still he was silent.

"Josiah, Josiah, tell me, is he wounded, killed?"

"No. I—I suppose it is all the other way. It is nothing to me. There, you can read it if you like."

With trembling hands Mrs. Lethbridge took the letter and read it.

"Oh, Hugh, my darling boy," she sobbed.

"What is it, mother?" asked Isabella. "What has he done?"

"He has received some order, some distinguished order for bravery. There, there, read it! Isn't it splendid? I was afraid he was killed or hurt or something. I didn't expect this. Oh, isn't it glorious? But it is just like him."

Josiah Lethbridge rose from the table.

"Shall we go into the library for our coffee and cigars?" he asked. He seemed to be making an effort to be calm.

"We must tell Mary," said Mrs. Lethbridge.

"You must do nothing of the sort," said her husband. "When I said, once for all, that we would have nothing to do with that woman, I meant it. Will you come this way, Barcroft and Mr. Erskine? Oh yes, the ladies can come with us if they do not mind tobacco smoke."

A few minutes later we were all in the library, where, in spite of Mr. Lethbridge's chagrin, we were not able to suppress our desire to talk about Hugh and what he had done. It appeared by the document received that he had, by his coolness and bravery, not only saved the life of an officer, but that he had rendered such important service to his battalion that a possible disaster had been turned into a victory.

"Ah!" I said. "How I envy him!"

"Envy him! In what way?" asked Barcroft.

"Envy his being able to serve his country," was my reply. "How a man with health and strength can stay in England at a time like this I can't understand."

"Are you referring to me?" he asked. And I noticed there was an angry look in his eyes.

"I was not referring to any one," was my reply. "I was simply stating what I felt."

"For my own part, I believe that a man who is looking after the finances of the country may be doing more for his nation than by wearing khaki," he replied. "Don't you think so, Miss Lethbridge?"

"I think too much is made of the so-called heroism of soldiers," she said, evidently with a desire to please him. "Of course it was grand of Hugh to do what he did, but he was always like that." And she looked smilingly into

Barcroft's face.

Again the girl angered me, and in my heart of hearts I despised her. But why should I be angry? Why should I care about her evident desire to please this young Cornishman? And then, realizing that my words were bordering on discourtesy, said:

"I expect the War Office will have written to his wife. Anyhow, I will see that she knows to-morrow that her husband is a hero."

At this, Isabella Lethbridge looked at her father and laughed, while he, having given me an angry look, talked about something else.

The evening, as far as I was concerned, was painful; and yet I was glad I had accepted the invitation, glad I had been there when the news of Hugh's bravery had arrived. Shortly after ten o'clock I took my leave, vowing to myself as I did so that I would never go there again. Indeed, as I reflected on what had taken place, I could see no reason for my being asked. I had nothing in common with Josiah Lethbridge, while, in spite of everything, Isabella Lethbridge was farther removed from me than ever.

"I hope you spent a pleasant evening, sir," said Simpson, as he helped me off with my coat.

I did not answer him. Why it was I could not tell, but my mind and heart were full of strange, tumultuous thoughts and feelings.

The next morning, I was on the point of sending Simpson for a carriage to take me over to John Treleaven's farm when Hugh's young wife burst into the room with a radiant smile upon her face.

"Have you seen this, Mr. Erskine? Have you heard about it?" And she laughed and sobbed at the same time. "It is about Hugh. He has got the D.C.M., and they have actually written to me about it, and I have got a letter from Hugh too! Oh, Mr. Erskine, I am proud and happy!"

"It is splendid," I said, "simply splendid!"

"Did you know about it?" she asked. "I only got the letter last night."

"Yes, I knew," I said, before I had time to think of the meaning of my words.

"Has he written to you? Have you heard from the War Office?"

"No, I have not heard from Hugh for weeks," I said, "neither have I heard from the War Office, but I was up at Trecarrel last night."

"And have they heard up there?"

"A letter came while we were at dinner."

"And were they pleased? Oh, Mr. Erskine, I am so proud and happy, and yet I am miserable too. You see, I am constantly wondering whether I did right. I cannot bear to think about it, although I am so happy."

"Think about what?" I asked.

"About Hugh being disinherited. His father has never written him once, and—and—and you know what I mean, sir."

"I hope it will all come right in the end, Mrs. Lethbridge," I said.

"Oh, but you mustn't call me Mrs. Lethbridge; you must call me Mary. You are Hugh's friend. Do you really think it will all come right? I pray a hundred times a day that it may. Somehow I think it will, because God has answered my prayer in keeping Hugh in safety. Oh, Mr. Erskine, I never prayed in my life as I have been praying lately. Somehow I never felt the need of prayer as I do now. Now that Hugh has gone and left me alone, and while he is in such terrible danger, I am obliged to pray. God has become more real to me lately; and seeing that He has answered my prayer in keeping Hugh safe, perhaps He will do the other also. Why, Mr. Erskine, his father cannot keep a hard heart against Hugh when he is such a hero! Have you seen the paper this morning? They have told all about it. Hugh did wonderful things, simply wonderful! Oh, he can't help being proud of his son when he reads it, can he?"

I did not reply, because when I remembered the look on Josiah Lethbridge's face I felt I could give her no comfort.

Still, Mary's visit did me good. Her simple trustfulness and her devoted love were such a change from the atmosphere at Trecarrel that her presence seemed like a ray of sunshine on a dark day.

After this, days and weeks passed without anything happening which needs recording. We had become used to the war, and while we still read our papers anxiously, there was not the great excitement there had been in its early stages. Our hearts thrilled at the story of the battle of Ypres, especially when, presently, the details of that terrible struggle became known; but the keen excitement and feverish desire to read what had taken place somewhat subsided.

Meanwhile, as all the country knows, the spy fever became prevalent. On every hand we heard that agents of the German Secret Information Department covered our country like a plague, and even here, in Cornwall, all sorts of stories were afloat concerning people who were suspected of giving information to Germans. Personally, I paid but little attention to these stories. I did not see how we, situated as we were, away in the extreme end of the country, could be in any way utilized by the enemy. Neither did I see how any one in Cornwall could render them service.

I was soon to be undeceived in this matter, however.

XVII

THE PHANTOM BOATS

It came about in this way. One morning in the early spring of 1915, it was unusually fine. For more than a week the weather had been cold and dismal beyond words, then suddenly, as if by magic, the clouds disappeared, the sun shone brightly, and it seemed like summer.

So much effect did the weather have upon my health that no sooner did I finish my breakfast that day than I made my way towards a high point on the cliffs, and having ensconced myself in a sheltered spot, where I caught the warmth of the sun and at the same time had a glorious view of sea and coast, I gave myself up to pure enjoyment. I felt very happy, I remember. A letter had come to me from Hugh Lethbridge, telling me he had received a commission, in recognition of services he had rendered, and that he was well, and almost happy. The winter had about come to an end, and while I certainly was not so strong as when I had come to Cornwall, I did not feel like dying. The bright sunshine and pure air seemed to give me a new lease of life, and at times I caught myself wondering whether I had not enough vitality in me to overcome the malady from which I was suffering, and which I so much dreaded.

I had not been there more than a few minutes when I heard the sound of voices. A man and woman were talking in the most casual way about the war, and I gathered that something had appeared in that morning's paper which promised well for our arms.

"It is splendid, isn't it?" It was the woman who spoke. "A number of trenches taken, and the Germans driven back nearly half a mile."

"It won't be long now," said the man. "We shall soon begin to work in good earnest. Did not Lord Kitchener say that he did not know when the war would end, but he knew it would really begin in May? This is only a foretaste of the good news which will come presently."

"The Germans are such brutes," said the woman. "There doesn't seem to be a shred of honor in the country."

"They are not sportsmen," said the man. "I was talking to a man the other day who had been to school there, and he told me that no German boy knew the meaning of 'playing the game.' All they have done is a repetition of that which commenced the war. 'It is only a scrap of paper,' said the German

Chancellor. 'Of course we signed the treaty, we gave our promise; but necessity knows no law.' That is Germany all over. Could anything be more devilish than to bombard those defenseless towns up north? As for their treatment of the Belgians—well, it is all a part of their gospel of frightfulness."

"It fairly makes me feel murderous," said the woman. "I am ashamed of having been friendly with Germans."

"That is exactly what I feel," said the man.

I heard every word they said plainly, although I was hidden from their view; and as everything they said agreed so perfectly with my own feelings, I felt like shouting "Hear, hear." Of course, I said nothing, but remained in the shelter of the great rock, basking in the sun and rejoicing in the soft spring air. A little later both the man and woman came within my view. Evidently they had not been conscious of my presence, for they started when they saw me.

"Excuse me," said the man, "but the sight of you was so sudden that it almost gave me a shock. You have discovered a delightful spot."

Then I remembered having seen the man before. He had come to see me immediately after my arrival, and I had had some little talk with him.

"Have you seen the good news this morning?" Apparently he was in a communicative mood.

"No," I replied. "I never get a paper until hours after other people have read and digested theirs."

"Ah!" he said. "Haven't I seen you before? Yes, I remember now. You live at yon little wooden hut, don't you? I saw you last summer, and your servant was good enough to give me a glass of milk. Have you not felt it very lonely through the winter?"

"Somewhat," I replied, "but I have got used to it now. Besides, such a day as this atones for a score of dreary ones."

"The news this morning is splendid," he said. "My sister and I have just been talking about it. I think we shall soon have them on their knees now, don't you?"

I did not reply. I was at the moment too much interested in watching the lady, at whom I am afraid I stared rather rudely. She was, perhaps, my own age, or it might be two or three years my junior. According to every standard of beauty I know, she was one of the most handsome women I had ever seen. Magnificently proportioned, simply dressed, a fine carriage, and a brilliant complexion, she would be noticed in any crowd. I wondered who she was;

wondered that even I, living the secluded life I did, had not in some way heard of her. Her eyes, too, were very striking—large, lustrous, brilliant.

"I don't know," I said, turning to the man. "With such an enemy as Germany, we have all our work cut out."

"Ah, but surely," and he laughed gaily, "you are not what the papers call a 'dismal Jimmy,' you are not a pessimist. The Germans are no fighters, they are only boasters. I admit they are very thorough in their preparations, and there is no doubt about it, they have prepared for this war to the minutest detail; but when it comes to hand-to-hand fighting, they are nowhere."

"You think so?" I queried.

"I am sure of it," said the man. "I have been in Germany a good deal, and they are blusterers, boasters, cruel if you like, but not brave. My sister and I were talking about them a few minutes ago, and we both agreed about it. Of course, they are mean and treacherous, they have no sense of honor. There are no depths to which they will not sink, in order to gain their own ends."

"Yes, you have had evidence of that," I replied. "But what angers me more than their treachery, is the treachery of our own people who have given them information. I saw in yesterday's paper that only English people could have given them signals on the Yorkshire coast whereby they were able to do their baby-killing."

"Well, we are safe down here, at all events," was the man's reply. "There is nothing for which they need come to Cornwall."

"I am not so sure," replied the woman, and her voice startled me, it was so clear, so musical. "They seem to have a hundred deep-laid schemes which are apparently innocent, so nobody suspects them. Even in a district like this there may be spies about."

Both the man and myself laughed merrily. Looking out over the blue waters, which glistened in the sunlight, we could see three great warships evidently patrolling the coast.

"We have no fear for what they can do here, Rachel, with those steel monsters about," laughed the man. "The Navy has been our salvation, and will be our salvation."

"I have heard," said the woman, "that Germans know this country to its minutest detail, that there is not a lane, nor a creek, nor a cave along the whole coast from Land's End to John o' Groat's House, but what they are aware of it."

"Nonsense, Rachel. I think you are like the rest of the women, carried away by fairy stories. How long have you been living here, sir?"

"More than nine months," I replied.

"The war must have broken out soon after you came?"

"Yes," I replied. "I came in May."

"My sister is awfully frightened, and is constantly manufacturing schemes whereby the Germans can invade us, and she fancies that every stranger is a German spy. Have you, living so close to the cliffs for more than three-quarters of a year, ever seen anything of a German spy?"

I shook my head.

"Never seen a sign of a German spy, have you?"

Again I shook my head.

"There, Rachel," laughed the man, "surely that should quieten your fears."

A few minutes later they passed on, leaving me alone. I watched them follow the pathway which led close to my house, then they mounted the hill at the back, and were lost to my sight.

That night I went to bed early. I had exercised myself more than usual during that day, and felt rather tired, yet I could not sleep. I could not tell why it was, but my mind seemed abnormally active. Perhaps it was because the time allowed me by Dr. Rhomboid was fast drawing to a close. If he were right, I had not more than three months to live. I got up and lit a candle and looked in the glass. My cheeks were certainly pale and hollow, my hands and arms painfully thin, and yet I did not feel like a dying man. I remember blowing out the light and putting aside the curtain and looking out on the sea. There was no moon, but it was a wonderful night of stars, and I could see the long line of breakers as they rolled against the cliffs. The night was as still as heaven, not a breath of wind stirred. The very thought of war, of tumult, of the roar of big guns, seemed infinitely removed from me. The night contained the very genius of peace. I went back to bed again, and still I could not sleep. Hour after hour I lay restless. Why it was I could not tell, for on the whole I slept well.

I yielded to what seems now a mad impulse, and putting on my clothes, I went out into the night. Soon my heart beat wildly, for coming round the headline I saw several boats. They made no noise, and yet, in the light of the stars, I was sure I saw them. How many there were I could not tell, but there seemed to be many. Each cleared the corner silently, and then, passing near to the cliffs, was lost to my view.

As I have said, the night was windless, but not a sound could I hear. No splash of oars, no throb of machinery, and yet, I felt sure I had seen the boats pass. Of course, I might easily be deceived; for, although it was a night of stars, nothing on the sea showed clearly—the boats were like so many phantoms. Once, as I crept closer towards the cliff, I thought I heard a rustling noise, but I was not sure. No matter how still the weather might be, the murmur of the waves was always heard, and my mind, excited as it was, could easily conjure up foolish fancies. How long I stood there, I do not know. It might have been an hour, for I was unconscious of time. Presently I felt myself shiver, then, realizing how foolish I had been, made my way back to my little wooden hut. I had barely reached my door, when I was certain I heard a rustling in the bushes, just above the spot where a spring of water gushed out.

"It was a hare or a rabbit, or it might be a fox," I said to myself, and yet, in the excited state of my mind, I was not satisfied. I had a feeling that something was happening around me. I called to mind the story of Father Abraham. I remembered, too, the repeated visits of the idiot lad called Fever Lurgy. What had become of him? I had neither seen nor heard anything of him for months now. What lay behind this feverish warning? Why had he told me to leave? I went back to bed, and in a few minutes was asleep.

When I awoke, it was broad daylight, and hastily dressing myself, I went to the spot in which I had stood the previous night. All was quite calm and peaceful. The day was wondrous in its glory, even although the sun was yet low in the heavens. Sea-birds floated overhead, uttering mournful cries. Out at sea the great steel monsters ploughed their way through deep waters, ever watching our shores.

After breakfast I clambered down the rugged footpath towards the beach. I felt a feverish desire to see the cave I had visited on first coming to St. Issey. The day was like summer; the sea rippled on the yellow sandy beach, and its music to me was like a long song. Everything caused my wild fancies to appear foolish. I looked carefully on the sand, but there was no sign of a foot-mark, no suggestion of a boat. Presently I found the fissure which led to the cave. This I entered, thinking as I did so of the quaint brooch of barbaric design which I had found there months before, and which I still possessed. Lighting a match, I looked at the sandy floor, and my whole body quivered with excitement. I saw many footmarks, and what seemed to me more important still, a piece of paper which had evidently been used as a wrapper of a bottle. On it was printed, in German, these words: "*Bremen's Special Whisky, Manufactured in Dusseldorf.*"

What seemed suspicious was, that any one in Cornwall should be drinking German whisky nine months after the war had commenced. Not even in peace-time had the English people been in the habit of patronizing German whisky distillers. In war-time it was unthinkable. More than that, I was absolutely certain that this paper did not lie here when I last visited the cave. Moreover, the footmarks were fresh. They had been made within the last few hours. I felt as perturbed as Robinson Crusoe was, when, walking on the beach of his lonely island, he had seen a man's footprint on the sand. What did it portend? I ransacked my brain, but could think of nothing. What could Germans be doing here? What advantage could it be to them? And yet, what I had seen troubled me. Leaving the cave, I carefully examined every portion of the cliff, but could discover nothing. No footmarks appeared. No place seemed to exist wherein anything could be hidden. I spent hours thinking, wondering, watching, all to no avail. When I reached my cottage it was lunch-time.

That afternoon, I remember, the sky became cloudy, and the sea, instead of a wondrous blue, became dark and forbidding.

"I will not go to bed to-night until I feel sleepy," I reflected. "I won't have such a restless time as I had last night."

I undid the wrapper of a new novel which I had ordered to be sent to me, and prepared to read. Simpson had gone to bed. The night was chilly, so throwing some fresh lumps of wood on to the fire, and drawing up a chair, I made myself as comfortable as possible. The book was by one of our younger novelists who, as it appeared to me, struck a new vein. He possessed what very few novelists have—namely, vision. He looked deeper into the heart of things than any man I had read for some time. I became so interested that I forgot the lapse of time, until, looking at my watch. I found it was past midnight. I had scarcely noticed this when I heard stealthy footsteps outside. I sat up and listened. A moment later there was a knock at the door—not loud but cautious. I waited a few seconds, and the knock was repeated. Standing close to the door I spoke, not loudly, but sufficiently clearly to reach any one who might be outside.

"Who are you? What do you want?"

"Let me in, and I will tell you."

"Tell me who you are before I do that," I replied. "It is a strange time of night to come to one's house, and I shall not open the door until I know who you are."

"I mean only your good," was the answer.

"That is easily said," was my reply. "As it happens, my man is sleeping only a few yards away, and I have a loaded revolver close beside me. I am a good shot, too."

I scarcely know why I said this. Perhaps it was because I thought if the man were there on evil intent I might frighten him.

"I have something to tell you, something vastly important."

"Who are you? What is your name?"

"One name is as good as another. I mean only your good; let me in."

"Very well," I said, "I will open the door. If you do not play the game fairly, expect trouble."

Whereon I opened the door, and saw an old, white-bearded man. He wore a long ulster and a soft, broad-brimmed hat which partially hid his features. He came in without invitation, and I shut the door and locked it, putting the key in my pocket. He looked at me steadily, questioningly. He appeared like a man trying to form an estimate of me.

"Won't you take off your ulster?" I said.

Without a word, he divested himself of the heavy coat, and placing his hat upon it, looked at me steadily again.

He might have been Adam in *As You Like It*. He was doubtless very old, but he was ruddy and hale. His eyes were bright and piercing, and I noticed that they were largely shaded by heavy white eyebrows. His hair, also, was thick and white and glossy. A kindly-looking old man he was, but alert, capable, strong.

"There," I said, pointing to a chair. "Sit down, and tell me what you have to say."

"Do you know you are standing on a powder magazine?"

The words came from his mouth like a shot, so tersely, so suddenly did he speak.

"Do you speak literally or metaphorically?"

"Maybe both," was his reply.

"Anyhow, it hasn't exploded yet," was my answer. "Won't you sit down?"

"You are very cool."

"I see no reason to be excited."

He chuckled, as though he were amused.

"Since you are so kind," he said, "I will sit down. Ah, that is a good cigar you have been smoking."

"Yes," I replied. "Won't you have one?" and I pushed him the box.

He lit the cigar with a steady hand, and seemed to be enjoying it, but I noticed that he gave me several quick, searching glances.

I was beginning to enjoy what seemed like an adventure. Although my strength had ebbed away considerably during the past few months, my nerves were still steady, and I saw no reason for being afraid. I knew that Simpson was within call, knew too that, at his oft-repeated request, I had obtained a revolver, which was within easy reach. But I had no thought of using it. The man's visit was evidently of a friendly nature, and I believed he had something of importance to tell me.

XVIII

FATHER ABRAHAM

"If I were you, I should leave this house."

"May I ask why?"

"Because your life is in danger. Yes, I see you smile, but I know; I have reason to know."

"No," I replied, "my life is in no danger at all. I gather you are thinking of murder. I happen to be a lawyer, and have studied criminal cases for the last ten years, and I can never remember a murder to have taken place without some grave motive for it. No one has a sufficient motive to kill me. As far as I know, I haven't an enemy in the world, my death would benefit no one, and there is no reason why any would-be murderer would endanger his life by killing me."

The old man looked at me with an amused twinkle in his eye. He seemed to regard me as an interesting specimen of humanity.

"You are talking in the dark, my young friend," he said.

"No," I replied. "I am not talking in the dark, I am talking common sense. If I possessed a secret which was dangerous to any one, if I had it in my power to hurt any one, if I had money which some one desired, if some one hated me very much, if I had done any one any great injury, if I had stolen some young fellow's sweetheart, I could believe there might be truth in your words; but I have done none of these things. I have lived the most commonplace, humdrum life imaginable, and I haven't an enemy in the world. More than that, circumstances have made it unnecessary for any one to kill me. My death will come in a perfectly natural way in a very short time."

"What do you mean by that last sentence?"

"Just as I told you. If you do not believe me, I beg you to refer to Dr. Rhomboid, R-H-O-M-B-O-I-D, of Harley Street, London."

"I see. But you are a cool one!"

"I have no reason to be other than cool."

"You say you are a lawyer, but there is no need for you to tell me that."

"Still," I said, "I am interested in what you say. You have taken the trouble to come here at midnight, when every one else is asleep, and you tell me my life is in danger. I cannot believe that in the slightest degree; but the bump of curiosity, as the phrenologists say, is largely developed in my cranium. Tell me why you came."

"I have found out all about you that there is to know," he said between the puffs of his cigar.

"That didn't take you long," I replied.

Again there was a silence between us, during which he watched my face closely.

"Let me tell you this, my young friend. A man with sharp eyes, as yours are, and a brain quick to think, as yours is, is always in danger while a certain class of people exist."

"What class of people?"

He ignored my question entirely.

"You said just now," he remarked, "that the bump of curiosity in your cranium is largely developed."

"Very largely indeed."

"What is your interest in this coast? Why have you been seen creeping along the beach examining the cliffs?"

"Put it down to curiosity."

"Exactly! Curiosity. And let me tell you this, my young friend, that if your curiosity should be rewarded, you will be a dead man within twenty-four hours. You might, instead of living here in a perfectly defenseless way, surround yourself by a thousand safeguards; you might have as many sentries as the Kaiser himself, but your life would not be worth a pin's purchase."

"And a pin will not purchase much," I retorted.

"Exactly! That is why I tell you to leave here."

"You evidently know what you are talking about," I replied, "or at least you think you do. You will have noticed that I have not asked you any questions about yourself. There has seemed to be no reason why I should."

"Why? What do you know about me?"

"Practically nothing," I replied. "I am no Sherlock Holmes, and even if I were, I have not had sufficient energy to satisfy my curiosity; still, I can give you a rough outline of who and what you are. You built this little hut here, built it with care and intelligence, for which I am very grateful. You had as your man Friday, an idiot who went by the name of Fever Lurgy. You lived here like a hermit for years, and were a mystery to every one. Still, people did not trouble much about you, as a good many unconventional people live along the coast. I find that about a mile farther on from here, in another little bay, several artists have built little huts similar to this. One or two writing fellows also live lonely lives on this Cornish coast. You became known as Father Abraham; you showed yourself to practically no one; then, suddenly you left. There were signs of violence in the little room where you slept, and where I now sleep, and it was given out that you were the victim of foul play, that possibly you were murdered. Evidently, however, you were not. As a consequence, there was a good amount of honest sympathy wasted."

The old man laughed. Evidently I had amused him.

"As a lawyer," I went on, "I have discovered that everything may be resolved into a matter of motive. You must have a motive for doing this. Your past life must be interesting! You tell me that I am in danger of being murdered. I do not believe it a bit. At the same time, there is a connection between your past life and your reason for telling me this doleful news."

"I like a man with a clear brain," he chuckled. "I like a man who can analyze, who can deduce, who has studied the laws of synthesis. You were a student of Socrates, weren't you, years ago? You loved the Socratic method of reasoning?"

"Your deductions are from insufficient data," I remarked. "But that is by the way. Seeing you have taken the trouble to pay me this visit, would you mind telling me what has caused you to prophesy such evil things about me?"

"I do not prophesy, I warn. More than that"—again he looked at me keenly —"your report concerning your health and your declaration of Dr. Rhomboid's verdict on you doesn't justify you in not heeding my warning. Even although a thousand doctors pronounce the death sentence on you, you can still hope that they are mistaken; and you long to live, you hate the thought of death."

I reflected a moment. Somehow the old man's presence and his quick intelligence had made me think rapidly.

"Do you know," he went on, "that there is a great deal of reason for the foreigners' opinion concerning John Bull's brains? Mind you, John Bull is a cleverer man than he is thought to be; all the same, they have their reason for their opinions."

"What might their opinions be?" I asked.

He laughed quietly, and again looked at me keenly.

"You, now. You are a clever man, you have had a lawyer's training, you are given to observe, to analyze, to synthesize, but you have the Englishman's fault."

"And that?" I asked.

"You always try to find out the thing which is lying a long way off from you. You never observe the thing which is close by."

"You speak in a detached way," I replied. "You speak of Englishmen in the third person. Why do you do that? You are an Englishman?"

"How do you know that?" he asked.

"Instead of answering that," I replied, "I will tell you something else. You have spent a good deal of time in Germany."

I was startled by the change which came over his face. I had evidently made him fear.

"Why do you say that?" he cried.

"There is such a thing as intuition as well as deduction," I replied. "Intuition and deduction act and react one upon the other. But, after all, you didn'tcome here because you were interested in mental gymnastics. You say I am in danger in this place; you have warned me to leave it. Why do you say this to me?"

"Ah, there is the English side of your character coming out! Will you not do as I tell you without my giving you a reason?"

"No," I replied.

"Then your own blood be upon your head. I warn you; I can do no more. I tell you you are in danger. You as a lawyer ought to know that a clever man, an observant man, even although he may know nothing of what is going on around him, can be a constant menace to those who work in secret. Now do you follow me?"

"Yes," I replied, "I follow you, but because you will not tell me plainly what is in your mind, you have aroused my curiosity; more than that, you have aroused the John Bull in me. I am too near death to be intimidated by what you tell me. As a consequence, you have made me more determined than ever to stay here, unless," I added, "you have decided to come back and live here, and drive me from this little hut, which, in spite of myself, I have come to love."

"Ah, you like it!" he said. "It is comfortable, is it not? The sea views are wonderful, the silence of the night is a revelation; but leave it, my young friend, leave it!"

"I have told you I shall not leave it," I replied, "until I have sufficient reason for doing so."

"But you can do no good by remaining here; if you could, I would not hinder you from your madness. But can't you realize, man, that England is at war? Now then, cannot you understand?"

"Oh yes," I replied. "I have had that in my mind for some time. I realized it when I told you that you had lived a long time in Germany."

"How did you guess that?"

"Oh, for one thing, while you speak English with an English accent, the construction of your sentences suggests a close acquaintance with German literature. You mentioned the Kaiser just now when you spoke of being guarded, and a look of fear came into your eyes when I said I knew of your connection with Germany."

He grasped the arms of his chair as I spoke, and looked at me without speaking, but I saw that I had touched him—saw too that there were thoughts in his mind which he dared not utter.

"You are afraid of some one," I went on. "Who, I don't know; possibly I shall not be able to find out; but you are. In spite of the kindliness of your nature, there is a horrible fear in your heart. Forces are at work in your life which I at present cannot understand. Look here, are you a paid tool of the German Government?"

"God forbid!" he cried. "No, no, God forbid; but—but——Look here, Mr. Erskine, have you discovered anything?"

"Nothing. I wish I had."

"Let me tell you this, then. You are watched, constantly watched, and the moment you do discover anything——" He shrugged his shoulders by way of concluding his sentence. "Every man has his own secrets," he went on; "as you say, motives govern lives. They guide our actions, control our words."

"If I am watched day and night," I said, "I must be a person of some importance; but more than that, you must be in danger in coming here."

"I fight the devil with his own weapons," was his reply. "I meet cunning with cunning, plot with plot, mystery with mystery. To be forewarned is to be fore-armed, and I have taken every precaution; but I cannot tell you what I know— that is why I beseech you to leave here. You, a poor invalid, weak as a rabbit, with one foot in the grave, can do nothing; yet your very presence is a menace. Therefore leave the neighborhood, or if you must stay in the

161

neighborhood, go into the village away from here."

"I should not be in danger if I went into the village, then?" I asked.

"Go into the village," he repeated. "There are lodgings there, simple perhaps, but clean, which would suit you just as well as this."

"No," I replied, "no place will suit me quite as well as this."

"Then your blood be upon your own head; I am sorry. I like you; I watched you directly after you came here. I discovered all that there was to be known about you. Leave the place, man, and give it out that it is haunted."

"Do you realize," I said, "that you have put yourself in danger, too? I do not mean from those enemies who are unknown to me, but from other sources. I happen to know three magistrates in this district. If I were to tell them what you have told me to-night, I could have you arrested as a dangerous character. I have a servant, too, who is in a room close by. Possibly he has heard every word which has passed between us."

He laughed like a man amused.

"No, Mr. Erskine," he said, "there is not the slightest danger of that. Your servant is asleep. Bah, do you think I don't know? Do you think I am such a fool as that? As for telling the magistrates, you could not do it."

"Why?" I asked.

"Because you are you. Do you think I did not estimate the kind of man I am speaking to before I said what I have said? But I am sorry. I must be going now."

He put on his heavy ulster as he spoke, buttoned it closely round his throat, and pulled his broad-brimmed hat over his forehead.

"If you discover anything," he said,—"I am saying this as an off chance, ay, a chance in a million,—leave this place as soon as you have discovered it, and send a telegram to me."

"Where?" I asked.

"Send it to John Adams, Chigwheal Post Office."

"And you will tell me nothing more than that?"

"I came here to warn, not to inform."

As he spoke I heard a sound outside, something like the cry of a sea-bird; it was a human voice.

"Good-night," he said, holding out his hand. "I am truly sorry, but I have done my best."

I unlocked the door, and he passed out into the darkness. I listened intently, and heard the rustling of the bushes. A minute later, there was a murmur of voices, and I knew that Fever Lurgy was near.

After having closed the door and carefully locked it, I sat for a long time thinking.

Part of the little success I had had in the law was owing to a remarkably retentive memory. I have sometimes thought that my memory is peculiar to myself. I do not quite know how to describe it. I have listened to a conversation which has interested me, and I have listened to evidence in court which has been of importance, and for three or four days I have remembered it in its minutest detail, and could repeat it word for word. At the end of three or four days, however, the details have passed from me completely, although I have retained the broad outlines of what I have heard. Now as I sat, the conversation which had taken place, every word, every look, every gesture of old Father Abraham was clear before my mind.

That the old man was sincere I did not doubt. He evidently believed that I was in danger. I was sure, too, that he had had some connections with Germany, and that his fears were connected with the war. But I doubted his judgment. I was not sure that he was altogether sane. He was obsessed with thoughts which had no objective reality, at least so I fancied, and yet his warning was grave. Not that I intended to heed it: I had not much to hope for in life; but danger or no danger, I meant to get to the bottom of what he had said. Evidently this hut was closely connected with his thoughts. Evidently, too, it had been under his observation ever since he had left it.

I reflected on all I had said to him, and was pleased that I had told him nothing of what I had discovered. Remembering all that had taken place in the country during the last few months, I determined to use whatever faculties I might possess in order to discover how I might be a menace to the enemy. If I could discover that, I should be able to help my own country.

When I awoke the following morning, I realized how truly Father Abraham had read my character. I could not make up my mind, even although I had tried, to tell any one that the old man was still alive, and that his actions were at least suspicious. For one thing, I did not believe that he was an enemy to our country; for another, I had my doubts whether any good could result in making a search for him.

That he was in hiding in some place in the district I did not doubt. Chigwheal was about nine miles from St. Issey, and he evidently lived near enough to that village to receive postal communications; but where he lived, or what disguises he might assume, I had not the slightest idea. That he was a man with a quick brain and of great resource I had no doubt whatever, and I felt sure he would know how to defend himself in case of danger. In addition to that, too, I felt that I should be acting against the interests which had been born in my heart, if I disclosed his possible whereabouts. I knew instinctively that he was kindly disposed towards me, and to tell of what had occurred would possibly hinder me from the course of action I had decided upon. Added to all this was a kind of secretiveness which hindered me from making known his visit to me.

As may be imagined, I had plenty of food for thought. It was evident that his interest in me was no new thing. Months had now elapsed since Fever Lurgy had given me the same warning. Doubtless the poor thick-witted lad was but a messenger from this mysterious old man. I carefully thought over every sentence he had uttered, and weighed their possible meanings.

My danger, if danger there was, lay not in the fact that any one harbored evil thoughts concerning me, but that I lived in this little hut. Evidently the hut itself occupied a position of advantage. It was at the centre of some operation. The old man had built it for some purpose, and then, for reasons unknown to me, had left it. I called to mind the fact that immediately after my arrival I had seen figures in the near distance who looked as if they might be watching my actions; but why? It was well known that I had no purpose in coming to Cornwall save to find a healthy spot where I might conserve my poor feeble life as long as possible.

One thing, however, Father Abraham had done for me. He had set me on my guard. I had for some months now taken an intelligent interest in what was going on, and had read the papers carefully. Like all other British people, too, my eyes had been opened to what militarism had done for Germany, and to the depths of meanness and baseness to which they were prepared to sink, in order to carry out their purposes. As I have said previously, I had visited Germany on more than one occasion. I also understood the language and could speak it and read it fluently. While in Germany I had talked with professors in the universities and officers in their army. I was aware, too, of their mastery of detail and of their thorough preparedness for everything they undertook. What I could not understand was how I, living in this obscure corner of the country, could be in a position of advantage, and how I could be a menace to my country's enemies.

I did not know then, neither did I dream, how my eyes were to be opened.

XIX

GOD ANSWERED OUT OF THE WHIRLWIND

Nothing happened for some days. At first I kept close to the house, and was constantly on the alert lest some evil thing should befall me. I watched vigilantly too. Remembering all that had been reported in the newspapers, my mind was filled with suspicions concerning the possibility of the enemy pursuing his work in this part of the country. Especially did I watch the cliffs around the little bay; but in no way was I rewarded. I began to think that I was the victim of a hoax, or that Father Abraham was little better than a madman obsessed with mad fancies. Thus it came about that after a few days I became careless of the warnings given me, and pursued my old course of life.

At that time, I remember, the black cloud of war hung especially heavy on our land. The Prime Minister had stated in the House of Commons the number of killed and wounded in our Army and Navy, and the appalling figures which he gave were added to daily by the lists given in the papers. The village of St. Issey had not suffered greatly. It is true that three men had come home wounded, but their wounds were not serious, and as they had been bright and cheerful during their stay, we had been led to hope that we should escape lightly. Then, suddenly, the horror of the whole business came home to us. Two of our lads were killed at sea. Then we heard that others had been taken prisoners and lay suffering in a German prison camp. Others still were lying wounded in the hospitals in France.

One morning—it was some days after Father Abraham's visit—I found on opening my newspapers that among the killed was one Edward Trelaske, who died in action. The name struck me, first because it was Cornish, and second because it was the name of our Vicar. I saw too that he was a captain in one of the battalions belonging to the D.C.L.I., and I wondered whether he were in any way associated with St. Issey.

Scarcely had I read this than a knock came to the door, and I saw the Vicar enter the room. He looked ten years older than when I had first seen him. I think I said, when describing our first meeting, that he was a hale and handsome man, ruddy and inclined to stoutness. Now his face was haggard and bloodless, the flesh hung loosely on his cheeks, and I judged from his eyes that he was a stranger to sleep. Immediately I connected his appearance with what I had just read. I did not speak a word, I thought it best not to; but I held out my hand, which he gripped almost convulsively. Almost unconsciously I looked at the newspaper.

"Yes," he said, "it is there."

"It was your son, then?" I said.

"Yes, my eldest son; both were in the Army. One is still alive, thank God; but Ned, my boy Ned——" Then for a moment he broke down, his whole body trembling violently. He recovered himself in a few seconds, however.

"I do not complain," he said. "In a way I am proud."

"I think I understand," was my reply.

"I shall never be the same man again," he went on. "It seems as though a part of my life is buried with him, away in that little French cemetery; but at this moment there is no prouder man in England than I. My son, my eldest son, has given his life for honor, for truth, for God."

He spoke like a man inspired. Every word was weighted with a new meaning.

"I don't know why I came to you," he went on. "I received the news days ago, and ever since, ever since...." Then he stopped. There was a far-away look in his eyes.

"You have my deepest sympathy, Mr. Trelaske," I said. "Words are poor at a time like this——"

"No," he interrupted, "words are not poor, when they convey what the heart feels. I rather resented it when my son expressed the desire to go into the Army. I fully expected it of Harry, my second son, and had had him educated with that object in view; but it has always been a tradition in our family for generations that one of the sons should go into the Church. But he would not fall in with my wishes; he was not fit, he said, and he wanted to be a soldier. The living here belongs to our family, has belonged to it for more than a hundred years. Now I know it ought not to have belonged to us."

"Why?" I asked.

"The Church," he replied, "has been but little more than a name to me, the vocation of a clergyman I have regarded as little more than a profession; that is why—why...." He stopped, as if unable to express the thought in his mind. "'What is the use of my becoming a parson?' said Ned to me. 'I have nothing to say to the people. How can I tell the chaps whom I have fought with, shot with, played cards with, about their souls, about God and about heaven?' I argued with him. I told him that when a man was ordained a priest his ordination gave him priestly rights. But he would have none of it, and insisted upon going into the Army. As I said, I was grieved and angry; but now I know that he served his God more truly than I, for what I have done has lacked a great conviction. I have looked upon my profession as—as a profession; but he, he gave his life for his country, and for truth, and for God. Perhaps he did not say so in so many words, perhaps he did not even think of it, but that is what he did; and I am proud—oh, I am proud. He died a hero, too."

"How?" I asked. "Tell me."

"He was wounded, not badly, but his arm was broken. He made light of it, however, and among the German prisoners taken was a German officer, a major who was badly hurt. He asked for water. My son, although he was in great pain, fetched water and gave it to him, and while he was giving it to him the German got out his revolver and shot him through the heart."

"What happened then?" I asked.

"You may guess what happened," he replied. "Some of our men saw it. It was terrible—wasn't it? But how could I wish my son to die a nobler death, even although that fiend shot him? Did he not die as a Christian, trying to bring succor to his enemy?"

There was a note of earnestness in his voice which I had never heard before.

"And you got this news days ago?" I said.

"Yes," he replied, "and I have been to see no one since it came until now. I haven't even been to see my old friend Treherne. At first, all the foundations of my life seemed to be broken up. I could not understand it. I thought I should never be able to bear it. Why should I, a man past my prime, with my work nearly over, be alive while my son, a lad of twenty-seven, should be killed?

"I revolted against it.

"I told God He was hard.

"By and by, however, my mind became clearer; I began to understand. Not that I could put my thoughts into words; I cannot now. Presently I began to pray. I do not think I had really prayed for years. I had read the prayers at Church, I had done my work as a clergyman, but I had missed the great reality of it all. But then I prayed. This morning I felt I must come to see you. You remember what you asked me when I came here first?"

"Yes, I remember," I said; "but please do not trouble about that now. You have your own sorrow to think of."

"I am ashamed," he went on. "I, a clergyman, set apart to give help, comfort, to those who might come to me, and yet when you asked me one of the greatest of all questions, I had no answer to give. I was dumb."

I waited in silence. I longed to know what was in the man's mind, but I felt it would be sacrilege to ask him questions then. I could see that he had been passing through deep waters, that the billows had gone over his head. He was no longer the ecclesiastic, no longer the man he had believed himself, set apart simply because a bishop's hands had been laid upon his head. He had seen beneath the mere conventions of his faith, he had got to the heart of things, or, at least, he had tried to get there.

"I am ashamed," he went on, "that I had no answer to give you. Even yet I have none to give. I am still in the dark, and yet—yet...."

He seemed like a man who saw something from afar, one who was stretching out lame hands of faith.

"I understand as I never understood before," he went on. "Do you remember that story of David standing by the gates of Jerusalem, waiting for news of his son, and who, when the news came, cried out, 'Oh, Absalom, my son, my son, would God that I had died for thee, oh, Absalom, my son!' I understand that now. I think I understand something more; I am not certain yet, but I feel as though—as though...."

And again there was a far-away look in his eyes. He rose and held out his hand.

"You will wonder why I came," he said. "I do too, except that I could not help coming. Do you remember what our Lord said about blind leaders of the blind? No, I am not blind, but I am like the man who was cured of his blindness by our Lord, who said he saw men as trees walking. It is a strange story, isn't it? But oh, man, what fools we are! What blind fools! And how God Almighty opens our eyes and shows us our foolishness!"

I longed to be able to utter some words of comfort, but I was in the dark myself. I had been asking questions ever since I came to Cornwall, but had received no answer. I would have given anything at that time to have been able to say something which would have been balm to the father's bleeding heart. But I could not. I could only tell him how sorry I was, and that seemed such a little thing.

That same afternoon, the weather being fine, I found my way into St. Issey. I had practically forgotten Father Abraham's warning, and longing to see human faces, and to get away from the questions which haunted me, I turned towards the village. I had, by this time, learnt to know a great many of the people. I was no longer simply the stranger who had a few months before come to live in Father Abraham's hut. I had now been living in the neighborhood for several months, and was regarded by many of the people as a friend. I had also got into the habit of dropping into the cottages and talking with the simple folk. I had barely entered the village when I saw a woman standing by her cottage door.

"Oh, Mr. Erskine," she said. "Will 'ee come in a minute? I 'ave somethin' to tell 'ee."

"What is it, Mrs. Rosewarn?" I had seen her once or twice at the Chapel, and knew that her husband was a local preacher.

"Ain't 'ee heered, my deear?"

"Heard what?" I asked.

"About my deear boy. He's killed, my deear."

"Killed?" I said.

"Yes, my deear. They Germans 'ave killed 'im."

Never did I hear such pathos in a human voice. There was no bitterness, no anger, no suggestion of vengeance in her voice, but there was pathos, deep unutterable pathos.

"'E was a deear, deear boy," she went on. "No better boy ever stepped in shoe leather. 'Is father were ter'ble against 'is goin' as a sojer, but 'e would go, and now 'e is dead."

What could I say? What comfort could I give to this poor bruised, breaking heart? Never did I realize, as I did at that moment, how vain and futile was the learning of men when brought face to face with sorrow and loss. I did not feel it so much when the Vicar had come to me that morning. At the back of my mind I had felt that he, the Vicar of the parish, ought to have had means whereby he could obtain comfort. He was supposed to be the spiritual head of the parish, and professed to believe in shibboleths of Christianity; but everything was different in relation to this poor cottage woman. I felt that I, who had spent years at a seat of learning, who had pored over musty law-books and professed to know something of the ways of men, should have something to say, some message of hope to give her; but I had nothing.

"Oh, my deear Mr. Erskine," she said, "the 'and of the Lord is 'eavy upon me, but I am not as those who sorrow without hope."

"No," I said. "What hope have you?"

"Oh, my deear, 'e was a good boy. 'Ere is 'is last letter, sir. Will 'ee read it, then?"

I took the letter and read it. I do not ever remember perusing a document with the same eagerness as I perused this letter sent from the trenches.

"DEAR MOTHER AND FATHER,"—I read,—"I have just got a few minutes to write to you, so I am just sending you these few lines to tell you that I am well and happy. While I write I can hear the booming of the guns, the sound of shrapnel, and the awful noise of shells which are shrieking above me; but I am safe here. The trenches are so made that even the German guns cannot hurt us. We are doing very well, and although it will take us a long time, we are going to lick the Germans right enough. I wish the war was over and that I was home among you once again. I expect you will be in Chapel now, or just going home, for it is half-past seven on Sunday night. If ever I live to go home again, I shall go to Chapel more regularly than I did. An hour ago some of us met here and had a prayer-meeting. Lots of the fellows came who never thought of going to a prayer-meeting at home. Somehow war makes us think of things differently. I never dared to pray in the meetings at home, but I did to-night, and you would have been surprised at some of the chaps that did pray, and hear what they said. It was very funny, but they meant it all right, and God understood. Well, I must stop now, for I have to go on duty. Love to you both.—Your affectionate son,

"Tom."

"Ed'n it wonderful?" she said to me, with streaming eyes. "Tom would never say a word about religion when 'e was at 'ome; but now, do'ant 'ee see, my deear Mr. Erskine? I know that Tom is saafe with his God."

"How did he die?" I asked. I felt the question to be out of place, but I could think of nothing better to say.

"I do'ant know, my deear. We was told that 'e was killed in action, and that is all. But I ain't got no feears, Tom was a good boy."

At that moment there was a knock at the door, and the next moment Mr. Trelaske entered.

"I ... I have just heard that Tom is killed," he said, "and I thought you would not take it amiss if I dropped in."

"Bless 'ee, sir, I be glad to see 'ee," replied the woman. "Mr. Erskine 'ere was just readin' Tom's last letter. Would 'ee like to read it?"

I passed him the letter without a word, and the Vicar read it carefully.

"Oh, yes, sir," said Mrs. Rosewarn, "Tom was a good boy, and I ain't got no feears. 'E 'as gone straight to God, 'as Tom."

The Vicar stayed for perhaps ten minutes, and during that time he uttered no word about religion. He spoke quite naturally about Tom Rosewarn's death, and expressed deepest sympathy with the sorrowing mother.

"Yes, sir," said Mrs. Rosewarn, "we 'ave to comfort each other now. I 'eerd about poor Mr. Edward, and I ain't forgot you, sir, in my prayers."

"Thank you, thank you," said the Vicar. "I need them."

"It do'ant matter, sir, do it, whether we be Church or Chapel at a time like this?" went on Mrs. Rosewarn. "I ain't ever been to Church in my life, 'cept to funerals and weddin's. I 'ave always been a Wesleyan, and somehow I thought that your religion was deffurent to ours, but now, sir.... Well, sir, perhaps you understand what I mean."

When the Vicar left I rose to go with him, but the simple woman persuaded me to stay a few minutes longer.

"Only think, sir," she said, when he had gone. "Why, he ain't ever been in my 'ouse before. 'E said that my 'usband was committing what he called sacrilege, by preachin'. 'E said it was a sin for ignorant men, like my John, to preach the Gospel, and now to think that 'e should come 'ere like this, and talk like 'e 'ave talked. And, sir, whether we be gentle or simple, we 'ave got 'earts to feel, 'aven't us, sir?"

When I left the cottage I felt that in some way I was leaving a sanctuary, and I realized that this woman possessed a secret which was hidden from me. Her simple faith was greater and more profound than all the learned tomes in the libraries at Oxford, greater than all the scholarship of men. I wandered along the road aimlessly; I did not know where I was going, I did not care, but I had not gone far when I found the Vicar by my side. Evidently he had been waiting for me.

"Do you know that woman, Erskine?" he asked.

"I have met her a few times," I replied. "I have got very friendly with some of the village folk."

"I, who have been the Vicar of this parish for many years, have never been to that house before," he said. "I looked upon her husband as a Radical, as a Dissenter, and therefore a dangerous man. I have been angry with him for usurping offices which I did not think it right for him to hold; but, great God! how a thing like this shows us what fools we are!"

I was silent, for I did not know what to say to him.

"Do you ever read the Bible, Erskine?"

"No," I replied. "I have not read it since I was at Oxford. The last thing that I remember reading was the story of St. Paul's shipwreck. I could not help thinking then what a fine piece of literature it was; but it seemed a long way off. I thought of Paul as one who lived in a superstitious age, and one who saw miraculous interventions in what were only commonplaces. Somehow it strikes me differently now."

"How is that?" he asked.

"I remember that Paul said something about the Angel of God standing beside him, and telling him that the ship should be saved, and that in the story Paul said, 'I believe God.' It was very fine, very graphic."

"Yes," he replied. "It was more than fine, more than graphic. Paul possessed a secret which some of us have lost. I wonder, I wonder——"

"Wonder what?" I asked.

"Have you ever read the Book of Job?" asked the Vicar, without seeming to notice my question.

"I have almost forgotten it," I replied. "I used to think in the old days that it was a very fine drama, compared with which even *Macbeth* was almost poor. But what of it?"

"Do you remember, towards the end of the story, that God answered Job out of the whirlwind? God seems to be answering me out of the whirlwind. He is just shattering all my poor little fancies, shrivelling up all my little beliefs. Why, that woman——Good-day, Erskine."

He walked away as he spoke, and I watched him enter the churchyard gates and find his way into the Church. A kind of curiosity impelled me to follow him, and silently I found my way into the old stone building, which had been erected in this quiet village in pre-Reformation days—built by men long since dead, built before even Erasmus let in the light of learning upon our country, before Luther's voice shook the world. How quiet it was! Not a sound disturbed the silence. Not even the murmur of the sea reached me here.

At first, I thought the place was empty; that the Vicar had passed through it on his way to the Vicarage. But I was mistaken. Kneeling at his desk, I saw him in prayer. His eyes were fixed on the stained-glass window over the Communion table, but I am sure he did not see the figures of saints and prophets that were placed there. He was looking beyond. I turned and went silently away. It was not for me to disturb him.

On looking back now, it seemed to me that that day was a day of great events. Not that much had happened. News had come to me that two lads had been killed in the war, and that was all. But there was more than that. I had seen, as I had never seen before, into the hearts of two people—into that of the Vicar of the parish, and into the heart of a simple woman. They had both lost their sons.

I climbed over a stile which led to a footpath whereby I could, by a roundabout way, return to my cottage on the cliff. I was in a strange mood, I remember. My mind was bewildered by what I had seen and heard, and I felt impatient with the philosophies which had somehow caused material barriers to be placed around me. I wanted to overleap those barriers. I was impatient with what seemed to place weights upon the wings of the mind and the wings of that something which we call soul. I hungered, as I never hungered before, for some assurance that life was deeper, greater, diviner than that suggested by the theories of men. A few months before I had been satisfied with the life I had been living. I was beginning to be successful at the Bar, and I had many pleasant friends and acquaintances. The possession of a good name and a respectable profession opened the doors of some of the best houses in England to me, and, as I said, I thought I was content. Then came Dr. Rhomboid's verdict, followed by my visit to Cornwall. After that the great war broke out, and life had become a maddening maze.

For some time now I had seen nothing of the Lethbridges. I had had two letters from Hugh, who told me he was well. He also sent me a photograph of himself, taken in his lieutenant's uniform. His letter, I remember, was a cheery epistle, intermingled with a tone of sadness. He asked me to visit his wife, and to try to cheer her; but there was no word either of his father or of his sister. Perhaps the thought of Hugh's letter made me think of the latter, for, as I found my way along the footpath, I reflected on our meetings.

Why was it that my mind was constantly reverting to her? I had, in a way, become almost sullenly resigned to the fact that, if Dr. Rhomboid were right, I had only three or four months longer to live, and yet, in a way for which I could not account, I constantly found myself thinking of Isabella Lethbridge. I told myself again and again that I did not love her, and I was sure I was right. Indeed, after my experiences with the Vicar and with Mrs. Rosewarn, I felt angry with her, angry with myself for constantly thinking about her; and while this feeling possessed me, I met her. She had come by a pathway from her home, and the two paths met just as we came in sight of each other. A kind of madness possessed me as I shook hands with her.

"Have you heard from Hugh lately?" I asked, after our first greetings.

"No," she replied. "My father has forbidden both my mother and me to receive any letters from him."

"Surely that is a foolish command on his part," I said. "He cannot stop Hugh from writing, neither can he forbid the postman from bringing letters to your house."

"No," she said, with a laugh, "but my father has the key to the letter bag, and he can decide as to what letters reach us." She spoke, as I thought, flippantly, and as one who did not care.

Perhaps it was the tone of her voice and the look in her eyes which caused me to say what I did.

"Have I to congratulate you, Miss Lethbridge?"

"Congratulate me on what?" she asked.

"On your engagement," I said.

"Engagement! To whom?"

"To Mr. Barcroft?"

She laughed as though I had perpetrated a joke.

"What made you think of such a thing?" she asked.

"The look in his eyes when I saw him at your house, and your evident liking for each other."

I felt how incongruous my words were, how utterly out of keeping with the scenes of sorrow I had witnessed that day; but, as I said, a spirit of madness was upon me.

"Men are such fools," was her reply.

"Yes, they are. But we cannot help that. Men were born to be fooled by women. But surely Mr. Barcroft is a happy man now if what rumor says is true."

"And what does rumor say?"

"That he is favored above all other men," I replied. "That Miss Lethbridge has consented to make him happy."

"Was it not Shakespeare who said that 'rumor was a lying jade'?" And again she laughed, as I thought, flippantly, heartlessly. "Poor man, I cannot help what he feels."

I felt that her words were those of a vulgar woman, and yet, as she stood there that day, with the early spring sunlight shining upon her, her face flushed with the hue of health, her eyes shining brightly, I had never seen any one so beautiful.

"And is rumor a lying jade in this instance?" I asked.

"Of course it is," was her reply. "Did I not tell you once, somewhere near here, that I did not believe there was such a thing as love?"

"And did you ever tell him so?" And I think there was an angry note in my voice as I asked her that question.

"Have I ever given you the right to ask that?"

"I don't know," I replied. "But I want to tell you something. I have no right to tell you, but I am in a strange humor to-day. I have been talking with Mr. Trelaske, whose son has been killed in the war. I have also been to the house of Mrs. Rosewarn, whose boy Tom is dead."

"Of course, that is very sad," she said; "but I don't see what that has to do with what you have to tell me. Come, I am impatient to hear."

Reflecting on it since, I cannot think why I yielded to the madness which possessed me, but I am setting down in this narrative what actually occurred. I suppose I acted like a boor, and I know that, judging by every canon of good taste, I am to be condemned.

"Miss Lethbridge, do you know that more than once since I came to Cornwall I have believed myself in love with you?"

She stared at me with wide-open eyes.

"I have sometimes thought," I went on, "that I would give worlds to possess your love. Had I not been a dying man, I would not have said this; but it does not matter now. Besides, I do not love you."

"Thank you," she replied. "But really——"

"No," I interrupted. "Do not retort by saying that you never wished for my love, and that if I offered it you would decline it with thanks. I am in a strange humor, or I should not say this. In a way I do love you, love you more than words can tell or imagination can fancy; at the same time, I know I do not love you at all. I love the woman you ought to be, the woman God meant you to be—if there be a God."

She looked at me like one startled.

"You have tried to play with my heart," I said to her, "I who am only a dying man. No, do not deny it, but you have. You have flashed looks of love at me. You have tried to make me think that you love me, and all the time you have not cared a straw about me. There have been times when I have been ready to worship you, but I could not do it, although, as I said, I have loved you—that is, I have loved the woman you ought to be, that you were meant to be; but it was not you. Do you know, Miss Lethbridge, that you have been a baleful influence in the lives of men? It does not matter to me now, I am beyond that; but since I have been in Cornwall I have met three fellows whose lives you have blackened. You won their love, you made them think you cared for them. Why have you done it?"

Her face from rosy red became ashy pale, but her eyes gleamed with hot anger.

"Really, Mr. Erskine," she said quietly, "you mistook your profession. A burlesque actor is your role."

"Your retort is poor," I went on. "I am not acting, but am in sober earnest. Perhaps I have no right to think of such things, but there have been times when I became mad about you, would almost have sold my soul to possess you. Why, even now my heart cries out for you. I love you more than life or being, and yet it is not you I love at all; it is the woman you might have been."

She stood looking at me for some seconds, again with wide-open eyes. Once or twice she seemed on the point of speaking, but she uttered no word. Then she turned and walked away. Her head was erect, and she carried herself proudly.

I knew I had wounded her deeply.

XX

THE VICAR'S SERMON

On the following Sunday I went to Chapel in the morning, and to the Parish Church in the evening. As I wended my way thitherwards, I reflected how strange it was that I should make it almost a habit to go to a place of worship on a Sunday. Prior to coming to Cornwall, I had not been inside a Church of any sort for years; indeed, such a thing was alien to my life. I had no interest in it, neither did I see its utility. Indeed, even then I could have given no explanation for my action. Neither Church nor Chapel had given me an answer to things I wanted to know.

As I tried to analyze my reason for going, it seemed that something in the atmosphere of Sunday in Cornwall made it natural. Besides, it gave a kind of mild interest to my life. I had but few friends, and living alone as I did, I grew tired of reading and thinking; thus, when Sunday came, the ringing of the Church bells seemed to call me to a house of prayer. I dare say that if I had been in a country where Mohammedanism or Buddhism was the established faith of the people, I should have gone to their mosques or temples just as I went to Church and Chapel in Cornwall.

To speak quite frankly, I had, up to the present, received no benefit from either. Mostly the pulpit at the Chapel was occupied by some layman, who spoke in a language different from my own. These laymen had read no books expressing the thought of the age, neither did they at all understand the attitude of my mind. That they were simple, earnest men I did not doubt, and yet I often wondered at their daring to occupy the position of religious teachers. What distressed me, moreover, was the fact that most of them appeared very anxious to convince their congregation that they had prepared a fine discourse, rather than to help people. The note of deep experience was too often lacking; and yet almost Sunday by Sunday I found my way there, until my presence caused no remark whatever.

In spite of all this, however, I could not help reflecting that since I came to the little village of St. Issey a subtle change had come over the congregation. Not that the Chapel was very much more largely attended; but there seemed to me to be a spirit of yearning, a deep undertone of feeling among the worshippers. That morning especially did I realize this. The preacher was John Rosewarn, the father of the boy whose death had been recorded the previous week. I will not try to reproduce his sermon.

Intellectually, John Rosewarn had practically nothing to say to me, and yet my heart was moved strangely. The shadow of his loss was brooding over him, and although he had no great mental acumen, he seemed to be feeling his way to the heart of things. There was a deep tenderness in his voice, a new light in his eyes. He made no mention of his son's death, but the fact was felt throughout the whole Church. Many wondered, I myself included, how he could have conducted the service that day, yet he did; and although his message from an intellectual standpoint was poor and unconvincing, there was a sense of reality which I had seldom felt in the homely little building.

The congregation felt this too, and especially was it manifest during the singing of the hymns. One hymn, I remember, the people sang with great fervor. I had never heard it before, and from the standpoint of poetry it had nothing to recommend it, but as these people sang it, it was weighted with meaning.

> "We know, by *faith* we know
> If this vile house of clay,
> This tabernacle sink below
> In ruinous decay
> We have a house above
> Not made with mortal hands…."

I saw the tears rolling down the faces of the people as they sang, and I thought I noticed a note of triumph.

When the service was over, John Rosewarn came down from the pulpit into the vestibule and spoke to me.

"Thank you, sir, for calling at our house the other day," he said. "It is a terrible loss, sir, but we shall see our boy again."

I went back to my little house on the cliff thinking deeply. Yes, a subtle change had come over the little congregation. The first excitement of the war was over, but something, I could not define what, had created a new atmosphere. Personally, I was still as much in the dark as ever; and the faith, the suggestion of which I had realized that morning, seemed to rest on utterly insufficient foundations; but I could not deny its existence.

In the evening I found my way to the Parish Church. I saw at a glance that a larger congregation than usual had gathered. I noticed that old Squire Treherne was in the great square Treherne pew. Noticed, too, that Mr. Prideaux, father of young Prideaux, whose name I have mentioned, also several of the larger farmers who seldom came to Church of an evening, were present. What had drawn them there I could not tell, for it was in no way a special service. And yet, perhaps, it was special, for I knew that the sympathies of the people were drawn out towards Mr. Trelaske.

The Vicar did not look so haggard as when he had visited me, but the marks of suffering were plainly to be seen on his face. There was no change in the order of the service. The usual evening prayers were repeated, the Psalms were sung, and the village schoolmaster read the lessons as he was wont to do, and yet here, too, was a suggestion of a change. A deeper note was struck, a new meaning felt. I asked myself why it was so, and wondered if the change were in me or in the people around me. The Vicar conducted the service like a man who was very weary. There was no suggestion of triumph or even conviction in his tones. He seemed to be bearing a heavy burden. When presently the hymn before the sermon was being sung and he left his stall in the choir to go into the pulpit, I wondered what he could say. Had he a message to deliver? Had his sorrow brought him hope, faith?

He preached the shortest sermon, I think, I ever heard. Altogether, I imagine it did not take more than five minutes in its delivery, but the people listened as they had never listened before during the time I had been in St. Issey. He chose for his text a passage from the Psalms: "The fool hath said in his heart, there is no God." When he had read the passage, he waited for some seconds as if not knowing what to say.

"Has it struck you, brethren, that during this ghastly war, in spite of the fact that the greater part of the world is under arms, in spite of the fact that hellish deeds are being done, in spite of the welter of blood and the unutterable carnage, that we have heard no one deny the existence of God? I thought when the war first broke out and assumed such awful proportions, when I realized the misery it was causing, that people would have doubted God, that they would have said, like the enemies of the Psalmist of old, 'Where is now thy God?' I thought that atheism would have lifted its head again and uttered its desolating cry; that men would have said, 'If there is a God, He would not have allowed these things.' And yet worse things have happened than we, at the commencement of the war, thought possible, but I have heard no one deny the existence of God, neither have I heard any one seriously doubt His goodness. Why is it?"

He paused a few seconds and seemed to be communing with himself.

"Brethren," he went on, "we meet under the shadow of a great loss. Some of you, even as I at this moment, feel that we are in the deep waters, and in our heart's agony we cry out to God. We cannot help it."

He ceased again, and a silence, such as I have never known before in a Church, pervaded the building.

"Brethren," he went on, "will you pray for me, and I will pray for you? Pray

179

that we may be led out of darkness into light."

I thought he was going to finish here, thought he was going to utter the usual formula at the conclusion of a sermon, but he went on.

"God is teaching us many lessons—teaching us how foolish we are, how paltry have been our conceptions of Him; teaching us, too, our need of Him. Will the Church, will religion ever be the same to us again? I think not."

Again he stopped, and the people breathlessly waited, as if wondering what he would say next. To me he seemed like a man in doubt as to whether he ought to utter the words which had come into his mind.

"In the past," he went on, "religion, even in our quiet little village, has seemed as though it were divided into two camps. I have avoided the Chapel people and the Chapel people have avoided the Church. I need not say why. I am sure we shall never settle our differences by arguments or by criticisms. There has been too much of that in the past. This is a time when we need to pray, and so I am asking all the people in the parish, whether they belong to Chapel or to Church, to meet in the village schoolroom to-morrow night, to pray—to pray that God will bless our soldiers and sailors, and all who are seeking to help us to destroy this awful scourge of war, to pray for broken hearts at home, to pray that God will lead us all into His light."

He made a long pause here, and we wondered what was to come next. Then suddenly turning his face, as was his custom, he repeated the formula:

"And now to God the Father, God the Son, and God the Holy Ghost, be all honor, power, and dominion, world without end. Amen."

The little service was at an end. Quietly we left the old building and found our way into the churchyard. As I reached the gates, I felt a hand upon my arm and saw Squire Treherne standing by me.

"Will you come up and have a bite of supper, Erskine?" he said.

"Thank you, Squire, but I dare not. I ought not to have come out to-night."

"I am glad you did, anyhow," was the Squire's reply. "My word! this business is giving us a shaking up. Trelaske has never preached such a sermon before in my hearing."

I could not help smiling, for in truth he had not preached a sermon at all.

"I see what you mean," said the old man. "For that matter Trelaske never could preach; and, mind you, I have been as bitter against dissent as any man, but—but he has done more for religion to-night than he has done for many a long year."

"Are you going to the prayer-meeting, Squire?" I asked.

"What, I! I go to a prayer-meeting!" And he laughed as though it were a joke.

"Yes," I said, "why not? That is, if—if you believe it has any meaning."

"Yes," he said, "why not? After all, why not? Are you sure you won't come up to supper?"

"Quite sure, thank you."

I wandered slowly back to my little house, thinking of what the Vicar had said. Yes, he was quite right. Never, during the beginning of the war, had I heard any one deny the existence of God. It might seem as if there were no God at all, when one remembered the deeds that had been done; yet no one seemed to doubt that God lived and reigned.

I had scarcely reached the footpath which led to my little copse when, to my surprise, I saw Mr. Josiah Lethbridge coming towards me. I judged that he had been to my house, though I did not know why he should do so.

"The evenings are stretching out, Mr. Lethbridge," I said, "aren't they? It is nearly half-past seven, and the daylight has not yet gone."

"Yes, the evenings are stretching out," he said, with a sigh.

"Have you heard from Hugh lately?" I asked.

"No, I have not heard from him. I—I do not expect to; you know that."

"I had a letter from him a few weeks ago," I said, as cheerfully as I could. "He sent me his photograph in his lieutenant's uniform. Have you seen it?"

He shook his head.

"Would you care to?" I asked. "It is in the house close by."

"No," he said, and his voice was almost harsh. "No, I do not wish to see it."

"I have just come from the Parish Church," I said. "The Vicar has received a terrible blow, hasn't he?"

"The Vicar believed in that kind of thing—I never did."

"No," was my answer, "I do not think the Vicar believed in it any more than you. He regards war only as a ghastly necessity. But would you, knowing all you know, realizing all our sufferings, and all we shall have to suffer, have had us do differently?"

"You mean——?"

"I mean, would you have the Germans work their will, and dominate the world by material forces? Would you have had them glorify militarism, and set a war-god upon a pinnacle to worship? Would you have Europe accept the teaching of Treitschke and Nietzsche as the gospel of the future, while we did nothing?"

At this he was silent.

"I was at the Wesleyan Chapel this morning," I went on. "I did not see you there."

"No, I did not go."

"John Rosewarn was preaching," I went on. "John has lost his boy Tom."

He hesitated for a few seconds and I thought he seemed on the point of saying something to me, then he held out his hand.

"Good-night, Mr. Erskine," he said, and a few minutes later he was lost to my view.

"That man is deeply troubled," I said to myself as he walked away. "I wonder what he has on his mind."

When I entered my cottage Simpson had not yet returned. He had asked my permission before I went to Church that night if he might be out a little later than usual, as some old friends of his had asked him to supper. Of course I gave my consent, but when I found myself alone in the house I felt almost sorry. What I should have done without him during the hours of the long winter nights I do not know, for although his conversation was not very illuminating, it was always a source of comfort to me to know that he was near.

I sat down to the simple little meal that he had prepared, and then, throwing myself into an armchair, saw the previous day's newspaper lying by my side. I picked it up almost listlessly, and a few seconds later found myself reading an article on the ravages which were being caused by German submarines. This article detailed the list of disasters caused by this method of warfare, then asked questions which had been troubling the writer.

This gentleman, who seemed to know what he was writing about, stated that there must be secret stations along the British coast where the Germans could be supplied with fuel, therefore many traitors to their own country must exist in England. He also insisted that although the shores were constantly watched, hour by hour, and every precaution taken, the Germans had, by some means yet unknown to us, been supplied by people in England with what was essential to their devilish work.

"Has the Government," the article concluded, "been sufficiently stringent in their treatment of enemy aliens? Has it inquired with sufficient care into the means whereby our enemy has caused such appalling losses?"

I must confess, although everything seemed conjectural, that my interest was aroused, and acting on impulse I opened the door and went out into the night. It had now become very dark. Clouds hung heavily in the sky, there was no moon and not a star appeared. The night was not stormy, although a fairly strong breeze was blowing. The tide, I remember, was high, and the sea swept upon the rocks at the base of the cliff on which my hut was situated. I peered into the darkness, calling to mind as I did so the night on which I had seen, what seemed to me, phantom boats appearing round the headland and then becoming lost to view. I waited for a few minutes and then found myself shivering with cold. When I got back to the house Simpson had returned.

"Have you heard the news, sir?"

"What news?" I asked.

"Another vessel sunk, sir, by the submarines. It was struck without warning, and it is feared that every one on board has been lost."

"Where did this happen?"

"I don't know, sir, but some men in the village had got hold of a Sunday newspaper and were talking about it. I heard too that two people, one an English woman, and the other a German man, have been taken up as spies. It seems that they have been supplying the Germans with petrol."

The man's words seemed almost a commentary on what I had been thinking, and I turned, almost unconsciously, to the newspaper I had been reading.

"The Germans are too clever for us, sir, and there is no dirty trick of which they are not capable. I am told they jeered at the people who were trying to save themselves from drowning, and even shot at them. I am not very proud of my county, sir."

"Not proud of your county! Why?"

"Why, sir, there are dozens of young fellows in St. Issey who won't enlist, and I was told to-night of seven of them who are off to America."

"Off to America! Why?"

"Why, it seems that the Squire has been at them and told them they are cowards to stay at home at a time like this. It seems, too, sir, that poor Tom Rosewarn's death, as well as that of the Vicar's son, has roused some of the people terribly, and these young fellows have been called such names that they are ashamed to remain at home, but rather than join the Army, as they ought to do, they are leaving for America. I have never been a believer in conscription, but the stories have very nearly converted me to that way of thinking."

When Simpson had gone to bed, I put on a thick overcoat and again went out into the night. I wondered whether the fancies that had been in my mind had any foundation of truth, and whether I ought not to go to the authorities and make my suspicions known. There were a great many things against such a course of action, however. Local officials were not very clever, and did not act with much finesse. The Germans would be prepared for anything they might do, and if anything were done at all, it must be done dexterously and secretly.

By this time I knew, or at least thought I did, every inch of the cliffs around my home. I had discovered, too, an opening through the bushes which led far down towards the sea. Again acting on impulse, I found this little opening, and scrambled down the steep cliff-side until I came, perhaps, within forty feet of the water. I was entirely hidden from view, as at this part thick brushwood grew to within a few yards of the beach. Besides, it was very dark, and I knew that if I went farther I should risk my life. Up above me the wind soughed its way through the little copse, and over the heights of the beetling cliffs which rose darkly beyond. Out at sea I could hear the sad monotone of the waves. Now and then I heard the cry of a sea-bird, as though it were disturbed in its nest among the rocks.

It was now perhaps eleven o'clock, and every one would, in all probability, be abed, with perhaps the exception of the coast watchers who patrolled the coast. I was on the point of returning to the house when I was startled by the sound of a human voice. I was at this point sheltered from the wind, and my ears, having become accustomed to the noise of the waves and the night winds, could hear plainly:

"Is that the lot?"

There was a reply to this, but what it was I could not say. How long I waited I could not say either. That something was taking place that ought not to take place I was sure. Else why should men be in this lonely cove at midnight on a Sunday? Presently I heard a grating sound, then above the sound of the waves was the splash of oars. I looked intently, but could see nothing, and by and by when I had returned to my house I reflected that my vigils had been in vain. Yet not in vain, for I determined, whatever might be the danger accruing from my action, that I would not rest until I had in daylight again examined every inch of the cliffs.

Strange to say, I did not feel much worse for my night vigils, and when I awoke on the following morning my brain was clear and every faculty alert. I was arranging to carry my resolutions of the previous night into effect when Simpson placed the morning paper on the table. The next minute I had forgotten all I had intended to do.

XXI

MISSING—DEAD

On turning to the list of casualties which appeared, I saw to my horror that Hugh Lethbridge was missing. What that might mean I could not of course tell, but the news made my heart as heavy as lead. During the months I had known him I had become much attracted to the young fellow and had conceived a strong affection for him. If he had been my own brother I do not think I could have felt the news more keenly than I did. But more than that I reflected upon the sorrow of his young wife, and the pain his mother would be suffering. I called to mind the last letter I had received from him.

"Of course, we live only from hour to hour here," he said; "in fact, only from minute to minute. I have known chaps who have been laughing and joking one minute and have been hurled into eternity the next. That might happen to me. I am feeling very fit just now, but what may be my fate to-morrow, God only knows. I do not trouble so much about myself, but it is Mary I am constantly thinking about. She writes me often, and on the whole is very cheerful, but I know what she is feeling. I do not fear death so much except for her and for mother. As for father and Bella, I do not think they would care much. Anyhow, I would rather be killed than taken prisoner. From what I can hear, those Germans act as devils towards English prisoners."

I wondered what the term "missing" might mean. Of course, he had been lost sight of, but whether he had been taken prisoner or not was not clear from what the paper said.

"Going out, sir?" said Simpson, as I put on a light overcoat.

"Yes, Simpson, I am going up to Trecarrel."

"Any bad news, sir?"

"Yes," I replied. "Mr. Hugh Lethbridge is missing."

"Dear, dear sir!" Then lapsing into his old formula when he did not know what to say, he added, "Yes, sir; thank you, sir."

I had scarcely come within sight of Trecarrel when I had an attack of my old malady. It was not severe. Nevertheless, while it lasted it was terrible. I thought I should have fainted on the footpath on which I walked. Presently it passed away somewhat, and, undeterred by my suffering, I made my way towards the house. At that moment my last meeting with Isabella Lethbridge had no weight with me whatever. In fact, I did not anticipate seeing her. However, she must have seen me as I came up the drive, for it was not a servant but she who opened the door.

"What is the matter? You are ill!" she cried. "I—I never saw you looking like this before."

"That does not matter," was my reply. "I am all right now. I came up because —because...." I did not finish the sentence. I was startled by the look in her eyes. I saw her lips quivering. "Your father and mother are in?" I queried.

"Yes, but—but I do not think you had better see them now."

"It may not be so bad after all," I said, trying to speak cheerfully. "The paper only reports him missing."

"Oh, but haven't you heard? No, of course you can't have. But you ought not to be here. You look so ill, so terribly ill."

"She must care for her brother more than I thought. She speaks like one in terrible distress," I reflected. "Oh, no, I am not ill at all now," I said aloud, "but I saw the paper just now, and I could not help coming. It is not so bad as it might be, is it? While there is life there is hope."

"But there is no hope," she said. "Hugh is dead."

"Dead! Why, the paper——"

"Yes, yes, I know; but we have had a special message. It came late last night. Hugh is dead. Hugh is killed."

I stood like one stunned, I could not speak. The news had struck me dumb.

"Can't you say something?" she cried. "No, of course you can't. And you ought not to be here either. I will order a carriage to take you back," she added like one distraught. Her words came almost in gasps.

"And your father and mother?" I asked, without seeming to notice what she had said. "I hope—I hope——"

"Mother is wonderful. You see, she expected nothing else. She always said from the day that Hugh went to the front that he would be killed. Oh, yes, mother is wonderful, but my father.... Perhaps, after all, he will see you. Shall I tell him you are here?"

"Perhaps it would be better not, after all," was my reply. "I suppose I ought not to have come here; it was foolish; but I was so overwhelmed with the news that I could not help myself."

She looked at me for a few seconds in a way that I had never seen her look before, and then left the room suddenly. Presently I heard heavy footsteps coming towards me, and then Josiah Lethbridge entered the room. He looked years older than on the previous night, but the same stern strength of the man manifested itself. He held himself erect, and hid any emotions he might have felt.

"Excuse me for coming, Mr. Lethbridge, but although I had known Hugh for such a short time, I loved him as if he were my own brother."

"It is very kind of you to come," he said almost coldly; and then, "But you ought not to be here."

At that moment Mrs. Lethbridge entered, and I could not help being struck by her appearance. There was a new dignity in her every look and movement. A kind of holy pride shone from her eyes, although it was easy to see that they were not strangers to tears. The suggestion of inconsequence which had struck me when I had first seen her was entirely gone.

"I am pleased to see you," she said, holding out her hand. "You were Hugh's friend."

"I came to tell you how—how grieved I am."

"You must not speak like that," she said quietly. "My boy died in a holy cause. 'He saved others, but himself he *would* not save.'"

"Yes," I said, "that is true. One cannot think of him as dead in the ordinary way. When one gives his life willingly for what he believes to be the highest and the holiest, death has lost its sting."

"Oh, he is not dead!" she said. "I could not think of him as dead. The spirit which led him to do what he did can never die. Have you seen what they have said about him? Here, read his Colonel's letter, will you?" And she passed me a missive which I could see had been stained by many tears.

It was the letter of a plain, blunt soldier who was not gifted with great literary powers, and yet because it was so simple, so straightforward, it was more eloquent than if it had been written by a master of words. It described how Hugh, in the face of almost certain death, had undertaken work which might mean incalculable advantage to the British Army—that he had led his men forward in the face of withering fire, and that he had done what he set out to do. At first it was thought that he had been taken prisoner, as no signs of him were to be seen, but presently his body was discovered, almost mutilated out of recognition, yet plainly to be identified by infallible signs.

"He died a hero," concluded the plain, blunt soldier, "died for his country and his God. Had he lived, I should have recommended him for a captaincy right away, but he has received his promotion in a better world."

"That is it, don't you see?" said Mrs. Lethbridge, "he has received his promotion."

I could not keep back the tears which started to my eyes. I longed, no one knows how I longed, for the assurance which filled the mother's heart. Nevertheless, I could not help being gladdened by her faith.

"He will not come to me, but I shall go to him," she went on. "Do you know, Mr. Erskine, a few days ago I began to hope that he would return, and I pictured him coming back to St. Issey well and strong. I saw the people doing my boy honor; but that was pure fancy on my part, and it does not matter now. Yes, I shall go to him."

I could not help glancing at Josiah Lethbridge as she spoke. I wondered what he, who had driven his son from home, felt at that moment; but his face told me nothing; he might not have heard his wife's words. It was hard and stony and emotionless. But he did not rebuke his wife as he would have rebuked her the day before. He who had forbidden his family to mention Hugh's name sat silent, his face grave, ashen, his eyes fixed on the floor. What he felt or thought I could not tell, but I could not help believing that he shared his wife's pride. How could it be otherwise? After all, Hugh was his son.

"Bella told me that you looked terribly ill," went on Mrs. Lethbridge. "Certainly you do look pale, but better than she led me to believe. May I order you some refreshments?"

"No, I am better now," I replied, and glancing towards the mirror, I saw that my face had resumed its normal color.

Scarcely had she spoken than I heard the sound of wheels on the drive outside, and a minute later Squire Treherne was shown into the room.

"I could not help coming," said the bluff old man. "The last time I was here I told you—but never mind what I told you—that is over now. I just glanced at the paper this morning, and then, before I knew what I was doing, I was on my way here. We must hope for the best! He is only reported as missing."

But Josiah Lethbridge did not speak a word. Instead, he looked out of the window as though interested in the trees which were just bursting into life.

"Excuse me, Mrs. Lethbridge," went on the Squire, "I did not notice you; it was very rude of me."

Mrs. Lethbridge did not speak a word. She simply handed him the letter of Hugh's Colonel.

"God bless my soul! I did not know this," he stammered. "No—no, I did not know this, but—but——"

"I never felt so proud in all my life," said the mother. "I always knew that my boy was a good boy; now I know that he was a hero. He laid down his life willingly."

Still Josiah Lethbridge did not speak. His eyes were still fixed on the trees in the park.

"I know what you are feeling," said the Squire, after a few seconds of almost painful silence. "I know, I know. I lost my only son in the Boer War, and I—I have never been the same man since. Can—can I do anything for you?" he added.

"I was just going to suggest," I said, "that I should go over to John Treleaven's farm and see Hugh's wife. She will, of course, have heard the news."

"Thank you, Mr. Erskine," said Mrs. Lethbridge, "but that is my work. It is my duty to go and comfort my son's wife."

Again I noticed the new tone in her voice. The last time I was at the house she would not have dared to suggest such a thing. She would have feared her husband's anger, but now she stated her intentions naturally. She did not even look towards Josiah Lethbridge as she spoke, but I, who glanced at him at that moment, saw that his face never moved a muscle.

"If you would do something for me," said Mrs. Lethbridge, "take care of Mr. Erskine. My daughter told me just now that he was very ill and ought not to have come here."

"God bless my soul! you do look seedy," said the Squire. "What is the matter?"

"I only had a slight attack of my old trouble, and I look a great deal worse than I am."

"All the same, I am going to take you back with me," said the Squire. "No, no, I shall take no denial. That hut of yours on the cliff, with only a man-servant to look after you, is certainly no place for a man who feels seedy. You —you are sure I can do nothing for you, Mrs. Lethbridge? I do feel for you, God knows that. All the same, I do envy you. I wish I had another son to give. Yes, ten sons; I should be prouder than words can say to send every one of them. Somehow this terrible business makes one think differently of life, makes one feel that we have had wrong ideas of everything. Somehow we have confused existing with living."

Surely that was a morning of happenings, for scarcely had the Squire spoken than a servant entered the room bearing a letter. It came from the Vicar.

Josiah Lethbridge took the letter without a word and read it through with the same unmoved countenance. After he had done so he passed it to his wife.

"This is kind of Mr. Trelaske," she said. "He must be burdened by his own sorrow, yet he sends this letter to us. Of course he does not know all the truth."

I rose to go. I felt that I should be intruding if I stayed longer. I held out my hand to Mr. Lethbridge, who took it almost mechanically.

"It is very kind of you to call," he said. "And—and take care of yourself; you are not strong, you know."

When I reached the hall I found Isabella Lethbridge standing there.

"That letter from the Colonel is simply splendid," I said. "Of course your loss must be terrible, but you must be proud of your brother."

She made no reply, neither could I understand the look on her face. It was not so much sorrow I saw, as wonder and amazement.

"Funny family!" said the Squire to me, as we drove away. "Did you notice that the man never spoke a word?"

I nodded, and the Squire went on:

"My God! what must he be suffering! Drove the boy from home too! But— but, don't I wish he were my boy! Anyhow, there is going to be a change in that house."

"What do you mean?" I asked.

"The atmosphere is different. Did you notice Mrs. Lethbridge's face? Did you hear what she said?"

When we reached St. Issey, I asked the Squire to tell the driver to drop me, as I could easily walk to my house; but the old man would not have it.

"No, no, Erskine," he said, "you must come up and spend the day with me; I have nothing to do. Do you know, I have often felt condemned at leaving you so much alone; but you seemed as though you did not wish for society. Still, I have got you now! Yes, yes, I will send word to that man of yours, telling him what has happened to you."

A few minutes later I was snugly ensconced in the Squire's library, while Mrs. Treherne and her daughter fussed about me as though I were an invalid. I must confess that it was pleasant to be ministered to by a woman's hands. Simpson was all very well, but I do not think that any man knows what to do in the time of illness as a woman does.

"What are you thinking about, Erskine?" asked the Squire presently, after he had placed a box of cigars before me.

"I was thinking about Mr. Lethbridge's face," I said. "I was wondering what he must be feeling."

"A hard man, Erskine, a hard man. A man who has lived to make money; a man who has always had his own way. Whatever he has touched has turned to gold, whatever he has willed has come to pass." The Squire sighed as he spoke. "He has pulled all sorts of people into his net," he went on, "and got all sorts of people into his power. He does not say much, but he could ruin lots of us if he willed so to do."

I called to mind what Hugh Lethbridge had told me, and I fancy I knew what the old man was thinking.

"Sometimes, deep down in my heart," went on the Squire, "I have called him a Shylock; but I am not going to think about that now. He is passing through deep waters."

After lunch, I again announced my intention of returning home, but was again dissuaded; not only the Squire, but neither his wife nor his daughter would hear of my going.

"We will have an informal dinner at six o'clock," said the old man, "then you must come with me to the prayer-meeting."

The idea seemed so incongruous that I could not help smiling.

"Yes, I know what you are thinking," said the Squire, with a laugh. "I have never been to a prayer-meeting in my life, and I had no thought of going until you kind of suggested it to me yourself after last night's service; but when I came to think about it, it seemed natural and right. We are in for a stiff job, Erskine. I never realized it as I do now. Those Germans stand at nothing! Nothing is too devilish for them to do! Poisoned gases, poisoned wells, sinking passenger ships, killing defenseless women and children, murdering our soldiers, even when they are in the act of doing them a kindness,— nothing is too bad for them. But they are strong! They are strong! We do not realize yet how strong they are. They have utilized all the resources of their country to beat us, to crush us, and we shall have to use every ounce of strength we possess to come out on top. As the Prime Minister said, we must be prepared to shed our last drop of blood.

"But that is not all, Erskine. I know I have not been a religious man in the ordinary sense of the word, although I have gone to Church and tried to act straight, but it seems to me as though God wants to teach us a lesson. He is wanting to bring us to our senses. Never in my life have I realized the need of God as I do now, and if we are to fight His battles we need to go to Him for help. I have seen, too, how paltry is the spite which exists between the sects. God bless my soul! What, after all, does the Almighty care whether we go to Church or to Chapel? And it may be that this war will teach us how silly we have been. That is why, in spite of my prejudices, I am glad that Trelaske announced the meeting for to-night. Yes, I am going, Erskine, and I hope you are going too."

At seven o'clock that night the Squire and I stood at the door of the village schoolroom, for we had both determined to go to the prayer-meeting.

XXII

A DISCOVERY

I must confess that it was with a strange feeling that I took my seat in the little village schoolroom that night. I had been born and educated in a Christian country, and yet I had never been to a prayer-meeting in my life. As I have previously said, until I came to St. Issey, I had not, except for a wedding, entered a Church for years, and here was I, an avowed agnostic, who had little faith in God and none in a future life, obeying the Vicar's call to prayer.

I was startled to find, on looking round the room, that not only Mrs. Lethbridge and Isabella, but also Josiah Lethbridge had come. Their faces formed a curious contrast. Mrs. Lethbridge looked proud, almost triumphant, in spite of the marks of the sorrow which were plainly to be seen on her face. I noticed, too, that after the meeting commenced she entered heartily into the singing of the hymns.

Her daughter's face, on the other hand, was not easy to describe. In one sense she looked callous, bored, indifferent; in another, there was an expression of amazement, bewilderment, which I could not explain. But she made no sign of any sort. She sang none of the hymns, neither did she bow her head during prayer. As for Josiah Lethbridge, his face remained stern and immovable during the whole of the meeting.

Some one spoke of him afterwards as looking like a "graven image." Years before, I was told, Josiah Lethbridge used to pray in the prayer-meetings at the Wesleyan Chapel; but he had ceased doing so for a long time, although he had never severed his connection with the Church and had rigidly maintained his observance of the outward form of religion. More than once I wondered why he was there, for he must have seen the curious eyes that were cast upon him. Of course every one had heard of Hugh Lethbridge's death. Every one knew, too, that the father had driven his son from home because he had joined the Army, and because he had married the girl he loved. Besides all this, it was common talk that John Treleaven's daughter Mary had never been bidden to the great house at Trecarrel. The gossips had talked about it freely, and many remarks, not complimentary to Hugh's father, had passed. Still he was there, his face as stern as ever, his eyes keenly alert to all that took place.

Just before the meeting commenced we were somewhat surprised to see not only the Vicar, but the Wesleyan minister ascend the platform together. The Vicar explained this circumstance at the commencement of the proceedings.

He repeated what he had said the previous night, and described how the Church and the Chapel had for years been regarded as opposing camps.

"My dear friends," said the Vicar quietly, "I have been a Churchman all my life, and shall remain one until my death; but the troubles through which we are passing have taught me to see many things. I suppose we shall never see eye to eye, but we are all believers in the same God and in the same Saviour. More than that, we are all English people. Lads from the Church are fighting at the front, side by side with the lads from the Chapel. They are all fighting for a common cause. We all have our sorrows, too, and I have been led to see how foolish I have been in being so exclusive. Yes, God has taught me many lessons. That is why this morning I drove to Mr. Bendle's house. He is the minister of the circuit of which St. Issey Wesleyan Chapel is a part. We talked together, prayed together, and he has come here to-night to help me in this meeting."

I cannot say that I was much impressed by what took place, and yet in a way I was. I had no convictions of my own, but I could not help realizing the convictions of others. Somehow reality was taking the place of unreality. Most of the praying was done by the Chapel people, as none of the people from the Church had been taught to pray in public. Indeed, only one Churchman, with the exception of the Vicar, took part in the meeting, and that was the Squire. I will not try to reproduce his prayer. It was very unconventional, and yet the fact of this man taking part in such a meeting was significant of much. I noticed, too, that the Squire was as nervous as a child.

When the meeting was over, Mr. Treherne took hold of my arm.

"Wait for me, will you, Erskine? I want to speak to Trelaske a minute, and then I am going to drive you up to your place."

The room was nearly empty at this time, and no one but myself saw Isabella Lethbridge come towards me.

"Mr. Erskine, you do not understand, and because you do not understand you are hard and unsympathetic," she said.

She gave me no chance of replying, and I was left wondering as to the meaning of her words.

The next morning the newspapers were again full of accounts of the work of the German submarines. Three trading vessels had been sunk, and many lives lost. This reminded me of the determination to which I had come on the previous Sunday night, and directly after breakfast I made preparations for carrying out my plans. If there was any truth in old Father Abraham's warnings, however, it was necessary for me to be careful, so I made a point of reconnoitring the coast before taking any definite action.

I dressed myself as if for walking, and arming myself with a walking stick, and putting the revolver, which Simpson had persuaded me to carry, in my hip pocket, I went to the highest point of the cliff. It was one of those dull days when a thick mist enveloped everything, and although this mist, unlike a London fog, did not entirely hide the view, it shut out everything except what lay in the near distance.

I had scarcely reached the summit of the headland when I heard a cry of pain. With some difficulty I located it, and after investigation discovered a poor little mongrel dog, lying wounded. The creature looked piteously up at me as I approached, as if to solicit my aid. On examining it more closely I found that it had received what seemed like a wound from a pistol or a rifle, but of this I was not sure. I did not think it was mortally wounded, although it bled freely. I had never seen the dog before, nor could I imagine who could be its master.

"Poor little chap," I said, as I patted its head. It gave a slight yelp, as if in recognition of my act of kindness. "Simpson has always been wanting me to keep a dog," I reflected. "I wonder if this little thing would live if I took it home and cared for it?"

For a moment the incident, slight as it was, drove from my mind the purpose I had in view. I was preparing to carry it back when I heard the sound of voices. Immediately the dog gave a cry of fear and pain. Perhaps it shrank from my endeavors to carry it. I placed it upon the ground, reflecting that I would return to the house and obtain Simpson's assistance, but at that moment a man and a woman came within my view. I remembered in a moment that they were the people who had spoken to me, as I sat basking in the sunlight, a few days before.

"Ah, what have you there?" said the man.

"I have only just found it," I replied. "I came out for a walk, and heard the poor little thing moaning."

"The little wretch has been poaching, I expect, and somebody's gamekeeper has shot it."

"I should not think that likely," was my reply. "This is common land here, and no one, as far as I know, has attempted to preserve it. The only man who owns a gamekeeper in the immediate district is Squire Treherne, and his woods are at least two miles away."

The man looked at the dog, as I thought, indifferently, while the woman shuddered at the sight of blood.

"Have you any idea whose it is?" he asked.

"Not the slightest," I replied.

"I should let him stay, if I were you," said the man. "He is an ugly-looking beast, and I should judge that his teeth are poisonous. There is no trusting that kind of dog, they will bite even those who try to help them."

All this time the poor little thing was whining and whimpering piteously.

"I shall take it back to the house," I said. "I am afraid it is badly wounded, but I should like to save its life if I could."

"Even if you do, you will never win a prize at the shows," said the man, with a laugh. "I hate those mongrel dogs. By the way," he went on, "is not this a bad morning for you to be out? You look very ill, and have the appearance of a man who ought to be in bed."

To this I made no reply. To say the least of it, I regarded it as an impertinence for the man to make any remark at all on my appearance. I knew nothing of him, and beyond the occasions I have mentioned I had never met him.

"You are a hard-hearted brute," said the lady, speaking to her brother. "I think it awfully kind of you, sir, to take so much interest in the poor little thing."

"Excuse me for asking," said the man, "but since I have met you I have often wondered at you living alone at that little hut." His manner appeared to invite confidence.

"I expect I am somewhat of a hermit," I replied.

"But whatever induced you to live in such a place? Are you not afraid of tramps and that sort of thing?" and he nodded towards my little house.

"Tramps!" I replied. "I have not seen a tramp since I have been in Cornwall."

"Well, different people, different tastes!" and he laughed as he spoke. "But if I were you I should not live in such a lonely spot as that for whatever might be given me. Even in Cornwall it is possible to dispose of people, and you would be fair prey to any strolling vagabond."

"He might be wanting to frighten me," I said to myself. "I wonder what his purpose is?" and I could not help connecting him with old Father Abraham.

"Rather bad news of the war again," he went on, as if desiring to change the subject.

"As to that," I replied, "I thought it was rather good news, except for what the German submarines are doing."

"Yes, yes, the submarines, they are very bad."

"What brutes the Germans are," chimed in the woman. "They make me feel just murderous. Oh, I wish I were a man that I might join the Army."

All the time the poor little creature was whimpering as if in pain.

"Let me throw it over the cliff," said the man, "and put it out of its misery."

"No," I replied, "I am going to take it back to the house."

"Yes, yes, do," said the woman. "May I help you? I am awfully fond of dogs. I have kept them all my life and know a good deal about them. I have saved two that the veterinary surgeons had given up."

I picked the little creature up carefully, and was wending my way back to the cottage when the woman rushed to my side.

"You will let me help you, won't you?" she said. "I am so sorry for the poor little thing."

Badly as I wanted to refuse her help, it was impossible to decline a woman's proffered kindness, and a few minutes later both the man and the woman had accompanied me to my little house, and I stood watching her, as with deft fingers she washed the poor little dog's wounds.

"There!" she said when she had finished. "I think he will be better now. May I ask your servant to get me a basin of clean water so that I can wash my hands?"

As I have said in describing our last meeting, she was one of the handsomest women I had ever seen, and I quickly discovered that she was more than ordinarily intelligent. How it was I do not know, because I am not quick to form acquaintances, but in a few minutes I had ordered Simpson to bring refreshments, and was talking with them freely. They told me that they were staying at a furnished house near St. Eia, that they had been staying there for some months and intended remaining instead of returning to London.

"I hate London," said the woman, "and I love the quiet peacefulness of this neighborhood. Besides, I do not think it is safe to live in London. The Germans intend to raid London, and they will throw bombs all over the city. No one will be safe."

This led to a general conversation about the war, and about the cruelty and baseness of the Germans in attacking defenseless ships and murdering women and children. In spite of myself, too, I found that I was subjected to a kind of cross-examination, and yet no one listening could have detected a question which could have in the slightest degree been regarded as suspicious, but here my lawyer's training came to my aid, and I was careful to drop no hint of any suspicions I might entertain.

When they had gone I heaved a sigh of relief, although, truth to tell, the woman's presence had fascinated me. I wondered who she was, and could not help asking myself if there was not some motive behind that which appeared on the surface, actuating them to find their way into my little cottage.

"Simpson," I said, when they had gone, "what did you think of those people?"

"I think they are a very nice lady and gentleman," he said. "The lady herself was very charming."

"You liked her, did you?" I said.

"I always say, sir, that when a dumb animal takes to a person there is nothing much wrong with that person. Now that little dog, sir, was afraid of his life of the man, but did you see how grateful he was to the lady? And no wonder, sir! She treated him as if he were a Christian."

"Which way have they gone, Simpson?"

"They went towards St. Eia, sir."

I hesitated a second. I did not like to take Simpson into my confidence, neither was I pleased at the thought that I had been discussing my visitors with him; still, he was an old servant, and, as I have frequently said, I regarded him more in the light of a friend than a servant.

"Simpson," I said, "just follow them, will you, and see where they go and what they do."

"Yes, sir," he said, but I could see that he was astonished at my request.

Half an hour later he returned.

"Please, sir," he said, "they went along the St. Eia footpath, and then turned off as if they meant to go to Chy-an-Wheal."

Of course there was nothing suspicious in this, and yet my mind was not at ease. I had never been a man given to morbid fancies, and had always been too much a materialist to pay attention to people who profess to believe in premonitions; and yet my meeting with this man and woman had again stirred a thousand fancies in my mind, while the little creature sleeping on the rug seemed in some way to cause vague fears to come into my mind. Perhaps this was because of the state of my health. It seemed to me that my life, humdrum and commonplace though it might appear, was surrounded by mystery. I had vague intuitions which had no basis of reason.

After a time I rose and went out. I wanted to shake off the feelings which possessed me. A few minutes later I was scrambling down the cliff-side, hidden by the thick scrub of bushes. Presently I had a view of the whole of the little bay, which seemed absolutely deserted. I was far from fit to undertake what I had planned to do, but I could not resist the impulse which possessed me. I descended farther, and soon I was at the foot of the cliffs, looking eagerly around me. I found my way into the cave, but there was nothing suspicious there. Evidently no one had visited it since the last high tide. The sandy floor was untrodden; there were no marks of any one having been there. I crept out again, but still no one was visible.

"What a fool I am," I said to myself. "I am like a nervous child following a will-o'-the-wisp of my own fancies."

Still, what I had seen and heard could not be without meaning. I could have sworn to the fact that I had heard people at this very spot only a few hours before. I had heard a man say, "Is that the lot?" and some one had given him an indistinct reply. Of course this might have meant nothing, and yet I was sure it had. Again I examined the rocks inch by inch, but my search was altogether unrewarded. I passed the little fissure which led to the cave again, and this time I saw what I had never seen before. In an obscure corner, not far from the entrance, was another fissure. It was very narrow, but still wide enough for a man to squeeze his body through. I wondered why I had never seen it before, but on reexamining it I realized that it was so curiously formed, that any one with only a match to illuminate the cave could easily miss it. I squeezed myself through the fissure, and found myself in a cave far larger than the first.

In an instant the mystery of the last few months became plain to me. The new cave was as perfect a hiding-place as could possibly be found. Altogether there must have been some hundreds of cans of petrol placed there. This petrol was by different makers. Evidently it had been bought in comparatively small quantities at various places, and had been brought there to be ready for use as necessity arose.

I understood now the meaning of the words I had heard only a little while before.

"Is that the lot?"

What the speaker meant was evident. He had brought a consignment of petrol to this lonely spot, and his words referred to what I saw around me.

I realized also the significance of what Father Abraham had said to me during his midnight visit. Evidently he knew what the cave contained when he said that I was standing on a powder magazine. According to my calculations it was almost immediately under my little wooden hut. When I had asked him whether he spoke figuratively or literally, he had replied, "Both."

I remembered, too, the article I had seen in the London newspaper. The writer of this article had asked where the Germans had been able to obtain the petrol which enabled them to do their devilish work by means of submarines. Now it was plain. This cave, curiously hidden in the rocky cliff in a quiet, far-away spot on the Cornish coast, suited their purpose admirably. I myself had visited the outer cave on more than one occasion and yet had not discovered it. How many lives, I wondered, had been lost by the stuff which had been stored in this place! I called to mind the times when I had seen phantom-like boats coming round the headland. I remembered how I had puzzled as to what they might mean. Now all was plain; this rocky cliff, although far away from the centre of operations, was important beyond words. Evidently those who had been engaged in this work had cleverly avoided the coast watchers. Quietly and unsuspectingly they had brought cargo after cargo, and when the submarines had need of petrol they had been able to supply them.

All this flashed through my mind in a second, then the match by means of which I had made my discovery went out. I realized the awful danger by which I was surrounded; doubtless all these cans were carefully sealed, yet I knew that one spark might ignite this highly combustible fluid, and I should be burnt to death. But that was the smallest part of my danger. I knew that the men who were engaged in this work would stop at nothing; that the spies who had sought out this lonely cave would be ready to do anything in order to keep a secret.

A hundred wild fancies surged through my brain. I saw now why Father Abraham had been driven from his hut. What his connections with the Germans were I had no idea, but evidently he had been regarded as dangerous to their plans. That, doubtless, was the reason why the old man had warned me. His words came flashing back to my mind, and revealed to me the fact that I had been under constant surveillance. Then I thought of the man and woman who had lately visited me. What was the meaning of their interest in me? Were they what they pretended, or had they some sinister motive in asking me questions?

My discovery made the necessity of action imperative. But what could I do? Here was I, a poor invalid, and, if Dr. Rhomboid was right, I had only a few weeks longer to live. I had, as it seemed to me, only kept myself alive by my strong will power and determination that I would not yield to death. But what could I do? I had by this time learnt something of the police officials in the neighborhood, and I knew how utterly incapable they were of dealing with the matter. I was acquainted with some magistrates in the district, but I feared to go to them; a man like Squire Treherne would be utterly incapable of dealing with such a delicate situation. I knew that in his blunt, straightforward, honest way he would muddle everything. It is true I might write to the War Office or to the Admiralty, but, rightly or wrongly, I did not form a high estimate of their way of doing things; and yet I could see nothing else for it. Even now I might be watched. Even now German agents might be waiting outside the cave to pounce upon me.

I lit another match, and saw something which had hitherto escaped my notice. It was a slip of paper. I snatched at it eagerly and carefully read it, my heart beating wildly all the time.

The light again went out.

How long I remained there in the darkness I do not know, but it seemed to me as though I lived years in a few minutes.

A wild scheme flashed through my brain. I would deal with this matter alone! I could not fight for my country, but I would serve it in my own way.

I listened intently, but could hear nothing save the dull monotone of the waves outside. No whispering voices reached me. The darkness of the cave seemed to intensify the silence. I crept into the outer cave and again listened; still all was silent. Then I made my way into the daylight, taking every precaution before doing so. No, as far as I could tell no curious eyes were watching me. I was alone.

XXIII

A CLUE TO THE MYSTERY

I seemed to have a fresh lease of life as I clambered up the rocky cliff towards my hut. I had no sense of weariness or weakness at all; it might seem as though all my fears had been groundless, and that Dr. Rhomboid had been utterly mistaken.

I expect this was because of the great excitement under which I labored. Every nerve in my body was in tension; at that moment nothing seemed impossible to me. My mind, I remember, seemed as vigorous as my body, and I felt as though I was walking on air. The possibilities of what I had discovered might mean putting an end to one of the greatest dangers which had been threatening our country. From what I could judge, this might be one of the principal store places of petrol. I realized, as I had never realized before, the cleverness of the German mind. No one, I imagined, would think of this out-of-the-way district as a possible centre of their operations. Naturally the whole of the East Coast from Dover to the extreme North of Scotland would be watched with the greatest care; but who would have thought they would choose this out-of-the-way spot on the North of Cornwall? It might seem as though Providence had led me thither.

More than once on my way to the house did I stop and look eagerly around me, but I was always assured that no one watched me, and that I was utterly alone; besides, I could not have chosen a more perfect day for my investigation. Although it was now near noon and the weather showed signs of breaking, a thick damp mist still enveloped the whole countryside, thus making observation from a distance almost impossible.

"Everything all right, sir?" asked Simpson, as I entered the house.

"What should be wrong?" was my reply.

"Nothing, sir, only you might have seen a ghost; you look terribly strange and excited, sir."

I laughed aloud.

"I have not felt so well for months, Simpson."

He looked at me dubiously, I thought, and seemed anything but satisfied.

"Are you ready for your lunch, sir?"

"Lunch?" I replied. "Haven't I had lunch?"

Making my way into my little bedroom, I caught a glimpse of my face. I hardly recognized myself! Pale as I had always been since my illness, my pallor had been nothing to the white, drawn, haggard face which I saw in the glass. But for the wild glitter in my eyes, it might have been the face of a dead man, and yet every particle of my being seemed instinct with life.

After pretending to eat some of the lunch which Simpson had prepared for me, an unusual languor crept over me, and throwing myself on the couch, I quickly fell asleep.

I was awakened by a sound of voices at the door, and I started up quickly. As far as I could judge, I suffered no evil results from the excitement through which I had passed. Whatever had caused me unnatural strength, its influence had not yet departed.

"Simpson," I said, "whom have you got there?"

"I beg your pardon, sir, but I have just told Mr. Lethbridge that he could not see you. I did not think you looked well, sir."

"Show Mr. Lethbridge in. I am perfectly all right."

"I am afraid I should not have called," said Mr. Lethbridge, as he entered the room. "You do not look well."

"I am better than I have been for months," was my answer. "Sit down, won't you?"

He gave me a quick, searching glance, and then took the chair to which I had pointed. There were marks of suffering in his face. Although he was calm and collected and showed no signs of emotion whatever, I thought I saw in his eyes a strange, haunted look.

"I am afraid I did not receive you very cordially yesterday," he said presently. "You see it—it was the shock."

"Of course it was," was my answer. "I understand how you must be feeling."

"Do you?" he replied wearily. "I don't."

"Don't what?" I asked.

"Understand. I understand nothing. I am bewildered. I am in hell."

He spoke very quietly although his voice was strained and somewhat hoarse.

"You didn't sleep last night," I suggested.

"No," he replied, with a sigh, "I didn't sleep. I suppose I am regarded as a hard man, Mr. Erskine?"

To this I made no reply. I knew he was passing through a terrible experience, and, strange as it may seem, I wanted to do nothing to lighten his burden.

"I don't know why I have come to you at all," he went on. "You are a comparative stranger to me—indeed, a few months ago I did not know of your existence—and yet something drew me here. I suppose it is because you were fond of him."

"I loved him almost like a brother," was my reply. "If I had been his father, I should be a proud man."

He looked at me steadily for a few minutes in silence.

"I have learnt one thing anyhow," he said at length.

"What is that?"

"That one cannot destroy the ties of blood. Yes! Yes! I know I had disinherited him; driven him from home; told him he was no longer a son of mine. Yes! told him that I had put him outside my life. But it was a lie! I had not! I could not! Oh, the tragedy of it!"

"Yes, tragedy in a way," I said.

"Oh, the tragedy of it!" he repeated. "No, it is not death that makes the tragedy, it is something else. I can't understand it. Mr. Erskine, I am a just man."

At this I was silent. I could not for the life of me assent to his words.

"Yes, I am a just man," he repeated. "That is, I have tried to be just. I did what was right, too; he ought to have obeyed me. I was his father, and it is the duty of a son to obey a father; besides, I had done everything for him. I sent him to one of the best public schools in England. After that I sent him to the University. I had great plans for him. But he disappointed me. He married the girl I told him he must not marry; he did that which I forbade him to do; therefore I was right in driving him from the house. But it was all of no use; he was my son still."

"Of course he was," I said.

"Ah, yes! but there is the tragedy of it. He has died feeling that he was not my son, remembering what I said to him. That is the tragedy! Oh, how God Almighty must be laughing at me!"

"Not if there is a God," I replied.

"Why, don't you believe in God?" he burst forth almost angrily.

"I don't know," I replied. "But if there is a God, He pities you."

He started to his feet and paced the little room while I stood watching him.

"God! how I loved that boy," he broke out, "and he didn't know it!"

"Yes," I said, "that is the tragedy. That is the unforgivable sin."

"Go on," he said. "Say what you want to say."

"Hugh was hungering for your love, just hungering for it; but he didn't believe you cared for him. You ask me to speak plainly, Mr. Lethbridge, and so, at the risk of offending you, I am going to do so. You had your hard-and-fast ideas about life; you worshipped success, position, power, and money; you wanted Hugh to conform to your iron rules and laws, and because he was a live, human boy you tried to crush him."

"Yes! yes! I know." He spoke almost eagerly. "But even now I cannot feel right about it. After all, war is murder. How can I, a Christian man, a believer in the teaching of the founder of Methodism, believe that my son was anything but murdered? After all, is not a soldier a paid murderer? I think if I could only get that right in my mind I should be happier. Look here! Do you honestly believe that Hugh did right?"

"I don't believe; I am sure," was my reply.

"Ah! but you don't believe in Christian teaching. You told me months ago that you were an agnostic. Legalized murder cannot be right."

"Mr. Lethbridge," I said, "supposing there lived in this neighborhood a band of men without moral sense, without honor, without truth; men to whom you could not appeal because their standards of life were utterly opposed to yours. And suppose that by rapine, cruelty, and murder they sought to rule this district, to rob people of their homes, to outrage everything sacred in life. What do you think it would be your duty to do?"

"Yes! yes! I see what you mean. But are the Germans like that? Aren't they as good and as honorable as we are?"

"Listen!" I said. "I have just been reading some German books and reviews, and this is what some of the leading men in Germany have lately said. Mark you, they are not men in the street. They express the thoughts which dominate the population of Germany. Here is one by a leading General: 'We have been called Barbarians; we are, and we are proud of it. Whatever acts will help us, we shall commit them, no matter what the world may say. Germany stands as the Supreme Arbiter of her own actions, and however the world may rave at our cruelty and our atrocities, our devilry, we shall commit these deeds, we shall rejoice in them, and we shall be proud of them.'"

"Who said that?" he asked.

"A leading General in the German Army," I replied.

"Here is another statement by a renowned Doctor of Philosophy and an educationist: 'Children in our schools and the youths of our universities must be taught a new doctrine, the Doctrine of Hatred. They must be educated to hate as a duty; it must form a new subject in our curriculum of education, "And now abideth Faith, Hope, and Hatred, and the greatest of these is Hatred.""'

"You don't mean to say that any man taught that?" he asked.

"Here is the article in a German book," I replied.

"My God!" he said.

"Here is another statement," I went on, "by perhaps the leading journalist in the German Empire: 'Our might shall create new laws. Germany has nothing to do with what other nations may think of us. Germany is a law unto herself. The might of her armies gives her the right to override all laws and protests. In the future, in all the temples, the priests of all the gods shall sing praises to the God of War.'"

He looked at me steadily without speaking.

"Hugh gave his life to kill that," I said. "Is not that a Christian thing to do?"

He sat, I should think, for five minutes without speaking a word, while I watched him. Then he rose to his feet and held out his hand.

"Thank you," he said, "thank you. My God! what a fool I have been."

He left the house without speaking another word.

I went to the door and watched him as he made his way along the footpath through the copse. I saw that the mists had now passed away and that the sun was shining brightly. Strange as it may seem, I did not at that moment realize the inwardness of my conversation with Josiah Lethbridge; I only reflected upon the fact that although he was a magistrate I had said nothing to him concerning my discovery of that morning. He at least was a keen, capable man, he could act wisely and promptly; yet I had not uttered a word. But after all I had done right; the problem he was facing was different from mine, and he would be in no way in a fit condition to help me. Besides, I had made up my mind to carry out my own plans.

No one else came to see me that day, and during the remainder of the afternoon and evening I remained alone, thinking of what I ought to do. I still felt strong and capable. I suffered no pain, neither did any sense of weariness oppress me.

"That little dog, sir," said Simpson, coming into the room about sunset.

"Yes, Simpson? What of it?"

"It is a lot better, sir. The wound was not a bad one at all, and now he is getting quite frolicsome."

The dog had followed Simpson into the room and was sniffing at my legs in a friendly way.

"Poor old chap," I said, patting his head; "you are not very beautiful certainly, but you look as though you had faithful eyes."

He gave a pleased yelp and licked my hand; after this he lay down on the rug and composed himself to sleep.

"Evidently he has adopted us, Simpson," I said.

"Yes, sir. He makes himself quite at home."

"Simpson," I said, "you have the name and address of that man and woman who came to see me this morning?"

"Yes, sir, here's the card: Mr. John Liddicoat. There's the name of the house, sir."

"Do you know where it is, Simpson?"

"Yes, sir; it is a house just behind Treveen Tor. It is a biggish house, sir, but lonely."

That night when Simpson had gone to bed, I left my hut quietly and made my way along the cliff footpath towards Treveen Tor, which stands at the back of the little town of St. Eia.

I still felt well and strong, no suggestion of my malady troubled me. I could not help wondering at this, as I walked briskly along, and yet in my heart of hearts I knew that my abnormal strength was but a transient thing; I knew I was buoyed up by excitement, and that presently I should suffer a terrible relapse. That was why I was eager to do what I had to do quickly. As I skirted the little town of St. Eia I saw that the lights were nearly all out. I looked at my watch, and found that it was eleven o'clock, and the people had nearly all gone to bed. It was a wonderful night of stars, and there was not a cloud in the sky. The moon had not yet risen, but I knew it was due to rise before midnight. During the whole of my journey I had not met a single person. The night, save for the roar of the waves, was still as death.

Leaving the cliff footpath, I struck across the country towards Treveen Tor, and went around the base of the hill towards the spot where Mr. John Liddicoat's house stood.

Had any one asked me the reason for going there, I should have been unable to have given them a satisfactory reply. But in my own heart I was satisfied. I had carefully thought out the whole series of events, linking incident with incident and word with word; and although I had no definite hopes as to the result of my nocturnal journey, I felt sure that by taking it I should at least clear my ground.

Presently I saw the house plainly; it was, as Simpson had said, situated in a lonely spot, and only approached by a lonely lane from the St. Eia side and the footpath by which I had come. The house itself was in complete darkness; not a glimmer of light shone from any of the windows. I saw that it was surrounded by a garden, perhaps half an acre in extent. This garden was, as far as I could judge, altogether uncultivated. The fence around the garden was low, and scarcely any vegetation hid my view. The district around here was almost treeless. The land on which the house was built was, in the main, hard to cultivate. I saw, however, that two stunted trees grew at some little distance from the house.

I waited about a quarter of an hour without making any attempt to climb over the fence. I reflected that if my suspicions were correct, I must use every precaution. At the end of a quarter of an hour I crept cautiously over the fence and made my way towards the house.

Still all was dark. I carefully examined the ground around the two stunted trees I have mentioned, and presently I caught sight of something which set my heart beating violently. I was on the point of making a closer examination of what I had already seen, when a ray of light shone from one of the windows and I could hear the sound of voices. Again looking around me eagerly, I saw what looked like a large clump of rhododendron bushes. These offered me not only a hiding-place, but a post of observation. I had scarcely crept between the leaves when the door of John Liddicoat's house opened and two people came out. They were the man and the woman whom I had seen that morning.

Almost at the same time the moon rose behind a distant hill, and a few minutes later the garden was flooded with its silvery light.

"Have you got it all?" It was a woman who spoke.

"Yes, all except ..." and I could not catch the last word.

"You bring it, will you?"

They made their way towards the stunted trees, where they dropped the things they had brought. Then the man left the woman and appeared a little later bearing a light ladder.

I saw the man place his ladder against the tree and mount it, carrying something with him, what it was I could not tell. The moon had now risen high enough to enable me to see more plainly and to show me that the two worked swiftly and dexterously, as though they were accustomed to their work. Presently they had evidently finished, for they stood still and waited for something.

"I do not expect we shall get anything to-night." It was the woman who spoke.

"There is no knowing," replied the man; "besides, we have our orders. It is a calm night, too."

"What time is it?" asked the woman.

"Close on midnight," was the reply. "Anyhow, we must wait here until half-past twelve; if nothing comes by that time we shall hear nothing until to-morrow night. My word, if that fool of a fellow who lives in the hut on the cliff only knew! For my own part, I am not sure he does not suspect."

"What makes you think so?"

"I thought he was very guarded this morning," replied the man, "and I must use every means to make certain; if we bungle this we shall be in a bad way. Anyhow, he is closely watched night and day."

After this there was silence, save that I thought I heard a faint clicking noise. The minutes dragged heavily. It seemed as though nothing were going to happen. The moon rose higher and higher, revealing the outlines of the man and woman still more plainly, and presently I saw that their waiting had been rewarded. There was a clear repetition of the sounds I had heard previously. Then the woman said, "Have you got it?"

"Yes," replied the man; "we will take it in, and then our work for the night is done."

A few minutes later the man climbed the ladder again; evidently he was detaching something he had placed on the trees.

I waited and watched perhaps for another ten minutes, and then they went back into the house which had remained in darkness all the time.

XXIV

PREPARATION

How I got back to my little hut that night I do not know. I have not a distinct remembrance of any incident on the journey, or of any spot that I passed. I was unconscious of all my surroundings; I must have walked two or three miles, being utterly oblivious all the time of where I was.

I felt no sense of weariness, being still upheld by the unnatural strength caused by my excitement. A part of my journey led me to a footpath which skirted the cliff, and for hundreds of yards I walked on the edge of a precipice. But I knew nothing of it.

What I had seen and heard told their own story. My life, which had promised to be so uneventful, proved to be exciting beyond words. I had by some curious chance happened to come upon a spot which was, in some respects, the centre of German operations. What had been a mystery had now become plain to me. The scrap of paper I had found in the little cave had made all sorts of things possible. It had led me to John Liddicoat's house; it had enabled me to understand actions which would have otherwise been enshrouded in mystery. Who John Liddicoat and the woman who called herself his sister were was plain—they were German spies. Whether they were English or German I could not tell. Certainly they spoke the English language as though they had been born and reared on the British Isles; but that they were paid agents of the Kaiser there could be no doubt.

I little thought at the time I had paid my visit to the wireless station at M—— that it would have been fraught with such vital import. It seemed to me as though the hand of Providence had guided me there, and had led me to form an acquaintance with the young fellow who had insisted upon teaching me the secrets of wireless telegraphy. What I had learnt offered me boundless opportunities. The little apparatus, which not long before I had regarded as an interesting plaything, became of vital importance. Vast avenues of action opened themselves up before me; by means of this little apparatus which I had found such interest in constructing, I might do very great things. The man Liddicoat, by means of the two stunted trees in his garden, and the apparatus which he had fixed there, had been enabled to receive messages from the enemy. He had been able to learn when new supplies of petrol were to be brought, and when consignments of this same commodity had to be taken to the German submarines.

Nothing could be more cunningly contrived; the little cove was hidden by huge promontories, which rose up almost perpendicularly on the rock-bound coast. The spot was far away from all centres of population, and was such an unlikely place that no suspicion would be attached to it. Liddicoat was an English name, and a name closely associated with Cornwall. St. Eia was a little town where visitors often came, and thus he would be able to do his work unhindered and unsuspected. Evidently the Germans in their vast preparations had learned of this cave long before the war and had seen its possibilities; what I had discovered was the outcome of a carefully prepared plan. Of course there was much mystery which I had not yet been able to solve. The part which Father Abraham had played was not yet clear to me, and I found myself hazarding all sorts of conjectures, as to why he had built the hut there and why he had left it. But everything resolved itself into one interpretation—the Germans had foreseen this war, they had conjectured the course it would take. They understood the means which would have to be used, and they had made their preparations carefully, scientifically, and with vast forethought.

But what could I do? Evidently I was suspected. Even now, my house was being watched night and day; Father Abraham knew this, and had warned me to leave it. Unseen enemies might strike me down at any moment. And worse than all, although at that time I was buoyed up by an unnatural strength, I was little better than a dead man. I realized that I was opposed to those who were entirely unscrupulous, and who would allow nothing to stand in the way of the accomplishment of their schemes.

Doubtless, my wise course would be to write an exact description of all I had seen and heard and send it to the Government authorities without delay. If, as I suspected, Liddicoat was associated with an unscrupulous set of people, he would not hesitate to end my earthly career. In that case, unless I communicated with the authorities at once, my discoveries would be valueless; and yet with a strange obstinacy I determined that I would not do this. As I have said repeatedly, I was at that time buoyed up by an unnatural strength, and my mind was abnormally active. That is how I account for a determination which, in the light of after events, seems insane. Government authorities would be in an infinitely better position to deal with this combination of circumstances than I. Not only would they have every facility at their disposal, but they would have a vast knowledge of German methods. I, on the other hand, had but few facilities. I was almost entirely ignorant of the means they were constantly using, and I was alone!

Yet I adhered to my determination with that strange obstinacy which characterizes a man who is in an unnatural condition of mind and body. I vowed that I would see this thing through myself; that I would put together all the pieces of this intricate mosaic and bring the guilty persons to justice; then, when I had done my work, I would present it to the Government.

This and a thousand other thoughts flashed through my mind during my midnight journey from John Liddicoat's house to my little hut. I was conscious of no danger, and I am afraid I was heedless as to who might be watching me. I found myself in my little room without realizing that I had opened the door and entered. Almost like a man in a dream I lit my lamp and threw myself in an armchair. I had no thought of sleep, and my mind was still preternaturally active. Then a sense of my utter helplessness possessed me and a great fear filled my heart. I went to the door, opened it slightly, and listened. It was a wonderful night; the moon sailed in a cloudless sky, and I could see the shimmer of the sea far out from land. No sound reached me save the roll of the waves on the sandy beach; not a breath of wind stirred, not a leaf rustled.

Locking and bolting the door, I drew some paper from a drawer and commenced writing. How long I wrote I do not know, but I did not stop until I had penned a fairly comprehensive precis of what I had seen and heard. Why I did this I cannot tell; I only know that I was driven to it by some force which, to me, was inexplicable. This done, I signed the paper, giving the hour and date when I had written it.

I heard Simpson turning in his bed in the little room close by.

"Simpson," I said, going to him, "are you awake?" He yawned drowsily.

"Simpson, are you awake?" I repeated.

"Yes, sir," he said, starting up. "Is anything the matter, sir? Are you well?"

"Quite well, Simpson."

"Is it time to get up, sir?"

"I—I—what time it is I don't know, Simpson, but it is not time to get up."

He looked at me like one afraid.

"Can I do anything for you, sir?"

"Simpson," I said, "I want you to take this paper and put it away in a place of safety. You must not open it unless something happens to me."

"Happens to you, sir? What can happen to you?"

"I don't know—nothing, most likely. But I am giving this to you in case there should. Don't be alarmed. If nothing happens to me, let it lie in a place of safety, and give it to me when I ask for it, but if anything should happen...."

"Yes, sir," he said eagerly, as I hesitated. "If anything should happen, sir?"

"Then—then you will take this to Mr. Josiah Lethbridge!"

"Mr. Josiah Lethbridge, sir?"

"Yes, take it to him immediately. You must not delay a second."

"But what can happen to you, sir?"

"I know of nothing," I replied. "I am only taking a precaution. That is all, Simpson. Good-night."

I held the lamp in my hand as I spoke, while Simpson sat up in his bed staring at me.

"Excuse me, sir," he said, "but—but——" and then he put his hand under the pillow and took out his watch. "It is half-past three, sir, it won't be long before daylight; and—and haven't you been to bed, sir?"

"Good-night, Simpson," I said, and then found my way into my little room. Five minutes later, I had got into bed, and blown out the lamp. I was still strangely awake, and was again living over my experiences of the night. I heard Simpson groping cautiously around the house, and I knew he was looking at the fastenings of windows and doors.

"I shall have a busy day to-morrow," I said to myself. "I must see that my little wireless apparatus is in good order. I must be careful, too, that I arouse no suspicion in placing it on the spot I have prepared." After this I began to arrange my plans concerning the work I had to do. Then, little by little, things became hazy and indistinct to me. "I am falling asleep," I said to myself. "This is wonderful; I never thought I should sleep to-night."

I seemed to be passing through one world into another, from the world of realities to the world of dreams, and yet the latter was as real to me as the former had been. I had a kind of consciousness that I was asleep, and yet the stuff of which my dreams were made was just as vivid as my experiences of that night.

I was far out at sea, but it was not such a sea as I had ever known. I felt the movement of the waters, and heard the roar of the machinery. But I could see nothing. A great weight seemed to weigh me down. I felt, too, as though I were moving amidst great sea-monsters, the like of which I had never imagined before. I had a difficulty in breathing; it seemed to me as though the air which passed through my lungs was artificial. I had the use of my senses, but those senses seemed to respond to new conditions. I heard, but my hearing was confused; I felt, but with a kind of numb consciousness. I heard sounds of voices, but the voices might have been hundreds of miles away. It was as though I were speaking to some one through a telephone, a long way off. I was in a kind of a room, but it was such a room as I had never seen before. It had neither shape nor dimension. Little by little, that which had been shadowy and unreal became more definite. I saw a table, with three men sitting beside it; in front of them was a chart.

"She will be there on Thursday," said one, placing his hand on a certain spot on the chart. "It's a long distance from here and we shall want more petrol."

"It will be easy for us to get it," said another; "we have everything in training. We must let him know."

As I said, the voices seemed to be hundreds of miles away, as though they were speaking through a long-distance telephone. Yet every word was plain.

I realized at that moment that they were speaking in German, and saw, too, that the men had German faces, and wore German clothes.

I was not in the least surprised or disturbed. It seemed to me as though it were all a part of a prearranged plan. The sense of wonder had altogether departed from me.

"There will be a greater yell than ever about German atrocities," laughed one of the men. "After all, it does seem a devilish thing to attack passenger vessels."

"What has that to do with us? We must obey orders."

"But what good will it do?"

"God in heaven knows, I don't. I suppose the idea is to frighten the people, so that they will sue for peace."

"The English are not to be frightened that way; besides, it won't even touch the British Navy. They are masters on the sea, whatever we may do."

Their voices seemed to become dimmer and dimmer; they still went on talking, but I heard nothing distinctly after that. Indeed, the things by which I was surrounded, which had at first been comparatively clear, now became indistinct and unreal. I felt as though I were losing consciousness, and then everything became dark.

The next thing I can remember was opening my eyes to see Simpson standing by my bed.

"Anything the matter, Simpson?" I inquired.

"No, sir, except that it is ten o'clock, and I didn't know what time you meant to get up, sir."

"Not for a long time yet, Simpson; I am very sleepy and very tired."

Indeed, at that time an unutterable languor possessed me, and I felt as weak as a child. Simpson did not move, but looked at me intently, and I thought I saw fear in his eyes. But I was too tired to care. Then slowly life and vitality came back to me. While I was in a state of languor I remembered nothing of what I had seen in my dream, but little by little everything came back to me, until all was as vivid and as plain as I have tried to set it down here on paper. When I again opened my eyes, I saw Simpson still standing by my bed.

"I am going to get up, Simpson."

"You are sure you are well enough, sir?"

"Well enough! I feel perfectly well."

And I spoke the truth. It seemed to me as though a great black shadow which had paralyzed me, rolled away from my life.

"Prepare breakfast at once, Simpson; I shall be ready in half an hour."

Simpson took a last look at me, and then left the room, with his old formula: "Yes, sir; thank you, sir."

I got up and looked towards the sea. The sun was shining brightly, and the waves were glistening in the sunlight. It was a day to rejoice in. The air was clear and pure.

I moved briskly around the room, feeling no sense of weariness. My long sleep had restored me; my mind, too, was as active as it had been on the previous night. I fell to thinking about my experiences, and philosophizing on what I had seen in my dreams. "The real I," I reflected, "was not lying at all on that bed all last night. My spirit, my thinking self, my understanding self, was hundreds of miles away, where I don't know, but I was not here. I saw what I saw, and heard what I heard, without my body. I had other eyes, other senses. My real self was not a part of my body at all during that time. Therefore I have a self distinct from the body, independent of it. My body is only a machine whereby my real self does its work, therefore the death of the body would not be the death of me."

I took pleasure in ruminating in this way, even although there were at the back of my mind many doubts. The wish was only the father to the thought, and the thought did not carry conviction to my consciousness. It seemed to me that I had intellectually realized something which went to prove the immortality of the soul, but which really proved nothing. I could only be certain of that through some deeper process, something which went down to the very depths of life.

All the same, I found pleasure in it, and I remember humming a tune as I dressed.

Directly after breakfast, Simpson put the morning paper before me. Mechanically I opened it, and turned to the list of casualties. My heart sank as I read, for I found the names of three men who had gone from St. Issey among the list of killed.

"Are you going out, sir?" And Simpson looked at me anxiously.

"Yes," I replied, "I am going to the village. I see that Mrs. Searle's boy is killed."

"You are sure you are well enough, sir?"

"Quite," I replied. "By the way, Simpson, you have that paper I gave you last night?"

"Yes, sir; I locked it away carefully, and I understand what you said, but I don't understand what you mean, sir. Are you afraid that——"

"That's all right, Simpson; be sure not to forget my instructions."

A little later, I found myself at Mrs. Searle's door, and on finding it open, I entered. A second later, I blamed myself for the liberty I had taken. It is not uncommon for these simple folk to enter each other's houses without giving notice in any way, and I had fallen in with the habit of the people. But I should have known better. Mr. and Mrs. Searle were both on their knees praying, and there was an expression on each of their faces which I shall not try to describe. Sorrow, pain, even anguish, were expressed there, but beyond all this was an unutterable peace. I suppose I must have made a slight noise, for they opened their eyes at my approach and rose to their feet.

"Have 'ee 'eerd the news, Mr. Erskine?" It was Mr. Searle who spoke.

"Yes," I replied; "I have just read it in the newspaper. I came to tell you how deeply I sympathize with you."

The man held out his hand and grasped mine, and I saw the tears trickle down his cheeks.

"Mr. Erskine," he said, "the Loard's ways seem very hard, but He doeth all things well. I'd bin gittin' cold; the Loard 'ad bin prosperin' me, and some'ow I was forgittin' God. Then, three weeks ago, we 'ad a letter from Jim, tellin' us that 'e was right up in the firing line and that the danger was ter'ble. Some'ow that brought us back to God; we felt the need of God, Mr. Erskine, as we 'adn't felt it for years. And we prayed as we 'adn't prayed for years."

He still held my hand, looking at me through the mist of his tears all the time.

"When the news came yesterday," he went on, "we felt as though the 'eavens were black, as though nothing mattered. But that is over now. God alone knows what we 'ave suffered at the loss of our boy. But it is only good-bye for a little while; he isn't dead, sir. Now we can say, 'Bless the Loard, O my soul, and all that is within me bless and praise His Holy Name.'"

"What would I give," I said to myself, as presently I walked from the house, "if I knew their secret?"

Evidently the news had affected the life of the village greatly, for I found groups of people standing together talking about it. I joined a number of miners, who were working "afternoon core" and as a consequence had their morning at liberty.

"Ter'ble, sir, edn't it?" said one man to me. "John Searle and his missis took it all right, because they've got their faith to sustain them; but there's Harry Bray, 'e's going about like a man maazed; 'e don't believe in anything, sir, and as a consequence there's no light in his darkness."

"No light in his darkness?" I repeated.

"No, sir; he became a backslider and gave up God! This is what we was talking about when you comed by. What comfort have the world to offer at a time like this? Here be thousands and tens of thousands of people, all over the world, grieving because their dear ones will never come back again. Mothers grieving about their sons, wives grieving about their husbands, maidens grieving about their sweethearts. You now, sir, you be a scholar and a learned man. Do you know of anythin', anythin', sir, 'cept faith in an Almighty God, that will 'elp people at a time like this? What can science do? What can philosophy do? What can money do?"

"Nothing," I said almost involuntarily.

"No, nothing. Tell 'ee what, sir, this war is bringing us all back to our senses; we've thought that we could do without Almighty God, sir, but we ca'ant. A man who was preachin' at the Chapel on Sunday night called this war 'The World's great tragedy.' He was right, sir; but God is overruling it. He is answering men out of the whirlwind and the fire, as He did Job of olden times. Forty boys have gone out from St. Issey, sir; how many of 'em will come back again?"

I shook my head.

"Exactly, sir. Here is a wisht story in the newspaper. A poor woman, sir, who 'ad lost her husband and three sons in the war, wrote to the editor and asked him to give her some explanation of it all, to offer some word of comfort. So the editor wrote to a lot of clever men, sending them copies of the woman's letter, and asking them what they 'ad to say. Here are their answers, sir. They are from a scientist, a politician, a philosopher, and a literary man, and that's what they 'ad to say by way of comfort. She asked for bread, and they gave 'er stone."

I took the paper, and saw that the man had spoken truly. The answers which our leading scientists, politicians, philosophers, and scholars had to give were utterly in the negative. They could say nothing that would help to heal the poor woman's bleeding, broken heart. All their scholarship, all their learning, all their philosophy was Dead Sea fruit. Only the man of faith, the man of vision, could give her comfort.

I left the village wondering: I realized as I never realized before the impotence of mere intellectualism, of material success, of the advancement of physical science, in the face of life's great tragedies.

Then suddenly my thoughts were diverted into another channel, for coming towards me I saw Isabella Lethbridge.

XXV

PREMONITIONS

Our greeting was cold and formal; it seemed to me as though a barrier of reserve stood between us. I remembered what had taken place when we last met in a way similar to this. I also called to mind what she had said when she came to me at the little schoolroom in St. Issey.

"How are your father and mother?" I asked presently.

"Mother is wonderful, simply wonderful! As for my father, I can't understand him."

"No?" I said. "He called to see me yesterday."

"Indeed!" She seemed to take no interest in his visit, neither did she ask anything concerning his purpose in coming.

An awkward silence fell between us, and I was on the point of leaving her, when she broke out suddenly:

"I came out in the hope of meeting you! Seeing it was a fine morning, I thought you might be tempted to walk into St. Issey. If I had not met you, I think I should have gone to your house. I wanted to speak to you badly."

"What about?" I asked.

"I don't know," was the reply. "I have nothing to say now I have met you."

"Was it about your brother?"

She shook her head, and I saw her lips tremble.

"As you know, I have no brother now; he is dead. What a ghastly mockery life is, isn't it? But for mother, I think I should run away."

Each sentence was spoken abruptly and nervously, and I could see she was much wrought upon.

"Mr. Erskine," she went on, "you were very cruel to me a few days ago."

"Yes," I said, "perhaps I was. I meant to be. I am sorry now. Had I known about your brother, I would not have spoken."

"You were cruel because you were so un-understanding. You were utterly ignorant, and because of your ignorance you were foolish."

"Ignorant of what?" I asked.

"Of everything, everything!" And she spoke almost passionately. "Was what you told me true?"

A wild look came into her eyes, such a look as I had never seen before.

"I don't think I had any right to say it," I replied, "but was I unjust in my accusation? Did you not try to fascinate me? Did you not try to make me fall in love with you?"

"No, yes—I don't really know. And what you said is true, is it not—you don't love me?"

"You were very cruel," I said. "You knew why I came here—knew that the doctor had written my death-warrant before I came. It is nearly a year since I came here, and a year was all Dr. Rhomboid gave me to live. To-day I feel as though the doctor's prophecy will be fulfilled."

"That you will die before the year is out?" she almost gasped.

"Yes," I said. "That was why it was cruel of you to seek to play with a dying man's heart. But you didn't succeed; you fascinated, you almost made me love you. If you had done so, you would have added mockery to mockery. But I never loved you, I only loved the woman you were meant to be, the woman you ought to be."

I saw anger, astonishment, and yearning, besides a hundred other things for which I could find no words, in her eyes as I spoke. For a moment she seemed to be struggling to find some answer to give me. Then she burst out angrily, almost furiously:

"You are blind—blind—blind!"

"Blind to what?" I asked. "You care nothing for me, and you know it. You need not tell me so; I can see it in your eyes. You have won the love of other men only to discard it."

"Mr. Erskine," she said, "do you remember our first conversation?"

"The one when I first dined at your house?" I asked.

"No, the one when we met in the field yonder. It is nearly a year ago."

"Yes, I remember. You said you didn't believe that there was such a thing as love—although even then you were trying to make me lose my heart to you."

"I told you," she went on, "that some of us were born into the world handicapped, and I asked you whether, seeing nature had prevented us from getting our desires in natural ways, we were not justified in overstepping conventional boundaries."

"Yes," I replied, "I remember. But I never could understand what you meant."

"No," she went on, "you were blind, blind! I don't think a man can understand a woman. You were at the prayer-meeting the other night—do you believe in God?"

"I think there must be a God," I said. "I have just come from Mr. and Mrs. Searle's house. They have lost their boy; he has been killed in the war. They have no doubt about God's existence, they were even rejoicing in their sorrow; and it is all because God is real to them. Yes, I think there must be a God."

"If there is a God, He must be awfully unjust," she said bitterly. "If there is a God, why did He create us with barriers around us which we cannot break down, and which we long to break down? Why did He give us longings which we cannot satisfy?"

"What longings? What barriers?" I asked.

Again she seemed struggling for speech, and I knew there was something in her mind which she wanted to express but could not.

"Tell me," she said, "were you really serious when you said you thought the doctor's verdict was soon to be fulfilled?"

"Yes," I said, "perfectly serious."

"And you think you are going to die soon?" Her voice was hoarse and unnatural.

"Yes, I feel quite sure of it."

"And yet you are here talking with me about it calmly."

"What else is there to do?"

"It cannot be! It cannot be!" she cried passionately. "You must not die."

"If I could believe what John Searle believes, I should not care," was my answer. "If I could believe that this life is only a fragment of life—that death is only the door by which we enter another life, the fulfilment of this life; if I could believe that at the back of everything is an Omnipotent, All-Wise, Ever-Loving, Beneficent God, I should not mind death, I think I should laugh at it. Then what we call death would not be death at all. That is my difficulty."

"And you want to live?"

"Yes, I have an intense longing to live. I have a passion for life. But what can I do? When the poison of death is in one's system and science knows no means whereby that poison can be destroyed, all is hopeless."

"And the doctor gave you no hope?"

"No, he said nothing could save me. Yesterday I felt as though I could not die, as though life was strong within me. To-day life seems only a matter of hours."

"And yet you are able to think and talk and walk."

"Yes, that is the mockery of it. Do you believe in premonitions, Miss Lethbridge?"

"Premonitions?"

"Yes, premonitions. I have a feeling that within a few hours I shall be dead."

"From your illness?"

"I don't know, I suppose so."

She stood looking at me wonderingly. Never had I seen her look so fair, so wondrously fair, as she looked that morning, in spite of the fact that she showed marks of having suffered greatly. As she had said, I could not understand her. In one sense she seemed my ideal of what a woman ought to be. Even although I knew the shadow of death was creeping over me, I felt the power of her presence; felt that it would be bliss to love and be loved by such a woman. But I knew she had no love to give me; knew she had tried to play with my heart as she had played with the hearts of others.

"You would have made a poor conquest if you had made me fall in love with you," I could not help saying bitterly. "After all, I could only have been your slave for a few weeks."

"Don't, don't taunt me!" she cried; "it is cruel, bitterly cruel of you. Besides, I cannot believe that what you say is true. You are not near death—you must live!"

"What would I not give if your words were true, Miss Lethbridge! I never felt life so full of possibilities as now. If I could live only a month, a week, I feel as though I could render great service to my King and my Country."

Why I was led to say this I cannot tell, but something unloosened my tongue.

"How could you render service to your King and your Country?" she asked. "Have you discovered anything?"

"Yes, I believe I have. I believe I know more than all our Secret Service officers do."

"But surely you will not keep your knowledge to yourself?"

"Just now you called me blind," was my reply. "I don't think I am blind, but I am obstinate. Dying men have strange fancies, and I have a fancy that I can do what no one else can. I have a feeling that if I told my secret to the officials they would bungle my plans; that is why I am going to act alone."

"Are you going to place yourself in danger?"

"What matter if I do? I have only a little while to live, and if—if...." I stopped suddenly, for I realized that I had told her more than I meant to tell any one, that in my excitement I had been reckless and foolish.

"You speak in riddles," she said. "You have no right to put yourself in danger. I don't understand at all what you are saying. Tell me what you mean, will you?"

I shook my head. "Everything is so much in the clouds, so visionary, that it would be foolish to try to tell you anything. Good-day, I must be going now." And I walked away without another word, leaving her at the gates of her own home.

As I reflected afterwards, I had not played a very magnanimous part. I had been rude almost to a point of brutality, and yet I had not been able to help myself. Something in her very presence aroused my opposition, my anger. I cannot tell why, but when I was with her, feelings which I had never known at other times almost mastered me. I knew then, as I had known all along, that I had no love for her, and yet I was conscious that I was within an ace of throwing myself at her feet. Such was the power she had over me; but all the time I knew there was an unbreakable barrier between us. Something, I could not tell what, repelled me, made me adamant.

At that time, too, I was in a strange condition of mind. All I had told her was true; although I felt strong and full of life, I knew that the Angel of Death had spread his wings over me; that, in spite of my power to walk and act quickly, death was even then undermining the citadels of life. In a sense life was not real to me at all; everything was intangible, visionary. I was like a man in a dream.

It is now early in May, and, as I said to Isabella Lethbridge this morning, it is within a fortnight of the end of the year which Dr. Rhomboid gave me to live. I commenced writing this narrative last autumn, when the days were shortening and the long evenings were dreary and lonely. I feel now that I have got to the end of my story, and that I shall never tell of what may yet happen to me. I don't think I am a nervous or fanciful man, and, as far as I can remember in what I have written, there is nothing in my history to suggest that I am superstitious or carried away by old wives' tales. And yet I have a conviction that I have come to the end of my life; that I shall soon learn the great secret—if there is any secret in death. I don't feel ill, rather my body seems instinct with life; I am buoyed up by an unnatural strength; I am capable of thinking, of acting—yet something tells me that I am near the end.

I have been writing for hours, so as to bring my records up to this point. Why I have done so I cannot tell, except that I have obeyed an overmastering impulse.

At six o'clock this evening I arranged my wireless apparatus, so as to be ready for any news that should come to me. I have also sent Simpson to St. Issey with certain instructions which seem to be necessary, and I have taken all precautions of which I can think to render what I am going to try and do effective.

What will the future bring forth, I wonder? What will be the result of my plans? Will everything come to nothing, or will my dreams be realized? I know that if I acted according to the dictates of common sense, I should at once send Simpson with a long telegram to the authorities at Falmouth or Penzance. But with that strange obstinacy which possesses me I refuse to do this; I am acting according to impulse or intuition, rather than in obedience to reason.

Concerning the deeper things of life and death, I am almost as much in the dark as I was when I came here nearly a year ago; and yet not altogether. The subtle change which has come over the life of the village has affected me. The faith which has been renewed in the lives of so many people has created an atmosphere which I cannot help but breathe. Even now, although I feel death to be so near, I have a kind of intuition that I cannot die. I cannot say that I believe in God, but there is only a thin line of partition between me and that belief. Life is the same as it has been, and yet it is not the same. A new element has appeared, a new force has made itself felt, but what that force is I cannot tell.

During the last few weeks, although I have said nothing about it, I have been reading the New Testament, a book I had not looked at since I left Oxford. Especially have I studied the Gospels. They are very wonderful, in some parts sublime. But I have not learnt the secret of the Man Jesus. I cannot rid my mind of the thought that He was a visionary. And yet I don't know; there are times when I cannot get away from the belief that His words were founded on the Rock of Truth. When I came back from the prayer-meeting the other night, I felt as though Jesus said to me what He said to the man in olden times who asked Him questions, "Thou art not far from the kingdom of God." But everything was transitory and passed away in a moment, and I was left dull and unconvinced.

And here I leave it. I am a young man, little over thirty years of age, with life's work undone and life's problems unsolved. If this life is all, then it is a mockery, a haggard failure, an unfulfilled promise, an uncompleted plan. And yet I don't know; even although I were certain that there is nothing beyond, I am still glad that I have had my life. But if there be a Supreme Being, would He give me life and hope, and volition and possibilities, only to destroy that life? I felt as I never felt before—that my body is not my real self; that the essential I is distinct from the body. These premonitions of mine, what do they signify? Certainly they prove a sensitiveness to something which is beyond my power of understanding; but is that all?

Never did I feel as I feel now the utter uselessness of mere intellectuality, of material advancement, of scientific discovery, and the thousand other things which men strive after when divorced from faith, divorced from God. I feel that Science, Philosophy, have no answer to give me, and the wisdom of men is but as the voice of the wandering wind. If I believed in God, if I were sure of God, sure of the message which Jesus proclaimed, I could laugh at death; for I should know that out of discord would come harmony, and that out of incompleteness would come completeness. But that secret is not mine. I only dimly hope.

But I will follow my fancies no further. I have my work to do. I have to carry out the plans I have made.

XXVI

MIDNIGHT

Again I take up my pen to continue the narrative commenced long months ago. Since I last looked at these pages, wonderful things have happened, so wonderful that I do not expect to be believed; but I will set them down nevertheless, and I will record them exactly as they took place.

In order to do this I must go back to that May evening in the year 1915, when, as it seemed to me, I had come to the end of my life. As I have set down in these pages, I had, as I believed, made a discovery which seemed of importance to the nation, and pierced a mystery which had been baffling our Government. Events have proved that I was not wrong in my surmises, and that I had become of importance to the nation's welfare. As I said, I had placed my little wireless apparatus on what seemed to me a suitable place for receiving messages.

That I took every precaution in placing it may be imagined; I knew from the conversation I had heard between John Liddicoat and the woman who acted with him that I was a suspect, and that they had taken every precaution against me. I knew, too, if my suspicions were correct, and those suspicions almost amounted to a positive certainty, that I was constantly watched, and that I had, more by chance than by cleverness of my own, kept John Liddicoat in the dark.

It was a little after six o'clock in the evening, as near as I can remember, when I returned to my cottage after having visited my wireless apparatus, and made sure that no messages were being received. I had barely entered my room when Squire Treherne paid me a visit. I cannot say that I was glad to see him, much as I had grown to like him, for I felt that I was on the eve of great events and was impatient at interruption. Yet I knew he had not come without reason, and I could not tell him that his visit was untimely.

As I have said before, I treated Simpson more as a friend than as a servant, and while I had not in any degree taken him into my confidence, he knew of, and had become interested in, my little wireless apparatus. Indeed, he had rejoiced in my hobby, because he believed it took my mind away from unpleasant things. Moreover, he had proved himself, especially during the past few weeks, an exceedingly sensible fellow, and one who was able to keep his own counsel. Seeing Squire Treherne, therefore, I told Simpson to station himself in a spot from which he could not be observed, to keep a sharp lookout on my little instrument, and to warn me if any one should come near, and especially to take care that no one should learn of its location.

Having taken this precaution, I went back to Mr. Treherne, who, judging from his countenance, had important things to tell me.

"I hope you are well, Erskine," said the old man kindly, at the same time looking anxiously into my face.

"As well as I shall ever be," was my reply. "Do I look ill?"

"No, I can't say you do, but you look strange. Nothing the matter, I hope?" And again he looked at me anxiously.

"It is good of you to come and see me," was my response.

"Not a bit of it! Not a bit of it!" and his reply was eager. "The truth is, I want a chat with you. I have told them at home to put off dinner until eight o'clock in the hope that I may persuade you to come back with me. I have a trap close by."

I shook my head.

"I am afraid I am not up to it, Squire. But I hope you have no bad news?"

"Oh no, no bad news at all; quite the other way. But I say, my lad, I don't like the idea of your being alone here night after night, with only your man to look after you. You really don't look well. Come and pay me a week's visit, will you? I feel it would do you good."

"You are awfully kind, Squire, but do you know I am a good deal of a hermit. I have come to love this lonely life of mine, and every one is so kind that I don't feel as though I lived amongst strangers."

"That's right, that's right; but promise me you will come back with me."

"Not to-night, Squire; I really can't."

"Well, then, come over to-morrow. Come and spend a week with me; we should all love to have you."

"We will talk about that after I have heard your news," I said; "for I am sure you have news. What is it?"

"I don't know why I want to tell you, but I feel as though I must. Josiah Lethbridge has been converted."

"Converted! What do you mean?"

"The age of miracles is not past;" and the Squire laughed as he spoke. "You know what my opinion of Lethbridge has been; you know, too, that he is regarded as a kind of Shylock. I told you about our quarrel, didn't I?"

"Yes, I remember perfectly."

"I hate war;" and he spoke as though he wanted to change the subject. "I can't sleep of a night when I think of all the misery, all the agony it is causing. I know that we as a nation could do nothing but what we have done; but when I remember people like poor Searle, and the hundreds and thousands all over the land whose hearts are broken, I feel like going mad. It is simply hellish, man! Not that we can stop it. We must go on and on, no matter what it costs us, until war is made impossible for the future. No, Kaiserism, militarism must be crushed, destroyed forever! Still I feel, Erskine, that there is a tremendous alchemy in war. It is brutal, but it is purifying. It is hellish, but God uses it, and over-rules it for His own purposes."

"I hope you are right," was my reply. "But what is your particular reason for saying this now?"

"It is Lethbridge. You know what a hard man he is, don't you? You have heard how he has got people into his grip, and ground them to powder? You have been told how, like a spider, he has attracted them into his web and imprisoned them? I don't say that, in a way, he has not been a just man. He has never done anything that has violated the law. But he has been cruel and merciless. He has demanded his pound of flesh to the fiftieth part of an ounce. He has never forgiven an injury, and has always been impatient of any one's will but his own. But there, I needn't enlarge on that; you have heard, you know."

"I have heard a good many stories," I replied, "but as a lawyer I always deduct about seventy per cent. from the total. You see, people are given to exaggerate."

"Yes, yes, that may be. But Lethbridge was as hard as nails, as cruel as death; that is why the wonder of it comes to me now."

"The wonder of what?" I asked.

The Squire hesitated a few seconds, and then went on: "He got me into his meshes. Doubtless I was foolish, in fact I know I was. I speculated, and then, although I was bitten, I speculated again. I don't say Lethbridge encouraged me; but he made me feel that things would be sure to come out right. They didn't, and I had to mortgage my estate. I hated going to a bank for money, and Lethbridge helped me out. Little by little he got the upper hand of me, until—well, for the last few years I have been like a toad under a harrow. You can understand the position. I never thought I should tell you this, in fact I have always kept my troubles to myself. All the same, I have been mad at the thought that the estate which has been in my family for I don't know how many generations should be handed over to a man like Lethbridge."

I was silent, for there seemed nothing to say.

"This morning," went on the Squire, "he came to see me. At first I met his advances coldly, for although he has had me in his power I have always held up my head. To my unspeakable astonishment, he came with a proposal which will enable me to be my own man again in five years. Just think of it, Erskine! I feel as though an awful weight were lifted from my back."

"Why did he do it?" I asked.

"That brings me back to what we were talking about. There is some wondrous alchemy in war. It may debase some, but others it humbles and ennobles. He said he had had a talk with you, and you had made him feel that his son had died a hero, and was a martyr to his faith. In short, Hugh's death has changed Lethbridge—shaken him to the very depths of his life—revolutionized him. It seems that he has had further messages about Hugh. From what I can understand, Hugh gave his life for his enemy. At the risk of his own life he rescued a German officer, and was killed while he was in the act of doing his glorious deed. The message does not seem very clear, but that is the meaning of it. The thing happened in the night-time, and the soldiers who told Hugh's Colonel were not altogether sure of the details, but this they all insist on: young Lethbridge was a hero; he might have saved himself, but wouldn't; he rescued an enemy at the risk of his own life, and then paid the penalty of his action."

I gave a long quivering sigh. I could not help being sad at such a splendid life being cut off in the middle.

"Yes, yes," went on the Squire. "Hugh was a splendid boy. It seems awful that we shall never see him again—at least, this side of the grave. But that lad's not dead, Erskine. A boy who could do a deed like that could never die. He had eternal life in him. Anyhow, Josiah Lethbridge is not the same man. You should have seen the look of pride, and more than pride, in his eyes as he told me about it. And what he has done for me, he has done because he says he believes Hugh would have him do it. 'My boy is speaking to me from heaven,' he said; 'that's why I am doing it.'"

The Squire dashed a tear from his eyes as he spoke.

"Would to God I had a son like him! I tell you, Erskine, I would not have minded losing my estate so much if I knew that he was coming into it. But there, I have told you what I came to tell you. I thought you would like to know. It is a miracle, nothing less than a miracle. He has made me ashamed of myself. Here have I for years been going around thinking hard thoughts and saying hard things about Josiah Lethbridge, and now I feel as though I had been a mean, contemptible sneak. I have scorned him because he is a Dissenter, I have said hard things about people who are not of my way of thinking. I say, God Almighty is giving us a shaking up, and showing us what blind fools we have been. As though He cares what Church we belong to, what place of worship we attend, and what form of prayer we say! I don't read the Bible much, Erskine, but there is a passage which has been running in my mind all the way over here: 'What doth the Lord require of thee, but to do justly, to love mercy, and to walk humbly with thy God?' That goes to the heart of things, doesn't it? All the rest is trimmings, trimmings. But there, I must be getting back. Now, won't you come with me?"

"I can't to-night, anyhow," I said.

"Well, to-morrow; promise you will come over then. You will add to my happiness, my boy. You will really!"

The Squire's proposal put a thought into my mind which had not occurred to me before. I had determined on another plan, but our conversation had suggested a better one.

"I will come over to-morrow for a week, provided I am able, on condition that you do something for me," I said.

"Of course I will do anything for you, my boy. But what is it?"

"Do you know Colonel Laycock?"

"Perfectly well. I dined at his mess the other night."

"You are on good terms with him?"

"Of course I am. Why?"

"I am going to ask you to do a strange thing, Squire," I said. "I have got a scheme in my mind. I am not going to tell you what it is. I am afraid—I am afraid to tell any one. Why, I don't know; but it is a fact. It is possible that to-night I shall send you a message—possible that I shall ask you to do something which will not appeal to your judgment. But I want you to do it. Will you?"

"But what is it, my dear fellow?"

231

"I cannot tell you; I want you to trust me. I believe big things are moving, and if you will, I am sure you can help me to accomplish what I have in my mind. If the thing comes off, I will write down detailed instructions, and I want you to act on those instructions. You are a magistrate, and therefore have considerable authority."

"Magistrate!" he said. "Is it something to do with law, then?"

"It is, and it isn't," I said. "The message may not come to-night, may not come till to-morrow night or the next; but when it comes, I want you to act on it. Will you?"

"Then will you come and spend a week with me?"

"If I can."

"I never like acting in the dark, Erskine, but you are a cautious fellow, and I trust you implicitly. Yes, I will do it; but for the life of me I can't see what you are driving at."

"Maybe it will end in nothing," I said, "in which case nothing will be done. But I'll tell you this: if my plans bear fruit, as I think they will, then—then— you will be glad you trusted in me. I am not asking you to compromise yourself in any way; all the same, I tell you this: it seems to me a matter of life and death."

For a few seconds the old man looked at me as if he doubted my sanity, then he gripped my hand.

"I trust you completely, Erskine, and I will do what you ask. But I must go now. Good-night, my boy. God bless you!"

Directly he had gone I went out to relieve Simpson, and on visiting my wireless apparatus, I found that no message had come through. For the next two hours I was on tenter-hooks. My mind was filled with a thousand doubts. Fears of all sorts haunted me. What if my little apparatus were not powerful enough? What if I had misunderstood the whole situation? Everything seemed shadowy and unreal. I doubted myself, I doubted everything. That little apparatus which I had prepared to receive messages seemed as valueless as the toy of a child. How could messages move across great spaces and affect the little instrument which I had manipulated with such care? How could I expect to frustrate the plans of people who were skilled in plotting, and who had been plotting for years? Were not all my hopes and beliefs as baseless as the stuff of which dreams are made? What could a man with the Angel of Death flying over him expect to do under such circumstances?

Still I held on to my faith. Foolish as it might seem, I believed that my reasoning was sound, that I had discovered the truth, and that by carrying out my plans I might save hundreds of lives.

It was now dark; the moon, which was on the wane, would not rise till far past midnight. Although the night was windless it was cloudy. This fact made everything so dark that I did not dread watchful eyes.

Nine o'clock, half-past nine, ten o'clock, yet my little instrument was silent. Had I misunderstood what John Liddicoat had said? Was I mistaken when I heard him tell the woman that he must expect another message the next night? I was in an agony of suspense. Then my heart gave a great leap—the little instrument began to move, while I, with fast beating heart, wrote quickly.

Ten minutes later I had locked myself in my little room and was eagerly studying the slip of paper before me. I knew that the message, whatever it might be, had emanated from a spot within a comparatively limited radius, for the simple reason that my apparatus was not of sufficient capacity to receive long-distance messages.

It is impossible for me to convey on paper the state of my mind as I read the words which had been transmitted. My excitement was tense beyond words. I felt my heart beating wildly; I scarce dared to breathe.

And yet the message looked innocent enough. It was simply this: "One hour after midnight to-night. Completeness essential."

That was all; there were no explanations by which any one who was not in the plot could gain any information. It might be received by a score of wireless stations, and any one ignorant of what I knew would be none the wiser. It gave no clue even to the most subtle mind whereby action could be taken. It might be read by any one with perfect safety. No Government official, whatever his position, could understand it. Neither would he see any importance in it. The words were innocence itself, and yet, as I believed, they meant the safety or the destruction of perhaps hundreds of lives. So innocent did they seem that it appeared like madness to take action, but remembering what I had seen and heard, connecting incident with incident, and placing link to link as I did, my chain of reasoning seemed flawless. If I were wrong in my conclusions, I should not only be an object of ridicule, I might indeed be placing myself under menace of the law.

Still I decided to act. Rapidly I wrote a letter to Squire Treherne, giving him the minutest details of what I wished him to do. My brain, I remember, was clear, and I was very careful to insist on all sorts of precautions. This done, I summoned Simpson to me.

"Simpson," I said, "I want you to take this to Squire Treherne immediately; it is a matter of great importance. It may be that you will be in danger on the way; but that must be risked. You must speak to no one. Take the footpath through the fields, and don't delay an instant."

Simpson looked at me steadily as though he doubted my sanity, but evidently there was something in my eyes which told him how much in earnest I was.

"Yes, sir; thank you, sir," he said, and then he hesitated.

"What is it, Simpson?"

"You will be here all alone, sir."

"I can't help that; I shall be all right. Do as I tell you."

"Shall I find you here when I get back, sir?" he asked.

"No, Simpson, I was going to mention that. You will not find me here when you get back. But take no notice of that; wait here until a quarter past one."

"Quarter past one, sir! What, an hour and a quarter past midnight?"

"Wait here until a quarter past one," I repeated, "and then, if I do not appear, make your way down to the copse, by the footpath, to the beach. You know the cave which is almost immediately beneath the house; go straight to the mouth of the cave and look for me."

Again Simpson looked at me as though he doubted my sanity, but, like the well-bred servant he was, he made no reply but "Yes, sir; thank you, sir."

A minute later I heard Simpson leaving the house.

I felt that the air was laden with tragic events. It was now past eleven o'clock, and I had two hours in which to wait, but I could not stay indoors. Strange as it may seem, I felt no weakness, while the malady from which I suffered gave me no pain at all. I was still buoyed up by the same strange, unnatural strength. I crept towards my little wireless apparatus, but there was no further message. I remained in the near distance for some time, waiting and watching; once or twice I thought I heard a rustling among the bushes, but I was not sure. Although I had no reason for my suspicion, I believed that some one was near me, that furtive eyes were watching me; but I had no tangible reason for believing this. At midnight I went back to the house again; Simpson had not returned. The little dog I had rescued a few days before came and sniffed at my feet, wagging his tail as he did so. Evidently the poor little wretch was rapidly recovering from his wound; indeed he seemed quite well. I put on an overcoat and prepared to go out. The dog still wagged his tail, as though he thought he was going to accompany me.

"No," I said to him, "you must not come."

Whereupon he began to whimper piteously. I left the house, locking the door, but I had not gone more than a few steps before I stopped. The dog had begun to howl. "This will never do," I reflected. "I will let him come with me, he can do no harm." I opened the door again, whereupon the little brute rushed to me and capered with joy. "Be quiet," I said. "If you follow me you must make no noise."

He seemed to understand, for he followed closely at my heels, making no sound as I carefully made my way through the undergrowth. When I had passed through the copse I stopped and listened; at first I thought I heard a rustling sound behind me, but evidently I was mistaken, for all was as silent as death. The night was still dark, although here and there between the clouds I saw stars twinkling; not a breath of wind stirred, and no sound reached me save the soughing of the waves. Some miles out at sea I saw the revolving light of the Dead Man's Rock Lighthouse. My descent to the beach was precipitous and somewhat dangerous, but I knew the pathway, and noiselessly made my way down, the dog keeping close to me all the time. A few minutes later I had reached the beach, and again I listened. My eyes had become sufficiently accustomed to the darkness to see that the dog was also listening. Once or twice he gave a slight whimper, but at a whispered command he was silent.

I found my way to the shelter of a rock close to the fissure by which the outer cave was entered. Creeping into the hollow of the rock, I took a little electric lamp from my pocket, and in its light saw that it was nearly half-past twelve. Minutes at that time seemed to me an eternity. Again I passed through all sorts of doubt, and more than once called myself a madman who had followed a will-o'-the-wisp of a wild fancy. Still I held fast to my resolution. From my hiding-place I could see the fissure which led to the cave. At least it would be difficult for any one to approach it without my seeing him. All the time the little dog sat close by my side with eyes and ears alert. I think he understood the condition of my mind.

Minute after minute passed slowly by, and there was neither sound nor sight that gave me warning of any one's approach. I looked anxiously to the right and to the left, seeking in vain to pierce the darkness of the night; but nothing happened; I was alone and in silence.

I think I must have fallen into a kind of waking dream, for, as it seemed to me, some moments passed when I had no consciousness of my surroundings. Then suddenly the dog at my feet gave a savage yelp. It was well he did so, for I saw two forms close by me, both of which seemed to be in the act of pouncing upon me.

I have read somewhere of a man who, when facing a great crisis, felt that he lived a lifetime in a few seconds. I realized now that this can be true. Within a few seconds of the time when the dog yelped, the whole panorama of the past twelve months, and all the details of that panorama, flashed before my eyes. It came to me with a vividness which I had never realized before. That I was indeed at the heart of a scheme whereon depended the lives of many people; that these tins of petrol were intended for German submarines; that this little cove had been used as a storehouse for the fuel whereby the Germans had been able to do their fiendish work; that in some way unknown to the authorities, hundreds of cans of this spirit had been stored there from time to time, and then, as they were needed, taken to those deadly monsters which operated beneath the sea; and that I had, partly by chance, partly by reasoning, but more by intuition, got at the heart of it all. I felt, too, that on me depended the failure or success of the German scheme. By some means or other Liddicoat, or one of his minions, had discovered or suspected what I had done.

It was one of those moments, so tense, so weighted with vital issues, that the human body and the human mind are made capable of what in ordinary circumstances would be impossible. Without waiting a second, without giving time to think, and yet feeling all the while that I was acting upon reason rather than upon impulse, I leapt upon what seemed to me the form of a man, and was instantly engaged in a deadly struggle. Even now that struggle does not seem to me real. It is like the memory of a dream rather than something which actually took place. But that it did take place I have tremendous proof. I do not remember making any noise of any sort, but I do remember the deathly grip which was laid upon me and the fight which I knew was to the death. I cannot explain why, but life never was so dear to me as at that moment. I felt, too, as though Dr. Rhomboid had been somehow mistaken in his diagnosis; that life was strong in me, but that passion was swallowed up in a greater passion, a nobler passion—it was to render service to my country, to save the lives of my fellow-countrymen.

Even while I struggled I saw what the success of my plans meant; what their failure meant. I remember, too, that I wondered why the second person I had seen took no part in the struggle; why, although there were two who prepared to attack me, only one fought me. Yet such was the case; it was man to man. Who the man was I was not sure, although I had a dim consciousness that I was fighting with the man Liddicoat; neither had I any clear conception as to the meaning of that deadly struggle; all the same, I knew that I must struggle till I had mastered him. I did not remember the precautions I had taken or the agencies I had set on foot; everything was swallowed up in the one thought— I must master the man who I was sure meant to kill me.

How long the encounter lasted I have not the remotest idea; indeed, as I think of it now, I was robbed of all human personality. I was simply Fate, and as Fate I must accomplish my purpose, heedless of everything.

I fancied that I was gaining the upper hand of him; fancied, too, that others were coming upon the scene of action; but of this I was not sure, for a great darkness came upon me suddenly, and I knew nothing more.

XXVII

VISION

And now I have come to that part of my experiences which I find difficult to relate. It is probable that if these lines are read by eyes other than my own, they will be disbelieved, yet I will set them down as I remember them. This is no easy matter, for I feel as though I were recalling the incidents which happened in a far-off dream rather than something which actually took place. And yet not altogether. What I am going to tell is very real to me, even although the reality is utterly different from what I ever experienced before. Even as I remember, I find myself thinking out of ordinary grooves, and my thoughts are of such a nature that I find no language sufficient to express them.

I was dead. I knew that my spirit, my essential self, had left my body, and that I was no longer a habitant of the world in which I had lived.

My first sensation, for I can find no better word to express my thought, was that of freedom, and with that sense of freedom came a consciousness of utter loneliness. I felt as the Ancient Mariner in Coleridge's immortal poem must have felt:

> "Alone, alone, all alone,
> Alone on a wild, wide sea,
> So lonely it was that God Himself,
> Scarce seemèd there to be."

I felt no pain, no weariness, and I was free; but I was alone.

I do not know that I felt fear; no terror possessed me; I did not think of my past life with dread, neither did past scenes haunt me. My thought of the past was rather the thought of emptiness, of purposelessness, of vacancy; it seemed to me as though my life had been a great opportunity of which I had failed to avail myself.

I had a feeling, too, that it was very cold. I seemed to be floating in infinite space, through sunless air.

Kipling, I remember, in one of the most vivid poems he ever wrote, described a man who, when he died, was carried far away:

> "Till he heard as the roar of a rain-fed ford, the roar of the
> Milky Way.

Till he heard the roar of the Milky Way die down, and drone
   and cease....

Then Tomlinson looked up and down, and little gain was there For the naked stars gleamed overhead, and he saw that his soul was bare. But the wind that blows between the worlds had cut him like a knife...."

But the poet's imagination never saw in his vision an experience like mine. No winds blew between the worlds; there was no roar as of a rain-fed ford; all was silence. Not the silence of narrow spaces, not even the silence of night, when the ears of listeners are filled with noise made by silence; it was the silence of illimitable spaces, the silence of eternity.

I thought my spirit was mounting; at least that was the impression left upon me; I was going upward, not downward. But here words fail me again, because, as it seemed to me, there was no upward and no downward. More than that, there seemed to be a lack of standards whereby one could measure anything. There was no more time, and as a consequence there was no past, no present, no future. Everything, as I thought, was formless, meaningless.

I know I have failed to give a true idea of what I saw and felt. As a boy, I was for a short time fascinated by the study of astronomy, and I remember being made afraid by the thought of the distances between the worlds. Now all that was changed; I was floating, it appeared to me, between unnumbered worlds, but in a way they were near to me, so near that I could see what was happening on them.

How long I was alone I do not know, for, as I have said, time had no meaning. In a sense I felt as though I wandered through the silences for æons, although scenes flashed before me with the speed of light. My experiences make me think of the words of the old Hebrew poet:

"A thousand years in Thy sight are but as yesterday,
   when it is passed, and as a watch in the night."

I have said that the worlds I saw were near me, so near that I could see their inhabitants and watch their movements and activities. But even in this I convey a wrong impression, for while I had this sense of nearness, I had also the consciousness that they were separated by vast distances. It was just as though I had a glimpse of the Universe. There were millions of worlds around me, and all were inhabited; everywhere was life, life that expressed itself in thought and action. On every hand were sentient thinking beings who played their part and did their work in the world from which they drew their life.

A sense of unutterable awe possessed me. I was between the worlds. I could watch what was being done on those worlds, and I felt myself to be the merest speck in infinity.

As I have stated, the thought which possessed me was that I was utterly alone, and that while I suffered no pain, and while I had a consciousness of freedom which made me exultant, my loneliness was beyond all thought....

I felt a presence; at least that is the only word I can think of to express my thought. I had no consciousness of a person being near me, and yet that Something was all around me, an Intelligence, a Will, a Power. What it was I could not tell, but that Something answered the questions which came to me....

The one predominating thought or consciousness which flooded and overwhelmed everything was the consciousness of God. While I had been in the body, something hid from me the reality of God; now everything was God. I lived in God; everything was submerged in this one great Fact of Facts, and I wondered at my blindness when I was alive. And yet I was overwhelmed by what, for want of a better word, I call the immensity of everything. I remember asking myself how God could care for such a life as mine; how He could take an interest in the myriads of beings who inhabited the worlds; how He, Who controlled planets and suns, could care for the little lives of men. For I seemed so infinitely little; I was but a speck in infinite space, less to the Universe than the tiniest insect which crawled upon the face of the globe on which I had lived.

But even as the thought came to me came also the answer: because God was infinite in thought, in love, in power, so His Being enveloped all; that because He governed the infinitely Great, so He cared for the tiniest speck of life He had created....

I saw the world from which I had come; I was able to locate my own country. Europe stretched out before me like a plain, and there I saw the nations at war. At first the war appeared only like the struggle of ants upon their little hills, and it seemed of no more importance as to which army should conquer the other than if they had been so many insects at war.

"How little we must be to God!" I thought. "On earth we regarded the European War as something beyond all thought, all comprehension, yet seen from here it is less than a struggle of gnats. What does it matter to God whether England or Germany wins in what we call the Great World Struggle?" But even as the thought flashed through my spirit came the answer that God did care; that because we were the breath of His life we had a destiny to fulfil, a work to do; that the energies of God were on the side of those who sought to express His will.

It was all infinitely beyond me; I could not understand, and yet I had the consciousness that God watched the struggle of the creatures He had made, and that He was on the side of those who, perhaps unknown to themselves, were moving towards His own purposes. As I watched, the world seemed to become nearer to me, and such was my power of vision that I was able to visualize all the struggle and all the deadly warfare from Russia to France. I heard the boom of guns, I saw the flash of bayonets, I could plainly see the men in their trenches and could hear them talking with each other. I saw shells flying from the mouths of the guns, I watched their passage through the air. I beheld them as they fell, and I saw the stain on the battle-fields. I realized everything as I had never realized it before. I saw men in their death agony, I heard their groans, their shrieks of pain. I saw thousands of torn, mangled bodies, bodies which a moment before were full of life and vigor.

Then, as it seemed to me, I beheld the agony of the world. I saw blighted homes, broken lives, bleeding, broken hearts.

"O God!" I cried out, "let me not see! I cannot bear it!"

For death was horrible to me, and life a mockery. How could God care when He allowed these young lives, so full of hope and promise, to perish in a moment?

Then out of all the mad carnage and above the din and horror of war came a voice that filled my being and rang through the worlds:

"Fear not them who can kill the body, but are not able to kill the soul."

I saw that the great tragedy of the world was not the tragedy caused by war, but the tragedy of men killing their souls even while their bodies lived; that the death of those on the battle-fields was as nothing compared to the death of those who seemed to live and yet who were dead, because they had sacrificed truth and honor and love, and that death was impossible while honor and truth and love lived.

Then I looked again, and behold, the heavens were full of the spirits of those who had offered their all on the altar of duty, and that for them there was no death. I saw that instruments of war had no power to touch the real life of these men; that each had a Divine Spark of life, and that that life was still under the overshadowing wing of the Eternal love....

Ages appeared to pass; how long I knew not, cared not, for time had no meaning. I saw that the Eternal Love and the Eternal Life, which was everywhere, was bringing out of all that at first seemed a meaningless chaos an infinite order; that even the War of the World in which men lost their lives by thousands and hundreds of thousands, in which unholy passions seemed to prevail, and in which Death stalked triumphant: I say I saw evolving out of all this, confused and contradictory as it all appeared, a higher life and a higher thought—a movement towards the Eternal Will and towards the Eternal Purpose which was behind everything.

I know I have badly expressed all this, because I find no words wherewith to make clear that which came to me; for in truth thought was lost in consciousness, and language fails to express that consciousness. I only know that I saw order coming out of chaos, light out of darkness, love out of hatred, divinity out of bestiality, life out of death.

For life and love were all.

I did not see God—that is, I was not able to visualize His Presence. I did not talk with God as a man talketh with his friend, and yet my whole being seemed to be filled with His Light and Love and Peace. I felt that I was breathing God, because God was all; that nothing was outside His Care, that nothing was too small for His Love. I wondered at my doubts and at my absence of faith, for God was everywhere, in everything; in all purposes, plans, desires. I was conscious that He was shaping and directing and controlling all the thoughts of men, and that everything was moving towards His Eternal Purposes.

In the light of what I saw, pain and wrong and misery were being overruled by the Eternal Love, so that even they were speeding men towards the greater, fuller life, and that in the march of untold ages Life and Love were everything.

A sense of triumph, of exultation filled me, bore me up as if on the wings of eagles. I saw everything from a new perspective. I realized as I never realized before the meaning of the words of the Apostle:

"Our light affliction, which is but for a *moment*, worketh for us a far more exceeding and Eternal weight of glory."

I saw that all things—all wrong, all pain, all darkness, everything which made life dark and terrible—were only for a *moment*, and that they were overruled by the Eternal God, so that those who suffered them merged through the ages into Eternal Love and Eternal Light.

How long I was in this state I do not know, for, as I have said, time had no meaning to me. All life's standards seemed to melt away. I only knew that I was, that I felt, that I was filled with an overwhelming joy, because I knew that darkness would end in Eternal Light, that pain would end in Infinite Peace.

Then slowly everything began to fade away; the worlds by which I was surrounded ceased to be. I lost the power, of visualizing; my thoughts became dim and indistinct. Presently all became darkness save for one speck of light. Sometimes that speck of light became very small; sometimes it grew larger, but it was always there, and I was conscious of an unspeakable peace.

XXVIII

THE NEW LIFE

The first thing I can remember after coming to consciousness was the feeling that strangers were around me. I could not see them, but I knew they were there. I remember trying to open my eyes, but I could see nothing; I heard whispered voices, however.

"Is he dead?"

"I am not quite sure. No, he's not dead, his pulse still beats!"

"Will he live, do you think?"

"Difficult to say. He came out of it all right, but his vitality is very low."

"Was the operation severe?"

"Yes, very severe; it is a miracle that he has lived as long as he has. I must go by the Riviera express to-morrow morning, but I will call about eight o'clock."

"Have you any further orders to give?"

"No, you can only do what I have told you. His life hangs on a thread; he may live, but I doubt it."

I listened in a detached kind of way, scarcely realizing what I heard; I was perfectly indifferent, too. It had nothing to do with me, and even if it had, I did not care. Then darkness came upon me again and I no longer saw the bright speck shining.

After that I had quickly fleeting moments of consciousness; things around me became real for a moment and then passed away. Doubtless I was in a semi-comatose condition; sometimes I imagined I heard fragments of conversation, but I can remember nothing definite.

After that followed a time of intense weariness. I felt as though I were too weak even to lie down; I could not move my limbs, and the weight of my own body on the bed seemed to weary me, but I was not sufficiently conscious to realize the full extent of my weariness. I have a vague remembrance of being fed; I call to mind a woman standing by my bedside holding something to my mouth; but as I reflect now these things seem only phantoms of the mind.

After a time I became conscious of intense pain, and I have a recollection of being able to move my limbs, and I remember hearing a voice saying:

"He is stronger anyhow, but I never saw a man so utterly exhausted."

A long space of time, how long I do not know, but it seemed to me interminable. Day appeared to follow day and week to follow week, and yet I have no distinct remembrance. In recalling it all, I am like a man trying to remember a far-off dream.

Suddenly I became awake. I was fully conscious that I was living; I could outline the room in which I lay, I could see the sunlight streaming in at the window, I could hear the birds singing. I was very weak, but I was alive; I was able to think, too, able to connect thought with thought, although my memory was dim. Incidents of my life passed before me like shadows; I saw them only in part, but I did see them.

The room was strange to me. This was not my little bedroom by the sea; the apartment was bigger than the whole of my cottage. The ceiling was high, and the window through which the sun shone was large. I did not care so much where I was; all the same, I was curious.

"What has happened to me, I wonder?" I asked myself, "and why am I here?"

I could see no one in the room, and all was silent save for the singing of the birds and the humming of the insects. I had a vague consciousness that the feeling of summer was in the air, and a delicious kind of restfulness possessed me. I was no longer too tired to lie down, rather I felt the luxury of being in bed. I suffered no pain either, although at my side, where I remembered suffering exquisite agony, was a kind of tingling sensation which I associated with a wound in the act of healing.

I saw a woman come to the head of my bed; she wore a nurse's uniform, and had a placid, kindly face.

"Who are you, and where am I?"

I know I spoke the words, but I did not recognize my voice at all; it seemed far away, like a whispering among breezes.

The woman said something, I know, but what, I could not tell. I imagine the effect was soothing, for immediately afterwards I found myself going to sleep.

Again I was conscious, more vividly conscious than before. The outlines of the room were the same, and I was able to recognize some of the furniture which I had previously seen. I remembered, too, lifting my hand from the counterpane and noting how thin and white it was.

The door of the room opened and a man entered. I saw at a glance that it was Simpson, and I looked at him through my half-closed eyes. He came to my bedside and looked steadily at me, then he placed his hand gently on my forehead; his touch was as soft as that of a woman.

"Simpson," I said, and this time I was able to recognize my voice. "Is that you, Simpson?"

"Yes, sir; thank you, sir."

His old-time formula acted on me like a tonic; it made me want to laugh. Yes, I really was alive then, and Simpson was with me; but what was the meaning of this strange room?

"Simpson," I said, "am I really alive?"

"Yes, sir; thank God, sir."

I thought I saw the tears gather in his eyes, and I am sure I saw his lips tremble.

"Have I been ill, Simpson?"

"Yes, sir, very ill, but I believe we have beaten them, sir."

"Beaten who?" I asked.

But this time he did not answer. The woman came in again bearing something in her hand. There was a whispered consultation between them, and then I remember drinking something, after which I went to sleep again.

When I again awoke I felt sure it was morning. I had no reason for believing this, but I had no doubt about it; the air was morning air, the sounds were morning sounds. The birds were chirping in the trees, the cattle were lowing in the meadows, the poultry were cackling in a yard near by, a thousand whispering voices everywhere told me that I had awakened to the dawn of a new day. I moved in my bed; yes, I had strength enough for that, and the movement caused me no pain. In an instant I heard footsteps, and Simpson again came to my side.

"Can I do anything for you, sir? How are you to-day?"

"I feel like a man reborn, Simpson," I said. And it was true. A life was surging in my veins which I never remembered before; I felt as though my whole being had been made clean and all my powers renewed. I was unutterably weak, but I felt all a child's health and joy.

"Tell me what this means, Simpson," I said; "this is not my room, not my bed."

"No, sir, but I am your man, sir," and his voice was husky.

"Yes, I am glad you are with me, Simpson. It is good to wake up and find you here."

"I hope I shall never have to leave you, sir," and I saw him wipe away his tears.

"Tell me about it, Simpson—tell me where I am and what has happened to me."

"I am forbidden to talk, sir; the doctor won't allow me. You see——"

"What doctor?" I interrupted.

"Dr. Rhomboid, sir."

"Dr. Rhomboid? Dr. Rhomboid?" The name was familiar to me.

"Where am I, Simpson?"

"You are at Trecarrel, sir; Miss Lethbridge insisted on——"

"Miss Lethbridge! Miss Lethbridge!" Then like a flash the veil dropped from my memory. I called to mind the struggle on the beach, the hand-to-hand fight, the plot which I had determined to expose.

"Miss Lethbridge insisted on my being brought here, did she, Simpson?"

"Yes, sir; you see, sir, that man Liddicoat struck you with something heavy. I —I—but there, I mustn't tell you."

"Yes, you must, Simpson; I insist upon knowing everything. I remember all that happened now: I was leaning against the rock waiting, when the dog barked, and the man Liddicoat sprang upon me. I struggled with him for a long time, and then suddenly everything became dark."

"Yes, sir, after they had finished——"

"Finished what?" I asked.

"I can't tell you now, sir; but Miss Lethbridge insisted on your being brought here. And really, sir, the road is easier here than it is to our house, and I gave in."

"But how did Miss Lethbridge get there?"

"I don't know, sir. I expect she will be telling you herself as soon as you are strong enough. Then I insisted upon sending for Dr. Rhomboid, and, sir, as Providence would have it, he was staying at the Tolgarrick Manor Hotel. The Squire had heard of it, sir; that was why, as soon as you were brought here...."

I felt that my mind was weakening, and that I had no longer any strength to grasp the things which Simpson was saying. I lost interest in them, too, and I remember falling asleep with the thought in my mind that I was in the house where Isabella Lethbridge had insisted upon bringing me.

I awoke again, and I knew that I was stronger; everything was outlined more clearly to me. Not only the objects by which I was surrounded, but my thoughts seemed more definite. It was now night; the room in which I lay was only illumined by a candle, but I saw everything plainly. Sitting by my side was the nurse whom I remembered previously; she started up on hearing me move and looked at me anxiously.

"You need not fear, nurse," I said. "I am better; the cobwebs have gone."

The nurse smiled, then she placed her hand upon my wrist.

"Yes," she said, "you are better, stronger. Can you bear to have this in your mouth a minute?"

"I can bear anything, nurse."

Evidently she was pleased with me, for a minute later she smiled confidently.

"Your pulse is normal and you have no fever," she said.

"Why am I here, nurse? What has happened to me? Tell me everything."

"No, no; go to sleep now, and in the morning you may be strong enough to bear it."

"I should sleep far better if I knew everything," I replied; "don't be foolish, nurse."

"What do you want to know?"

"Dr. Rhomboid has been here, I am told," I said. "What did he say about me? When I saw him in London he wrote my death-warrant."

"Now he has given you a reprieve," was her reply, "and more than a reprieve. In fact, he said that if you got through the operation you would live!"

I was not surprised; I felt that life, and not death, was surging within me.

"Don't try to keep things back from me, nurse," I said. "I remember everything that took place. I remember the struggle on the beach and the darkness which followed. Simpson tells me that I have been brought to Mr. Lethbridge's house, and that, as if by special Providence, Dr. Rhomboid was staying at the Tolgarrick Hotel. What was his verdict?"

"He sent for a London surgeon," said the nurse, "and he told us that if you recovered from the operation you would live. You have recovered."

"Then he made a wrong diagnosis in London. That means I had something growing in me, and now it's cut out I shall live?"

The nurse nodded and smiled.

"That's all I must tell you now," she said; "take this and go to sleep."

I obeyed her like a child; a feeling of utter contentment possessed me, and I felt myself dropping into a deep, untroubled sleep.

When I awoke again I had a feeling that it was morning. I knew that the dewdrops were shining on the grass, that the day was new-born; I knew, too, that the sun was rising in a cloudless sky, that the time was summer.

I was in the same room, but somehow it was different. A new atmosphere pervaded it; I saw vases of flowers, flowers that were wet with the morning dew, flowers that had been gathered that morning. Their perfume was as sweet as the spices of Araby. A feeling of delicious restfulness possessed me; I was as weak as a child; but there was new life in my being, a life that would overcome everything. I closed my eyes with the consciousness that all was well; nothing troubled me, no thought of care weighed upon my brain or heart. I caught myself remembering those lines of Browning:

> "The lark's on the wing,
> The morning's at seven,
> The hillside's dew-pearled,
> The snail's on the thorn;
> God's in His heaven,
> All's right with the world!"

I heard a sob close by my side.

I did not know how it was, but the sob seemed to be in accord with my thoughts, for it contained no sorrow.

I opened my eyes and saw Isabella Lethbridge leaning over my bed. I didn't speak, I couldn't; my life was filled with wonder, a wonder which I cannot put into words.

She was dressed, I remember, all in white; this I thought strange, because I imagined she would show some kind of mourning for her dead brother; but I gave it only a passing thought, for it was of no importance; the thing that impressed me was the new light in her eyes, the new joy in her face.

The barrier which had always stood between us had melted away; she was transformed, glorified. There was no need to tell me that a wondrous change had come over her; that some joy to which she had hitherto been blind possessed her; that a new power was pulsating in her life: Isabella Lethbridge was transformed, beautified beyond all thought.

We looked at each other without speaking a word; there was no need for words; words at that moment would have seemed like sacrilege.

A thousand questions flashed through my mind, but I did not ask them; there was only one question which I longed to ask, a question which embraced everything.

Still we did not speak; we remained looking in each other's eyes, as if each were trying to find what we looked for.

Then I saw the tears well up, saw them trickle down her cheeks, saw her lips quiver, and then she could no longer hold back her words.

"Don't you know, don't you know?" she sobbed.

I held out my arms, and a second later our lips met, and we were uttering incoherent words which none but those who know the language of the heart can interpret.

"You know now, don't you?" she said at length.

"Yes, I know," I said.

And yet it was all a wonder to me. When last I had spoken to her an invisible barrier stood between us. I had admired her beauty, her keen intelligence; I thought, too, that I saw wondrous possibilities in her nature; but I did not love her. Something, I knew not what, forbade that love. I had told her so, told her that I did not love her, that I only loved the woman she ought to be. Now it seemed as though a magician's hand had swept away the barrier; that some divine power had illumined her life and filled it with a new and divine element. I saw her ennobled, glorified; the old repellent look had gone; those eyes which had flashed with scorn were now filled with infinite tenderness. Why was it? And what had wrought the change?

Presently she lifted her head, and I saw a look of fear come into her eyes.

"You said you didn't love me; is that true?"

"You know," I replied.

"But tell me, tell me!"

"I can't," I replied; "words only mock me; they would only suggest the faintest shadow of what fills my life. The barriers are gone! What has wrought the change?"

"Are you sure you are strong enough to hear? Oh, it is wrong of me to speak to you like this, and you so weak!"

"Your every word is giving me new life," was my reply; "tell me everything."

"And you are sure, sure—that—that——"

"That I see in you the woman God meant you to be," was my reply. "But what has wrought the change?"

"I can hardly find words to tell you, it seems so unreal, so—so beyond the power of words to express. But—but years ago I could not love; I longed to love and could not; something held me back, what, I didn't know. I tried to break down that something. I—I was called a flirt, you know," and she laughed nervously.

"Yes, yes, I remember," I said.

"I did it as an experiment. I fancied that somehow if I won the love of some one, the casement around my heart would break, would melt away; but it was no use. And all the time I knew that I was missing the joy of life. Then you came. Yes, you were right; I thought I saw in you one who might break the hard crust around my heart, and I tried to fascinate you, tried to—to—do what you said. You remember?"

"Yes, I remember."

"But you were right. If you had loved me then, I had nothing to give you. At the centre of my heart there was a burning fire; but that fire was confined; I didn't love you; I wanted to, longed to, but I could not. And yet all the time I knew that if ever love came to me it would be for you, only you."

She ceased speaking for a few seconds, and I heard her tremulous breathing.

"Do you understand? Do you forgive me?" she asked.

"Yes, I understand; go on, tell me."

"Then came that day, before—before—the awful night. You know when you told me that you believed you were going to die, and you hinted that that very night you were going on an enterprise which meant danger, possibly death, I think I went mad; I have no remembrance of anything except the feeling that I must watch you, save you! So all that evening I waited around your hut unseen. I saw you at your little wireless station; I saw you send Simpson away; I saw you go down through the copse towards the beach. I followed you, watching all the time. Even then I didn't know my secret; I acted as though I had no will of my own, as though I were driven by some power I could not understand. I didn't know your plans, but I felt that I must be silent and watch. Then when that man leapt on you something seemed to break within me, something was liberated, I didn't know what; but I knew that I loved you, I knew that the power of love had come to me, and that I was ready to die to save you. Without thought or comprehension of what I was doing, I flung myself upon the woman, and—and…."

"Oh, my love, my love!" I murmured. "Thank God for all His goodness!"

For some time we were silent.

"Tell me all the rest," I said presently.

"That's all, isn't it?"

There was a great deal more, but I cared nothing about it. At that moment it seemed to me that all I had tried to do and hoped to do for my country was swallowed up in the one great possession, the one great fact which overwhelmed everything.

"Am I doing wrong in telling you this?" she asked. "It seems as though there is nothing else in life now but that, because it has meant everything else— faith, religion, God. It has made the world new, it has broken down all barriers and glorified all life. Oh, my love, my love, do you understand?"

"I understand," I replied, "I understand."

And then the truth which had contained everything, the truth which was the centre and circumference of all that came to me during the time I thought I was dead, flooded my heart and brain.

"Life and love are everything, for these mean God."

I did not ask her the result of my struggle with Liddicoat, or the outcome of the plans I had made. I wanted to ask her, and yet I did not; somehow that did not seem to matter.

I heard the birds singing in the trees around the house; heard the lowing of the cattle in the meadows; saw the sunlight streaming through the window; breathed the sweetness of the morning air.

I had indeed entered the light and life of a new day; the world was flooded with a glory that was infinite; barriers were broken down because I had learnt the secret of life!

For some time we were silent; again there seemed nothing to say, because everything was too wonderful for words.

"During the time your life hung on a thread, and when the doctors doubted whether you could live, even then I had no fear," she went on presently. "That which had come to me was so wonderful that it seemed to make everything possible, and—I cannot put it into words—but while I was almost mad with anxiety, in spite of a kind of certainty which possessed me, I knew that all was well, I knew that somehow—somehow we should be brought together and that life's secret would be ours."

A knock came to the door and the nurse entered.

"How is the patient, Miss Lethbridge?" she asked.

"I feel wonderful," I replied; "far stronger than I was when you were here last, nurse."

"Yes, you are all right," said the nurse smilingly. "Miss Lethbridge came directly you fell asleep, and insisted on my going to bed. I am sure it was awfully good of her to relieve me."

"She has proved a good substitute, nurse," I replied; "but you must insist upon her going to bed now if she has been watching all the night."

"Yes, and you look as though you need washing and your hair brushed," laughed the nurse. "You must not get on too fast, you know."

"I shall be quite well enough to receive visitors soon," was my reply.

"Visitors!" laughed the nurse; "you will be inundated with them as soon as you are strong enough. A man has come all the way from London to see you; he wants to interview you for one of the London newspapers. You see, having succeeded in exposing that German plot, and causing the arrest of a lot of dangerous people, you have been the talk of the country."

"I was successful, then?" I said.

"Successful! Oh, of course you don't know; but you will hear all about it later, as soon as you are stronger."

"How long is it since it happened?" I asked curiously.

"I have been here just five weeks," replied the nurse.

XXIX

CHRISTMAS 1915

Of course the facts are old now, and I need not detail them here. All the world knows that Colonel Laycock's soldiers came up in time to get hold of, not only Liddicoat and his accomplice, who proved to be dangerous German spies, but several others who had been in the enemy's service for the purpose of conveying petrol to the submarines. The little bay in which I had lived was of great importance to them, and the cave I had discovered was their principal storehouse for petrol. Indeed, since their plot was exposed and our Government officials got hold of the facts, submarines have done their work under increasing difficulty.

Of Father Abraham I heard but little. This, however, is the news which came to me: Years before, he had been sent from Germany to act as one of their agents, but later on, when he discovered what would be expected of him, he left the neighborhood; but before doing so he did his best to create the idea that he had been murdered, and that his body had been disposed of. It seems that he stood in deadly fear of the Germans, and believed that he was constantly watched. He was afraid to confess that he had been acting as a German agent, and that was why he didn't tell the English authorities what he knew. Why he was so anxious to save me from danger I cannot fully comprehend; all I know about him I have set down in this narrative, and those who read this must draw their own conclusions. Certain it is that he was never seen in the neighborhood of St. Issey again.

My own recovery was longer than I had hoped for. I grew gradually stronger, but the operation which I had undergone was more serious than I had imagined, and it was several weeks after I awoke to consciousness before I was allowed to leave my room.

Dr. Rhomboid, who came twice from London to see me, was very insistent on my taking no risks, and also kept the many visitors who desired to see me from entering the room.

Thus for some time after the incidents I have recorded, with the exception of the doctor, who, by the way, was not Dr. Wise, the only persons I saw were the nurse, Simpson, and Isabella. As may be imagined, however, I was well looked after, and was not at all sorry at being deprived of the companionship of my neighbors. Perhaps, however, I have said too much. I did want to see Squire Treherne, and I should have been glad of a visit from the Vicar; and bearing in mind what Squire Treherne had said, I wanted to have a chat with Josiah Lethbridge.

At the end of three weeks I was pronounced sufficiently strong to receive visitors, and the first who came was Josiah Lethbridge. I had expected to see a change in him, but not so great as had actually taken place. He knew nothing of what had passed between Isabella and myself, because we had arranged to keep everything a secret; but he could not have treated me more kindly had I been his own child. When I uttered my apologies for the trouble which I had given the family, his lips quivered and he seemed on the point of breaking down.

"Please don't mention that," he said. "If you only knew the joy it gives me to know that you are in the house, and that I am in the slightest degree able to be of service to you, you would not talk in that way. But I must not try to explain now; the doctor has only given me three minutes to be with you, so I will only say that I am glad you are here, and that I am eagerly looking forward to the time when we shall see more of each other and know each other better. I have a great deal to tell you, my lad. God only knows how much."

Of the visits of Squire Treherne and Mr. Trelaske I will not speak, save to say that I well-nigh broke down at the old Squire's behavior.

"God bless my soul!" ejaculated the old man; "we will give you a time when you get well! No, no, not a word from you; you must not talk; but we *will* give you a time! We will have the whole countryside *en fête*! It is not only the German plot you have exposed, it is other things, my boy! God bless you!"

It was not until the beginning of August that I was allowed to leave my bedroom and find my way down-stairs. The nurse and Isabella walked each side of me, supporting me at each step I took, and when I reached the living-room I found Mr. and Mrs. Lethbridge awaiting me. I had barely spoken to Mrs. Lethbridge when I heard a child's cry in the room, and, looking, I saw Mary, Hugh's wife, holding a baby in her arms.

"Yes," said Josiah Lethbridge with a laugh, "this is a secret that we have kept in store for you. This is Hugh's child!"

"Then—then...." I stammered.

"As soon as my son's wife was well enough I insisted upon her being brought to her true home. Mary, my love, bring your baby here where Mr. Erskine can see him. Isn't he a beautiful boy? He was christened a month ago."

"And what is he called?" I asked.

"There was only one name to give him," replied Josiah Lethbridge proudly

—"Hugh."

As I looked into Mary's eyes a sob rose in my throat. I saw the joy of motherhood there, I saw infinite tenderness, and more than tenderness. It was a joy chastened by sorrow, by loss unspeakable, by hope eternal.

"I am so glad, Mary," I said, "so glad. It is as it ought to be, isn't it?"

"Isn't he just like his father?" said the young mother proudly. "See his eyes, his chin—why, he's Hugh all over again!" Then her lips became tremulous, and tears welled up into her eyes.

"He is a beautiful boy," I said, "and—and...."

"He's made the house a new place," cried Josiah Lethbridge. "I have made Mary sleep in the next room to mine so that I can hear him when he cries in the night. It does me good to hear a baby cry. Oh, my boy, my boy!" and his voice trembled as he spoke.

I knew what he was thinking about—knew that he remembered, with a great sadness in his heart, that he had driven his only son from home; knew that he suffered unspeakable sorrow; and I could see that he was a different man.

"Isn't God good to us?" he said huskily; "and—and—Mary's forgiven me too, haven't you, my love?"

He put his arm around the young widow's waist as he spoke and kissed her.

"It's the baby who has done everything," said Mrs. Lethbridge. "The news that he was born came in the middle of the night, and when Josiah heard that both mother and child were well, he could not stay in bed; he got up and tramped around the room like a man beside himself. 'She must come home,' he said, 'home, and bring her baby with her.' Oh, it's wonderful, wonderful!"

"And you, Mary," said I, "are you well again?"

The simple-hearted girl turned to me with a wan smile.

"When the news came to me first about Hugh," she said, "I thought I should have died; I wanted to die; life seemed hateful to me; then—then—when my boy was born, oh, he made all the difference! I know Hugh is not dead, he lives in heaven, and he is watching over us. You believe that too, don't you, Mr. Erskine?"

"I don't believe in death," I replied; "there is no death, only seeming death."

"Do you remember what I said to you, Erskine, when I saw you months ago in your little hut?" said Josiah Lethbridge. "I said that God Almighty must be laughing at us. Now I know I was wrong."

"Yes?" I said questioningly.

"God Almighty never laughs at us," said Josiah Lethbridge. "He is revealed to us by His Son, and Jesus wept at the graveside of Lazarus. He weeps at all the sorrow and pain of the world. Jesus wept even although He knew He would raise Lazarus from the dead, and God weeps at our follies and our madness even although He, in His Eternal Love, is working out for us all a greater salvation. Oh, we are fools, my lad! We measure His purposes by our little foot-rule; we explain His Will according to the standard of our puny minds; we measure events by days and years; but God lives, and works His own Sovereign Will. It has all come to me lately. I have gone through deep waters, my lad; the waves and the billows have well-nigh overwhelmed me; but that little baby has made all the difference; my boy lives again in him."

I was silent, I remember; there seemed nothing to say. What were words at such a time as that? Deep had called unto deep, and the Voice of God had been heard in the mysterious happenings of life.

I found my way to a chair close by a window, through which I looked out on the lawn, and at the flowers which surrounded it. It was about three o'clock in the afternoon, and the sun had begun to sink, although the day was yet glorious. Beyond the trees of the park I could see the wild moorland, and between two rugged tors I caught the shimmer of the sea.

The nurse had left the room by this time, and none but the members of the family except myself remained. I could not help realizing the change that had taken place. When I had first entered the house the atmosphere was cold, hard, unpleasant. Josiah Lethbridge was in the height of his prosperity, and he had his wife and children around him; his life did not seem to be touched with care or sorrow; no clouds seemed to hang in his sky. Now the death-reaper had come and had taken his only son; yet it was a far happier home than then. Josiah Lethbridge had been embittered towards his son, because the latter loved a simple-minded farmer's daughter; he had even driven his son from home, because the lad would be true to his heart and marry the girl he loved. Now he had taken this girl to his arms; he had brought her and her baby to his home. There was sorrow in the house, but it was a chastened sorrow, a sorrow illumined by faith and love.

"Oh, if my boy had only lived!" said Josiah Lethbridge; "if he had only been spared to see this day, I think my cup of happiness would be full; but God Almighty never makes a mistake."

"No," I said, "He never makes a mistake."

"Do you say that, Erskine?"

"Yes, I say it," I replied, thinking of my own experiences and remembering the life that had come to me. "Yes, I say it."

"It is a ghastly thing, is this war," he went on. "I become bewildered, maddened, when I think about it. I can't explain it, I can't even see a far-off glimpse of explanation, when I think of this life only. When I think of the suffering, of the waste of life, the sorrow, the unutterable sorrow of tens of thousands of homes;—it's all so foolish, so—so—mad. But that is not God's doing, my boy; besides, even in it all, through it all, He's working His Will. Life is being purified; men are learning their lessons. I know it, Great God, I know it! The nations of Europe were in danger of forgetting God, and now are realizing their foolishness. But oh, if my Hugh had lived! If I could see him coming across the lawn as I used to see him, if I could hear him laugh in his old boyish way! But he is dead."

"No, Mr. Lethbridge," I said, "he is not dead; there is no death, of that I am certain; there is no death. God lives, and because He lives His children live always. I agree with you about the ghastliness, the sinfulness, the madness of war; but this war has told me that the eternal life in man laughs at death. What we call death is not an end of life, it is only a beginning. This life is only a fragment of life; that at all events I have learnt."

I looked around the room and found that we were alone. Mary had taken away her baby, while Mrs. Lethbridge and Isabella had, for some reason, left the room.

"You speak like one who knows," said Josiah Lethbridge; "you talk like a man who has seen things."

"Yes," I said, "I have seen things."

"And you have rendered great service to your country too. Have you read what the papers have said about you?"

"No," I replied, "I don't know that I have troubled about them. After all, those were only incidents; there are more important things than those."

He looked at me curiously.

"I know what you have experienced and suffered," I said, "and I know what your suffering has done for you; but you know little of my story; I want to tell you more about it."

"Yes, yes, tell me!" he said eagerly.

And I told him—told him of the doctor's verdict; told him of my longing for life; told him much that I have set down in these pages.

"I can't explain it," I said, when I came to describe the experiences through which I had passed after the great darkness fell upon me, "but I KNOW, I SAW."

"You felt that, saw that?"

"God and immortality are not matters of faith to me now, Mr. Lethbridge; they are matters of consciousness; that is why I am so certain about Hugh. He is not dead. A lad who could do what he did had Eternal Life in him. God is here all the while; it is only our blindness that keeps us from seeing Him. Hugh is still your son. There are only two eternal things, Mr. Lethbridge."

"Two eternal things," he repeated, "only two?"

"Life, love. That leads me to what I want to say to you now."

He looked at me with keen interest.

"I love Isabella," I said simply. "Haven't you guessed it?"

"What! Do you mean——?"

"I do," I said. "Will you give her to me?"

"I—I have seen a change in her lately, and—and——But, my dear boy——"

"I am afraid I am what you will call a poor match," I went on. "The doctor says it will be months before I shall be fully strong again, although he promises me that I shall be able to resume my old profession in a couple of months from now. Perhaps my clients will have forgotten me; still, I think I can get some new ones; my reputation seems to be better than I thought it was. Besides, if I become fully strong again, I shall feel it my duty to offer my services to the country; so I shall be a poor match, I am afraid, but I love her."

"And she?" he asked.

"She knows all I have told you," I replied.

"And—and—that has made all the change in her then. Why—why——"

"Will you give her to me, Mr. Lethbridge?" I repeated. "Will you let me take Hugh's place as far as I can? I will give my life to make her happy."

His astonishment seemed too great for words; several times he attempted to speak, but broke down each time.

"But, Erskine, my lad," he said at length, "Erskine——"

"You will, won't you, dad? If you don't, I shall run away with Frank!"

I had no knowledge that Isabella had been there, but, turning, I saw her standing behind me with love-lit eyes.

"Oh, dad, you won't refuse, will you?"

"Refuse?" he cried. "God bless my soul!—but—but—it's the very thing I would have chosen!" and then this stern, strong man sobbed like a child.

"We are having tea on the lawn," said Mrs. Lethbridge, entering the room at that moment. "Why, what's the meaning of this?"

When she knew what had taken place, she threw her arms around my neck, and kissed me.

"I have seen it for months," she declared presently. "Oh, yes, you needn't laugh at me; I saw—trust a mother's eyes."

That was the happiest evening I had ever known. I will not try to describe it, words seem so poor, so utterly insufficient. We were like those who had come safe into harbor after a voyage across a gray, trackless, stormy sea. We shuddered at the thought of the voyage; but we were glad we had undergone the suffering.

"I never knew dad so happy in my life," said Isabella to me as she bade me good-night. "Do you know, that in spite of everything I was afraid that he might—he might refuse? Oh, my love, my love, if Hugh had only lived to see us all!"

"He does see us," I ventured.

"Yes, but if he could be here amongst us, if he could see how father treats Mary, how he loves the baby, how happy mother is, and how—I—I——Oh, how I hate bidding you good-night, but we shall meet again in the morning."

"Yes, we shall meet in the morning," I said, with a glad heart.

I thought my story had come to an end here, that I had no more to relate, but an event has just happened which I must set down, or this narrative will be incomplete.

I had returned to London and taken up my life where I had dropped it. I was still comparatively weak, but strong enough to do the work which fell to me.

As the weeks passed by, clients came to me as of old, and I found myself having to refuse briefs. I was glad of this, because I wanted to show Josiah Lethbridge, when I went to Cornwall for Christmas, that I was not helpless, and that I was able to provide a home for his child. I found, too, although the doctors refused me when I offered myself for the Army, that my strength was daily increasing. Indeed, so far had I recovered myself that near the end of the term I was able to carry through a difficult case, and in spite of being opposed by a barrister of national reputation, I was able to win it.

I had hoped to go to Cornwall at the beginning of the Christmas vacation, but I found that my success had led to so much work that it was not until Christmas Eve that I was able to get away.

"Simpson," I said on the Thursday night, "I want you to get my bag in readiness in time for me to catch the Riviera express to-morrow morning. You know what things I shall want, Simpson; I shall be away about a fortnight, I hope."

"Yes, sir."

But Simpson didn't leave me as usual.

"What is the matter, Simpson? Is there anything you wish to say?"

"Well, sir, as you are going to Cornwall, I thought—that is—you see, there might not be room at Mr. Lethbridge's house for me; but the little hut on the cliff is still empty, and I could sleep there."

"You want to go, do you, Simpson?"

"Well, sir——"

"All right," I laughed, "you be ready to come with me." Whereupon he hurried away with a glad look in his eyes.

Isabella met me at the station on Christmas Eve. It was about five o'clock when the train drew up, and when I stepped on the platform she sobbed like one overcome.

"What is the matter?" I asked.

"I—I was afraid you would not come—afraid lest something should happen."

"Why, what should happen?"

"I don't know, only—even now it seems too good to be true. But there, you have come. Let me look at you again and make sure."

"Have you any visitors?" I asked presently.

"No; dad would not have any, but he's inviting Mr. Treleaven and his wife over to dinner to-morrow. You see, he's so anxious to make Mary happy. Do you know, Frank," and she laughed joyfully, "he seems to think of himself as your guardian. He has asked me twenty times to-day what time you are coming, and whether I have had any telegrams from you, and hosts of other things. I have been waiting at the station for an hour. He ordered Jenkins to bring around the car an hour too soon. He has read all about that trial a dozen times, and he is—he is proud of you, Frank!"

Oh, it was good to be in Cornwall again, good to breathe the pure air, and to smell the salt of the sea. As the motor dashed through St. Issey I thought of the time I had first seen it, and remembered the weight that had rested upon my heart.

"I have spent all the morning helping to decorate the Chapel," said Isabella, looking towards that structure as we passed it. "We are going to have a special service there to-morrow. Oh, it is good to have you, Frank."

A few minutes later we drew up to the entrance of Trecarrel, where both Mr. and Mrs. Lethbridge stood waiting to greet me, while behind them was Mary, holding her baby in her arms.

"Is he not a beauty, Frank?" she said, holding him up to me. "He is beginning to know such a lot of things too. He knows grandad, granny, and Isabella; you should see him laugh when they come into the room!"

"Now, Frank, warm yourself before you go up to dress," cried Josiah Lethbridge. "Mother, is the fire in Frank's room all right? He will be cold and tired, you know."

"Nonsense, Josiah; the fire has been burning there for hours."

"Well, I ordered it to be laid this morning," said the old man, "and when I went into the room at twelve o'clock the servants had not done it. Ah, but you are welcome, my boy; we will have a grand Christmas," and then he sighed.

I knew what he was thinking about, but I was so happy that I had almost forgotten Hugh when I entered the drawing-room and found Isabella awaiting me.

"I have got this new frock especially for you, Your Lordship. How do you like it?" she said, and my heart leapt as I saw the light in her eyes.

"If you had a decent figure it would look very well," I said, with a laugh; "but you know, even dressmakers can't ..."

After this I had to show contrition for my rudeness.

"You should have seen the hampers that dad has sent to the trenches," she said presently. "All the men in Hugh's company have been remembered. Oh, Frank, there is such a difference in dad; he is not the same man he used to be. He is great friends now with the Vicar, and with Squire Treherne, and all of them."

Precisely at seven o'clock we found our way into the dining-room. The apartment was resplendent with Christmas decorations; everywhere the feeling of Christmas abounded. There were only five of us to sit down to dinner—Mr. and Mrs. Lethbridge, Mary, Isabella, and myself—but six chairs were placed. The empty chair was at the end of the table opposite Mr. Lethbridge, and everything had been arranged as though the chair was expected to be occupied. All of us noted it, although no one spoke aloud concerning it.

"Dad ordered it," said Isabella to me; "he would have it so."

We took our places at the dinner-table, and then Josiah Lethbridge said:

"We will sing the old Grace, children."

> "We thank Thee, Lord, for this our food,
> But more because of Jesu's love.
> Let manna to our souls be given,
> The bread of life sent...."

But we never finished the last line; we heard a quick step in the hall outside, a bustling noise, then the dining-room door opened, and Hugh Lethbridge, pale and wan, but still tall and erect, clad in an officer's uniform, came into the room!

For a moment he seemed to be dazzled by the light, and walked with uncertain footsteps, while we stood silent with amazement. Then he caught the look on his wife's face.

"It's Hugh!" she gasped.

Hugh rushed towards her, and a second later they were locked in each other's arms.

"My wife! My Mary!" he cried.

I will not try to describe what followed, nor attempt to tell how the mother fell upon her boy's neck with fond words of endearment; how Josiah Lethbridge put his hand upon his boy's head, felt his shoulders and his arms, and patted him with infinite tenderness as though he wanted to assure himself that it was really he and not his spirit; how Isabella kissed him again and again, with all sorts of endearing terms; and how Hugh and I shook hands at least twenty times.

"And it is not vacant after all," said Josiah Lethbridge, as he saw his son sitting in the chair which had been placed opposite him. "Oh, thank God! Thank God!"

Of course Hugh had a long story to tell. It seems that in the excitement of battle, after the German officer had shot him, he was left for dead, and then, before the stretcher-bearers came to him, he had crawled away, and it was believed that he had been buried with the others who were killed that night.

Hugh's description was extremely hazy, because he himself scarcely knew what happened to him. When he awoke to consciousness he found himself in a French peasant's hut within the German lines, and here he was kept and nursed by the owners. It seemed a miracle that he should have escaped, but these peasants, seeing that he was English and hating the Germans, kept their secret well. Month after month he lay ill, and even when at length he was well enough to get up, his memory had gone, and he could tell nothing about himself nor what he wanted to do. By and by, however, when his faculties were restored to him, he realized the difficulties of his situation, and for a long time he schemed and planned how to get through the German lines and find his way back to his friends.

I will not trouble the reader with a recital of all he went through; suffice it to say that he at length succeeded, and was received by his old comrades as a man risen from the dead. As may be imagined, no sooner did he get among the English than all his difficulties vanished. A new uniform and money were given to him, with a lengthy leave of absence. He was careful, too, to impress upon his superior officers that he didn't want any news concerning his safety to arrive in England before he himself got there. He wanted to give his people a surprise, he said. This being easily arranged, Hugh returned to England, and arrived in Cornwall on Christmas Eve. He decided first of all to go straight to John Treleaven's farm, where he hoped to find his wife, but learning that she had gone to Trecarrel, he with a great wonder in his heart had hurried to his old home.

The lights of Trecarrel never went out that night. It was Josiah Lethbridge's will that they should not. Besides, we all had so much to say. Hugh would have the baby brought into the room, and Josiah Lethbridge insisted that Mary's father and mother should be fetched immediately. And then Hugh had to tell his story at least six times over, and we all wondered and exclaimed at each recital.

The wonder of that night will never leave me. I had thought that I could never be so happy again as on the evening when Josiah Lethbridge told me he would give Isabella to me for my wife. But that Christmas Eve when Hugh came and the Christmas morning which followed were more wonderful still. Never shall I forget how the soldier lad held his baby in his arms, and looked at it with infinite tenderness and wonder; while his wife, who had believed him dead, clung to him, uttering fond, endearing terms all the while. Never shall I forget how Mrs. Lethbridge went from one to another, with tears of joy streaming down her face, or how Josiah Lethbridge, the old hard look gone from his eyes, told his children again and again how he loved them.

I will leave my narrative here. My tale is told, even while it is not finished. While I write, guns are booming, and the war between the nations goes on;

but I do not fear.

> "For Right is Right, since God is God,
> And Right the day must win."

This great world carnage is horrible beyond words, its madness is inexpressible, but beyond all is God. He has many ways of teaching His lessons, and He is now speaking to us out of the whirlwind and out of the fire.

9 783752 332629